PERSISTENT RUMOURS

Also by Lee Langley

Novels
Changes of Address
The Dying Art
From The Broken Tree
The Only Person
Sunday Girl

Stage Play
Baggage

PERSISTENT RUMOURS

LEE LANGLEY

MILKWEED
EDITIONS

Printed in the United States of America
Cover design by Adrian Morgan. Cover photograph by Robert Flynt/Swanstock.
94 95 96 97 98 5 4 3 2 1
First Edition

Milkweed Editions is a not-for-profit publisher. We gratefully acknowledge support from the Elmer L. and Eleanor J. Andersen Foundation; Dain Bosworth Foundation; Dayton Hudson Foundation for Dayton's and Target Stores; Ecolab Foundation; General Mills Foundation; Honeywell Foundation; Jerome Foundation; John S. and James L. Knight Foundation; The McKnight Foundation; Andrew W. Mellon Foundation; Minnesota State Arts Board through an appropriation by the Minnesota State Legislature; Musser Fund; Challenge and Literature Programs of the National Endowment for the Arts; I. A. O'Shaughnessy Foundation; Piper Family Fund of the Minneapolis Foundation; Piper Jaffray Companies, Inc.; John & Beverly Rollwagen Fund of the Minneapolis Foundation; Star Tribune/Cowles Media Foundation; Surdna Foundation; James R. Thorpe Foundation; Unity Avenue Foundation; Lila Wallace-Reader's Digest Literary Publishers Marketing Development Program, funded through a grant to the Council of Literary Magazines and Presses; and generous individuals.

Library of Congress Cataloging-in-Publication Data

Langley, Lee.
    Persistent rumours / by Lee Langley. —1st ed.
        p.   cm.
    ISBN 1-57131-001-0
    1. Scholars—Great Britain—Psychology—Fiction.   2. Mothers and sons—Andaman Islands—Fiction.   3. British—Travel—Andaman Islands—Fiction.   4. Married people—Great Britain—Fiction.   I. Title.
PR6062.A5335P47   1994
823'.914—dc20   94-6454
                                                                                        CIP

This book is printed on acid-free paper.

To Mary
a sister rediscovered

PART ONE

Chapter 1

Whiteness around him; walls of net. The bed was hot, sticky, the child restless. When he saw her in the doorway, he feigned sleep, but through his lashes and through the misty veil of the net he could make out her shape: the pale arms and hair, a dress the colour of violets – or was he confusing that with the scent she wore?

She drew aside the mosquito netting and the sweetness flowed over him, heavy on the warm night air. She smoothed back his hair, barely touching him, and murmured a phrase, something quite brief. Then she turned away, the light gleaming for a moment on her cheek.

He lay still, his eyes closed now, listening to the crickets. He slept. Later he woke in tears, screaming, waking others, causing alarm and confusion.

The servants came running: the ayah who slept across the threshold of his room; the bearer, looking tousled and disreputable without his white turban; the chowkidar hurrying from the gate. They stood round the child's bed, anxious, helpless, while he screamed. His mother was more practical: it was a bad dream, she explained. She lit the oil lamp, dispelling the shadows, soothing him. Just a nightmare, she said. It was the first of many.

The 747 began its descent. His wife touched his shoulder, waking him. 'Nearly there, James.' He stirred, still sleepy, and glanced out of the window at the piercing blue sky. Ten hours ago they were in London, shaking rain from coat collars and hair. It all seemed very undramatic and easy. An occasional turbulence; a headwind which delayed them slightly. Deliberately, he shut his mind to what lay ahead. The journey was almost certainly doomed to end in disappointment, everyone concerned long dead or dispersed as Daisy had already pointed out. And in any case what was he seeking? Evidence of a betrayal? Of a tragedy? Lies and excuses had been part of it for so long, why start digging now? At the end of it all, what did he expect to find? Would it still be there, the house, and the room where he once slept, where a woman with pale yellow hair leaned over his bed –

'Please fasten your seat belts.'

The scent of violets dissolved in the dry, pressurised air. A dress like flower petals – no. He concentrated: like butterfly wings. And the phrase she murmured as she turned away, what was it? He shook his head, defeated as always. Far below, surf crawled up a shelf of sand, slipped away. His wife was fiddling with the safety belt, her elbow pressing into his ribs. The jet was about to land in Madras and he badly needed to have a pee.

Elizabeth Oakley. Her Journal.
October 20th 1899. The voyage out has begun: the dock crowded, people waving, such a clamour. Our cabin is filled with flowers and fruit; hampers, and necessities of all kinds that Henry thinks necessary – indeed vital: brandy and soda water, Bovril, a spirit stove for brewing tea. There is a doctor on board but Henry has a medicine chest with chlorodyne and laudanum. I pray we shall not need them!

In the beginning it was all gaiety and excitement; newness. The surge of movement, the smell of engine grease. Other passengers observed them indulgently, the tall man with the small, childlike wife absorbed in each new discovery, astonished by porpoises, exhilarated by storms. She could be glimpsed early in the morning, striding round the deck, the sea mist dampening and darkening her bright hair, hanging on her lashes like tears.

Not all the passengers were indulgent; some had misgivings: Mrs Oakley, newly married, was perhaps too eager in her ways, too receptive. She talked too freely to crew and servants, asked questions of new acquaintances, speculated aloud about natives and idol worship. Major Oakley's bride would need breaking in. No great difficulties need arise: she was already seventeen and ready for responsibility, but occasionally her responses caused dismay.

'Must one be taught everything, then?' Elizabeth had asked, when one of the old hands, a matron with two decades of experience, offered to initiate her into the rights and wrongs of station life. 'Would it not be more interesting to find out for oneself?'

Mrs Brinkham dispensed a brief smile. 'It is most important to know what is required. In the beginning we all need to be shown the ropes.'

'So that we may be tied down?' Elizabeth said, more statement than question. She saw the look on Mrs Brinkham's face and laughed, turning the remark into a pleasantry: 'Secure, I mean.' She gestured towards one of the crew nearby, methodically checking knots on a lifeboat. As the older woman moved away, Elizabeth approached the man: 'What do you call that knot? Please show me how to do it.'

It was then, on the voyage out, that she recorded in the pages of her journal the first hint of a closing in.

. . . the cabin is airless, the porthole sealed. As the weather grows warmer I feel increasingly restricted by my clothes, the tight-laced stays, the petticoats, narrow sleeves, stockings, stiff collars and hats.

That morning, when she adjusted the little veil on her hat before the mirror, her reflection peered back at her through the mesh like a creature in a cage.

I wonder that we do not adopt a more suitable mode of

dress, surely a loose cotton shift would be more comfortable?
When I suggested as much to one of the ladies, she became
quite severe and told me it was most important to maintain
our British standards. We must not, it seems, give in to India.
Can a place be so dangerous? I have been studying the maps:
the subcontinent is so vast, with such varied countryside.
Desert, jungle, mountains. Palaces and temples. And there are
elephants, tigers, wild boar, crocodiles. Henry has warned me
that it will be hard. The conditions are in some ways primitive,
he says. I must be prepared for anything. This makes me the
more eager to be there, in those primitive surroundings.

She had known Henry for most of her life: it was Henry
who taught her card tricks and later, backgammon. When she
was still in the schoolroom with the governess he was off to
Sandhurst. She accompanied her mother to Baden-Baden. He
went to India with the regiment. With her hair up, ready to
enjoy her first London season, she found Henry home on leave
and seeking a wife. What more natural than to marry him?
Surely she loved him? Certainly her mother approved.

In his uniform, so well cut, displaying his slim figure, he
looked very dashing. He had a way of stooping slightly as he
talked to her, a tender, deferential drooping of the head that
touched her. She found him after all these years suddenly quite
dazzling.

She had thought some aspects of her new life would be
disturbing, disagreeable even. Girls talked vaguely of the terrors
to be faced on the bridal night, but when the time came, Henry
found Elizabeth interested and happy to participate in the
unfamiliar rituals of the marriage bed. The wedding service
itself aroused speculation, expectation:

'Matrimony,' the vicar intoned, eyes on the page, 'is not to
be taken in hand inadvisedly, lightly or wantonly, to satisfy
men's carnal lusts and appetites like brute beasts that have no
understanding. It is a remedy against sin and to avoid
fornication . . . for such persons as have not the gift of
continency . . .' She listened carefully, impressed by the practi-

cality of the Solemnisation of Matrimony: so marriage was, it seemed, a way of legally satisfying men's carnal lusts. She was intrigued to learn that Henry, who seemed so gentle and so understanding, must also possess these . . . appetites. When the priest enquired later, 'Wilt thou obey him and serve him and be fruitful in the procreation of children?' she consented with tempered enthusiasm.

But the wedding was not consummated on the first night, nor the second. Elizabeth felt unwell, flushed and feverish, and Henry thoughtfully decided to postpone matters until the honeymoon voyage.

In their stateroom he was courteous, gentle. He had feared she would be frightened, find some of it unpleasant. Instead she was curious, 'Oh!' she exclaimed with surprise, and then, 'What is it called, Henry dear?' Embarrassment on Henry's part, taken aback by such frank interest. 'Surely there is some word – some term . . . among women . . .'

'I mean the *proper* name.'

Henry found himself incapable of speaking in such bald, clinical terms. He indicated that he would write of the matter in his journal.

And thus it became customary for Henry and Elizabeth to leave their diaries open, side by side so that each might read the other's entry for the day. This proved particularly useful in areas where Henry found it difficult to express himself freely in speech.

Elizabeth's difficulties were to come later, when she saw that her thoughts might cause Henry disquiet, even pain. For the present, her pages lay open to be read by her new husband.

Colonel Brinkham made it clear how fortunate she was: 'The Suez Canal, steam . . . journey over in a month or less! The first time we came out, it was round the Cape under canvas, ship loaded with cattle and hens, shocking cacophony, woke us at sunrise. Of course I was always up by then anyway.'

'I remember – ' Elizabeth began, to be cut off peremptorily, 'No, no. Before your time.'

7

She remembered a three-masted schooner . . . stars that hung so low in the sky she felt she could reach up and pluck them down . . . the crack of a mast snapped off in a storm . . . a meteor that streamed through the heavens, scattering brightness like a jewelled bird shedding diamond feathers . . .

'As a child,' Elizabeth said tentatively, 'I travelled – ' but her voice was soft and the conversation flowed on, over her words.

She remembered the smell of hay, the lowing of cows being milked for breakfast, and the other sounds – pigs squealing and the sickly, sweetish stench of blood that hung over the ship when they lay becalmed, seeping into cabins and staterooms. There was nowhere they could avoid the farmyard and the slaughterhouse.

She wanted to break in, to tell them more – as a child I once saw an albatross swoop on a sailor and strike his skull with its beak so hard he fell overboard and drowned – but people were now talking of the waters at Bath and Harrogate and she listened politely until it was time to change for dinner.

Each day I watch the sun set, I have the privilege of seeing a giant painting come to life in the sky, no two days the same. Yesterday it sank like a globe of fire in the cold, blue sea, swallowed into its depths, leaving just a smear of pink in the sky before the moon appeared. Today the whole sky glowed purple and peach and crimson streaked with green. Lavender-coloured clouds stood like a wall on the horizon, the edges gradually turning to burnished, molten gold. Surely the Artist who created this skyscape should be applauded?

Later, while a trio played in the lounge after dinner, she crept out to gaze at the darkness. In the moon's rays the brasswork on deck and the white paint had a ghostly glow and the sea lay ridged and glistening like the scales of a great fish.

Daisy was hungry. The airline meal had been acceptable in its plastic fashion but she had eaten little, stomach clenched in the cold, insidious panic that she felt in the face of all things

8

unfamiliar: wrenched away from the routine she had created and perfected, she felt exposed, frightened of taking a false step.

The plane banked steeply and she swayed into James's shoulder. He sighed.

'Sorry.'

She felt anxious and, as always, responsible, as though any approaching disaster would be her fault. As perhaps it was. She should have discouraged this trip. It was unlike James, usually so sensible, hating the unexpected, the different, the new. But the decision, of course, had been his. That was one of the things he did. He decided things. There were all sorts of areas which she had abandoned. Things she did not – or could not – do.

'Let me do that,' James would say brusquely. 'You can't climb that ladder/lift that suitcase/get the car into that space.' Gradually, there were more and more things which apparently lay outside her capability: with time she too was convinced, acknowledged herself unable to cope with them.

Dimly she could remember running an office, dealing with wine waiters, being decisive. Increasingly, there were times when she felt like asking James: 'What do I think about this?' to avoid confusion later. More and more they seemed to be drifting along parallel lines: close but not touching. And not talking.

At one stage, earlier on, when things were bad, she rang the Samaritans. It was wonderful: they listened. And they talked. They talked! 'My husband never talks to me about things that matter. I feel I'm not living up to expectations. Always given the feeling that I'm not living up to what's expected of me.'

Later things changed: he stopped expecting anything of her. She was simply another of life's unsatisfactory elements, something to be endured.

She rummaged in her handbag for some mints, but all she came up with was a loose cough pastille grey with dust and tasting of old make-up.

One night, with the moon behind her, Elizabeth leaned on the

9

rail and watched the sea flowing outwards from the iron walls of the ship, streaming away in an endless, widening wake. She saw that in the darkness under the stern the water blazed as bright as liquid jewels. The surface heaved and glittered like some fiery monster flexing its rippling muscles, green phosphoric light shimmering, dancing on the surface.

Elizabeth needed to know, without delay, what caused the green fire, and in what manner. Henry was busy, discussing politics over an after-dinner cigar, but further down the deck she could see a member of the crew who looked approachable.

When Henry appeared shortly afterwards, Elizabeth was seated on deck staring into a bucket of sea water. She begged him to fetch a glass tumbler, scooped water from the bucket and peered closely, trying to identify the source of the irregular green light brightening, fading and brightening again while she watched. Inside the tumbler glowing rings of light seemed to pulsate.

She bore the jar of liquid away from the deck, carrying it carefully, like a prize, excited, guilty, as though she had stolen fire from a sea-god's altar.

. . . I carried the tumbler to our cabin though Henry was concerned that the pitching of the ship might cause it to be upset, but I set it on a shelf beneath the porthole and lay in my bunk in the darkness watching the green flame glow and dim till I slept. Next morning I examined the tumbler and could now clearly distinguish the miraculous object that was the source of the pulsating light: a small creature like a worm, grubby and colourless, hung in the water. It did not move when I agitated the tumbler and it gave out no light.

She kept the tumbler of water safe, thinking that perhaps the creature slept by day. After dark she studied it again, shaking the imprisoned spirit, but the worm hung inert in the now cloudy water and she saw that it was dead. When she next returned to the cabin the tumbler had been removed.

The voyage was punctuated by social gatherings: waltzes and cotillons on deck in calm weather; lectures with lantern slides on the flora and fauna of the Himalayas. The gentlemen played cards, the ladies sewed and strolled and chatted. And there were the meals: the luncheons, the dinners.

. . . Today's menu: Mutton broth or Mulligatawny soup. Salt fish and egg sauce. Roast haunch of mutton. Boiled shoulder and onion sauce. Boiled beef. Roast fowl. Pillau. Ham. Haricot mutton. Curry and rice. For vegetables there were french beans, cabbage, boiled and baked potatoes, and for sweet, damson tart, rice pudding and currant fritters.

One of the gentlemen, finding what he called a foreign body in his soup, suggested that the cook felt such affection for us that he was sending us locks of his hair as a memento . . .

Each evening Elizabeth checked their position on the map and tried to calculate how a sailor might steer by the stars, as the engine throbbed beneath their feet and the sea streamed away from them in a long, curling trail of lace. And one morning she woke and saw on the horizon a smudge, a low-lying cloud, a blur of apricot and grey. She saw India.

Chapter 2

She dressed quickly, almost breathless, afraid the ship might reach it too soon; that she would miss the slow approach. Without breakfasting, she hurried up on deck and stood waiting, as the land rose higher out of the sea, to display its curves and ridges.

Like a child she hung on the rail, arms hooked over the polished wood. The ship steamed on and she waited. And India reached her before she reached it, carried on the warm wind: a smell, a combination of dung and incense and cheap native tobacco, of excrement and attar of roses and spice. A heady, heavy smell at once exotic and nauseating.

Slowly the town appeared, materialising like a mirage out of the low hills: a church and fort, rooftops, a lighthouse . . . The seagulls became noisy, drowning out, then themselves swallowed up by, other sounds: dogs barking and children's voices calling and men shouting to one another in a jumble of glottal notes. And beneath all that, a subdued roar, of creaking wheels, carts drawn slowly by oxen, more quickly by scrawny horses, filling the crowded streets, the undefined movement of people and the clattering of pots and pans, the beehive hum of Madras.

Henry, considerate as always, had a tray of tea and toast sent up for Elizabeth. Nevertheless, by the time they were close to shore she felt weak, not from lack of food but from excitement. She paid no attention to the little boats bobbing against the ship, the natives frantically selling shells, fruit, brassware, elephant tusks; to the small boys diving for coins carelessly thrown by the passengers. Her eyes were on the land, the crowded quayside where coolies scurried like thin brown mice and women in flowing saris of raspberry, saffron and violet walked with pots or bundles balanced on their heads. With a thrill of pleasure she saw how even the poorest seemed to manage some touch of decoration – one wore bangles of coloured glass, another, jingling anklets and, astonishingly, a tiny silver ornament piercing her nose. Elizabeth touched her own naked nose, thoughtfully.

The plane door opened and the heat engulfed them. It was, Daisy thought, rather like opening the oven door at home: the same blast of hot air that stung your eyes, seared your skin and sucked the breath from your lungs. She was startled: she had never experienced such dramatic heat.

'It's like an oven –' she began, but her voice emerged as querulous. James, misunderstanding, sighed and moved away.

Madras Airport was stark and cheerless: cement and rusting iron, the walls streaked with stains that looked like dried blood. The new arrivals joined the straggle from an earlier flight still waiting for baggage, Customs, Passport Control. Only immediately beneath the overhead fans was there any trace of cool air. Daisy sniffed apprehensively.

'Drains? Or perhaps . . . I hope nothing's wrong –'

'It always smells like that.'

'What, you mean everywhere? In the hotel too? Will the hotel smell like that? Of drains? Surely not!'

She heard her voice going on, embarking on unnecessary repetitions, slightly shrill. Why did she do this? Menopausal nerves? A need to reach James, even by irritating him? In fact, there was more to the smell than drains anyway. She could distinguish spices and a perfume, oily but appealing, like the heavy fragrance of some night flower: Nicotiana?

Jasmine? Perhaps James would know what flower it reminded her of.

'James, does the smell – '

He cut in sharply, 'We'd better get our luggage. I think it's this way.'

He strode ahead of her, a tall figure, his walk slightly ungainly, a lack of co-ordination in the movements, head turning this way and that, impatiently; the wiry white hair ruffled. He looked rumpled and travel weary; the stubble on his chin was silver, not a five o'clock shadow but pinpricks of glinting metal that caught the light when he moved. He looks a tired old man, she thought, surprised by the fact. His quick temper, impatience, his enthusiasms, were all so full of vigour that most of the time he seemed little different from the man she had married thirty years before. His blue eyes were still bright and sharp, his back straight. But he was seventy-six. She followed him out into the orange-tinged, late afternoon sunlight.

※

Elizabeth was given a tour of Madras in a horse-drawn Victoria: she found it impressive, the buildings classically proportioned, the flowerbeds bright with formal splendour.

'And where is the bazaar?' she asked.

The junior officer looked surprised. 'Well: I have not myself visited . . . the neighbourhood is not – '

'I should so like to see the bazaar.'

Driving through the narrow streets in the well-sprung carriage, she seemed to float above the dirt and noise, as though separated from it all by an invisible wall.

'Perhaps we might stop for a moment?'

In the club that evening, as the Regimental ladies embroidered and sipped fresh lime cordial on the veranda, Elizabeth mentioned her explorations.

A young wife paused in mid-stitch: 'You did not *walk* in the bazaar, I trust?'

'Well yes. How else – ?'

'That was unwise: the dangers of walking in the native quarter are well known. Your escort should have explained the situation.'

The wives, it seemed, kept away from the dirt and the noise, repelled by it all, incurious.

'But such colour, and the wonderful smells – '

'– smells indeed!'

'Indians use colour as a consolation,' an elderly woman murmured to Elizabeth, kindly, 'it helps to soften the terrible harshness of their lives.'

But they had been smiling, the women in the bazaar, the girls drawing their saris across their faces shyly as they gazed at the white woman in her stiff, bell-skirted dress and bonnet. Their eyes, black rimmed and lustrous, had been full of laughter.

Above the clubhouse a blue veil of mist trailed across the sky, blotting out the flame of sunset. The ladies put away their embroidery. Elizabeth sat on for a few moments as around her the chairs scraped and shifted, the ladies prepared to move indoors. Where would Henry be posted when they had served their term in Madras? Perhaps she would see Delhi, or the far north – the Himalayas . . . Beyond the steps the lawn was already being swallowed up by darkness and the crickets began to fill the night with their insistent creaking.

*

It was already hot by nine, the morning losing its freshness, moisture evaporating from the grass. Flowers watered earlier by the gardeners grew dull and dry as the sun rose higher. Daisy swam a few lengths in the hotel pool and sipped her milky tea. She had ordered tea with lemon, but fortunately James had overheard: unwise, he warned, they almost certainly would not have washed the lemon whereas the milk was always boiled.

'You'll get the trots. Mark my words.' He was right, of course. She asked for milk.

James was at his worst in hotels, reacting against what he regarded as spurious intimacy. Checking in yesterday, he had looked unsmilingly into the smiling face of the reception clerk.

'You are making your first visit to Madras, sir?'

James signed the registration form and carefully replaced the top of his fountain pen. 'No.'

'So you are knowing the city already. Next week will be our – '

'I'm afraid we're leaving on Monday.' The tone was crisp.

The clerk's face closed up; his eyes grew dull and flat and he withdrew into ritualised obsequiousness. James, impassive, was aware of Daisy's nervous movements beside him.

She smiled brightly at the clerk to try and redress the matter, but he had turned to someone else and did not catch her eye. This happened frequently, she found. She recalled a time when such gestures had been reciprocated, when one smile met another. But she was less certain, these days, of her place in the scheme of things. She had lost her sense of timing. Her once-confident entry into a room of strangers had become a sidling, an ingratiating movement that called forth no welcoming gesture.

At the deep end of the pool she floated on her back, gazing up at the sky through the branches of a jacaranda tree. Backlit by the sun, the purple blossom glowed like silk. Men in white jackets were hanging strips of coloured lights about the trees, putting up temporary pavilions and setting out spindly gilt chairs. A private party was to take place later in the hotel garden. Another Fortieth Anniversary celebration she supposed. Forty years of Independence, of freedom. Freedom from us, she thought, self-consciously identifying herself with the departed imperialists. Freedom from the British yoke. And yet she could detect no hostility in the liquid brown eyes. The smiles seemed genuine.

'You're a tourist. A source of revenue,' James said, shrugging, when she mentioned this. 'Of course they'll smile. But they don't forget who we are. What we were.'

Not her. This was not *her* old country and she had neither guilt nor nostalgia to draw on. She had been surprised when he first mentioned going back.

'But everyone's dead,' she objected, 'who would you talk to, now?' He had answered vaguely: it was, he said, a question of updating memories, tying up loose ends. He disliked being questioned, particularly in areas where probing could reveal scar tissue, evidence of old wounds. And in any case the reasons were confused, not entirely clear even to himself. James had never been a man to share his thoughts or plans.

Her hair was soaked. Soon she would have to dress, hurrying. James disliked waiting when he was ready. She had suggested earlier that he might go without her: old histories and atlases were his field, she would be unable to judge their worth or merit.

'A closed book to me,' she thought, splashing, startling a bald man who was slowly lowering himself into the warm water.

'Go without you?' James had said sharply. 'What would you do? You'll only get bored or try and go for a walk and get lost . . .'

What did he make of her, the bald man, Daisy wondered: a straggly haired Englishwoman well into her fifties, wearing a rather dull two-piece swimsuit, paddling childishly by herself. She was something of an anachronism, with her silly name, and a cleavage unseemly in a middle-aged woman. She was like one of those Thirties creatures with their nicknames and P & O labels. All wrong, like a butterfly born out of season, beating its wings against a hostile sky. She smiled at the bald man and swam towards the steps on the far side. She had a good smile, once it had been an asset, winning allies, bridging rifts. Nowadays it served to disguise her condition. Most people were unaware that Daisy was unhappy.

Chapter 3

The weather was changing. Each time it took Elizabeth by surprise: winter was perfect for riding in the cool, early morning as the sun cast sharp horizontal shadows across the countryside and the horses steamed and snorted. It was still pleasant for the rounds of call-making later in the day, the leaving of cards and the taking of tea.

... To the Musgroves' this afternoon. Amy fretting because the handsome young captain she met at last week's ball has failed to call and leave his card. When Mrs M. was out of the room, Charlotte Belling, also present, made scandalous suggestions to Amy how she might awaken his interest. The social round is most exhausting, and hierarchies must be observed – though Charlotte for one does not always do so! She is incorrigibly frivolous and flirts with the young officers – keeps them dangling, as she puts it. She advises me to learn to 'play the game'. It can be tedious here, for a woman, she says.

Rereading her journal entry, Elizabeth recalled that Henry would almost certainly read the page. She crossed out the last two sentences.

She found their world irritatingly stratified: the 'At Homes', and formal dinners consisting of many courses, followed by dancing, or theatrical entertainments; the meticulous observance of good housekeeping. Each activity had its place and was attended to in great detail.

The men had pig-sticking and polo and shooting. And they

had their tours of duty, the occasional uprising or rebellion to put down. Work. The white woman's burden, she realised, was leisure: leisure that prevented them from using their time in anything other than time-marking forms of inactivity. There were exceptions: she heard of women who ran missions, opened native schools, helped up-country doctors. But they were labelled eccentrics. For Elizabeth, as for the other memsahibs, the social round and domestic supervision expanded to fill the day.

True, there were moments, under the mosquito net, when inert bodies were galvanised into temporary life; when Henry, for instance, cradled Elizabeth in his long arms and found ways to relieve the tedium. She appreciated these moments but it seemed to her sometimes that the exertions demanded were excessively exhausting; the reward, when it came, insufficient. Slippery with perspiration and the excretions of bodily pleasure, suffocating under the weight of Henry's body, she decided that in a cold climate she might enjoy marriage more. And as once again it grew hotter, lethargy and discomfort drained the days of interest. Handing out measures of rice and flour and sugar . . . checking bazaar accounts . . . everything took so long. Waiting for bath water to be heated, to be carried to the tub in earthenware urns; personal 'arrangements' that ranged from the austere to the revolting – it all took time, sapped energy. And, unmentioned, but sitting at the back of everyone's mind was a collective memory: the Mutiny. They all knew the stories, the oldest among them had been there at the time. Bitterness and fear persisted. Indians could smile and salaam. They could also slaughter, and they had. Perhaps they would again. So they must be kept busy. Elizabeth must provide work to keep the servants out of mischief: 'They so need duties to keep them occupied that it is a positive service to drop one's clothes on the floor in order that they may pick them up,' Amy informed her.

. . . the duty of the British to provide work for idle Indian hands is as far as Amy's interest in the country goes as a rule. But I am invited tomorrow to drive with her and Charlotte

20

to an Indian celebration. She will say no more. Perhaps there is to be a wedding? I feel a great lassitude, and long for a bracing Sussex breeze...

Arriving in Charlotte's carriage to collect Elizabeth, the girls were filled with animation and repressed excitement.

'You cannot imagine, my dear, the most astonishing spectacle, we missed it last year, but we hear – '

'It must be seen, so do come, dear Elizabeth!'

Reluctantly, feeling heavy, dragged down by the heat, Elizabeth put on her bonnet, took her parasol and joined them.

The road at first was smooth, the carriage bowled along smartly, but when they turned off towards the open space at the edge of town, the spindly wheels bounced and jolted in the pot-holes. Locals streamed along on foot, on bullock-carts, in rickshaws pulled by scrawny, sweating men, all heading the same way, the women wearing their best saris, the children with eyes kohl-rimmed, giving velvety, innocently seductive glances at passers-by. The noise lapped at the carriage like surf, and Elizabeth found it hard to concentrate on Amy and Charlotte, who chirped in counterpoint.

'It is an ancient festival – '

'Terribly Indian – '

'- and rather discouraged by the British – '

'Why?' Elizabeth enquired listlessly.

'Well they are savages, Elizabeth, you know that.'

They drove past holy men smeared with ash, sacred cows, their horns decorated with tinsel and flowers. Ahead Elizabeth saw the *maidan*, a big open space filled with people; tall, gibbet-like structures rising above the crowd. She felt suddenly apprehensive.

'Is it a public execution?'

Charlotte giggled and patted her hand reassuringly. 'Of course not! It is a festival. See how happy they look!'

The carriage reached the edge of the *maidan* and halted. Elizabeth could see other Europeans dotted about in their carriages, the ladies protected by parasols, veils, hats, gloves, cologne-soaked handkerchiefs and fans. Their flurryings and wavings and fanning gave an impression of constant movement in the carriages, like small birds pecking and twittering in their nests. Elizabeth found them somewhat contemptible: to be so affected by a little heat and noise. Shading her eyes from the low-slanting sun she strained to make out the scene before them: people milling about; stalls selling sweetmeats and garlands of tinsel and marigolds, slices of water-melon and coconut, sugar-cane juice. Music from some unseen band of players threaded through the voices. Some distance away, above the crowd, rose posts about thirty feet high, crossed at the top by a horizontal bamboo from each of which a figure seemed to be suspended. A rope hung from the other end to the ground.

'What is it? What is going on?'

'It's the swinging by hooks,' Charlotte said, her eyes bright. 'I can't recall their name for it – '

'They are doing penance for their sins,' Amy explained. 'I suppose it's a sort of Hindu version of a Catholic saying ten Hail Mary's – '

'- except that some rich sinners pay a poor man to do the penance *for* them – '

They chattered on: 'Later there will be fireworks, and a party at the Maharaja's to which we are invited. He does an excellent banquet – '

She tried to shut out their voices, to allow the muted uproar from all around to penetrate her brain, but all the while, slowly, the carriage had been edging forward through the crowd, and suddenly Elizabeth saw quite clearly what was going on: the men swinging above their heads were suspended from heavy iron hooks, two through the flesh of their back, and two piercing the chest. She felt a buzzing begin in her head and glanced quickly at the face of the nearest man: he looked drugged, but he was quite conscious and threw sweetmeats and flower petals on to the crowd below him. His white loincloth was gradually turning pink as the blood from his mangled chest and back seeped into the cloth. The men holding the rope ran frenziedly, like people dancing round a maypole, and he suddenly swung out, wide, reminding Elizabeth, incongruously, of a swingboat at a fairground.

The driver urged the horses forward, just as the crowd parted for a moment, and they were carried closer, right beneath the first swinging post. As the man twirled, he cried out in a combination of agony and religious ecstasy, and scattered his offerings: a sweetmeat, sticky and soft, struck the bodice of Elizabeth's pale blue dress. She screamed and felt a stabbing pain deep inside her as she clawed frenziedly at the sweetmeat, trying to dislodge it, staring down in revulsion at the reddish brown splodge: it looked like a fragment of flesh torn from his chest by the hooks.

She began to retch, unable to fight off the nausea which swept over her. Amy and Charlotte, too, were distressed yet pleased in a way, their belief in local barbarity confirmed. They ordered the driver to return to town immediately. Smelling salts were produced and a damp handkerchief, cries of comfort and reassurance. Still, they pointed out, it was what one expected of savages, was it not? They were surprised that Elizabeth, usually so resilient, should be so disproportionately upset.

Later the doctor confirmed what she already knew: blood had soaked the petticoats of the pale blue dress; her white bloomers were clogged with viscous crimson: a baby, hardly formed, was lost.

'No serious damage,' the doctor said jovially. 'You'll soon be fit to try again.'

The heat increased, day by day, sucking the air out of the narrow streets, pressing against the chick-blinds at the bungalow windows. As fast as the sweeper sprayed cooling water on the blinds, the warm breath dried the matting so that it clattered against the windows, smelling of heat and burnt brushwood. Yellow dust hung in the air like fine muslin, coating the lungs, gritty against eyeballs. Elizabeth lay, sapped of energy, on her daybed, indolent and no longer curious. People continued to give her good advice: she must keep her head covered or the sun would burn out her brain. She must take exercise, she must rest. She must wear cotton, she must wear wool, she must wear linen. She no longer took her morning rides or her carriage drives along the sea-front at sunset, watching Indian families grouped on the sand, the rosy light painting their clothes pink, turning the sand to copper.

Increasingly, she felt imprisoned in the bungalow, shut in by the dried-grass screens at the windows and the mosquito net over her bed; restricted to the compound, its high wall topped with shards of broken glass. She was hedged about with restrictions which cut her off from the world around her. She felt like a perpetual visitor.

*

Why had she done it? Why insist, voice rising high with tension, that she could manage on her own? That just because James did not wish to see the temple towns, was she to be deprived of them? What was the point of coming all these thousands of miles and not look at anything? And so on.

James had used the old arguments – cited instances, commented ironically on her famous self-sufficiency – and then, unexpectedly, given in: 'Well, why not?'

'What?' (A sinking feeling; a sense of rug being pulled from under her.)

'Go ahead. Book a car. You'll have to do it yourself, I'm going to be pretty tied up, bloody airline still hasn't confirmed the flight for Monday.'

So it was arranged. Daisy would be driven to some hand-picked temples, shown round and brought back safe to the hotel. There were rather more temples than she had bargained for, and the driver, insistently informative, was reluctant for her to miss the slightest detail. So the day had been long, and filled with ancient Hindu statistics and the importuning of temple beggars. Lunch was a disaster because, unable to decide whether to opt for the antiseptic safety of an international hotel dining room or take a chance on the colourful uncertainty of the wayside eating house (fragrant spices, flies, germs . . .), she had gone without, and was now faint with hunger.

The driver waved towards a huge monolithic shrine by the roadside: 'The Pallavas, madam, possessed no iron, but as you see they were carving temples out of solid rock. How did they cut the huge rocks, you are wondering?' He smiled. 'They dropped a seed into some tiny crack in the rock. In time the seed grew into a tree. The roots grew strong, until finally they split the rock, no matter how big. In this way, madam, we see how a small thing, taking root, can break a big thing.' He laughed comfortably. He had eaten something that looked delicious, served on a shiny leaf at a stall, while Daisy drank lukewarm bottled water from her flask. At least one of them was not hungry, she thought resentfully.

'That seems a slow way to build a temple.' Her voice was sharp.

The driver shrugged. 'Madam, they were in no hurry.' He said, casually, 'That is the Indian way. When you are weak, how else to fight? A seed, a drop of water, with time, with repeating, can overcome great strength.'

That was the Indian way. Something James knew about.

The car was not air-conditioned, the suspension had long ago given up any struggle, and she had spent seven hours being bounced along streets filled with dust, lorries, scooter rickshaws and the noise of a thousand car hooters.

Surely they could not be far from the hotel now? The car was coming up to a major intersection and she knew from James that one did not ask questions at such times. She waited, leaning forward from her seat in the back, as the driver gunned his way across at full speed. Just ahead and to their left a cyclist decided to change direction. Without warning he turned sharply right.

The driver slammed on the brakes and Daisy shot forward, hurled against the front seat. For an instant the cyclist was framed in the windscreen like a fish in a glass case, motionless, suspended in time, perfect as a picture; then came the crash, jolting, horrible, not the jarring impact of a solid object, but with a yielding lurch. One moment he was hurtling towards them, and the next he vanished as the windscreen turned into a wall of diamonds, a glittering screen that slowly bulged, then shattered, scattering broken glass over the car's occupants as he came through it in a tangle of metal and flesh. Brilliant fragments like a jewelled sandstorm sprayed Daisy's face and arms, clattered against her sunglasses. She heard the driver swearing very quietly and with great force. From all around came screams and shouts and the driver leaped out of the car. He reappeared holding the cyclist, half carrying him. One white sleeve was bright crimson from shoulder to wrist, the colour of bougainvillaea. Blood poured from his head down his shirt, and from his knees, darkening the flimsy cotton pants. A moment later he was in the front seat, leaning against the window, bleeding profusely over the seat cover, moaning quietly. Daisy's eyes flickered away from the welling gashes and she focused on a printed sticker on the dashboard next to him: 'Have Fun!' In the centre of the glittering windscreen was a huge hole, and around it, hanging loose, swinging with the motion of the car, strips of crazed glass dangled like chain mail.

'Madam, are you all right?'

Twisted round in his seat, the driver was smiling at her anxiously. He went on apologising: 'It is most unfortunate – '

She said, her voice shaky, 'Please keep your eyes on the road.'

The cyclist groaned loudly and the driver broke off to address him in a rapid stream of Hindi, giving quick, sidelong glances at his passenger.

'Where are we going?'

'To find hospital, madam.'

The main road left behind, they drove down side streets shaded by trees, driving fast, hurtling round corners. As they cornered, the loose diamonds piled up on the dashboard shelf slid noisily from side to side, scattering, gathering in small heaps, sparkling in the sun. The cyclist bled quietly in the front seat. Daisy thought: the police will want me as a witness. It could keep me here weeks. We have a plane to catch; James will be furious. He'll say – you see, you can't be trusted on your own. And he was quite right: if James had been in the car he would have anticipated, he would have noted a certain recklessness in the driver's approach to traffic lights and cross-roads, he would have told him to slow down. No matter that the cyclist had not looked before turning: the prepared mind would have taken measures. The crash would have been avoided.

She found herself wondering whether she could claim that she was not a witness to anything, that she had closed her eyes when it happened, had seen nothing. As hope tentatively surfaced, she was overwhelmed with shame: the man is badly hurt, bleeding, and I'm thinking about how to get away without delay, about what James will say.

Gingerly she began to shake broken glass out of her clothes.

Chapter 4

Dressing for the fancy-dress ball, Elizabeth was grateful for the comfort of her classical Grecian muslin robe. Charlotte would be even cooler: she had announced she was going as Salome – 'towards the *end* of the dance, my dear'. Elizabeth was never sure whether Charlotte was joking, and when she seemed at her most outrageous, she might well be perfectly serious. She was a married woman now and the condition suited her: slightly plumper, she moved through drawing rooms and garden parties with a radiant confidence. Elizabeth sometimes sensed scandal hovering over Charlotte's head like the dove in her illustrated New Testament of John the Baptist at the Jordan.

Amy, as Queen Elizabeth, would be perspiring in a red wig and a stiff, beaded costume with pleated ruff. Henry would not be in costume. Or rather, he would be in his own costume: military uniform was, after all, fancy dress, with its brass buttons and bright colours.

Elizabeth had heard stories about fancy-dress balls past: tales of indiscretion, of young wives newly arrived who turned the heads of junior officers. Escapades become folklore.

Nothing like that happened these days. With the death of Queen Victoria a pall of mourning had dropped over the social scene, and even now there seemed to be a cautious tone to the jollity.

The sound of the orchestra came faintly from the ballroom as she stepped out on to the lawn. The light from the tall windows fell across the grass in pale rectangles. Beyond, the darkness was full of movement: leaves rustling in a breeze that brought no breath of coolness, insects swarming, bats swooping. In the bushes tiny lights glowed and pulsed. Going closer, she could discern insects busy among the twigs and branches: quite ordinary, unprepossessing little bugs flickering like sapphires in the darkness. Elizabeth watched them, her face so close she was blinded by their blue-green brightness. She thought, guiltily, of the magical phosphoric light, the pulsating green fire she had captured – briefly – in a glass tumbler on board ship.

That too had seemed beautiful, shining and brilliant. She saw that the true nature of an object could be obscured as much by light as by darkness. Through the windows she could see the assembled company dancing, drinking champagne and eating water ices. Pale-skinned people in silk and satin, covered with jewels, wearing fine uniforms. How beautiful they seemed to be, and how ugly the native holy man they had passed in the road on the way to the ball: naked except for a rag tied at his groin, hair wild, bare feet in the dust, black skin smeared with white ash. Put him in the crimson and gold regalia, the gem-starred turban of a maharaja and Amy and Charlotte would say he was a fine figure of a man. But they would be admiring the glitter not the pulpy human animal. Was Henry a handsome man? She had never before considered the question. He was tall. Without fat. In his uniform – ah yes, a fine figure of a man. In his night-shirt . . . or out of it . . . he looked a little like a stork. Long, thin legs, long neck, a white body.

She wondered sometimes who he was. Behind the smooth, composed face, the deferential droop as he listened to the woman seated next to him at dinner, lay a stranger she had only a glancing knowledge of. Some day she meant to know him better. But there seemed never to be time.

High overhead, the palm trees jutted black against the thickly starred sky. The air lay still and hot and the moon burned like a great balefire, not with the silvery delicacy of home, but with a fierce blaze. Elizabeth felt it on her bare shoulders; the moonlight seemed to burn her skin.

This was their last night in Madras. Tomorrow they would take the boat, four days at sea, the hold filled with criminals in irons. Four empty days during which Elizabeth planned to question those on board, to learn something of the place they were bound for. 'There is no need, my dear,' a senior wife had assured her. 'One posting is much like another.' But not this one, surely? She was not to see the palaces of Delhi, the princes who walked on cloth of gold and garlanded their elephants with emeralds. Delhi could be as agreeable as London or Bath if you kept to the right neighbourhoods, the wives said. And the hill stations – ('quite like Baden-Baden') – would remain unvisited. Even Madras was civilisation. The ladies at the club had dispelled any doubts about her own destination: 'The Andaman Islands? You'll be crossing the black water my dear, that's what the natives call it. *Kala pani*. You will hear them moaning below decks, they know they won't be coming back.' There was no coming back for convicts serving life sentences on what Elizabeth visualised as a sea-girt hell: Henry was taking her to a penal colony. And what of the garrison? she wondered. How long would they stay? Would they ever come back? The climate, she heard, was inclement, the funerals frequent. The islands were mysterious; no one knew much about them – or wanted to. She became aware that the music had changed. She must go back: Henry would be wondering where she was.

*

'The city is *en fête*!' the bookseller exclaimed, spreading his arms as though offering the whole of Madras to Daisy as a gift. Above his head the sign proclaimed 'N. K. Ramachander and Brother. Antiquarian Booksellers. Rare Prints and Volumes.'

'Forty years of Independence, of freedom from the British Raj . . .' A smile of complicity: 'To paraphrase the Bard:

nothing in your Reign became you like the leaving it – wouldn't you agree?' He laughed uproariously.

James studied a book of geographical engravings, holding it up to the light, slowly turning the pages. It was left to Daisy with her bright smile to rescue Mr Ramachander from mid-air.

'Well, the Americans celebrate the Fourth of July, after all.'

He gave a small, delicate shrug. 'To be sure. But you know, Indians love to celebrate. Any excuse. People say India is changing. India has always been changing, its condition is flux. The losses and gains of so-called civilisation. From colony to troubled democracy is progress of a sort. But what next, one wonders? Still: paint the oxen's horns red. Fireworks and flower petals. Bread and circuses. They are simple people.'

'They'? Daisy wondered. Why does he talk as though he were somehow apart from all that? Mr Ramachander stood by the window, plump and uncrumpled in his dark suit and stiff white collar; his smooth, pale hands and silk tie seemed to be made of the same material. Outside in the dusty street a man in a dhoti blew his nose against the roots of a tree; another loping past in ragged cotton pants and thong sandals spat heavily, the gob of phlegm shining in the sunlight as it flew through the air and hit the gutter. Mr Ramachander was right: he *was* apart from all that.

James had made his choices: 'These two.'

Mr Ramachander took the books, smoothing the covers as though stroking a cat, glancing at the titles.

'Ah yes . . . Interesting volumes. Might I enquire: you have a special interest in our Andaman and Nicobar Islands?'

Daisy waited for James to reply, uncertain whether the special interest was to be public knowledge.

'We're spending a few days there.'

Daisy saw that Mr Ramachander was not to be privy to more information. There was a pause. She made her small contribution, breaking the silence.

'I hope we have nice weather.'

The bookseller said tactfully, 'Well, you know, the

islands . . . They can be . . . a little . . . unsettled at this time of year. Makes it more interesting, don't you agree? Look here, if you're going to be in the Andamans, I have some family connections – '

James was reaching impatiently into one pocket after another, shifting from foot to foot.

'We're rather pushed for time; if you could tell me how much . . .'

Mr Ramachander nodded, opening and closing the pages at random like someone seeking lost letters or concealed bank-notes between the leaves. He arrived gracefully, almost absent-mindedly, at a price and James took out his wallet and paid. He never bargained or haggled. If he felt the price to be unreasonable he simply left. Mr Ramachander looked slightly taken aback. Daisy suspected that he might have preferred the chance to lower his price – or at least defend it. Instant capitulation robbed him of an expected joust. But James was in a hurry.

With the books wrapped in flimsy paper under his arm, he propelled Daisy from the shop.

'*Bon voyage!*' Mr Ramachander called after them. 'Mention my name to the harbour master, it may prove useful!' He began to say something more but the blaring of a car horn blotted out his voice.

James walked fast, with his uneven, shambling stride, and Daisy, trying to keep up with him, began to sweat. She felt a prickle of perspiration break out over her breasts and a stab of pain in her foot.

'Why don't we take a rickshaw?' she said fretfully, not really expecting an answer. 'I didn't realise we'd be doing all this walking. I think I got a splinter of glass in my heel – ' 'All right.' James signalled a moped rickshaw jingling past. Daisy looked surprised. Usually she had to complain for longer before James took notice. She settled herself in the seat, cramped by his bulk.

She wondered about the cyclist, last seen being half carried into the hospital by the driver, who reappeared almost immediately and drove rapidly away from the hospital gates.

'Is he all right?' she had asked.

'Oh yes, madam. I will give him some rupees and mend the bicycle.' Private arrangements, accommodations arrived at to keep the authorities out of things – that was the Indian way. Less trouble for all concerned. Less chance of being caught in the mesh of bureaucratic corruption.

'I wonder if I should ask the hotel doctor to have a look at my foot, if there *is* a bit of glass in there it might go septic.' No response. 'With all the germs about . . .' She paused. 'I can feel my feet swelling. The heat – '

She sensed rather than saw his movement of impatience. She should stop now, allow silence to grow, expand between them like a buffer. But she heard her voice chirping into its next question.

'He said it would be unsettled, the bookseller. Will it be very hot, on the islands? What about humidity?'

Surely she had asked that before? But James did not give the familiar, exasperated sigh. He hesitated. He even thought about the question for a moment.

'I'm not sure,' he said, 'I don't remember.'

Chapter 5

There were about ten British on board, and the hold 'full of murderers', one wife whispered to Elizabeth. 'If they should get free – ' ('from leg-irons?' Elizabeth questioned doubtfully, but silently) ' – we should all be killed in our beds!'

Not beds, bunks. Elizabeth would have liked, for once, to offer information, rather than be instructed, but dinner was about to be served and Henry was approaching, ready to take her in.

Meals were simpler on this journey: no P & O banquets. No *soirées musicales*, no *conversazioni* at which Elizabeth might have been instructed by those more experienced than herself. 'Where shall we live?' she had asked Henry.

'On Ross,' he said. 'I believe a house is ready.'

Ready? What did he mean? Was it a new house, a bungalow freshly built, or an old house lying empty? And why empty? Where were the previous occupants? ('Crossing the black water, the *kala pani*, the convicts know they will never go home.') Had those others, for whom they were the replacements, gone home?

*

Breakfast was served during the flight to Port Blair. Indian breakfast. The smell of curry so early in the morning aroused a feeling of nausea in Daisy: she longed for the familiar comforts of buttered toast, crisp bacon, marmalade. The plastic tray lay untouched on her folding table, while next to her James tucked in without any apparent difficulty.

'Does the hotel have a swimming pool?' she asked, for something to say.

He chewed at a square of chapati. 'Shouldn't think so. I gather it's right on the beach. Nice spot. We used to drive through the forest to get there. No hotel in those days of course; there wasn't even a road, not a proper one, but the horses didn't seem to mind.'

He was more talkative than usual. Daisy seized the moment. 'But we're on the main island, aren't we? I thought you lived – '

'– I've told you. We lived on Ross. Sometimes', he added, 'we went across by launch. For swimming parties or picnics.'

'Was it safe for swimming?'

'Oh yes: the servants used to beat the water to keep the sharks away – '

Daisy glanced at him, sure he must be making one of his jokes, but he was perfectly serious.

'How appalling: did the sharks ever attack anyone? The servants, I mean. They must have been terrified.'

He looked surprised. 'I'd forgotten all about that . . . it does seem a bit . . .' He paused. 'I don't recall them complaining.'

'But didn't you think – '

He leaned back and closed his eyes, shutting her out. She stopped in mid-sentence. A stewardess in a blue-and-red sari was collecting the trays, moving slowly down the aisle.

Sending the servants in to frighten off the sharks: it did seem . . . what? What was the word? He felt panic nibbling at him: this had happened more than once recently. Last week he had been unable to close his mental fist on a word he sought: a material used in building. He had reached for it in conversation, to find himself coming up empty-handed. A moment's terrifying blankness. He had done a fast scan of possibles, recited to himself all the other materials he could think of: wood, tin, marble, plastic, iron, chalcedony, alabaster. But surely his elusive word had three syllables? He tried triple syllables at random – porphyry, gravadlax, honeymoon. The word hovered, half formed, in his mind, dissolving as he neared it. Hours later it floated serenely into his consciousness: asbestos. Of course. Now here it was again, that sense of helplessness, of facing a blank wall where there should have been a niche comfortably stocked with the right word. What was the word, the word? Sending the servants in had surely been a bit . . . *what*?

He felt increasingly uneasy: the droning of the engine, the sensation of floating inescapably towards some dreadful fate, unable to move from your seat: it reminded James of a bad dream. And he was an expert on them. Dreams of falling, of embarrassment; dreams of anxiety in which he tried vainly to locate his baggage, catch a train or find his way through a labyrinth. In dreams, he had noticed, sensations like loss, sorrow, fear, sexual excitement – even fulfilment – were experienced with vivid clarity. But he never felt the heat of the sun. Blue skies, yes. Brilliant sea, dazzling rocks; he could examine it all in the minutest detail, but with no sensation of warmth. Often there seemed a shadow on the scene, even in bright sunlight, a sense of impending storm, the sea banked up like a wall, suddenly ominous. Dreams of drowning. Flashes of darkness heralding pain.

A mosquito net draped about a bed. A troubled sleeper. A woman with yellow-gold hair in a dress like butterflies' wings. A pale creature who rose in the air, weightless, and floated high over the trees and away to sea. He cried out, trying to follow her, held back by bonds he struggled to unfasten.

Daisy was aware that James had drifted into sleep: he twitched; clawed at his safety belt, gave a muffled groan. She shook his shoulder gently. He mumbled something and slumped back into sleep.

A tiny movement caught Daisy's eye: a fly was buzzing slowly just above her head. It must have flown into the plane in Madras. The doors closed, the fly remained on board. The plane took off. Daisy thought: when the doors open again and the plane empties, the fly too will emerge, and find itself on an island seven hundred miles from home. Will it be lost? Puzzled? Frightened? Will it die? Or simply buzz out of the plane door and go in search of food? Perhaps it will settle down for a snooze in a luggage rack, and take the return flight to Madras.

Outside the windows the bright blue was suddenly blotted out by thick grey cloud.

'We have some turbulence, ladies and gentlemen. Please return to your seats and fasten safety belts.' The message was repeated in three languages. James sat up, blinking. Daisy looked at her watch.

'Less than an hour to go. We're halfway there. I hope we're not going to have a storm. It could be stormy at this time of year. We should have come earlier. Or later.' Unsettled, the bookseller had said. The guidebook called it hurricane season.

'James – '

James grunted and closed his eyes. The plane lurched.

Chapter 6

The weather turned stormy two days out: the blue sea that
had sparkled at Madras was now sullen. The waves surged
alarmingly, their crests tipped with dirty curls. Where the sea
met the sky, leaden clouds hung over the angry waters in a
blur the colour of a bruise.

The approaching straits were dangerous, everyone said so.
This was typhoon country: ships were blown off course, lost
at sea. There were stories of shipwreck, sharks . . .

As the little ship ploughed on, Elizabeth tried to visualise
this dreadful place they were bound for, this cluster of hostile
islands with reefs that could tear the steel of a hull as if it were
paper; a place with two monsoons, with murderers on every
side. Henry sensibly said speculation was fruitless: in two more
days they would see the islands. Until then he proposed to
read, smoke his pipe, write his journal. Elizabeth, filled with
curiosity and without the soothing consolation of tobacco, went
walking on deck and met Mr Pilkington.

She had seen them boarding the ship at Madras, Mr and Mrs
Pilkington and their babe in arms. Mrs Pilkington was pale,
frail and unhappy looking. Her husband was a whippet of a
man, quivering with energy, notebook always at the ready,
sharp eyes taking in everything. He whirled about the ship
with spring-heeled grace, seeing how the engine room worked,
looking in on the sickbay, talking to the cook, learning to
navigate. He played the violin, 'with more enthusiasm than
skill', he admitted, and having heard the sounds emerging from

his cabin, Elizabeth privately agreed that he spoke no more than the truth.

The crew began by resenting his intrusiveness, but after two days the sharp-featured little man had won them over, eyes screwed up, face pulled into a ferocious scowl of concentration as he nodded, grunting encouragingly, scribbling in the ever-present notebook, drawing charts or jotting down technical information.

He was the only passenger who managed – or desired – to see the convicts. Elizabeth heard from Henry that Tom Pilkington had gone below, into the foetid darkness of the hold, and talked to the manacled men. Henry felt this had been unwise: frontiers should not be blurred. The military men were uneasy with Pilkington, they mistrusted his curiosity.

He was, of course, the perfect travelling companion for Elizabeth: together they paced the deck, noting cloud formations and marine life, searching the reference books for information.

'One theory is that the name comes from the Malay word for the islands: "Handuman" – the Place of Savages. Understandable when you consider that for centuries the Malays loaded up their ships with Andamanese and sold them as slaves. As to the aboriginals, I'm told the Onges can be approached – with caution. The Jarawa would appear to be hostile and dangerous ... there's something in Takakasu's edition of I-Tsing ...'

For Elizabeth it was as thrilling as following a trail through a labyrinth:

... the Chinese called them Yen-t'o-mang ... the earliest authentic reference to the islands Mr Pilkington has found comes from two Arab travellers in the year AD 871. In the eighteenth century, a French priest, the Abbé Renaudot, translated their accounts from the Arabic. Now I am translating Abbé Renaudot for Mr Pilkington –

'Au-delà de ces isles on trouve la mer appellée d'Andaman ... The people who live on the coast eat – er –

human flesh, raw. They . . . they have visages and eyes frightful – sorry, frightening faces and eyes, and big feet.'

Henry, coming to fetch Elizabeth, paused to gaze out over the empty sea, listening while her clear voice carried across the deck . . . 'and they go completely naked . . .'

Henry said in his unruffled way, 'Time for luncheon, Elizabeth.'

They sat with another military couple and Henry casually led the conversation round to Elizabeth's garden in Sussex, the problems of black spot and mildew. He found her preoccupation with the islands worrying: wives did not, as a rule, bother themselves with the details of their husband's next posting. The British community was small, tightly knit: it would be regrettable if Elizabeth were to be cast in the role of eccentric outsider. He wrote as much, taking a tone of gentle concern, in his journal, and she read it, wide eyes fixed on the page, while Henry enjoyed the last cigar of the evening in the smoking room. But next day, disregarding spray and mist, she was on deck, questioning, listening, while Tom Pilkington talked on, never pausing to search for a word or draw breath.

It seems that Mr Pilkington is engaged on an ethnographic survey of the tribes of Southern India and he hopes to include those of the Andaman and Nicobar Islands. He is to take photographs, and create lantern slides and also phonographic records of tribal songs and music. He is equipped with all manner of anthropometric instruments on loan to him from some learned society in Bengal, for he, poor man, is quite impoverished.

His plan is to begin by attracting the more friendly tribal natives by showing them his American 'illusion machines', which he calls pseudoptics, for demonstrating moving pictures through the use of light. And he will play them music on his phonograph (perhaps also his violin?), to encourage them to sing and play in their turn. In due course bulletins will be published and he hopes to attract benefactors to establish an anthropological laboratory.

Mrs Pilkington, Nora, was seasick a good deal and needed help with the baby. But when mother and child were resting, he was to be found on deck.

'My dear Mrs Oakley, we are here in the nick of time! The European influence is fatally changing the natives – diet, customs, dress: we will finish by wiping them out – '

'Surely not!' Elizabeth exclaimed, horrified.

'Oh, not with guns – though we do that too – but with our mere presence. We give them measles and syphilis; the birth-rate has fallen ominously . . .' He was unaware that his voice could be heard yards across the deck. 'We bring them wretched factory-made beads and bits of cloth that take the place of shells and bark and clay pigment. Yes, we will be the end of them.'

. . . poor Mr Pilkington: he had planned to establish an anthropological laboratory to study and record the lives and customs of his tribal Indians, but costs have outrun his means and the laboratory remains a distant dream. He is dreadfully short of funds for his expeditions but he cannot delay. He says the anthropological study had better be completed now while there are still tribals to be studied. Later there may be money but no natives. We may have the dubious privilege of seeing the last of them. It is a story I am familiar with: as with the Incas, now these aboriginals . . .

She recalled a windswept plateau in the Andes, the ancient terraces rising above it in giant steps, a puna hawk gliding, black against the sun, a Quechua woman and her child, expressionless, resigned. She remembered the sadness of the Peruvian Indians, the terrible passivity. Something had been taken away from them, something more than the Inca gold and treasure.

. . . Had I a fortune I would most certainly assist Mr Pilking-ton. But how best should we protect the aboriginals? By leaving them in peace, he says. So is Mr Pilkington not himself guilty of the interference he abhors?

41

In Henry's journal, lying open as always next to hers, Elizabeth read with mortification:

... Mr Pilkington lacks discretion and judgement. He is not, perhaps, the most suitable of companions for an impressionable young woman.

But he said nothing, and Elizabeth and Mr Pilkington continued to walk the deck.

That night the passengers had their introduction to the changing mood of the local waters. Elizabeth woke suddenly in a cabin where gravity appeared to have changed its laws: the world heaved, out of control. She found herself sliding off the bunk; water jugs crashed to the floor, objects flew through the air as if thrown by invisible hands. From all around came sounds of alarm – voices crying out, doors banging, and beyond that, a growing, continuous roaring that filled her head, the sound of the wind and the waves. There were slow, heavy rolls of thunder, the rumbling of a lethargic god; a lurid sheet of lightning lit up the porthole; then, sweeping the ship like a fusillade of bullets, a sudden hailstorm, an assault of white marbles drumming on the deck. Unable to contain her curiosity, Elizabeth disregarded Henry's shouted instructions to remain in the cabin. She staggered along the passage, clinging to walls that fell away without warning and as suddenly sprang back to buffet her. Inching up the companionway, clinging to the rail with one hand, she scooped up hailstones, feeling them melt icily in her palm, cramming them into her mouth, crunching, though the cold set her teeth aching. Blinded by the spray, soaked, she caught glimpses of watery mountains rearing beyond the deck, dropping away out of sight.

The icy slush filling her mouth tasted like liquid smoke, like dead water, and awoke a memory: another storm, a ship under sail, every timber groaning and twisting with the strain of the wild wind; her mother tying her to the bunk with a sash from her gown, waves pouring over the decks, smashing frail wood, sweeping livestock and crew alike towards the rail. Cattle, sheep, poultry, all tumbling in the crazy, leaping water, pigs squealing as if under the slaughterer's knife. A cook from the galley flung headlong, grabbing hold of a pig as it slithered past, the pig mad with terror snapping at the cook's hand, blood, the cook letting go and the pig swept in one cascading wave over the side . . .

Elizabeth's hand, clutching the companionway, slipped and she fell, tumbling to the foot of the steps, cushioned by her bunched skirts, into Henry's arms. From deep within the ship she heard a sound: high-pitched, almost musical, the pitiful calls and shrieks of the manacled convicts, trapped in the hold in darkness and terror.

All night the ship fought, the sea boiling against the port-holes. Then, as dawn broke, there was a pause, a silence: the eye of the storm.

'Is it over?' Elizabeth asked, but before Henry could answer she felt the vessel tremble under them, every bolt and joint straining in protest.

'Whirlwind,' said Henry, and held her braced against the tilting, see-saw movements as the ship spun. The cabin door flew open and the blast swept them, gritty and hot.

Gradually the sea calmed and the ship lay clumsily in the water, without headway or direction, heaving and shuddering still, like a body racked by slowly subsiding sobs. Then, cautiously, creeping from places of safety, the passengers began to reappear.

Chapter 7

An Italian with headphones clamped to his luxuriant grey hair drummed rhythmically on the back of James's seat. Even above the noise of the engine James could not escape the invasion, the electronic subsound of the unheard tune. He turned and glared at the man who stared blankly back at him through his dark glasses. James grunted irritably.

'What's wrong?' Daisy suspected that it – whatever 'it' was, must be in some way her fault.

'Nothing.' He closed his eyes.

She watched him for a moment, then glanced out of the window again. White clouds were piled up around them like stiffly beaten egg white, and below – she stared down, peering at the puckered surface of the sea: lying low, so thickly wooded that it had the appearance of a silhouette, an area of blackness against the sun and misty sea, was land. A sinuous shape edged by a narrow sandy strip. More shapes lay beyond; dull green, seemingly solid rain forest. The plane dropped lower, its shadow trailing them, flitting across the treetops as though seeking a landing place.

'James – ' He grunted.

'We're there.'

He leaned across her, looking down, his face expressionless.

'So we are.'

He sat back and closed his eyes again. His wiry hair was untidy, sticking up comically in silvery tufts, and he looked a little absurd.

Once, years ago, misled by an atmosphere of concord, she had in a lighthearted gesture of affection, reached out and ruffled his hair. He had pulled away sharply, instinctively, and she had railed at him, surprising them both, weeping, 'You shut me out! I can't reach you! I'm alone, alone . . .'

'What curious circumstances are you inventing for yourself now?' he enquired. 'We are never apart.'

'We never make love – '

'Try and avoid sentimental euphemisms if you can.'

She longed to shock him, shower him with the lusty vocabulary she had once used naturally, free herself from the strait-jacket of gentility and discretion he had imposed on her – ('Why don't you screw me, James?') – but the garment fitted too well now, could not be cast off.

'You never touch me.'

'As I understood it, there was some problem – '

'I changed the pills. Things are different, can't you understand?'

But James disliked scenes and the liberating quarrel she had hoped to provoke fizzled out in rhetoric. For James it served a different purpose.

'I'm obviously impossible to live with, why don't you leave me?' he suggested, urging her, encouraging the idea, giving his hate-filled, triumphant smile. He knew people could not be counted on, especially those who said they loved you. They were the ones who betrayed you.

The plane dipped and he heard the note of the engine change, the grinding sound of the wheels being lowered. The last time he had made the journey from Home, it took three weeks on a P & O liner that ploughed its way across the oceans. He had boarded eagerly, his head filled with questions: would there be storms at sea? Falling stars? Romance as the band played a foxtrot? Last time, he stood by the rail of the ferry from Madras, watching as they approached the shoreline, Freddy, at his elbow, already making plans. 'We'll get your old man to give us a few introductions – '

But there had been no introductions, the old man already too far gone for anything more than silent, dutiful vigils by the bedside. James had reacted bitterly to the unfairness of it: after all the years of never being able to talk about the past, never being able to ask the important questions, to be too late. But Freddy had been unsympathetic.

'It's your own fault. You back away, Jamie, you pull up the ladder.'

Freddy had been his best friend, or so he thought, but Freddy had slipped away somehow, as people tended to. They met for lunch once a year, until that too lapsed, replaced by a card at Christmas, proceeds to some appropriate charity. Then Freddy was dead.

'AIDS, I suppose,' Daisy said when she heard. James was astonished, upset, disproportionately angry.

'Why should you "suppose"?'

'Well I should have thought it was obvious – '

'And you would be the person to think it, if it's obvious.' James sliced the top off his breakfast egg, smiling a bitter little smile at her.

She left the table, abandoning him in what he later described as a moment of crisis. He read the letter again. Freddy gone. They never met, they never wrote, but James had always nursed the idea that one of these days, one of these years, they would pick up where they left off. He had been able to talk to Freddy, long ago. Perhaps – but now there was just the letter and then the obituary in *The Times*, quite brief but affectionate, paying tribute to his career in the City; his translations of Greek poets, his charitable work, the brave fight against his – unspecified – disease. The usual thing. No mention of the dangerous, glinting charm that drew strangers to him, that cluttered his life with emotionally unstable acquaintances who believed themselves to be more important to him than was the case.

At his memorial service James saw faces he had once known and long lost touch with; others were unknown to him, strang-

46

ers brought uneasily together by the snapping of the only thread that had connected them.

There were anecdotes, recollections, laughter.

'God, Jamie,' he had sighed once, 'people pop up like genies out of a bottle and there's no way to get rid of them once the game's over.'

And now the game was definitely over. Some actor, apparently well known, read Freddy's favourite poem, the Cavafy – 'He said once that it was what he lived by . . .'

> When you set out for Ithaka
> Pray that the road is long,
> Full of adventure and discoveries . . .

Adventure and discoveries, that was the aim, he had impressed on James when they set out on that earlier journey: 'Remember Stevenson, Jamie: "The unwearying search for something new in a new country"!' And on the way, keep Ithaka in your mind.

The celebrated actor was giving it his all, his voice unctuous with charm:

> But do not hurry the journey.
> You should be old when you reach your island,
> Old, rich, with all you have gained on the way . . .

James had always known Freddy's proclivities, but surely Freddy was too *old* for AIDS, that was a now-generation thing. Wrong frame of reference. But Freddy was gone and there would be no taking up where they left off. Freddy, too, had let him down.

Daisy gazed in dismay at the scene below: rusting corrugated iron sheds; a sprawl of industrial development. The sun glittered harshly on the little silver rectangle of tin rooftops, hurting her eyes. Dull green treetops spread away into the distance. Miles of raintrees and mangrove. And James had given her the impression it was like a tropical island paradise in a TV

47

commercial – white sand, palm trees, crystal sea and happy, laughing Third World folk.

She felt a web of resentment thickening around her: she had wanted a Greek island: antiquities, local honey and yoghurt in the Aegean sun, wine and black olives, the sense of myth and romance . . . But James had made the final decision, as he always did.

She could have argued. But the exhaustion of the inevitable defeat had swept over her and she turned away with a shrug. Still, she had thought at least it would be beautiful.

*

On the fourth day, before it was light, the ship began to seethe and clatter with the movement of people and the shifting of goods as they approached the islands.

Elizabeth listened to the sounds that came from deep in the ship: the moans, the cries, the clanking of chains as the convicts faced the prospect of their final destination. A dank hold filled with criminals, desperate men. The air rising from below pervaded the ship, rancid with fear and hate. Would she smell that fear, sense that hate, day after day?

'How long will you stay on the islands?' Nora Pilkington asked her when they met.

'Three years, perhaps a little more, Henry tells me.'

The Pilkingtons were already on deck when Elizabeth appeared, he with one of his notebooks and a look of keen anticipation, she pale and apprehensive, the child held against her shoulder, well wrapped up although the air already felt warm and humid.

'Well, Mrs Oakley!' Tom Pilkington looked up from making a note. 'Here we are. Ptolemy's cannibal islands, Marco Polo's land of dog-faced men. Are you not excited at the prospect of so much strangeness?'

'Oh indeed yes!' she exclaimed, unaware of Henry's fleeting, sidelong glance, the anxious frown shadowing his face.

She watched the shoreline emerging from the pre-dawn dimness: a harbour, low hills, a promontory. Slowly the helmsman brought the vessel round to its docking berth. With the gentlest of bumps, a nudge of hull against harbour wall, and a rope made fast, they were linked to the quay.

*

The plane skimmed the dusty runway. There was a roar, a throttling back that pressed them into their seats and the wheels bounced hard, once, twice. They sensed the braking, the wrenching pull, the protest from every metal joint as the pilot dragged it to an unwilling halt. A voice thanked Daisy and James for flying Indian Airlines and please remain seated until the plane has . . .

Everyone else immediately stood up and began to haul down belongings, push towards the exits. James and Daisy remained in their seats, though she was tempted to join the rush. 'Let them go,' he instructed her firmly, 'I refuse to jostle.'

'Sir?'

The blue-and-red sari was at his shoulder. 'Will you please follow the other passengers.'

He looked furious and Daisy felt an unwilling twinge of pity: this happened frequently: *he* behaved correctly, but others set the course. Unfair really.

*

The convicts staggered from the hold, stumbling, clutching one another, half-blind in the sunlight after days of darkness. They were unsteady on the jetty, still swaying to a sea-surge, one or two vomiting. Elizabeth and the luggage – the trunks and hatboxes, the hampers and crates – were taken smoothly in hand by the army.

'Welcome to the Andamans, Mrs Oakley.' The young officer saluted and waved her ashore. She suspected that had there been a puddle in her path he would have whipped off – well, not his own jacket, but certainly one from the nearest sepoy, and thrown it down before her.

. . . without delay, on our very arrival, I was faced with the strangeness of this place. On the quayside, quite calm, almost as though unaware of the soldiers and the convicts huddled in their chains, were some small, very black men: Onges, Mr Pilkington informed me, come to barter with us. One of them had a pair of curving shells of brilliant pearl marked with purple like butterfly wings. He grew impatient with the baubles we offered, and would not exchange the marvellous butterfly shells, shaking his head angrily. Then he pointed, suddenly, to the bright brass buttons on Lieutenant Harrison's jacket. To please me, it seems, Lieutenant Harrison took his sword, cut off one of the buttons and gave it to the fellow who gazed at it with delight. then he thrust the shells at me. There was something strangely alarming about the incident: the sword slicing through the thread, the glittering button held in the small, dark hands of the aboriginal, his smile, teeth gleaming like fangs. I wished it had not happened.

*

Passengers lined up at Immigration Control, hot and tired. Passports were slowly checked, visas examined, permits issued. A sign was nailed to the wall: 'Restricted Area. No photographs. Andaman and Nicobar Administration.'

The shed was airless; people milled about, calling loudly to each other. Indian visitors who knew the form infiltrated the queue and made faster progress to the front. Daisy felt limp and cross and started to say as much, but caught the look on James's face in time and swallowed the words.

Sooner than she expected they were at the counter. The grim-faced Indian official in starched white shorts and shirt took their passports, glanced mechanically, paused, glanced again. He looked up at James with a wide, surprised smile.

'Welcome back to the place of your birth, Dr Oakley.'

Chapter 8

It is not given to many to see their own name carved on a stone and set at the head of a grave, but when he was four and had learned to read, James walked up the hill to the cemetery on Ross and stopped at a neatly tended plot, spelling out the letters on the moss-greened marble stone:

JAMES
SON OF ELIZABETH AND HENRY OAKLEY
Born April 1st
Died October 29th 1902

He counted on his fingers: 'Seven months.' There was another grave nearby, another stone, to Maria Henrietta Oakley, born June 1905, who had lived only a matter of hours.

'What did he die of?' James asked, looking down at his other self, buried so firmly under the grass.

Of pneumonia, Elizabeth told him.

. . . *It is the festival of Diwali, and every corner of the house and compound is decorated with little lights, tiny lamps made from saucers of clay filled with oil and a wick, set along walls, the edges of flat roofs, the veranda railings and the jetty. In the native quarters around Aberdeen, where the families of Hindu convicts have settled, the little houses of wattle thatched with palm are outlined in tiny points of light, the lamps glimmer like fireflies in the darkness.*

Sometimes the women float paper boats with a clay lamp on

board, to ask for a sick person in the family to be made well. If the boat stays afloat, if it sails out to sea with the lamp shining in the darkness, the offering has been accepted and there is hope.

Elizabeth had watched them before, watched the frail boats launched, and tried not to see the look on the women's faces when one of the boats capsized or sank. Now, she had a sick child of her own, lying dry-lipped, blazing with heat, and the army doctor had nothing to offer. Elizabeth tried prayer: frightened, sick at heart, she implored God to help. The temperature stayed high, the pulse weakened.

That evening, as the sunset vanished into rapid dusk, Elizabeth made her way down to the shore, carrying a little paper boat hidden in her shawl. Henry would have been appalled: this was unquestionably going native. The ayah provided the clay lamp and the oil, then stood back a yard or two as Elizabeth bent to the curling lip of surf and carefully launched the paper boat, asking silently for her child to be made well. She watched it ride the calm surface, the little light bobbing on the gentle rise and fall, being carried out to sea. She glanced over her shoulder to smile at the ayah and turned back but she could no longer see the light. A sudden wave sent the water lapping higher, wetting her feet. She stared into the darkness, straining to catch a glimpse of pale paper triangle, flickering light. After a while they went back up the slope to the house, Elizabeth's shoes squelching on the path and the ayah's glass bangles clashing softly as she drew her white sari more tightly round her head. A few days later the child was buried in the English cemetery up the hill.

In that moist, untrustworthy climate horses and children died often of pneumonia. Or of dysentery, or dengue or malaria. Or some undiagnosed disease. Women and men too. Young officers, younger wives, arrived, settled in and succumbed. Replacements of horses and men were ordered from the mainland. More babies were born. In time, a second James took the place of the first.

When he understood, James found the grave troubling: he

felt sometimes that it was he who had died that day in October 1902 and was buried under the stone. Later, he came to feel that it was wrong of him to have survived when that other, earlier James had not. And did his mother really love him, as she said, or did that love belong to the James beneath the soil? He began to feel uneasy.

From the beginning he had asked questions, and Elizabeth always tried to answer them. She told him the names of flowers and birds and trees (where possible the proper, Latin ones), and how the tide worked and where the moon went when it disappeared.

She showed him an atlas of the world, tracing journeys she had taken: the route from Southampton to Madras, and then she drew a line with her finger from Madras to Port Blair.

'And here we are.' And long ago, she said, turning the stiff pages of the dark blue atlas –

'Long ago, when I was younger than you are now', there was a journey from Peru to Bristol, on a ship with sails and a mast that cracked in the storm, a ship that crossed the world as the sailors steered by the stars. (Later James realised that of course the sailors would also have had scientific instruments to navigate by, but the scene retained its magic in his mind: the Southern Cross, the meteor with its fiery tail, days becalmed on a glassy sea, or driven before the wind.)

There were tales of strange birds encountered in mid-ocean, of a blue shark twice as long as a man, caught and hauled on board –

'And inside the shark were twenty live young ones, each no more than twelve inches long.'

They swallow their young, she told him, when danger threatens, and disgorge them when it is safe. Lucky sharks, she said, smoothing his hair from his brow sticky with sweat, to be able to protect their babies.

He sat close, pressed against her, and cautiously stretched out his thin legs. No question: his mother could never swallow him, however great the danger.

Why had she been on the other side of the ocean when she was little? James asked her, his small finger slowly making the journey across the atlas page, and she explained that it was because of her father, whose work took him to faraway places, and whose wife went too, just as she accompanied Henry now. Wives, she said, went where their husbands had to go.

'And will we stay here always?' James asked.

'Oh, no. Your father will be posted somewhere else before long.' She spoke confidently.

They would be posted elsewhere. Another officer would take on the responsibilities of the stone jail on the promontory; the dispensing of justice, the allocation of punishment. When they first arrived she heard about the double gallows with the trap-door, the flogging block, where unruly prisoners were tied to receive their strokes of the lash –

'Barbaric!' Elizabeth was shocked. Henry tried to explain degrees of barbarity: how they strapped leather covering over the convict's lower back to protect his kidneys, and the back of his neck to protect the spinal column.

'They are flogged with care.'

'You mean neither too much cruelty nor too little? Just the right amount?' But he refused to be drawn.

There would be another posting, yes, she told the child; another family would occupy the house with the red-painted roof.

Elizabeth drew him little maps of the islands: one of Ross, with all the houses marked, and the tennis courts, the two churches, the library. Another of South Andaman, with Port Blair and Aberdeen dotted with English houses, and Mount Harriett and Hope Town jetty where Lord Mayo was stabbed to death by a convict one sunset more than forty years before, though she left that story untold. Nor did she tell him much about the Cellular Jail: that had been a source of conflict with Henry for too long, causing doubts to sour into recriminations. So she touched only lightly on the jail.

She shaded the interior with vaguely indicated tribal areas, some marked 'Dangerous', and on some of the outlying islands she wrote 'hostile aboriginals', on others 'uninhabited'. She was trying to give their world a shape. She told him the real name of the great banyan tree in the compound – *Ficus benghalensis* – and the flowers in the beds the mali watered so assiduously: canna and hibiscus, plumbago and lily.

But when she tried to explain to him what it had been like, at the beginning, she found it difficult: there were the red-roofed houses that she saw across the bay as the launch approached the island, the sound of the surf that could be heard wherever she stood or walked, even above the clanking of the convicts' chains . . . the padauk trees with their grey, soaring trunks and roots as hard and clean as giant ships' propellers, trees which were looped and crowned with flowering creepers and from which desperate men sometimes hanged themselves . . . Then she remembered:

'We arrived in the butterfly season,' she said.

They arrived in the butterfly season. To Elizabeth it seemed as though the whole island was on the move: every bush, every tree trembled with the flutterings of a thousand wings. Butterflies, orange, white, gold, tortoise-shell, splotched with patches of colour like inkblots or traced with lines of iridescent blue and green, hovered over branches and blossom like a shimmering veil, the beatings of their wings creating a movement in the air, imperceptible but part of a restlessness which seethed over the islands.

They fed on nectar, fastidious predators draining the flowers, moving across the land, leaving behind them used blooms which quickly faded and withered. And when the moment came, the migrating butterflies rose, abandoning their grazing grounds, and flew away above the treetops in a cloud so vast that it obscured the sun. Others simply joined the dead blooms they so closely resembled and decayed into them.

When James was older he remembered seeing the butterflies, watching them flutter over the bushes like a descending crop of flowers, but he did not recall their departure. Simply that one day they were gone.

Elizabeth explained the need for their departure, comforted him:

'They will come back,' she said.

The butterflies would be back next season, she told him. Afterwards he learned that it was a different generation that fluttered back to rediscover the islands: the original butterflies would not be seen again.

And in his nightmares, later, he saw his mother in her dress the colour of flower petals – or of butterfly wings – rise up in the air and fly away over the treetops, her dress gauzy and transparent in the sunlight.

When she first set foot on Ross, handed ashore from the launch by one young officer, taken charge of by another, Elizabeth was too occupied to pay proper attention to the butterflies. She saw a small, boat-shaped island rising to a low central hill, the slopes covered with two-storey houses and stone structures.

She thought the houses pretty from a distance: only later did she learn that they were painted red with solignum to prevent the termites from eating through the timber.

Her house looked modest enough, but twelve servants were lined up for inspection. Too many, surely, Elizabeth demurred. She had supposed they would live simply here. Even in Madras they had managed with –

The officer cut in: 'It serves a purpose: employment of convicts is a desirable condition and, besides, they cost so little.'

'Are these, then, convicts?' Elizabeth whispered.

'Of course.'

Most convicts, she learned, spent only the first six months of their sentence in the cells. After that they were allowed to live outside the prison, earn money by working, and dress in ordinary clothes.

Everyone employed convicts; the larger houses had perhaps twenty servants, the Chief Commissioner forty (three men were kept busy polishing the ballroom floor), and there were the road gangs, but these were men not yet out on ticket-of-leave, the clanking of their chains made a kind of hideous music in the background: there was the sound of birdsong, the susurration of surf on shore and the dull clanking of the convicts' chains.

She studied her servants, her convicts, lined up, smiling, bodies inclined in a respectful attitude as they were introduced in turn by the young subaltern.

'Head bearer, second bearer, cook and cook's boy, dhobi, chowkidar, bheesti, mali and garden boy, chaprassi for messages and so on, and the sweeper. And', he added, 'your ayah.'

'But we have no children,' Elizabeth pointed out.

'She will be your maid meanwhile.'

Elizabeth murmured, 'What crimes have they committed?'

'Murder for the most part,' the subaltern said cheerfully. 'Crimes of passion and village disagreements account for a good many.' There was no mention of hardened criminals or of political agitators against the British Raj. No point in arousing anxieties in a newly arrived Englishwoman.

Henry was needed at once at the Jail and the two officers strode off down the path to the jetty. Elizabeth was left to move in. The servants stood, waiting to be instructed. She started with the head bearer, impressive in his immaculate turban and white tunic.

'What is your name?'

'Head bearer, memsahib.'

'Yes, but your name?'

They were surprised, then pleased, as she went down the line. 'So, head bearer: Kushmar.' Kushmar had a noble profile, marred by a scar from nose to ear. 'Second bearer: Nirad; cook?'

'Ved, memsahib.'

Ved had a severed forefinger; carelessness in the kitchen, or quarrels at home? Cook's boy: Vijay. The dhobi, who would wash their clothes, Vinod. The chowkidar, clad in khaki, wore a leather belt. Hanging from it was a two-foot-long knife sheath,

curved and weighty. It was, Elizabeth observed, empty: a convict guarding the gate here did so without a weapon. But once
he would have carried a curved kukri knife, razor sharp and
never to be drawn without being used. 'You are a Gurkha
then,' she observed. He looked pleased, touching the sheath.
Few mems paid so much attention.

The bheesti who carried all the household water, the mali
who cared for the garden, even the sweeper, an Untouchable
employed to empty the bathroom thunderboxes, they all had
names and she learned them. The ayah, Madhur, plump and
calm, in her white sari, had already taken up her duties: she
relieved Elizabeth of her travelling case and stood by her left
shoulder awaiting orders. Possibly the memsahib would like a
tub? Hot water would be made available.

These people had all been involved in violent crimes – had
perhaps killed. Some, no doubt, were tragic figures, victims
of domestic upheaval, but the bheesti, for instance, with his
villainous eyes and powerful frame, or the gardener, decidedly
sly and menacing of manner, could they not be ex-bandits,
dacoits, who had killed and robbed professionally until appre-
hended?

'You have no need to fear them,' Henry said reassuringly,
when she put the question. 'There is virtually no crime on the
islands.'

'Virtually?' Elizabeth asked. 'So the flogging blocks and the
gallows, what are they for?'

'Very rare disturbances. Prison uprisings and so forth. We
are absolutely not in danger.'

'Then why do we have a man to guard the gate?'

'To give him employment, of course.'

Later she learned he had killed five men from another village
in Nepal – but in self-defence, he assured her earnestly.

Once again, as in Madras, she was to be kept busy handing
out the household stores, keeping accounts, planning menus,
overseeing the tasks that the servants were there to carry out.
But there was a difference, here: the servants were no mere

deferential shadows, they were people who had suffered upheaval: violence, jealousy, treachery, greed – or just bad luck – had shattered their lives. 'Saved souls' she called them: bodies that might have swung from the gallows had been ferried across the black water to a new life, of a sort.

'How many of you are married?' she asked Kushmar one day while weighing out the rice. He waggled his head.

'None married. Not many women on Andamans, memsahib. Women's jail closed now.'

Nevertheless, there are women here, I see them in Aberdeen market. When I mentioned this, Kushmar told me there is a 'marriage parade' from time to time: female prisoners wanting husbands are brought across from the mainland, and the ticket-of-leave convicts are assembled. The men and women are lined up face to face, and the selection takes place. I so hope that Kushmar will find a wife . . .

In Henry's journal, lying open, she read the observation that *on the whole it is unwise to encourage too much frankness in the servants: this can lead to misunderstanding and disappointment* – advice she all too soon found it impossible to follow. It was Madhur who first aroused her doubts: she found it hard to envisage this gentle and discreet woman as a criminal. Why was she here?

The ayah pulled her sari across her face. 'Memsahib, I am ashamed . . .' The small, unimportant tragedy unfolded: the young married woman, the 'bad man' who caught her outside the village and 'did a bad thing'. She had struggled, but the act had taken place. Bruised, bleeding, she had stumbled home, to be thrown out by her husband. Weeping quietly, twisting her fingers while the glass bangles jingled softly on her wrists, she relived her fear of the well-to-do rapist, her attempt to defend herself with a knife when the assault was repeated, the inevitable finale: local officials bribed, lies believed, the trial a farce . . . Elizabeth comforted the weeping woman: something would be done. She would speak to Oakley sahib at once.

The jail was part of Henry's world and Elizabeth was a

stranger there. Early each morning he strode off down the path to the jetty on Ross, stepped into the ferry and vanished till he returned for tiffin or dinner; today he might be off on some tour of inspection in the interior, or at one of the barracks. She climbed from the rickshaw and approached the high walls with curiosity tempered by uncertainty.

She heard the noise first: a roaring built from the cries of many men, some shouting instructions, some chanting in unison, grunting with effort, others yelling sudden warnings. And with the voices came a clanging, metal on metal, and the thud of hammering and a creaking of ropes and scraping of stone. Then, as she stepped through the main gate, flanked by two watch-towers decorated to look like crenellated castle turrets, the prison engulfed her, boiling with movement. Through a haze of red brick dust prisoners tramped back and forth loaded with building materials, balancing perilously on high walls, crawling like beetles along narrow ledges. Covered sheds were filled with men working ancient machinery; and beyond the main block, in the distance a chain gang strained at a huge iron girder, dragging it slowly towards the far wing. The red dust swirled, the prisoners worked on, the brick dust clogging their sweat and gathering on eyebrows and hair. Work-gangs plodded past, almost trampling her underfoot, too weary to alter direction. She stepped aside hastily, feeling in the way. In her white dress and shoes she seemed like some pale butterfly hovering over a turmoil of mud and metal and toiling beasts. She had not realised how unfinished the prison was.

In the compound a huge banyan tree cast its shade on to the beaten earth. Three men lay prone, faces cradled on their arms, huddled under the tree. Nearby a Eurasian warder stood, bored, flicking away flies. As she passed she heard the men groaning softly, moaning in pain.

Major Oakley, she learned, might be in the Administration Block. A warder showed her into an empty room and requested her to be seated. Major Oakley would be located instantaneously.

'Those men, under the tree – ' Elizabeth began, but he broke in.

'Unruly convicts. Troublemakers. They have', he said reassuringly, 'been flogged.'

Overhead a punkah slowly squeaked to and fro, the rope pulled by a convict squatting on the far side of the room. Elizabeth saw with astonishment that round his neck he wore an iron collar with a wooden tag. He tugged mechanically at the punkah rope, his eyes downcast. The room smelled of brick dust and damp. On a shelf lay reports and printed papers covered in a thin film of orange dust, curling at the corners. One, nearest to her, was headed in large letters ANDAMAN AND NICOBAR MANUAL SETTLEMENT ORDER – CELLULAR JAIL-ABERDEEN. She flicked her eyes down the list of instructions:

. . . the completion of the jail is a matter of great urgency . . . Settlement officers are requested to see if it is possible to utilise invalid gangmen where the work is light . . . advantage is naturally taken by convicts to remain idle when it is raining. With a view to preventing this and to utilise labour to the utmost –

'Elizabeth?' Henry, hurrying in, looked alarmed. 'Are you unwell?'

She shook her head, eager to give him her news: 'Henry, I have learned of a disgraceful case of official corruption: my ayah should not be here! There has been a miscarriage of justice – '

He came round the desk, took her elbow and steered her rapidly to the door, down the corridor and across the compound to the gate, without speaking, and with such speed that her feet scarcely touched the ground. At the gate he said, quietly and vehemently, 'Never, *ever* become involved in the rights and wrongs of the prisoners' cases. That is beyond our jurisdiction –'

'But injustice – '

'There is not a prisoner here who will not claim injustice of one sort or another. We administer here, and *here* they will be fairly dealt with. I can do no more. You have behaved foolishly, Elizabeth, and I trust you will know better in future.'

He summoned a rickshaw, and lifted Elizabeth bodily – and unceremoniously – on to the high seat. It was the first time she had seen him angry. She stared at him, eyes filled with tears of disappointment and indignation.

'You will not even listen?'

'I cannot.' To the rickshaw man he said, 'Ferry for Ross', handing him a coin. He turned and strode back inside the jail. As the rickshaw trundled downhill towards the harbour she allowed herself to cry, the tears gathering the brick dust on her skin into dark orange streaks that rolled down her cheeks and dripped like spots of blood on to her white dress.

Later, beneath the mosquito net, she cried and he comforted her; he was considerate, she eager to please. His tenderness was genuine, her response soon won. Indeed her response was ardent: Henry in anger had a masterful quality, a harshness that she found, to her surprise, attractive. It also reminded her that her safety lay in his hands. Bodies stickily entwined, they were once more in harmony. But later, half asleep, she remembered the blinding red dust, the pain of the prison. She remembered that she had meant to ask about the men groaning beneath the banyan tree and the iron collar worn by the man pulling the punkah.

'This is the most important man on the islands.' The Assistant Commissioner drew Elizabeth over to a burly, naval-looking man with big hands and an ill-fitting jacket. 'When you get your first bout of Andaman fever you will give thanks for Dr Wilcox and his little black bag.'

Bluff but, unlike some of his fellow medics, not a bully, Dr Wilcox poured quinine down throats, punched vaccinations into infant arms and legs and saved those he could. He had no wife and was cheated openly by his domestic servants, who also failed to keep his clothes in good shape. He gratefully accepted dinner whenever invited – 'Good enough fellow, my cook,' he exclaimed, mouth full of Elizabeth's chicken fricassee, 'but it's not real cuisine like yours, Mrs Oakley.'

'Yes, Ved is a treasure.'

Henry's expression did not change. 'The cook', he said, 'has skill. We are fortunate.'

Newly arrived from Madras, in touch with the outside world, Elizabeth and Henry were in demand. The social scene was limited: the small British colony welcomed them to the Club – ladies permitted until 6.00 p.m., after which it reverted to Officers' Mess.

The wives – about ten of them – gave dinners and luncheons, of a necessity less grand than in Madras, but almost as formal; the High Commissioner held an occasional dance; there were picnics and boat trips in calm weather.

The local beauty, Maud Innes, dark haired and honey skinned, could walk in the sun without burning, and swam every day in the tiny cove at the tip of the island. She played tennis with languid skill and amused Henry, usually immune to the charms of gossip, with her accounts of high life in Ooti, her husband's last posting.

Alone with Elizabeth she was less amusing: 'To get away from here, my dear Elizabeth, that is what I long for. Day after day, week after week, month after month, doing nothing. Waiting for the sun to set. Then one can admire the sunset. Waiting for the moon to wane, so that one may admire the new moon, turning one's wedding ring and making a wish. Always the same wish: let us leave the islands.'

There had been a child, soon after Maud's arrival, buried, like so many others, up in the walled cemetery on Ross, and she feared to have another –

'Not only because the child may die, but supposing the fevers, the snakes, the heat, prove insufficient to finish off the child, there is school to look forward to. Separation. This is something we all face: do we stay with our husbands or go

Home with the child? Whichever you do, you hurt someone, most of all yourself. Try and avoid having a child.'

'But . . .' Elizabeth, pregnant herself, was hesitant, 'we cannot choose.'

'We can do our best: for medical purposes, one may consume quantities of hot gin, one can have frequent, extremely hot tubs, gallop on horseback on the hard sand, jump downstairs two steps at a time – it can be remarkably effective at the right time.'

Maud's boredom on the island puzzled Elizabeth: her own curiosity was already aroused; there was so much to learn here, so much that was new. 'May I come to the jail again?' she asked. 'I am clearly ill informed. I should like to know more.' Reluctantly, Henry agreed.

For a while Elizabeth saw less of Tom and Nora Pilkington. With his odd, scientific purpose and unnatural preoccupation with the natives, Tom Pilkington formed a part neither of the Army nor of the Civil Service worlds, moreover he ignored protocol, turning up without warning, raising unsuitable topics at dinner. He behaved impetuously.

Elizabeth could sympathise: she too found the narrowness of their society chafing. One day, on impulse, she bought a sari in the bazaar. The ayah dressed her, pleating and folding the long strip of cotton round her mistress's body, smoothing her hair into a coil, adding a jasmine bloom, while Elizabeth regarded herself in the cheval glass. Unexpectedly early, Henry came home to find his wife twirling barefoot in the bedroom, silver anklets tinkling like cowbells. That was when he wrote in his journal about the dangers of mingling too freely, about loss of native respect and the imperatives of duty.

Elizabeth's pages next day were devoted to an account of a prisoner's death:

We are fortunate that the bulk of prisoners are happy with their incarceration and see no need to complain – though hunger strikes are not unknown: three months ago, a Brahmin deprived of the sacred thread his sect must wear at all times, began to starve himself and despite forced feeding, he has now died. Would we deny a Catholic priest his crucifix? Can it be that at times our administration is less than just?

Their diaries had become instruments of admonition on one side, provocation on the other, the early innocence lost. Elizabeth wrote:

Perhaps thoughts – fugitive things, sometimes disloyal or unfair, sometimes frivolous, should not be embalmed in ink and paper. To pin down thoughts is to attempt to catch quicksilver.

On the islands, it was clear, unconventional behaviour was discouraged.

'You know Mr and Mrs Pilkington, I believe, Mrs Oakley?'

'We came over on the same boat from Madras.'

The Chief Commissioner led Elizabeth in a slow waltz. Through the thin soles of her dance slippers she felt the smoothness of the wooden floor, freshly polished by his convicts.

Across the ballroom, Tom Pilkington handed Nora a water-ice. She gave him a rare smile, her expression for once not harassed or apprehensive. He leaned forward and kissed his wife lightly on the lips. Elizabeth was aware of a general stiffening, a rustle of disapproval around her.

'Today is Nora's birthday,' she said. The Commissioner did not reply. Clearly that was no excuse. Even in so small a community, etiquette must be observed. A ball at the Chief Commissioner's house was not a bedroom. The Pilkingtons were outsiders and Nora was aware of it. Tom, organising his survey programme, was too busy to notice.

'Progress!' he called out, impatient to pass on his news, dragging Nora over to Henry and Elizabeth. 'Progress!' He shook hands, seized a drink from a passing bearer. He had obtained permission to dig around the aboriginal settlements.

'You required no permission, surely?' Dr Wilcox asked. 'The Commissioner knows of your work – '

'I meant permission from the natives,' Tom said.

'Oh! The *natives*.'

He intended digging round their huts to examine the kitchen

middens, 'sift through the ancient layers of fishbones, mollusc shells, ossiferous remains of wild pig . . .' He was convinced there would be no human bones, even long buried. 'There is no evidence of cannibalism. Marco Polo got it wrong.'

Natives were also coming forward to answer questions and be measured, intrigued by his mechanical magic: the phonograph, lantern – 'and some modest bribes'. Elizabeth raised her eyebrows questioningly.

'Beads, cheroots and so forth.'

'I thought we were destroying them with those things?'

For a moment he looked guilty. 'All in the cause of science. Life is short, learned volumes are long. And in any case the process is irreversible.'

Ross and Aberdeen were English suburbs: genteel, neatly laid out, correct. People attended one of the two churches, played tennis on one of the two courts, borrowed books from the library and saw each other under formal, ritualised conditions. Elizabeth, expecting exotic strangeness and some hardship, was disconcerted:

The islands consist of rain forest and mangrove swamps which harbour mosquitoes and can smell very disagreeable. On the other hand the wild flowers are ravishing and the forest teems with brilliantly coloured birds. What I find odd is that we live so untouched by our surroundings. The ladies sew and meet for tea and look at magazines from London. Yet all around us there are aboriginal tribes, said to be cannibals, though both Mr Pilkington and Henry dispute this. They are small and very black, with frizzy hair, their bodies painted with clay. Many are quite naked, wearing only a girdle of rope or leaves, though a few have learned to hang a small apron of rag from their belts when they approach us. Mr Pilkington views this as a tragedy: creating guilt where none existed. Some of them are friendly, bartering rare shells for empty jam jars and bits of coloured cloth, others, such as the Jarawa, so hostile that not only the villagers but the troops go in fear of them. These I cannot describe since they are never

66

to be seen in the settlements. Mr Pilkington – Tom, as we are to call him – tells me the Jarawa possess formidable bows twice the height of a man, and iron-tipped arrows. Dr Wilcox says they have been known to attack villagers and convicts who venture into their territory and kill them most horribly. Last week a convict was found murdered and the police sent a party into the interior in search of Jarawas. There is some confusion about what occurred, but the party returned with two Jarawa heads hanging from a pole. Tom is shocked by this barbarous reprisal, and Henry agrees that it was wrong.

'The Andaman aboriginals are not in general cruel.' He paused. 'Except, it must be said, for the Jarawa.'

Tom Pilkington was waving his arms in disagreement. 'The Jarawa were not always hostile. I trust you are aware, Henry, that when we – the British I mean – first arrived, they welcomed us. Then they left us alone. They merely wanted to be left alone too. Of course that is never something we find easy, is it? We repeatedly misunderstood their actions, tried to impose bizarre laws on them, punished them severely for the most trivial of misdemeanours, and then proceeded to drive them out of what was, after all, their territory. Small wonder they turned against us, against everyone.'

'Misunderstood or not, they are dangerous,' Henry said sharply. 'I must warn you, Tom, that no landings are to be attempted on hostile islands. And of course, no expeditions into the interior.'

Dressed in immaculate white, the Commissioner's convicts offered drinks, discreetly removed glasses, hovered attentively.

Glancing about the ballroom, Elizabeth wondered aloud whether Maud was unwell.

Dr Wilcox drained his glass of whisky. 'She had a slight accident: got thrown from her horse. No bones broken. Still, I told her to stay in bed for a day or two.' He was about to add more, then shrugged, and signalled one of the servants for another drink.

It seems to me sometimes that life here is as unreal as a

*dream: we live surrounded by violent criminals, convicts who
cook our food, serve us breakfast, tiffin, dinner, who weed the
gardens and care for the children. Nobody finds this
extraordinary: we take for granted that our murderers will
not harm us. It is hard to imagine our own servants killing
anyone, but I know that domestic conflict can make murderers
of unlikely people. Kushmar's story – so sad – is such a case.
His parents borrowed a large sum to pay for his sister's
wedding. The money-lender cheated them, giving them less
than agreed, charging interest 'in advance', so that the dowry
was incomplete. As a result, the sister was so harshly treated
by her in-laws that she drowned herself and Kushmar in a
madness of grief killed the money-lender – who was armed
at the time, and gave Kushmar his disfiguring scar. So many
sad stories. I am told I must not be drawn in. But how can
one not?*

It seemed to Elizabeth that each community had a destructive
effect on the other: not only the colonised suffered damage.

*Determined not to be 'infected' by the strangeness, the
'otherness' of the natives, we guard against feelings in case
they lead us into dangerous waters. So we become
unfeeling . . .*

She saw the way the British could observe the brutality of
the jail, the sadness of the Indians, and the wickedness of taking
over the aboriginals' land, and remain unmoved by pity, or
shame.

. . . this immunity, too, could be a form of infection . . .

✳

The minibus left the airport – 'not that it's a real airport, is it?'
Daisy asked rhetorically. 'Just a shack and a runway.'

'The Japanese built the runway when they occupied the
islands during the war.' James looked ill at ease. 'All this was
green . . . It used to be the golf-course.'

Now it was a dust-filled dirt road populated by roving bands of stray dogs. A rusty tin sign proclaimed 'Site for Aviation Fuel Station'.

The driver called out above the noise of the engine, 'We are now approaching Aberdeen bazaar!'

Daisy flicked her eyes right and left and dabbed at her face with a handkerchief. 'Just the usual bazaar.'

James took a deep breath. 'What is the *usual* bazaar? I suppose it has the *usual* street, with the *usual* shops and the *usual* people – if looked at with the *usual* tourist's eye.'

He was amazed by Aberdeen, appalled: rust had reached its apotheosis here; every tin roof a dull reddish brown, corroded to the point where the ragged edges looked like lace. He remembered a street of beaten earth lined with tree-shaded stalls selling foodstuffs; a few small shops – little more than shacks – where cloth was sold. He recalled his mother taking him to buy cotton: the shopkeeper had brought out a rickety wooden chair for the memsahib to sit on while he showed her the bales of village weave. There was no dressmaker on the islands then, none of the clever copyists of Madras or Delhi who could reproduce a blouse or frock from a magazine illustration in a day. Here the wives learned to sew, or sent home for new garments. Now there were hardware and electrical stores, something called a Home Video Centre, and a shop where colour televisions could be rented. There was, it seemed, telex available and a secretarial agency. The shopfronts were brash and modern, neon signs competed with the brilliant sunlight. He felt dazed, disoriented, cheated. As usual, he took refuge in withdrawal, closing his eyes, leaning his head against the seat back and doing his best to block out the Italian voices behind him.

Daisy sat very straight, trying not to sway against him when the minibus swerved to avoid a bullock or a cyclist.

The arrival had been edgy from the start; the friendly Indian in Passport Control handing back James's passport with a knowing smile: 'In search of your roots, I suppose. We're getting quite a few of you old Andaman hands, these days, coming back to have a look at us. It can be painful sometimes. Things have changed, you know,'

James had ignored him, of course. Simply pocketed the passport and steered Daisy towards the exit.

Her eyes prickled. It would be easy to dissolve into tears; they were at the front of the bus, no one would notice. Wet cheeks could in any case easily be passed off as perspiration. She was saved by anger: no Aegean island, no dark blue sea or white rocks. They were now driving past a huge rubbish dump: the contents of a thousand dustbins; broken bottles, crushed tin containers, rusting iron. Scraps of plastic and dirty paper blew against the tall trees by the roadside and were caught up among the trailing creepers dangling from the high branches. Stepping daintily over the compacted filth, stray dogs and a goat or two browsed indolently. She looked away, disgusted, and found they were rounding a bend that brought them out on to the sea-shore. Across the bay she could see a small, boat-shaped island. She was aware that James had opened his eyes, was leaning forward as he stared intently across the blue-green water.

'That's it,' he said. 'That's Ross.'

Chapter 9

She sat on the veranda of her airy house on Ross, pregnant once more, and through Henry's brass telescope she watched the antlike figures of the native workers on Atlanta Point across the bay. Men bowed under heavy loads, carrying stone, hacking back the undergrowth. On the islands there was no escape: with a terrible irony, the convicts were building their own prison . . .

In the brick fields at Dundas Point and Minni Bay the convicts turn out 20,000 bricks every day. They collect the clay, they even make the lime used in the mortar by burning raw coral from the reefs around the harbour. At the Hope Town kiln they suffer burnt feet and hands from the scorching hot bricks; in the quarries at Namunaghar and the lime kiln they work ceaselessly, in shifts.

Henry tells me that the prison is based on a Quaker jail in Pennsylvania, a humane new concept in prison design: one man to a cell, with a window for ventilation, though high on the wall for security; a degree of privacy and dignity almost unheard of on the mainland. Certainly in Port Blair there are some who consider it a profligate use of space – a whole room for just one occupant could be said to verge on the luxurious! Alas, the prisoners are miserable in solitary confinement.

With its seven wings radiating from the central watch-tower, to the designers the Cellular Jail no doubt appeared a fine building. To Elizabeth's less admiring eyes it straddled the promontory like a malign octopus.

Earlier, there had been a prison on Viper Island in the bay, with an open-air gallows serving the old penal colony. In the harsher days following the Mutiny, convicts were kept handcuffed in pairs, night and day, and if they tried to escape, they were hanged from the gallows. The Cellular Jail had its own killing place, though there should have been small use for it: in theory prisoners were executed only if they committed fresh crimes while serving their sentence. More frequently used was the flogging block. (Three men under a banyan tree, groaning in pain. How many were flogged in a week, a month, a year?) 'It may seem harsh to us,' Maud told Elizabeth, 'but you must remember how numerous are the criminals and how few we are. If ever they attempted a rebellion we would be in a precarious position. Discipline *must* be maintained.'

Maud was in a bad mood: Elizabeth had been aware of undercurrents when she arrived for tea.

'Maud, is there something wrong?'

'Just this place, these people!' she burst out. 'I have been having ridiculous problems with the cook, I wonder if he is deranged, sometimes. I ordered roast pork for tiffin and he served chicken. Does he think I cannot tell the difference? It happens every time.'

'You will probably find he is Mohammedan,' Elizabeth suggested. Maud said impatiently, 'What of it? I do not ask him to *eat* the wretched meat, simply to prepare it!' Despite its golden surface, her face looked haggard, and when Elizabeth went home she heard Maud calling sharply for bath water to be heated, 'At once! *Jaldi!*'

To the British the Cellular Jail seemed an appropriately impressive symbol of imperial stability: people were happier when they knew where they stood. They had been confident that once the prison was established, properly run and administered, there would be no more trouble.

That 'trouble' persisted – sudden outbreaks of disobedience, refusals to work, violence, suicide – surprised and disappointed everyone.

72

Elizabeth watched the Jail take shape, growing, month by month, each wing occupied as it was completed, and wondered that no one else seemed aware of cries and moans of despair. She could not, of course, actually hear them on Ross – across the bay only birdsong and surf were audible – but she felt the anger and the fear that seeped through the stone walls; a despair clotting and coagulating until it seemed to take shape and cry aloud.

Her own walls were vulnerable to a different threat: white ants penetrated wood, plaster and brick. They came up through the floors, rugs and mats, and tunnelled into chests and wardrobes, eating their way through the contents. Table legs stood in saucers of water and the piano had its miniature moats to keep it safe from invaders. Clothes left draped over chairs would be shredded by morning, riddled with holes.

They consume laundry baskets, books, papers and pictures. Only indigo seems to deter them, they dislike either the smell or the taste, so we place runners dyed in indigo under armchairs and carpets. One rarely sees the creatures, they create secret tunnels, travelling unseen and consuming from within, unsuspected, until one of the servants lifts a box left standing for a few days, to have the bottom drop out, scattering a mess of filthy, ruined rags that was a fine set of linen a week before.

I have managed to observe the ants occasionally: not in fact white but grey maggot-like shapes with pincers waving at one end. Unpleasant, and yet they reminded me of my marvellous creature on the ship, the source of the green phosphoric light. That too was a dull grey bug, though with a special quality which transformed it.

The Pilkingtons came to dinner, and winged ants flew in through the doors and banged into the oil lamps, falling into their food and giving off an unpleasant smell. Tom launched into a theory concerning the diet of John the Baptist in the wilderness, scrutinising one of the insects on his plate, threatening to dissect it until Nora begged him to behave.

Elizabeth said, 'St John did not in fact eat locusts but the pods of the carob tree, some people call it the locust tree: *Ceratonia siliqua*. The pods are called St John's bread.'

Tom Pilkington gazed at her in delight. 'You constantly amaze me, Elizabeth. The locust tree! What other ancient lore have you got for us?'

Nora flinched from the winged ants as they buzzed in her ears, or were caught up in her hair. She batted at them frantically.

'You are quite wasted as a mere wife, Elizabeth! You should lead expeditions, explorations! Tom should have married someone like you, you share his fascination with horror.' Her voice was shrill and loud. In the dimness beyond the circle of lamplight, the bearers stood, waiting to remove plates, replenish glasses. Blending with the shadows, their faces were featureless blurs, only their white uniforms clearly visible.

Henry glanced over to where Kushmar stood. He said calmly, 'Bearer, I think Pilkington sahib's glass needs refilling – '

Nora's shriek drowned out his words: 'Oh God, now their wings are dropping off, they are crawling – they look like those disgusting maggots.'

Nora's special loathing, like that of most of the wives, was reserved for the white ants. Tom, of course, had a different view of them:

'It is true they destroy, and it is easy to be disgusted by them. But what we see as ferocious destruction of our goods is after all only their instinctive drive for survival. We are fortunate that our own social structure demands less of us.'

Dinner broke up early. Nora was unhappy about leaving the child, anxious to be home. Her ayah, though well behaved and apparently devoted to her small charge, was nevertheless a convict, 'and anyway, with Indians,' Nora murmured, 'one never knows: they do such cruel things in the name of their religion: barbaric – '

'They would consider far more cruel the banishing of seven-year-old children, taken from their mothers and packed off to a distant country, to be beaten and humiliated by strangers,' Tom observed, 'which we accept quite cheerfully. Shall we introduce boarding schools to them in due course?

'I see young tribespeople exchanging their leafy garments for factory-made cotton because they think it must be superior. Natives who lived on roots and honey and forest berries are learning to eat rice, which they cannot grow, and to smoke: will this improve matters for them? Their palm-thatched huts are being roofed with flattened kerosene tins that rust. Better?'

'I acknowledge that our presence has had an effect on their traditional way of life that is in some ways regrettable,' Henry said, 'but on their morality, perhaps for the better – '

The familiar Pilkington exclamation of despair; glass and cutlery rattled as fist banged tabletop. 'Morality? You think we should impose ours on them? You think that suitable? They live in harmonious monogamy; they lack sexual shame, they rarely murder one another. They share their food without profit. What we offer is corruption.'

Nora said slowly, as though continuing a train of thought, 'This place kills people.'

'Come now, Nora: you're perfectly safe provided you make sure you are properly accompanied and do not stray into the interior.' Henry did his best to sound reassuring.

She shook her head, unconvinced. 'Women and children wither and die here.'

She was about to say more, but she remembered in time that Elizabeth had no need of imaginary fears, her child lay up the hill in the cemetery. Mortified by her own outburst earlier, she whispered an embarrassed apology to Elizabeth as she donned her wrap.

They paused for a moment in the garden, Elizabeth breathing in the perfume of the night-scented blooms. Tom was left behind as the other three strolled towards the gate. Elizabeth retraced her steps to find him transfixed, gazing up at the stars. He spoke dreamily, his upturned eyes reflecting points of light.

'When I was a child I tried to find the mythological creatures who apparently inhabited the night sky: I was told Cetus was a sea-monster; Pegasus a winged horse, and so on. But I never could make the patterns fit the names. Finally I realised they are not actually visible in that form: it is simply our way of looking at the constellations, of joining up the dots of the stars. But it is all quite arbitrary, Elizabeth: other cultures join up their dots to form different pictures, and what we see as a bear may be a bird to them. We all form our own pictures from the given material – I see it one way, you another. Is one truer than the other?'

In the starlight his thin face took on the appearance of an ivory mask, the pale skin smooth and youthful. He took her arm affectionately. 'You are very good, to put up with my noise and nonsense. It is just my way, you know, of asking questions. Of trying to get at the truth.'

Ahead of them, Nora and Henry had reached the entrance. The chowkidar sprang to attention, hand instinctively falling to the empty knife sheath, and swung open the gate. Henry glanced back as Tom fleetingly clasped Elizabeth's frail wrist.

'Nora,' Henry said, ushering her through the gate, 'how's that mali of yours? Elizabeth has some plants for you . . .'

*

'Corbyn's Cove,' James said. 'We used to come across for picnics, go swimming – '

'You told me.'

The sandy bay was ringed with tall palm trees. The hotel lay beyond a garden bright with flowers. Beyond that rose a green hill topped by more tall palms. The sun glittered on the sea. No tin shanties in sight. Almost resentfully, Daisy conceded – silently – that the view was lovely.

As the minibus reached the hotel entrance and before it had come to a complete stop, the Italians were scrambling for the exit, talking, laughing, cheerfully pushing past the silent couple at the front.

At the reception desk, an elegant Indian was trying to make a telephone call. Blazer clad and immaculate, he flung up his hands despairingly: 'It's been out of order for three days now. Nothing works. Our ass of a prime minister has reduced the country to a shambles!' He shrugged his shoulders and wandered away. The Italians were signing in. Two young Indian girls, slender, fashionably dressed, exquisite, giggled softly with their absurdly handsome escorts.

'Our honeymoon couples,' the receptionist said, smiling at Daisy conspiratorially. A group of about thirty Russians, solidly built and mostly middle aged, straggled down the staircase and out towards the beach, skins seriously sunburnt. Outside the window, palm leaves, backlit by the sun, glowed a brilliant, tender green.

'I think I might go for a swim.'

James frowned. 'Oh, I shouldn't, not yet. You'll want to rest first.'

No, she wanted to contradict him, firmly, I *don't* want to rest first. I want to swim. I want to swim.

'I suppose you're right,' she said, 'I'll have a rest.'

She went up the stairs. James hovered at the reception desk.

'Do you have a local telephone directory?'

The manager stepped forward confidently. 'Of course! Of course!' He glanced about, snapped his fingers and addressed the receptionist in Hindi. 'She will attend to it.' He vanished into an inner office. The receptionist hunted about for a moment or two, lifting books and papers, dropping them back on the desk. She looked harassed. 'Can I perhaps be of assistance? Locating some local person, is it? Name?'

'What?'

'This person you are seeking. What is the name? We can put out enquiries. We will unquestionably be finding them for you, no problem.'

James became suddenly vague. 'No matter. Not important.
I'll leave it for now.'

*

*I have witnessed a marriage parade. Henry was reluctant, but
I so desired to observe one and he agreed. It was a dramatic
event: ticket-of-leave prisoners assembled in the jail courtyard,
women from the Madras boat lined up and so they stood, face
to face, soldiers around them in a large circle, like a parody of
a cotillon, couples lined up waiting for the music to strike up.
Some of the men were ugly, some pleasing. Some women had
a slatternly air, others looked frightened: who would choose
them? What future would they have here? Poor things, small
wonder that they drew their saris close about their heads,
some chewing nervously at a corner of the thin cotton.*

*To my delight, Kushmar was among the men, and Maud's
cook Khan, a sweet-tempered young Muslim. There was a girl
I noticed at once: alert, standing erect. Not beautiful but
intelligent and bright eyed. A shapely body beneath the folds
of her sari. Khan caught her eye and I saw a flash of interest
pass between them. The introductions and 'proposals' began,
men in a certain order approaching the women . . .*

*Later I saw Khan passing our gate and called out to him.
Had he found a wife? 'No, memsahib.' Was there no one he
liked?*

*'Oh yes, memsahib, one nice girl from Bengal like me. But
not possible.'*

*The girl was Hindu. And for the sake of her family, she
would not agree to convert to Islam. I could imagine the
outcome: the two of them staring at each other sadly, another
man leading her away. Oh, these divisions between people.
Tom pointed out that in her village she would have been no
more free to choose. And how free are we? When parental
approval – or disapproval – indicates the way, would it not be
considered lacking in dutiful sensibility to go against it? Those*

of us who marry for love are lucky indeed. Kushmar found a bride, a fat girl with merry eyes. But poor Khan remains alone.

Reading this passage in the open journal, Henry paused and tried to recall the past, his early encounters with Elizabeth. Had it been affection that moved her, then, or dutiful obedience?

Tom Pilkington had run into trouble with his anthropometric survey: the second monsoon brought a cyclone which delayed everything until after the flooding had subsided. The damage had to be cleared up. There was also reluctance on the part of the natives.

'Someone started a rumour that I'm looking for specimens! The poor things fear they will be killed and stuffed, and exhibited in a museum! I did persuade a few to come forward, but when I attempted to paint a white spot on their forehead to give me the position of the fronto-nasal suture, there were shrieks of alarm: they were convinced it would blister into a number on their skin, and serve as some sinister means of identification.

'As to measuring, that set more rumours going: they were to be imprisoned, I was measuring them for prison clothing – or the gallows!'

Elizabeth heard no more until Henry arrived at the house in a hurry, at an hour when he would normally have been busy with jail affairs.

'Nora Pilkington is in a state of prostration. Could you possibly go across and see her? No harm has come to her at all, but Dr Wilcox thinks she would benefit – '

'Of course.'

The Pilkingtons lived in a wooden house on Chatham Island across the causeway from Port Blair. The timber mill brought in elephants to move the wood, and from the Pilkingtons' windows the great beasts could be seen, patiently lifting and dragging enormous tree trunks. They made Nora nervous:

'Suppose one ran amok? We could be crushed.'

The torrential monsoon left the house standing in a small

brown lake. And when the flood drained away, Nora was filled with fresh fears: that the convicts might rise up in a rebellion, or the Andamanese decide to attack.

Elizabeth arrived to find her lying on her daybed, feverish and agitated. She seized Elizabeth's hand and at once began to weep. Slowly the story emerged: Tom had asked her to accompany him, to help with the measuring. The day had begun well, with about fifty Onges turning up, friendly and interested:

'They crowded round while Tom showed them pictures with his pseudoptic and he managed to get some measurements so that he can calculate nasal and cephalic indices. He gave them the usual cheroots, and some brightly polished coins, but then some of them began to look at my necklace, and then they began to pluck at my clothes – '

She stopped. She was shivering as though cold, though her hands felt dry and hot. Gently Elizabeth prompted, 'Did they harm you? Were they . . . rough at all?'

Nora shook her head. 'But if you could understand! It was horrible, the closeness, the plucking of their fingers all over my clothes, like being pecked by birds . . . I felt them on my skin, crawling like insects. Horrible.' She shuddered. 'It was like . . . being . . . violated . . .' She began to cry.

'You don't understand, do you? I can see you don't understand at all!'

Her eyes were red rimmed and sore. She clutched Elizabeth's hand until her grip slackened in sleep. Elizabeth covered her gently and came out to find Tom sorting specimens on the veranda table. Elizabeth put her finger to her lips, and they conversed in whispers.

'I thought we were making real progress! They found her clothes and decorations interesting, we could have begun – '

'She was frightened.'

'But there was no need!' He flung up his hands. 'They would not have harmed her! Would *you* be afraid of – mere curiosity?'

Elizabeth thought for a moment. 'Perhaps not. But – '

He seized her arm. 'Come back to the settlement! Help me, Elizabeth.'

She stared at him, shocked by the idea, knowing Henry would never agree. Then considering the possibility:

'But when?'

'Well. Now!'

The boat was little more than a canoe, moving slowly up a creek that ran deep into the rain forest. It was dark here, the air so moist she drank it in mouthfuls as she tried to breathe. High above them, hidden among the topmost branches, she was aware of birds. She could hear them: the flapping of wings, squawks, high trilling notes of song. Occasionally, a feather floated down, spinning slowly as it fell. They moved so silently that, passing close under the bank, Elizabeth heard the occasional popping of a seed pod, the sound like a chick breaking out of an egg. Lianas trailed across the water, brushing her face with wet fingers, leaving greenish marks on her bodice. The water was a dark, soupy brown, the surface thick with insects, fallen pods, flowers and feathers, forming a crust that rose and fell with the wake created by their craft. Occasionally, she thought she sensed a movement disturbing the surface: could there be crocodiles in these waters? She had never heard so, but there were barracudas that chewed the flesh of natives unlucky enough to fall among them.

The forest seemed deserted but she knew that the aboriginals must be around them, following their progress. When she caught a glimmer of light, a shining, in the gloom, she wondered if it might have been a pair of eyes reflecting the sun that filtered in slanting beams down through the canopy of leaves. Drops of moisture fell lazily through the thick, flocculent air, and her dress darkened from crisp white to a crushed, clinging grey.

Henry was surprised to find Elizabeth still absent when he arrived home. Perhaps Nora had needed more attention. Later he grew worried as the light began to die out in the sky, but when she returned, stepping from the little rickshaw that had brought her from the jetty, she ran so eagerly to the veranda before he could go to meet her, so buoyant, she seemed so relieved to see him, to be home, her face alight, that Henry forgot his prepared speech and caught the excitement that he sensed in her, clasping her to him protectively.

'What – ' he began, but she cut in, saying she had had to help the Pilkingtons, Nora and Tom had both needed her help. Henry knew that help must be given where needed, but though he said nothing, he felt the Pilkingtons imposed too much, were in their different ways too prone to problems. She must change, she said, and bathe. It had been an exhausting day. In the dusk Henry was aware only that her dress was somewhat damp, and that her hair was not its usual tidy shape.

. . . In the jungles of the Andamans, flowers mark the seasons. One after another the trees and creepers come into flower, pale mauve, purple, deep yellow, scarlet, blooming and carpeting the paths when they drop. Each has a recognisable odour and the aboriginals refer to the different parts of the year by reference to the plants in flower at the time. Their calendar is a calendar of scents. There is a beauty here which belongs to basic things. What we try and impose proves ugly. Poor Nora Pilkington has suffered an unfortunate experience. She supports Tom in his work but she longs to be gone from this place.

She said no more to Henry about the day's events than to assure him Nora had suffered no actual harm. The diary entry remained incomplete. She hesitated to cause him anxiety, and the incident was over.

*

James enjoyed his dinner. 'Jackfruit curry. Excellent. Spiced horseradish – '

'I long for something raw.' Daisy glanced enviously at the salad dishes heaped with sliced tomato and onion. 'It looks very clean. I'm sure – '

'Fatal. Asking for trouble. Only needs one man in the kitchen who hasn't washed his hands – '

'But everyone else is eating the salad.'

'More fools them.' He took some more curry. 'Try the jack-fruit.'

After dinner, too restless to read, Daisy picked her way carefully down the dark drive to the gates. Beyond them the sea glimmered, palm trees silhouetted against the steely surface. Far out she could see the usual patch of shimmering moonlight, but nearer, just beyond the surf-line, where the waves gathered themselves, flexing silken muscles for the final gentle rush to the shore, there was a sharp glitter, like molten silver.

Behind her, from the darkness, came the sound of singing. The Russians were clustered in the drive, forming a circle, singing, clapping in unison. As she approached, some of the big women smiled and nodded at her, breaking the circle, beck-oning her to join in. In the distance she could see James, sipping a whisky on the terrace. The Russian women in their dowdy print frocks and clumsy sandals, the men in crumpled trousers and open-neck shirts, began to dance in a ring; their steps precise, movements delicate, with an unselfconsciousness that she found touching. One of the men, brawny and red faced, with a flowing moustache, danced barefoot, ignoring the rough, sharp ground. It was an old dance, an old song, from some collective, tribal past. Not sad, yet Daisy felt the all too familiar pricking behind her eyes. From the hotel she saw the Italians coming, one with a video camera to capture the scene, make it real for them. She moved on towards the terrace and saw James. He had moved inside and was sitting by the window studying the old atlas from Ramachander's bookshop, lost in its pages.

*

'I hear your men have been decimating the Jarawa,' Tom called out to Henry across the clubroom.

'Tom!' Nora, once again, was embarrassed by her husband's candour.

Henry refused to rise to the bait. 'The tribe attacked when the men were making a routine tour of inspection, nowhere near their territory. Several of our chaps were injured. They decided they had to teach the Jarawa a lesson. Shot the lot.' He hesitated. 'They found a child.'

Tom blinked rapidly, a sign of increased interest. 'A child? Alive? Where is this child? Can I see him? Now?'

Dusty, dull eyed, squatting in the hospital compound, he was a disappointment to Elizabeth who had been expecting an aboriginal version of the lustrous cherubs of Madras. They stood round, studying the child, at a loss. He looked about three years old.

'What will become of him?' Elizabeth asked.

'He will be cared for,' the anglo-Indian doctor said reassuringly. 'Diet is always a problem: we are unsure what exactly he would eat in the normal way. Roots, grubs, possibly sea-slugs . . .'

The child gripped a rudimentary bow made from a pliant twig and a thread of liana, and scratched listlessly in the mud. He seemed to be searching for something. It was Tom Pilkington, observing him closely, who suddenly moved to some nearby bushes, broke off a short, straight twig and handed it to the child. The boy stared at the twig, then took it, calmly, and at once fitted it to the tiny bow he held. He got to his feet, raised his arms above his head and stood, aiming the bow at Henry. It was a touching, absurd sight: the naked infant, hostile and armed with his twig and bow, and looming over him, the tall, thin Englishman in his immaculate uniform, curiously at a loss.

Standing back a little from the group, Elizabeth was conscious of a moment of frozen stillness: the child warrior with his dusty black skin, the British officer staring down at him, and the thin man on his knees in the dust, leaning forward, bright eyed, smiling.

Henry broke the silence. 'We could achieve great things here: we can teach the child – '

'We may learn from the child. If he will let us,' Tom said. 'Yes! We may learn!'

Henry smothered a sigh. 'There are times', he said to Elizabeth later, 'when Tom's boundless enthusiasm can be somewhat tiresome.'

Elizabeth was busy for a few days, first with the garden, then organising a dinner for some visiting civil servants. She forgot about 'the piccaninny' as Nora called him. She was surprised when Nora arrived at the house, distraught.

'Tom is missing.'

Nora's anxieties were familiar: she worried about the boat when they crossed the bay, she feared heights, she disliked the climate and had a terror of the forests and the swamps. She was a frequent visitor to the hospital, taking her sickly child to be examined, or dosed for some possible ailment. Elizabeth once came upon her, wandering in the cemetery on Ross, studying the epitaphs on the gravestones.

'Look:' Nora drew her from one grave to another, stumbling over exposed roots from the towering rain trees. 'Look: gathered to God aged twenty-two . . . died aged four . . . aged three . . . aged thirty.'

'You could find the same in London, Nora.'

Nora's face seemed to have grown smaller, pinched, to have lost its smoothness, as a fruit shrinks before it withers.

'The proportion would be different. No one grows old here.'

From far below them, floating up through the trees and undergrowth, came the soft, insistent sound of the surf crashing gently on the shore. Nora touched a stone angel, rubbing her fingers over the foot that peeped from beneath the drapery.

'Shall we see old age, Elizabeth?'

Above all, she had a terror of the forest-dwellers, convinced that one day 'the savages' would surround the house and attack her and the child while Tom was busy elsewhere. Without him she never felt safe. And now Tom was missing.

Elizabeth accompanied her back to Aberdeen on the next launch and they made enquiries. Tom Pilkington had been seen the day before, with the Jarawa child. The child, it seemed, was also missing.

Nora said flatly, 'He has taken him back to his people.'

'That is quite impossible, Nora – '

Nora's voice sounded tired: 'He talked of the possibility. He had come to the conclusion the child would not survive here, that he should be returned to the tribe.'

Henry gave an exclamation of dismay. 'But surely – ' He stopped. 'I shall send a search party at once.'

He did more: he led it. They headed into the interior, crossing the leech-filled mangrove swamps and the narrow, seawater creeks, penetrating deep into the forest, venturing into Jarawa country, first in boats filled with soldiers crouching back to back, guns at the ready. Then, clumsily, on foot, cruelly exposed, rifles of small use when arrows could rain on them from the fastness of the trees before any trace of a shadowy body could be discerned.

They found Tom and the child without difficulty. The child sat tranquilly, as usual gripping his bow and a handful of tiny twig arrows. Tom was not far away, spread-eagled on the ground. His body had been deeply pierced and ripped by many steel-tipped arrows, skewering him like a boar on a pig-sticking hunt. His throat had been cut, not cleanly, but hacked at so that between head and body a dark, shredded mass of flesh lay exposed, blackening as it dried, and already swarming with busy red ants. His eyes were open.

'We do not belong here,' Elizabeth said bitterly when Henry gave her the news. 'We bring ugliness and death with us.'

'This must be hard for you,' Henry said awkwardly. 'I know you were . . . fond of him.'

She looked surprised. 'He was our friend.'

'Yes,' Henry said, 'of course.'

Nora left on the next boat for Madras. 'I always knew something terrible would happen in this place.'

'We shall see you again, I hope,' Elizabeth called after her, 'in Madras.' In due course they too would be leaving, when Henry's term of office was completed. What lay ahead was vague: probably a spell in The Nilgiris; a cool, quiet hill station. And surely after that Henry would be rewarded with a posting to Delhi or Calcutta? Surely they would see the great cities at last?

Henry said, 'Odd, the way things turn out: Nora always feared death here, for herself and the child. Tom never worried.'

'Tom should have worried,' Elizabeth said angrily, 'he should have taken thought.'

. . . Henry says that what occurred cannot be regarded as Tom's fault. No doubt he is right. But Nora is alone and I cannot help thinking of the Indian proverb Madhur recited to me once: 'Whether the melon falls on the knife or the knife on the melon, to the melon it is all the same.' The fate of melons and of women is alike in that: whoever's the fault, they are the ones who suffer.

The Pilkington affair was much discussed: Nora was pitied, of course, but there was an unspoken feeling that the Pilkingtons had never quite . . . fitted in. No one mentioned the native child; possibly no one thought of him. Except Elizabeth.

It was impossible, but somehow it happened: the small, pale woman ordered the aboriginal toddler to be taken from the army hospital to her rickshaw; transferred him to the launch, and installed 'the piccaninny' on Ross.

The child was not amiable, and attempts to be affectionate or playful failed. He simply searched for twigs, collected arrows. Elizabeth placed selections of raw vegetables and fruit next to him. Each day she spent time naming familiar objects for the child. Occasionally he drew patterns on the ground with a twig. They could be seen from far off, at the end of the garden, the yellow-haired woman, kneeling, the small black figure blending with the earth, an effigy, dust made flesh.

And then the posting came in, and she knew the child must be left behind.

When it was time to catch the boat she kissed Madhur good-bye; the plump woman with her white sari and softly clinking glass bangles had become a friend. Elizabeth remained unmoved at the Club farewell party, though she cried when Kushmar gave her an elephant he had carved from padauk wood, and the mali presented her with a box of seeds carefully saved from the garden blooms. She realised that she would miss her murderers.

The Jarawa child was left in the charge of the anglo-Indian doctor, with funds provided for his care. Leaving him at the doctor's, she looked back several times but the toddler remained staring at the ground, drawing patterns in the dust with his twig arrow.

When the islands sank below the horizon she thought she had seen them for the last time.

Four years later they were on their way back.

'Why?' Elizabeth asked. 'Why did it have to be you?'

'Because there has been trouble and I know the territory,' Henry replied. He paused, honesty compelling him to continue: 'I volunteered.'

Once, Elizabeth would have accepted his need to do so, admiring him for his sense of duty. Now she pressed her lips together and continued to fold clothes for packing.

'Someone had to go,' Henry said gently.

She nodded, smoothing back her pale hair. 'And it had to be you.'

In Mysore there had been a palace. Music recitals and painting classes for the memsahibs. There were regular newspapers from Home, and travellers passing through. There had been talk of a hill station in the North, perhaps Dalhousie, the prettiest and gayest, for their next posting. But Henry had volunteered.

She wrote for a long time in her journal that night. The pages were no longer open for Henry to read: Elizabeth's journal had become private property. For a while Henry left his journal open, and she cried sometimes, as she read between the lines the unuttered yearning of a man who needed more than she was now prepared to give.

*

James had disappeared. Daisy woke up feeling bleary and out of sorts to find his bed empty. Tiny birds flittered and swooped busily on the balcony, hovering over the scarlet and white hibiscus blooms. She watched them for a while, and then checked the bathroom: James had been known to spend half an hour at a time locked in the bathroom, especially when away from home. The first time he stayed with Daisy's parents, his long absences caused her father to ask her about the state of her fiancé's bowels.

'His bowels? I've no idea.'

'Very important. Take my word. Show me a man's bowel movement and I'll tell you what he's made of.'

'But what grand conclusions can you draw? I mean I've never thought about mine: it's just something that happens.'

Her father nodded. 'Exactly. You're an easygoing, normal creature. Now your mother's had the runs off and on for the last thirty years. I don't need to tell *you* she's nervy.'

James was not a man to enter into discussion of his bowel movements, but later, when they were married, she learned he had been constipated for thirty years. At school he blamed the lavatories (wet seats, harsh paper, insubstantial doors, no privacy). Later the army latrines. By then it had become chronic. But Daisy's father was not persuaded.

'A man who can't empty his bowels is clenched up. He's holding himself in. Doesn't want to look at what's inside him. You'll have trouble there.'

Daisy began to laugh: 'It's a curious approach to psycho-analysis.'

But in the course of time, Daisy's father had the last laugh. This morning, however, James was not locked in the bathroom. Nor was he on the terrace, where the Russians were gathering for a coach trip to the sawmill on Chatham Island and the factory producing matches. The Italians were trying on snorkels; a newly arrived British party waited patiently at the reception desk and the honeymoon couples lingered over tea and toast in the dining room. Daisy tried to read but the hotel's ubiquitous piped music filled her head with unwanted noise. In a burst of daring she decided to go for a swim.

On the beach, an Indian family looked for shells, calling out to each other in a mixture of Hindi and English. The girls, slender and pretty, stood on the surf-line for a moment, and then, fully dressed, they began wading out through the waves, their bright cotton kurtas and baggy trousers soaking up the water, clinging to their bodies, perversely revealing the curves they were designed to conceal in the cause of modesty. They immersed themselves, splashing about happily, their garments floating and spreading in the water like Japanese paper flowers. Daisy tugged at her two-piece swimsuit, feeling clumsy and exposed.

The Indian mother, proudly rotund and placid in her silk sari, retreated to the skimpy shade of a palm. Her husband, in Lacoste sports shirt, immaculate slacks and a dark red turban, kept watch on the girls. Daisy was unaware that he was keeping watch on her also until he called out, 'You should be wary of that area: submerged rocks are to be encountered. Very sharp.'

She looked startled. 'Oh! Thank you.'

He studied her with interest: 'You have children?'

'Yes.'

'How many children?'

'Two.'

'Ah! Boys?'

'A boy and a girl – Well, they're hardly *children* any more, they're grown up of course . . .' She submerged herself and swam steadily out to sea.

A boy and girl. Lizzie and Bill. Elizabeth, after James's mother, and William after Daisy's father. Cheerful, self-reliant, mature Lizzie and Bill. They had been so affectionate as children, so close, but somehow they seemed to drift away while she was preoccupied with other things. With James of course. She had never put the children ostentatiously first, as some mothers did, because she knew instinctively that James carried within him a terror of being excluded, left behind, abandoned.

On the other hand, he was determined that the children would never be 'sent away' to school: they must always be near, able to reach their parents in a moment of crisis or need. It was not his fault that the crisis never arose, that they were not, in fact, needed. And it was a bad day for James when the children, politely, gently, asked to go to boarding school.

'But why?' Daisy was hurt, bewildered.

'It's nobody's fault, Mum. But we just can't take the tension, the pressure.'

James, being James, retreated into silence and distance. Daisy merely felt she had failed them somehow.

It was a turning point, though she only recognised it as such much later. She had given up her job for the domestic round, and now she was redundant. The children did not, it seemed, require her presence. And James would no longer admit that he did. That had stopped long ago.

Lacking a convincing role in their lives, she became tentative, reduced to asking generalised questions, though later even that grew difficult, when she found she was unable to understand the answers.

'Have you read any Gerard Manley Hopkins?' she asked, when they came home one holiday. 'There's one I find so moving – '

Lizzie broke in, 'I have a problem with Hopkins: I can't take the circularity of his aesthetic.'

The . . . ? They tried to help, lent her volumes of John Ashberry, Wallace Stevens. But when she found a line she responded to, or resonant beauty in a phrase, they told her sadly that she had missed the point.

Lizzie and Bill rejected the overview, the broad brushstroke, the middle-of-the-road, liberal–humanist guidelines she clung to. Instead they built arguments from footnotes, special knowledge informed their responses. Their particularity defeated her, so that she took refuge in providing creature comforts, offering them vast meals, expensive presents, tickets to pop concerts and, later, the opera, all to give them something to talk about when they came together for Sunday lunch – it was important that they still enjoyed Sunday lunch together. Or so she thought until she overheard Lizzie one day on the telephone to a friend: 'Must go, got to help with lunch. Yeah, well, it's about as jolly as a reunion banquet in the house of Atreus, but there you go, that's family life.'

She could have left him – many women would have done so. But when? At what point? When the first view of the future began to take shape, while the children were still small? Too soon. Later, when she felt superfluous, knowing they were now able to take care of themselves, that might have been the time, but by then it was already too late, for her. She had grown timid, apologetic, in complicity with her own weakness.

Besides, just now and then, fleetingly, like a glimpse of sun between thundery clouds, James would bestow on her one of his rare, genuine smiles, would seize her arm in a moment of enthusiasm, remind her of some harbour or temple once visited, and her heart would be eased by a memory of happiness.

When she came out of the sea, the keen-eyed father in the red turban was still there. He watched her approach.

'May I enquire your age?'

No, you may not, she wanted to reply. It's none of your business. But he stood there so calmly, smiling so encouragingly that she found herself responding obediently, 'Fifty-four'.

His eyebrows went up. 'You have preserved your body exceedingly well,' he remarked, as though complimenting her on an antique mahogany chest of drawers.

She picked up her towel and walked away, attempting a

dignified stride, quite impossible in powdery, yielding sand which reduced her to a ducklike waddle.

She found herself hurrying as she approached the hotel entrance. Where was James? She was used to being excluded, not being consulted, not being informed of his plans. But he had never before vanished without warning. She acknowledged anxiety. James treated the passing years as something of no more than historical interest: he might groan, creakily, when putting on his socks or flex his back in mid-lecture, but he walked everywhere at punishing speed, and never carried an umbrella. He behaved as if he were invulnerable. She pictured him now, lying somewhere, struck down by sunstroke or a heart attack, in need of help. She had to face a fact that he regarded as an irrelevance: James was an old man.

The girl behind the reception desk stood with the telephone to her ear, neither speaking nor listening, simply waiting. Daisy finally caught her eye.

'I wonder if you've seen my husband . . . Dr Oakley? He –'

'Yes indeed. He has ordered a taxi. He has gone to Port Blair. I think he is seeking someone.'

Daisy was aware of the strident note in her voice as she said sharply, 'But he doesn't know anyone in Port Blair. Who could he be looking for?'

The girl began jiggling the telephone receiver and did not reply. Daisy found herself repeating, close to tears, 'Who could he be looking for?'

PART TWO

Chapter 10

James the second was born in the hospital on Ross on a windy November night in 1911. The tall rain trees thrashed and the palms rustled harshly, the sound mingling with the noise of the surf. It was a difficult birth and Dr Wilcox and the anglo-Indian midwife were relieved when it was over.

Elizabeth spent much of her time on a chaise-longue on the veranda. At the appropriate times she fed James, handing him back to the ayah to be bathed and put back in his cradle.

Only when he was several weeks old and pronounced healthy by the doctor did she tell Madhur to open the big tin trunk that held her store of baby clothes. Superstitious fears and previous experience of stillbirths and short-lived infants bred caution. But James had a rosy glow that suggested sturdiness. The rose would fade of course, and he would grow sallow, his skin losing its brightness; that was what this climate did to children. But he seemed strong. When the day came for his official naming, she decided to dress him in her own ivory satin and lace christening gown and the tiny cap that tied beneath the chin with long satin strings; there were white kid slippers as thin and soft as gloves and woollen bootees small enough to fit snugly on a woman's thumb. These were the things her own mother had dressed her in, carrying her through the damp air of Lima, through the *garua*, that sad greyness, not quite rain, through which the sun came as a veiled glare, a luminous haze that seemed always a part of her childhood.

The ayah threw back the lid of the trunk. From the veranda

Elizabeth heard the wail of dismay: some crack, some tiny pinhole had been searched out and invasion had stealthily taken place. Building their obscene tunnels as they advanced, the white ants had taken over the trunk inch by inch, their pincer jaws shredding and rending the lace, the fine lawn and delicate wool. Stained with their excrement, the remains of Elizabeth's precious baby clothes lay in rags, detritus from the bottom of some filthy dustbin.

Madhur comforted her, murmuring soothing phrases, and called the sweeper to remove the trunk. That night Elizabeth informed Henry that she needed a holiday: she and the child would spend some time in a mainland hill station – perhaps Ooti. Henry nodding, listening carefully and hearing more than the words, said he would book a cabin for her on the next boat.

He took her hands and held them, examining them carefully, almost with surprise.

'Such small hands . . .' Arms long and slender, narrow shoulders sloping gracefully, and a waist, even after childbirth, that he could span with his hands. He was swept with longing, with an urge to catch her to him and crush her as he had once, long ago . . .

But as always he found it hard to express the demanding emotions.

'I shall – miss you. A great deal.'

'I shall miss you.' She stopped herself saying more.

'How long do you think you will be gone?'

'A few weeks. Possibly a few months.'

He released her hands. It was important, suddenly, to get certain things said: 'I have always known . . .' A pause, a searching: 'I am a rather dull man – ' He raised a hand: 'Please do not deny it. I am dull, not stupid. But I have feelings and whatever you may think, you have always been the most important thing in my life.'

'More important than duty?'

He looked wretched. 'I speak of feelings. Duty is . . .' he

shrugged. 'Duty. Like honour or truth, not to be confused with personal feelings. I'm sure you know that.'

She said she was thirsty, would he send Kushmar with some lime juice?

The date for her departure was not immediately settled and she lay on the veranda, staring across the bay. On the promontory the jail was complete. It lay sprawled along the top of the hill, its cellular tentacles filled with human blood and bone and flesh, as though the convicts had been ingested by the giant stone octopus and become a part of its body. Occasionally, as she handed James back to the ayah, she found herself weeping, but by the following week she felt stronger, and the question of a holiday became less urgent; it was postponed, then forgotten.

Later, when James and Freddy talked, James always insisted that he remembered his early years with great clarity. 'I was happy then.' But what he recalled was a jumble of impressions, moments, fragments reflected in broken mirrors, each capturing a part, but never the whole picture.

He recalled, dimly, a hurricane, when he saw a giant tree dragged from the earth, roots waving like snakes, hurled through the air by the force of the wind; he remembered calm blue days when someone – it must have been Elizabeth, but her image remained insubstantial when he tried to focus on her – led him gently into the shallow sea, teaching him to float, face submerged and eyes open, to observe the shoals of tiny fish darting like jewels through the transparent water. There were sailors who saw dugong or manatees in the tropics, suckling their young, and came back with stories of mermaids riding the waves, but he saw them only as dark shapes, shadows on the sea-floor.

Of the jail he remembered only what he heard, snatches of conversation between grown-ups that meant little. Everyone considered that life for the convicts had improved considerably – 'Remember when they were handcuffed in pairs, round the clock? Remember the iron collars?'

So an outcry in the House of Commons, condemnation of

the 'living hell' of prison life on the Andamans, reported in the *Daily Telegraph*, caused distress and anger. The penal colony was the focus of criticism and the residents resented it. Worse was to follow.

'I hear we have a visitor among us,' the doctor told Elizabeth. 'A gentleman of the press. Young and personable. Fresh from London. Cut quite a swathe among the unmarried ladies in Madras.'

Elizabeth smiled, smoothing a strand of hair back into its golden coil. 'How do you know that?'

'Communications do get through, you know. I hear he was wounded at the Somme.'

'We must invite him to dinner,' Elizabeth said. 'He will have the latest news from Home.'

James, face pressed to the veranda railings, out of sight but in earshot, listened as they talked.

'Home' was often spoken of: at Home people went for bracing walks on the Sussex Downs, he was told, and the weather was different at Home. And quite close to Home, his mother had told him, there was something called The War and young men were dying to protect their King and country. In church every Sunday prayers had been offered for our brave soldiers at the front. And the prayers must have worked because now The War was over.

At Home, one of the mothers said, there were shops that filled whole buildings, that had wide staircases, marble floors and windows. Where you could look at elegant frocks, hats; have tea. All this had little connection with the shacks in Aberdeen bazaar. Home was special.

You went Home to go to school.

At the beginning this seemed merely odd: at four and five school was a long way off, like Home itself. You woke up and found the rains had begun, or the butterflies were back. One day there was a typhoon. Another day everyone went to the cemetery and the mothers cried. Some day there would be school too.

At six, school became something you talked about occasionally, like Christmas or birthdays, and then forgot.

At seven it became real: you found yourself being measured for grey flannel shorts and shirts, and a big tin trunk was brought in from the outhouse.

'How long will school last?' This was a difficult one, and nobody James asked knew how to answer it. Other people of seven or eight were as puzzled as he was, and older ones had already gone, and could not be questioned.

His mother had told him a story once, an old Indian legend about dragonflies which laid their eggs at the bottom of a pond. When it was time to hatch out, the larvae would float to the surface and then vanish, never to return. A frog which knew both worlds, above and below the surface, told the larvae that on the surface their brothers turned to glittering creatures with shining wings. And they promised each other that when *they* hatched out they would return with the truth. But once free of the pond, there was no way back in. James thought school seemed to be like that. 'How long does school last?' he asked his parents. School lasted a long time, but was jolly good fun, Henry said. He had enjoyed his own school-days enormously.

James noticed that, whereas Elizabeth usually answered his questions, it was his father who seemed to know all about school, but he was less good at answers, he missed the point sometimes.

'Where shall we live?' James asked once.

There was a small silence, like the pause before a storm, and then Henry said carefully that it would be a boarding school, surely he had explained that, and there would be dormitories. 'It's capital, you will have a great many friends – '

'But where shall *we* live?' James asked, looking at Elizabeth. 'Where will our house be?'

'Your father will have to remain here, of course,' she said, 'and,' she paused, 'and I must be with him. But – '

James could no longer hear her: he felt a tightness spreading from his stomach, up his throat, he thought that if he opened his mouth the tightness would pour out and make a mess. He swallowed twice.

'I thought you were coming with me.'

She had not moved from her chair but she seemed suddenly a long way away; he could hardly see her. She shook her head.

'But I shall come for a long visit when I am able,' she said.

The tightness in his throat grew worse, it moved into his face and suddenly spilled from his eyes, wet and hot against his cheeks. Salty, it ran into his mouth like sea water.

She wrapped him in her arms and wiped away the tears with her lace-edged handkerchief and murmured soft, comforting words. He continued to sob because none of the words said she would be coming too, none of the words changed anything.

The visitor from London was handsome but ill informed. Representing a leading journal of record, Albert Raith seemed to know nothing of the problems involved in running a penal colony; he was ignorant of the background and hazy about the history of the islands themselves. But he disarmed criticism by admitting as much to everyone.

'I feel the most frightful ass,' he confessed to Henry apologetically, 'coming here and taking up your time with all these wretched questions.'

Could he see the jail? he enquired, and 'glean a few facts, talk to a murderer-wallah or two?'

Did they ever try to escape? he asked. Stow away on a ship to the mainland, for instance? Henry shook his head. 'They would be discovered. Occasionally some go off into the interior, they will persist in thinking the land joins up with Burma in the east. Of course they either die of hunger or the Jarawa get them.'

'Didn't I hear about some servant heading into the jungle after a spot of unpleasantness with a memsahib . . . ?'

'That was a cook, a Muslim. The lady in question . . . was unwell: she had ordered him to supervise the hot water for her tub and apparently was dissatisfied with the temperature. She lost her temper, called him – well, she insulted him, I'm afraid. He picked up a kitchen knife and waved it at her. Then he dropped the knife and ran.'

'She wasn't hurt?'

'No, no. But of course, he knew what it meant: he would lose his parole, be back inside. We sent a party of troops and found him, before the Jarawa did.'

'Lucky man.'

'Not altogether. The jail was too much for him. He managed to get hold of some rope one day. Hanged himself. Sad business.'

Maud Innes had left the islands, granted her longed-for release when her husband got a new posting. Elizabeth found out about Khan from one of the servants. At the Club such things were not discussed.

Albert Raith – Bertie before long – was invited to the Club; he played golf and tennis with the husbands and amused the ladies with outrageous stories of London life. He never talked about the Somme.

His hair grew in tight curls that resisted barber and comb; he had small, merry eyes as black and shiny as boot buttons, and a quizzical, apologetic smile. Everyone liked him.

When he came to dinner, Elizabeth showed him the garden. James hung on the veranda rail and watched Albert Raith walking among the flowers with his mother.

Further along the veranda, from his study, Henry too glanced down at the couple. Their voices could be heard now and then, drifting back as they turned this way and that among the flowerbeds, as Bertie Raith told anecdotes – rueful, self-deflating stories of gaffes and social disasters that brought the rare gift of laughter into this normally staid household.

He came to the end of a story. Henry – and a few yards away James – both saw Elizabeth throw back her head and laugh till tears came to her eyes, saw her put a hand on Bertie Raith's arm. He was slender, almost frail, and only a few inches

103

taller than Elizabeth so that, heads turned to one another confidentially, their faces almost touched.

It was the first time James could recall hearing his mother laugh. Smile, yes, she smiled when they played together, but laugh? Henry saw how fronds of pale hair had escaped and waved around her cheeks as she shook her head in delight. He knew her smile, her gentle amusement as they sat together talking in the dusk, but this free, sudden laughter that seized her like a fit disturbed him.

There was a party one night, during the festival of Muharram, when the Commissioner's Muslim servants hung lanterns made of painted skeleton leaves in all the trees. James wandered among the guests, brushing past military trousers and evening skirts, edging past polished boots and pale shoes. Occasionally a face would bend towards him like a descending moon and someone would ask how he was. Across the garden he saw his mother, her face glowing in the light of the painted, gauze-like lanterns, laughing again, at some quip of Bertie's.

Everyone enjoyed Bertie's company, but not everyone, it seemed, was wholly happy about his visit. There was the episode of the tango: Bertie had a gramophone record and played it at the Club. None of them had heard the tango before, and certainly no one knew how to do it. Bertie volunteered to teach them. One by one the wives learned the Argentine step, the promenade position and the rocking turn. Elizabeth was quick to pick it up; she and Bertie Raith made a handsome couple, swaying to the music, feet flashing like knives. At the Club, after 6.30, when the ladies had gone, Bertie was occasionally discussed. 'The Poodle-faker', they called him. 'How long is the Poodle-faker staying . . . ?'

Once James overheard a snatch of conversation and asked his mother what it meant:

'Mama, what is a poodle-faker?'

Elizabeth's maternal smile faded for a moment. 'It is a foolish expression, quite meaningless and certainly not one you should trouble yourself with.'

Bertie Raith's article, when it appeared, caused outrage:

'He has twisted the facts.'

'Betrayed our trust!'

'Not the full picture!'

'Where did he get this information? Who did he talk to?'

'Disgraceful!'

Elizabeth read the article and handed the newspaper back to Henry.

'What do you think of it?' she asked.

'A very thorough job. A lot of what he says is true. I have myself raised some of these points in the past . . .'

'But?'

'But he fails to make the comparison. To describe the conditions in other jails, on the mainland. Many prisoners would be grateful for the way things are done here.'

It was not till some time later that James discovered the significance of the 'foolish expression' that had irritated his mother. His best friend, Freddy Tremayne, who slept in the next bed in the dormitory and who sometimes invited James home during the holidays, enlightened him.

As a couple drove past in an open sports car, Freddy raised his eyebrows eloquently and nudged James.

'Off for tea at Skindles I should think, trying his chances with the damsel. A real poodle-faker by the look of him.'

James looked startled. 'What do you mean?'

Freddy was worldly beyond his years. His parents were divorced and he lived part of the year abroad. James frequently found his vocabulary exotic and baffling. Now, however, it was all too clear.

'Well you saw how he looked at her, the way his arm lay on top of hers, definitely a ladies' man – '

He noticed James staring at him in dismay.

'What's wrong?'

James shrugged. 'Nothing.' A pause. 'Do all . . . poodle-fakers try their chances with . . .'

' – women? Oh yes. The life and soul of the *thé dansant*, the sort who suggest playing sardines at house parties. My ma knows a few.'

James walked on silently. His mother, too, had known one.

But driving in the Victoria through the forest to the picnic spot at Corbyn's Cove, when James had asked, 'Mama, what is a poodle-faker?' Elizabeth had told him a lie. She had told him, her smile fading, that the word meant nothing.

As the date for his departure came closer, James became difficult: he had always been an obedient, willing child. Now he demonstrated stubbornness in small things, and threw occasional tantrums. When Henry asked him what was wrong he said nothing, and his eyes swivelled to where his mother sat sewing. Surely she must know? Surely she must see how unhappy he was?

But when he yelled at the ayah, or broke her glass bangles (later flinging himself tearfully into the softness of her white sari and the familiar comforting lap) Elizabeth said nothing. When he was late at table, or pushed the food around the plate, prodding it viciously with his fork, she said nothing. When it was time for bed she came to his room as always, bending over to kiss him goodnight, engulfing him in the scent of violets, rearranging his mosquito net; still she said nothing. But on his last night, she returned to his room and, thinking him asleep, drew aside the mosquito net and reached out to smooth back his hair.

Lying still, his face shadowed, James watched her, saw a trace of something shiny on her cheek, a gleam of light perhaps. He saw the pale face and arms, the yellow-gold hair. The scent of violets flowed over him. She murmured something, a phrase, and turned away.

Then, alone, he cried into his pillow, soaking the stiff cotton, crying until his eyes were swollen and his cheeks felt tight with dried salt. At last he slept, and in his dream his mother came to him, leaning over his bed in the dress like butterfly wings, murmuring a half-heard phrase. Then she rose in the air, weightless in the shimmering dress and floated away, out of reach. The blue sky was pierced with flashes of darkness, he felt no pain yet knew that pain was coming to him. He cried out, waking, screaming.

The ayah was first into the room, followed by Kushmar and the chowkidar, distressed, alarmed.

His parents took charge, soothing him, his mother ordering warm milk. A nightmare, they said. Just a dream.

Chapter 11

The boys were allowed a photograph on their bedside lockers: some had parents, or a family group. Freddy Tremayne, in the bed next to James, had a snapshot of a wire-haired fox terrier. James kept his photograph of Elizabeth and Henry in a leather frame in the drawer of the locker, glancing at it when reaching for hairbrush or toothpaste.

Elizabeth wore a narrow white dress with a fine shawl round her shoulders. The strong sunlight had obliterated all detail, so that she emerged as a small white shape next to Henry in his golfing kit.

James recalled the day the photograph was taken: it was a Sunday. Bertie Raith had played golf with his father and come to lunch afterwards, crossing the bay in the launch.

His mother wore the white dress. It had a square neck and narrow sleeves with heavy lace at the wrists. The material had a sort of pattern in it, which he used to follow, tracing it with his finger, but he always got lost in the swirls and snaky shapes before long.

He stared at the photograph and imagined himself there, watching them that day. He closed the drawer and tried to recall their faces, their features. He could see his father, tall, with a moustache and kind eyes. He thought about his father's eyes: what colour were they? Brown surely? Brown and kind. And his mother, her fingers entwined in the thick, yellow hair that had a sheen like the newly braided rope for sale in Aberdeen bazaar . . . His mother, tucking a stray curl back behind her ear. She was smiling in the photograph, but he realised with alarm that her face was as blurred in his mind as it was in the picture. He felt a sort of terror that he could not remember his mother's face. He pulled open the drawer, snatched up the photograph and held it close to his eyes, which only made it worse: everything dissolved into shadow and whiteness, eyes became black holes and sent no message of love or laughter. It was all there, eyes, nose, smiling mouth, but she could have been anyone in a white dress and shawl.

He wondered when he would see them next.

'She said she would be coming Home as soon as possible,' James told Freddy.

'They all say that: we'll be down very soon. Then things come up . . .' Freddy threw a pillow at a fat boy two beds away.

'Alsopp! When did you last see your parents?'

The boy wrinkled his face, trying to remember. Freddy looked at James.

'You see?'

Elizabeth wrote often: short, cheerful letters full of news about the garden, with drawings of butterflies and flowers. The gold mohar trees were in bloom, she told him, and the road from the jetty all the way to Aberdeen blazed with the gold and crimson blossoms. There had been a hurricane, quite a small one . . . Was he well? she asked. Enjoying school?

James polished his black school shoes and placed them neatly beneath his bed. It was odd, learning to do things the servants had always taken care of.

There had been a bad moment, on the first day of term, when he had dropped his clothes on the dormitory floor, expecting a servant of some sort to be along to clear up after him and lay out clean garments.

Matron had been amused, but also firm:

'When you are older, James, you will have someone to do all those things for you. Not quite yet though.'

There were other ways in which he found himself ill at ease:

he did not know the names of some quite everyday items because they were to be found only here, at Home. Electrical appliances other boys took for granted, like the wireless, astonished him. To be able to switch on the electric light by your bedside was as good as a magic trick: there had been no electricity on Ross. And motor cars! Roaring everywhere in such numbers and such variety. The food was different and people spoke differently, quicker and using new words. Sometimes boys would laugh at him – or rather, not at him alone but at the boys from overseas. The oddities.

The nightmares were a problem: James, crying out, screaming, exasperated boys flinging pillows at him, Matron arriving in a camelhair dressing gown and hair-net.

'It must have been something you ate. You shall have a laxative tomorrow. Settle down everyone.'

When she had padded off in her sensible slippers, the questions began in the darkness:

'What was it, Oakers? Were you dreaming about the jungle? Was it lions and tigers?'

(A dress like butterfly wings, the smell of violets –)

'What were you dreaming of?'

'I don't remember.'

Sometimes he invented: 'A storm at sea', or 'Snakes'.

They liked that: 'Tell us about the snakes, Oakers.' So he made up scary stories about snakes that came up the water outlet in the bathrooms, or dropped from the tops of doors, and also about scorpions, centipedes that anchored themselves in your flesh, and leeches, and of course white ants. And sharks and the barracudas that attacked a young soldier who tried swimming across the bay and chewed little pieces off him till there was nothing left but a patch of red water.

But the nightmares were not the worst of it: that came when he was wide awake and thinking of the house with the red roof and the first floor veranda and the plumbago and cannas in the garden, and tried to picture his parents in the scene, and found only hazy shapes, figures in a landscape, blurred, like the modern paintings the art master showed them in class: figures that seemed to get smaller and further away every day.

There were other paintings they looked at: Rembrandts and Goyas and Dutch interiors. James discovered Piranesi's broken columns and a Fuseli the master dismissed as 'overheated imagination'. One day he showed them a Vermeer, 'The Officer and the Laughing Girl', and drew their attention to the way the artist had captured the light falling on the girl's face, the man's confident pose, the relationship between the two figures. James studied the picture closely and saw that on the wall behind the pair was an early map of North America. He asked about that.

In art, every second Wednesday they were allowed to draw whatever they wished. James drew maps, maps of islands small and large, with shaded areas and contours; with names and roads and labels. The art master seemed puzzled by these drawings, though impressed by James's attention to detail.

'Maps again, Oakley? Next week we must try and find another subject: something rather more lively perhaps.'

It had begun with Elizabeth's spidery sketch of the green, boat-shaped island, showing the child where he lived – here was the flight of stone steps to the church, there the cemetery, the library, here the steep, zig-zag path down to the tiny cove where they had secret picnics – a path so steep that James learned to use the exposed roots of trees as steps, bracing his small feet against them to stop himself sliding. In her neat, small hand his mother had written the names of the houses and drawn the contours of the land that rose to a small hill. Later she drew another map of Ross, this time a map of flowers and trees and butterflies, identifying the places, the species and the seasons in which they flourished.

'On the islands,' she told him, 'the natives have a calendar of scents, that is how they describe the different parts of the year, by the flowering seasons . . .'

His own maps came later, drawn from memory; invented, inaccurate versions of the islands he knew only in part, extravagantly decorated with tall trees, menacing sharks around the shores, and arbitrarily placed aborigines armed with huge bows and arrows. Maps which had as the centre of the universe the red-roofed house with its first-floor veranda, which quite properly occupied the centre of the page, the rest radiating out from there. Only when the geography master told him so, much later, did James learn that he was working in the tradition of the medieval map-makers who placed Jerusalem at the centre of the world – 'Have a look at the Hereford Mappa Mundi some time, they drew Palestina big enough to put in all the important Christian sites, which made it about the size of Russia . . .' Like his, those charts were rich with exotic decoration, monsters and marvels: 'Medieval geography was poetic rather than scientific for the most part. "The cannibals that each other eat/The Anthropophagi, and men whose heads/Do grow beneath their shoulders" . . . that sort of thing.'

It certainly left the life cycle of the frog and the repeal of the Corn Laws far behind in the interest stakes.

'You'll find a sixteenth-century map of the Indian Ocean in the British Museum,' the master told him, 'there's a rather fine sea-monster in that one. Your little islands are in there too.' He tapped James's exercise book. 'They called them the Andemaons.'

Maps, James found, led him through literature and history, they took him on journeys and taught him why men travelled; they made clear the need for laws, for boundary signs and charts for sailing ships to steer by; they marked the paths men took for the mining of gold and the search for the sources of rivers; the missionary routes to savage conversions and ships full of plundered treasure. But all that he learned later.

Saturday Evening Prayers. James filed out of chapel with the familiar sense of a ritual satisfactorily concluded: thanks for past mercies, a request for more of the same. And, as usual, a polite reminder that a family reunion in the near future would be appreciated. A one-way conversation, true, but he had a distinct feeling that God was at least listening.

The housemaster caught his eye, beckoned. 'Oakley, a word. The Head wants to see you. Right away.' He paused, then added, as though continuing a conversation, 'You'll be fine, Oakley, you'll see.'

James stared up at him, puzzled.

'Sir?'

The man looked embarrassed. 'I mean, the Head is not going to punish you or anything.'

'No, sir.'

James knocked on the heavy oak door and went in quietly. The Head sat behind his desk, a reading lamp shining on papers neatly arranged on the leather surface.

'Ah, Oakley, come in, come in, boy.'

James stood in front of the desk, which reached to his chest, and waited. The Head fiddled with a paperknife, looked at the boy over his spectacles.

'How are you getting on, Oakley? Settling in all right?'

'Thank you, sir.'

'Good, good . . .'

Just words. They meant nothing. James wondered why he asked. The old man with bushy eyebrows did not care, not really, how he was getting on. Just as his parents could not really and truly care about him or they would never have handed him over to Mrs Etheridge on the Port Blair quayside, to be delivered to school like a parcel. He was just another piece of luggage: one tin trunk, one leather suitcase, one wicker tuck-box, one boy.

He was expected to stand waving goodbye from the deck, next to Mrs Etheridge, but he said he felt sick and went below so that he would not see the figures on the quay, growing smaller as the ship pulled away.

'I know sometimes you boys from overseas . . . well,' the Head paused. 'It is not always easy . . . The climate for a start . . .'

'Yes, sir.'

There was another pause. James waited. The Head must have something he wanted to say, but he was taking his time. He leaned on one elbow, rubbing his chin, then said briskly, 'Look here, Oakley, I have a bit of news for you, from home – from India, I should say.'

'Yes, sir?' Perhaps there was to be a visit; they were on their way.

'This is rather difficult, my boy; bad news, I'm afraid.'

'Yes, sir?'

'Best not to beat around the bush. To put it plainly, your mother – Mrs Oakley is – she has, um, died.'

James stood with his eyes fixed on the Head, waiting. There was a silence.

'I'm sorry,' the Head said at last, as an afterthought.

'What was it?' James asked. 'Was it cholera? Malaria?'

'No. It seems she was drowned.'

James thought of the last swimming party they had been on, to Corbyn's Cove, splashing in the clear blue water, their carriages waiting under the trees, horses tossing their heads to dislodge flies. His mother slipping through the water, black swimsuit gleaming like sealskin, pale hair pushed under a swimming cap.

'But she swims – she could swim very well. And we always had other people with us – '

'Nothing more I can tell you, I'm afraid. All I have is a telegram.' He paused. 'Remind me how old you are.'

'Eight, sir.'

'Eight! So you're not a baby, are you. Yes. Well, it's a bad business, my boy. But you'll get over it. We shall all do everything we can to help. The boys, too.'

'Thank you, sir.' James found that his legs felt funny; to stop him falling over he leant against the desk. His chest was pressed against the edge. The desk was supporting him, he felt the wooden edge pressing into his ribs, hurting. The pain seemed to spread from his chest outwards until it filled his body. Dimly he heard the Head speaking.

'See Matron if you want an aspirin or something.'

'Yes, sir. Thank you.' There was a pause.

'Right. Run along then.'

He pushed himself away from the desk and walked carefully to the door.

The boys were keen to know more: clearly this could be a better story than even the soldier and the barracudas:

'Come *on*, Oakers, tell us what happened. Was it a shark? You said there were sharks; do they swallow people up whole – '

'– don't be daft, Matthews, that's Jonah and the whale!'

'– sharks *bite*! An arm or a leg at a time – '

'Shut *up*!' Freddy was nine, but sometimes seemed older than the housemaster. Usually, his slender, elegant features remained expressionless, or at most amused, but they could see that he was angry. James was hunched at a table in the study room, books open, and he stared down at them as though learning the words by heart. Freddy slammed down the lid of his desk and said pleasantly, 'If you idiots don't shut up and give a chap a bit of peace I'll get the gardener's boy to give every one of you a black eye.'

Freddy was slightly built and avoided scuffles. But the gardener's son was ten and big for his age. Freddy had found a simple way of protecting his own interests: gifts from his ample tuck-box ensured loyalty. The boys abandoned their quest for melodrama and turned to their books. Freddy was the only one who saw that on James's exercise book the neatly written words in the centre of the page had run together and dissolved into a large inky blob.

Chapter 12

It was not, in the normal course of events, a gathering he would have attended: Juniper Banks ran her dinner parties with an efficiency that approached the military. She planned, disposed and executed ruthlessly. James took fright at such drive, such confident manipulation of conversation and guests. But he was, in his field, a catch: an academic with a reputation spilling out into the posher Sundays and the Third Programme of the BBC. He fitted into her design for the current season.

He evaded, retreated, prevaricated, but he was finally trapped. Too far ahead for him to be feasibly otherwise engaged, the date was set. In petty revenge he arrived late and so failed to be introduced to the vivacious young woman in the white cotton piqué dress across the room. At dinner he found himself seated next to her and was able to observe that her hair had a sheen like rubbed bronze, but – monopolised by the child psychiatrist on his left through the stuffed mushroom starters and the Elizabeth David *boeuf en daube* – it was only at the lemon soufflé stage that he managed to catch her eye – eyes: pale grey and brilliant.

'I'm James Oakley.'

'I know.'

'But – ' He frowned. 'I don't know you.'

And yet, something niggled in his brain; some forgotten connection, something which struck a faint chord. He searched and failed to identify the source of his uncertainty.

'Have we met before?'

'Oh yes, More than once.'

'Impossible! I would remember – '

'It was many years ago.'

He looked doubtful. 'But you're so young – '

'Dreadfully young, I'm afraid.'

'You can't be more than . . .'

She helped him out: 'Twenty-two.'

He looked appalled. 'I'm twice your age.'

'But from now on the differential will be eroded,' she said confidently. 'When I'm thirty-seven, you'll be fifty-nine, and when I'm forty-seven – pushing fifty, that's over the hill for a woman, you'll be a mere sixty-nine, a mature man. Perfectly acceptable.'

'Acceptable for what?' he asked, and then, almost fretful, 'You're sure we've met before? But where? When?'

Madge's husband Noel, natty in his navy blazer and yachting cap, was very much the skipper, swinging a brass handbell, calling 'All aboard the *Skylark*!' James thought he looked ridiculous. Already in low spirits, he felt despair closing in on him: why was he here, on this gratingly jolly day at the seaside? It all sprang from a misunderstanding: he had envisaged a sailing trip, taking a turn at the helm, handling the ropes, bringing her about, feeling the spray in his face. Instead, it was a floating cocktail party. Difficult to leave now – a taxi to the station would be required and a train back to London, and good old Noel would be upset. No, there could be no escape. Stretching his lips into a tortured grin, James stepped on board and decided to see the day through as painlessly as possible. He moved as far from the rest as the size of the yacht permitted and squatted down with his back to the party. Against the sun the sea was ink-blue, the white, curling edges of the waves brilliant. Above his head the pennant fluttered with a brittle, clattering sound.

Children scampered about, tireless, noisy, pausing occasionally to stare at the severe young man who stared back, unsmiling. One of the smallest, a Mabel Lucy Attwell figure with a pot belly and pigtails, produced an autograph book from a pocket and proudly showed him the signatures she had collected: Jessie Matthews, Leslie Howard, Albert Einstein . . . She was a protection against unwelcome adult overtures and he permitted her to sit on his lap as they turned over the grubby pages.

The yacht headed out of the bay, catching the wind, skimming across the blue water. Listen to the sea, James told the child, 'it slurps and whooshes against the hull like an old man drinking soup'. He recited 'The Owl and the Pussycat' to her and as the breeze grew chilly he took off his jacket and bundled the fat little creature inside it and she fell asleep in the sun and dribbled on his shirt.

When the trip was over, Madge found him, still jacketless, leading the sleepy child along the deck.

'Oh James, what a shame, you've missed all the fun!'

He watched the rest of them leaping on to the quayside, laughing, linking arms, and felt a profound relief.

'Never mind,' he said.

'Well: thank you for looking after – ' she peered at the child without recognition ' – this little thing. The mother must be somewhere about.' She moved on, rounding up guests, dangling promises of more cocktails ashore.

Eighteen years later he sat next to a girl with bronze hair at a dinner party and she teased him, dropping hints of mysterious, long-ago encounters. He had forgotten everything. Even the autograph book.

The child tugged at his trouser leg and held up the autograph book.

'But I'm not famous.'

'I shall write you letters,' she explained, 'when I have learned to write. And you will write to me. And when I grow up we shall be married.'

'How old are you?' James asked.

'Four.'

'When you are grown up I shall be an old man.'

'How old?'

'At least forty.'

'That *is* old,' she agreed. 'But I shan't mind. I shall marry you and look after you. Write your name here.'

So he scribbled his name in the little book and she tucked it away, unaware that for a really satisfactory correspondence an address is generally helpful.

'You say we've met *twice* – '

'You know about maps,' she said, ignoring the question, 'let's talk about maps.'

He began to plan withdrawal strategies: he would need an excuse, possibly a reference to making an early start next day. This was an intrusion that must be blocked.

'You'd be bored. It's all rather technical. You don't want to know about theodolite triangulation and the difference between apparent and sidereal time, or the relative merits of hachuring and layer colours for contouring. Anyway, these days it's all electronics and automation. The romance has gone out of it.'

Daisy knew the woman's role in conversations of this sort. She nodded judiciously, pushing her plate away, leaning her elbows on the table, tilting her face towards his, creating a pocket of intimacy. He felt heat rising in his body, nerves on edge, his settled routine and certainties suddenly precarious.

'That's not how you told it in your last book.'

'You haven't read it – not all the way through?'

'Don't be patronising.'

'I meant – it's somewhat dry.'

'So is champagne. Would you abandon it halfway through the bottle?'

Her mischievous eyes caught the light, glinting like silver, dazzling him, for a moment. Her face swam towards him, he was aware of her shoulders, a shadow where her dress dipped low over her breasts; he felt it suddenly vital that she should not, after all, abandon the conversation. Perversely, having said she would be bored, he now wanted to hold her, and reached for anything that might prevent her from turning away, finding the guest on her other side more attractive. Alarmingly, she seemed suddenly to have lost interest.

'The maps have all been drawn now,' she said, shrugging. 'You can add a motorway or a new town and that's about it, isn't it? Not much left for us to do.'

'Every detail is important: without maps we wouldn't know what places are like, what they're composed of: the height of the hills, circumference of the lakes, where the river goes . . . When you're going somewhere new, don't you buy a map?'

'Primitive man didn't have maps,' Daisy retorted, 'he walked it and found out that way.'

'Ah, but with maps we know before we're there.'

She nodded. 'So there are no surprises?'

'If God had not intended us to look before we leap he wouldn't have given us eyes.'

'He gave us eyes so that we could look up at the stars,' Daisy said provocatively, 'not down at the Ordnance Survey.'

Unsettled by her clear grey eyes that seemed at one moment guileless, the next dangerously challenging, he fell silent, gratefully accepting the coffee passed to him, concentrating on helping himself to a mathematically precise amount of sugar, stirring carefully. This sort of frivolous badinage was not his style at all. He felt oddly breathless, shaky, as though in some undefined way threatened.

'. . . we all go in turn,' he heard Juniper announce in her firm, clear voice from the head of the table. She had a feeling for the changing mood, she paid attention to balance and mix. Tonight she had decided to introduce a note of challenge, shake up the slightly jaded formula. 'Gaps. You have to say what you think is the gap in the life of the person to your left. Then each of us must say what *we* think is our own gap.'

He was horrified. After-dinner games! He had always loathed games of all sorts: truth or consequences, word association, amusing definitions . . . He should never have come. He must go at once. But it was too late; down the table, coming ever closer, one by one, gaps were being described: sport, drunkenness, travel, cannabis-smoking, people admitting to the safe lacunae.

James peered closely at his coffee spoon while the grey eyes appraised him, the table waiting.

'I think James's gap is laughter,' Daisy said slowly. 'I don't think he's had laughter in his life.'

Nine sets of eyes, nine judgemental faces, an after-dinner jury disguising behind social gestures – smiles, raised eyebrows – their private summing up of fellow guests. James, mouth dry, shoulders twitching, hands restless, suffered and prayed for the evening to come to an end.

Desperately he improvised acceptable gaps for himself: 'Oh, opera . . . modern art.'

A podgy woman in an unflattering floral dress shook her head, waving away his contribution. 'That's just pastime stuff. Culture. We're after the gap in your *life*, James.'

The circle of faces blurred. He felt the pounding begin in his head. Flashes of darkness. Pain. A prickle of sweat in his armpits.

'I'm not very good at games,' he said. 'And it's past my bedtime.'

In the act of pushing back his chair he asked Daisy, seemingly as an afterthought, 'How does one find you?'

'I'm in the book,' she said, 'if one wants to look me up. Or one could find one's way in person. The A to Z should help: does one know how to use it?'

Chapter 13

My Dear Jamie,

This is an extremely painful letter for me to write and for you to receive. Your mother was very dear to me and I know we shall both miss her more than words can express. I shall be returning for a long home leave in the near future and we shall have a good talk.

Meanwhile I am sure you will give full attention to your studies as your dear mother would have wished.

Your affectionate father.

Henry read the words over with dismay: this was not the letter he wanted to write; he had intended something warmer, something that would comfort the child and at the same time cast a calming veil over the unhappy business. Crumpled up at his feet lay his first attempt: a sheet of paper on which was scrawled 'What am I to do? I cannot live without her.' Clearly, that was all wrong. But when he tried to think of the right thing to say to the child, he found himself quite lost for words.

When it arrived, the letter was not what James had hoped to receive: it explained nothing. He had expected answers and there were none. He felt confused. In time he became angry and frightened. It strengthened his feelings about the way things had happened, without his knowledge; the unfairness of it, dying behind his back like that.

During the day he found quite quickly that he was able to behave normally: learning his spelling lists, handing in his work, asking for seconds at dinner, giggling with the rest when one of the masters actually slipped on a banana skin one day on a town walk, and skidded into a lamp-post like Charlie Chaplin.

The others realised with relief that there was no longer any need to be 'careful' with Oakers. Even the kindest among them recognised that they could forget about the dead mother and let him take his share of being kicked, whipped with wet towels in the shower room and jumped on in the normal way, and everyone felt a great deal better. Except James, who was unintentionally leading a double life.

There never had been the promised 'good talk', for Henry discovered it was impossible to draw Elizabeth into the continuity of everyday life.

At the beginning, on the first home leave, James had been young enough to speak without restraint. He had asked about his mother's death.

Henry found it painful to discuss, and kept the explanation short.

'She was drowned.'

'Yes but where?'

'We are not sure exactly where.'

'What d'you mean?'

'We are not sure where it happened. It was at sea.'

Without warning Henry had started to cry and seemed unable to stop. James had never seen his father cry before and it shocked him, he was at a loss to know what to do. It was an appalling moment for both of them. He watched Henry, watched the way his face wobbled and seemed to blur, as though melting into the tears that ran down his face, lodging in folds and wrinkles. He gasped for breath, choking, making sounds in his throat. James felt sorry for him. His own eyes began to prick and sting and then to fill up, and he was on the point of crawling into his father's arms, when Henry took out his handkerchief, blew his nose and briskly apologised for his behaviour. James realised that crying was something to be ashamed of. Henry too had learned something: after that, afraid of breaking down again, of making a fool of himself in public, he behaved as though his wife had never existed, excising her from anecdote or conversational reference.

But in the red-roofed house on Ross he felt her fingertips in everything he touched, breathed her in with the smell of flowers and, home on leave, when he looked at James, Henry saw Elizabeth in the curve of his son's cheek, recognised a certain tilt and half-turn of the head that, catching him unawares, brought the tightness of unshed tears to his throat again.

On his next home leave, Henry visited James at school. He had agreed to play in the Fathers v. Boys cricket match, but the day was not a success: one of the boys asked him what he had done in the war. Henry told him he had been in India; he had taken some pains to explain that officers and men had been needed there to keep the Empire safe, but James watched Alsopp's face and knew that the reply was inadequate.

'Webber's father', Alsopp said, nodding at a passing boy, 'was in Flanders. His legs were blown off.'

James knew already that other fathers had fought in the war. He realised that other boys had lost fathers in glorious battles with foreign names, but Henry had not been among them, and Henry was safe and whole.

When the match began, his father strode manfully on to the pitch, lost his footing in a patch of slippery mud and got a large grass stain on his flannels. He flourished his bat confidently and was out for a duck a minute later. Freddy Tremayne's new stepfather, young and slim, got fifty and James wished that Henry had not come.

Over tea James told his father that one of the boys had invited him home for part of the holidays.

Henry looked disappointed. 'I thought we would spend the holiday together.'

'PC's dog is going to have puppies,' James said, as though explaining.

Henry looked down helplessly at the small, closed face. 'Well. If you really want to, of course.'

Charles Mitchell, Bonny Prince Charlie – PC for short – lived in a stone mansion in East Lothian. His father was a silent man with whiskers, his face whipped red by the wind; his mother was a gaunt woman with large feet and pale eyelashes who spent a great deal of her day writing letters to brothers and sisters Abroad. The house was chilly and dark, and the beds damp. James stayed for a week and thought it perfect.

The pleasure had nothing to do with Mr or Mrs Mitchell, and not much to do with his friend. On the first afternoon, PC tugged James away from the puppies newly born in one of the barns, and led him up the back staircase to a landing at the top of the house. He knocked, turned the handle and pulled James into a big, stuffy room with a sloping ceiling, dormer windows and a coal fire burning in a small iron grate although the day was warm.

'This is Nanny Baines,' he told James. 'Hullo Baines,' he said conversationally, and then to James's astonishment dived into the lap of the small, plump woman in a sagging armchair, hugging her, pulling her hair, laughing noisily.

At school PC was, like James, a serious, rather silent boy, but sitting in front of the fire in Nanny Baines's room he was full of stories, never still, poking the fire, rummaging in the mending basket, sprawling on the rug, fidgeting cheerfully.

Baines had brought up PC's father and older brother, as well as PC himself until he went off to school. Now she seemed to exist in the attic room for the purpose of being visited – not only by the child, but also by his father, who could be found occasionally, sitting silently in one of the rather worn spoon-back chairs, adding to the stuffiness of the room with his pipe.

James sat eating scones and jam while PC chattered and Nanny Baines poured the tea: she reminded him of his ayah at home, the one who picked him up when he tripped over and grazed his knees, clucking in sympathy, washing off the blood with strong soap and painting the cut with iodine. When the ayah moved, there was the constant sound of her brittle glass bangles, a soft clashing, a musical clicking, as the thin, weightless hoops of red, green and yellow glass slid up and down her plump arms. She wore a white sari, and her feet were bare. Nanny Baines wore a black dress and buttoned black shoes pushed out of shape by her bunions. The ayah's hair was pulled back into a sleek black bun; Nanny Baines's frizzy white hair escaped from its pins and stood out round her head like a dandelion clock. She asked no questions, and yet at the end of three days James had told her everything.

When the visit came to an end James thanked the Mitchells with rather more than the expected ritualised courtesy: 'I really and truly loved it here,' he said fervently. Mrs Mitchell made a mental note not to invite him again: 'Odd little boy.'

*

The first time James took Daisy out to dinner she chose the wine – though she took care to phrase her suggestion deferentially. They talked about ancient cartography and James was surprised by her acuity and charmed by her interest: she was accomplished in the role of educated listener. Later, while waiters hovered, removing and replacing dishes, fussing over cutlery, there came a pause which developed into a silence, and when she put in a question about his childhood – had it been happy? – he was disconcerted, confused, for reasons only partly connected with her question; connected more with his thoughts about her at that moment. He took refuge in brusqueness:

'Is that a conversational gambit? Are you exercising your social skills to put me at my ease?'

She smiled. 'Why should you think that?'

He raised an eyebrow and attempted an ironic, quizzical distancing; an indication of unfathomable depths. But looking into her face, words eluded him. He found himself considering how tender her lips were, the unusual way they curled into a questioning half-smile; the phenomenon of her blue-grey eyes glinting like granite in the sun. He wanted to make some kind of grand gesture: take her hand and cover it with kisses, disregarding the stares of other diners. He picked up his glass and waved it recklessly. His table napkin had slipped on to the floor and he bent to retrieve it, banging his forehead severely on the table's sharp edge. Biting back a yell of pain and spilling only a drop or two of wine, he asked calmly, 'Am I so transparently not at my ease?'

'One must observe the form. It's called getting to know each other, you must be aware of that, you're too old to be inexperienced.'

'Thank you,' James said drily, spirits nosediving.

'I meant it as a compliment. Older men are dangerously attractive.'

James felt his stomach contract; the inside of his head emptied of even the most inconsequential comment. He swallowed a mouthful of wine and tried to look enigmatic.

'You can't possibly be interested – '

But she was. He dismissed his schooldays as 'average: one doesn't analyse . . .'

He went through the motions of thinking further about the question, frowning, rubbing his chin and generally making movements to indicate uncertainty . . .

Boys, noisy, restless, living in the present. There was Freddy and fat Jolyon Alsopp, the Berger brothers and the boy whose home was somewhere in Scotland. James had stayed with him once, he recalled, but the friendship had not deepened. There were occasional educational trips to France or Germany, but on the whole holidays meant Aunt Laura's place near Oxford.

The Bergers, David and Daniel, had an older sister who came with their parents to watch her brothers run one Sports Day and talked to James. She had dark, curly hair too unruly for a fashionable bob, and a sprinkling of fine brown freckles across her creamy cheeks. James thought her beautiful and kind and

127

offered to bring her strawberries and cream when it was time for tea. She noticed his painfully bitten fingernails and nervous movements.

'That boy, the one getting me strawberries: he's nice.'

'Oakley? Mm.' David watched James coming towards them with his uneven, jerky stride. 'He's a sort of semi-orphan. Father in India, and he lost his mother when he was quite small.'

'Poor boy! How dreadful.'

'Don't *say* anything,' David warned her quickly, 'he doesn't talk about it.'

James hurried up to them, handed the glass dish of strawberries and cream to Sarah and found himself invited to stay in the holidays.

The Berger house, a solid nineteenth-century villa, was set in a garden that ran down to the river on one side and overlooked open fields on the other three. There were clipped hedges and rhododendrons and a rectangular ornamental pond. Tea was served under a vast cedar tree.

Sarah saw James arrive, getting out of the car sent to meet him at the station.

'Here's your friend,' she said to David. Without getting up from the grass her brother waved lazily. James stood, uncertain, waiting by the house. She left the others, and crossed the lawn towards him. She was wearing a light dress that blew about in the breeze, showing her knees.

'Hullo James. How lovely to see you.'

He looked wary: he did not altogether believe her.

She would have kissed his cheek, but he thrust out a hand, deliberately keeping a distance between them.

'Hullo.'

She took his hand, holding on to it for a moment, smiling up at him.

'After tea we are to play croquet. Why not put on something comfortable and join the battle?'

His sports jacket, collar and tie felt hot and itchy, but as he hesitated, a burst of laughter reached him from the group lolling on the grass beneath the cedar tree. He screwed up his eyes and glanced quickly across: bronzed and suntanned young hearties in white slacks and open-necked shirts were assembling hoops, mallets and balls, encouraged by two languid young women. They looked confident and in command of the scene. Already he regretted coming. His face tightened.

'I think I shall watch, if you don't mind.'

She led him over, calling to Daniel and David, introducing him to the others. Like Sarah, most of them were a year or two older than James, some already at university. He became stiff and remote, answering questions briefly, assuming an air of ill-concealed impatience.

When the game began he watched for a while from a deck-chair, looking bored. As the competition became increasingly ferocious, the shots viciously calculated to knock out the opposing team, the players grew boisterous, yelling, applauding, throwing themselves down on the grass in despair, challenging in mock fury a particularly wicked shot. Sarah, who was out of the game early, sat on the grass by James, enjoying the spectacle.

James, wretched and distraught, became convinced she had got out of the game from a sense of duty in order to keep him company. Consumed by guilt, and quite sure she regretted having him there, he was determined not to be grateful. He shrugged, raising his eyebrows in what he hoped was a sophisticated sort of way.

'Outdoor activities are terribly banal,' he said. 'So pointless.'

Sarah's smile remained undimmed. 'Would you rather do something else? We have a gramophone, you could play some music.'

'I shall go for a walk.'

'I'll show you the river.'

'You mustn't. You'll miss all the fun,' he protested, knowing she wanted to see the end of the game, encouraging her to abandon him, putting her to the test.

'I've seen them play before.'

They wandered down to the river. To his relief Sarah seemed to feel no need for social exchanges and they stood silently, listening to the sound of the water and the birds.

Near the bank he watched a dragonfly darting like a sliver of fire across the surface. He remembered a long-forgotten story . . . Sarah, also watching the dragonflies, caught his eye and smiled. 'My mother – ' he began. 'A long time ago. When I was a child. There's an Indian legend about dragonflies whose eggs hatch out at the bottom of a lily pond . . . The larvae float to the surface, and are never seen again. Those left behind wonder what has become of them . . .' He stopped. 'I'm afraid I can't remember how the story ended . . .' They watched the dazzling blue threads shooting across the water for a moment or two. He tried to think of something witty to say.

'Shall we go back?' he suggested. 'I need a wash . . . beastly soot from the train . . .'

After dinner Daniel put records on the gramophone and they rolled back the rug for dancing. There were foxtrots and quicksteps and a Charleston, and one of the languid young women offered to show James how to tango, but he refused. He sat in an armchair watching the laughing figures, the light from the chandelier gilding hair and faces. The jewels round the girls' wrists and necks sparkled and the thin silk frocks rippled against their flesh. He looked away, staring out of the french windows, into the blackness. Daniel, irritated, ignored him. David and Sarah tried once more to draw him into the circle. He said he rather thought he would go to bed, he did not care for dance music.

As he went up the staircase, he looked back and caught a fleeting expression on Sarah's face: a blend of regret and dismay. He knew she wished he had not been invited, that she did not, after all, like him. He carried on up the stairs, triumphant: he had suspected as much, and he had proved his point.

'It's all so long ago. A lifetime,' James told Daisy, defensively.

'Sometimes,' he added, to head off further questions, 'I stayed with people. It happens when you don't have family – '

'– Didn't you have family?'

'– And I seem to remember, later on, there were always house parties going on. Dancing. Picnics. Long weekends.'

'It all sounds incredibly P.G. Wodehouse; I'm surprised you enjoyed it.'

'That's because you're too young to know what life was like before the war,' he remarked pompously. 'You know what Talleyrand said.'

'Of course. But just remind me.' She leaned towards him and widened her eyes in parodic, exaggerated expectation.

He glanced quickly at the gentle hollow of her neck, just above the collarbone. He reached out and reverently touched the soft, firm skin.

'A work of art,' he said. Her smile faded. She looked across the table at him with the dawning realisation that she had achieved her heart's desire.

*

'La Rochefoucauld said history never embraces more than a small part of reality. Maps, too, for a long time, showed only a small part of the real world . . .'

James glanced about the hall: there they all sat, slack faced, bodies awkwardly disposed on ill-designed seats, the mood for the most part somnolent. Why did people attend lectures? They were here, but were they interested? The girl in the front row was about ten or eleven, probably dragged along by her mother who thought it would be 'educational'. The child was gawky, her hair bound into punishingly tight plaits which hung below her shoulders. She had light, piercing eyes which James found unnerving.

'The word "cartography" – the craft of map-making or the study of maps – comes from two Greek words: a leaf of papyrus, or paper, plus the verb "to write" . . .' The pale eyes were fixed on his face. He looked down at his notes, took a sip of water and moved rapidly on: historical development, the Mappa Mundi, the influence of printing. In passing he mentioned his book, though he found it unlikely that a north London, middle-class audience with no academic interest in the subject would be much drawn to a comparative study of primitive stick charts.

'Protected by taboo and secrecy, the charts were memorised by the navigator before a voyage. They were too precious and too fragile to be taken on the voyage.

'This is one of the curiosities: the precariousness of map surfaces.'

James shuffled the papers before him on the lectern, a nervous reflex: he had no need to consult his notes.

'Maps have been drawn on papyrus, clay, fragments of pottery or limestone, the skins of goats or cows, palm leaves, spherical gourds. American Indians drew maps on birch bark and hung them from trees – '

Mothers have been known to draw maps in notebooks: maps to mark the coves and indentations of small islands, to show the forests and hills, the known and the unknown, the places of danger. Disconcerting the way extraneous information could surface without warning in the interstices of his mind, in mid-lecture . . . Is it perfume from a dress that makes me so digress . . .

'There are canvas maps, maps on parchment, even cloth. The early silver and copper engraving plates were too precious to be preserved. Luckily for us, some copper plates were used as a base for oil paintings on their smooth side, and so escaped being melted down.'

Daisy gazed up at the lecturer unwinkingly, taking in the sardonic, angular features, the blue eyes narrowed in concentration, the wiry fair hair, the occasional, nervy movements of his big, bony hands.

'Ancient maps were cut up and used as bindings for books; the Cantino world map of 1502 formed part of a wall-screen in an Italian butcher's shop for years before someone realised what it was . . . It really is something of a miracle that any old maps have survived . . .'

In the front row, the girl's mother shifted restively, crossing and uncrossing her legs. The girl herself sat still, not fidgeting or yawning, but expressionless. James knew she must be bored. He felt a twinge of pity: surely she deserved better on a warm summer evening than this punishment? Abruptly he changed gear: began to talk of guesswork, fantasy and lies.

'The blank spaces – *terra incognita* – that was the lure. To attempt to fill in, find solutions to the mysteries of the blank spaces was the great task and the attraction for those early cartographers. Sometimes their enthusiasm got the better of their honesty. Jonathan Swift was rather rude about them, as you probably recall:

> 'Geographers in Afric-maps
> With savage pictures fill their gaps;
> And o'er uninhabitable downs
> Place elephants for want of towns.'

The girl smiled. He felt he was on the right track:

'Not only elephants but Anthropophagi, man-eaters who drank from human skulls, and men without necks, their faces growing from their chests, and dog-headed men and troglodytes . . . You might find India missing from one important map, and Ceylon five times the size of France in another, but imagination was given free rein.

'The first reference in Western literature is in Herodotus, but he too was rather keen on the wilder shores of cartography: when Rabelais wrote about the Mappa Mundi full of wonders, prodigies and strange creatures, he commented on Herodotus, Pliny, Solinus, the ancients, "all writing beautiful lies" . . .'

There was always a place for lies, beautiful and otherwise. Lies make the world go round . . .

A bit of potted history, a biographical sketch or two, a spoonful of Lewis Carroll:

> ' "What's the good of Mercator's North Poles and
>   equators,
> Tropics, zones and Meridian Lines?"
> So the Bellman would cry and the crew would reply
> "They are merely conventional signs." '

He paused. 'When I was about . . . eleven – ' In the front row, plaits twitched, pale eyes narrowed – 'We read *Travels with a Donkey in the Cevennes* at school, and the English master asked what struck us most about the book. I said "The author's duplicity!" Clearly he had a map and studied it. All that stuff about going down the spine of France, the streams running into the Garonne on one side and the Loire on the other – he was cheating of course. Stevenson never mentions a map in the book, but he must have had one. I'm afraid the English master was not impressed with my approach to literary criticism. But at eleven, I felt Stevenson should have given due credit to his map! I still think so.'

After the lecture, drinks with the committee, and the child from the front row staring silently while her mother gushed, thanking him for the 'wonderful evening'. She added, archly, 'You won't remember, but we've met before . . .'

'Forgive me – '

'Oh it was ages ago, I'm a friend of Madge – Madge and Noel Guthrie? We were fellow guests on their yacht once, it must have been five years ago – '

Seven, Daisy said, but not aloud. She flipped one of her plaits impatiently over her shoulder. James, suspecting the child was probably longing to get away and play with her dolls, was aware of her mother's expectant smile. Reluctantly, he dredged up the appropriate question: 'Have you seen Madge lately?'

'Not for ages. She joined the WRNS you know.' A gleam of

malice, 'But she and Noel . . . not a success, I'm afraid . . . she spent the war somewhere rather dashing – '

Lucky Madge. He had spent the war in a faceless bit of English countryside, in a derelict stately home requisitioned for use by military personnel. 'Intelligence' they called it, which sounded vaguely sinister and menacing and he had expected to be trained and dropped by parachute somewhere hostile, use his languages perhaps. But, of course, it had come down to maps in the end. He was an expert after all. So it was a matter of analysing aerial reconnaissance, adjusting grid references and making educated guesses at troop movements. He turned abruptly to the child and gave her one of his better smiles.

'Were you *very* bored by the talk?' he asked. She shook her head, staring up at him, bursting with words, passionate, shining; words that filled her with lightness so that she floated off the ground, words that threatened to explode inside her, scattering her like stars across the sky, words full of secrets and wonder.

But when she opened her mouth the words jostled, fought, got in each other's way; the dazzling sentences fell apart, damaged, and she remained silent.

Belatedly, recalling whose idea it had been to attend the lecture, Daisy's mother began to say, 'My daughter – ' but the chairman of the programme-planning committee chose that moment to reclaim his speaker and James was drawn deftly away, so he did not hear the name of the grey-eyed girl with the plaits, whom he had in fact met before.

'Let me refill your glass . . .' The chairman was assiduous. He paused, eyes flicking: 'I believe you know . . .'

A thin face, dark eyes, good suit. 'David Berger – '

'Of course.'

'We haven't met since – '

' – Before the war,' James said swiftly. He remembered exactly when. 'How's your brother?'

'Somewhere in Greece. Or is it Egypt this week? Business.'

He had not kept in touch with the Bergers – not with the

brothers at any rate. Sarah, with her fine bones, curly hair and freckles, whose knees he had covertly admired when her light frock lifted in the breeze that weekend long ago, he had remained friends with, for a while. Then she had married a German philosopher and gone to live in Vienna – and to die there, or not far away, when Hitler took charge of affairs. Sarah had been a lifeline of sorts; at Oxford, drawing him into her circle, undeterred by his gestures of alarm and rejection, defending him from casual dismissal or the impatient hostility of those he succeeded in upsetting or irritating.

Somehow, she got past all defences without causing him the discomfort of discussing them. The brothers, less forebearing, teased their sister with flippant references – "Kierkegaard said we should keep open the wounds of possibility, but James must have misread him: *he* keeps open the possibility of wounds, always on the qui vive for offence or betrayal – '

'And sooner or later we always let him down, that's our function: to feed his insatiable need for victimisation.'

'But he *has* a wound,' Sarah said. 'It's not up to us to decide whether he should have recovered from it. The wound is his. And incidentally, he's coming in for sherry – '

'What! The wretched Oakley?'

'Oh lor!'

Outside the door of her room, hovering on the landing, early, James could not help but overhear.

When she left for Vienna he went to the station to see her off. There was a crowd and he lurked at the back, carrying a bouquet he now regretted as redundant: he saw that she had so many flowers already.

She found her way to his side and hugged him: 'Flowers! Thank you, James.'

'You don't need more; we may as well chuck these away now – '

'Don't be silly.' She took the flowers. 'I hope you'll come and visit me. Stay with us for a while, use the libraries, would you like that? No one will bother you.'

Why did you bother with me? he wanted to ask; why did you persist? But there were people calling out, the brothers checking baggage, taking photographs. The train would soon be leaving.

He had regarded this invitation as a mark of his special status: the friend chosen to wave her off to her new life; he was chastened to discover he was just another among many. He turned and walked stiffly towards the exit, hoping she would notice his departing head above the crowd, hoping she would feel remorse.

Her brother had the same dark curls, the shadowed eyes, but his expression was quizzical, slightly malicious, as it had been even at school.

'Well, James. Your old maps turned out to be a good thing.'

Patronising bastard. James forced the usual smile, easy hatred rising, finding an outlet:

'Sorry about your sister.'

Watching the smile vanish, the eyes lose their sparkle, James was appalled, sickened by his own words, the breezy reference, as though regretting a prize not won, a minor inconvenience. Sorry about your sister. He wanted to reach out, mourn with the bereaved, rend his garments, and instead –

'Dr Oakley, allow me to introduce . . .'

The young publisher shook his hand warmly and told him he was a born communicator.

'Have you thought of doing a book of more general interest? We're in for a post-war boom in travel abroad . . .'

James looked pained. 'I don't think guidebooks are quite my field – '

'Or mine. I had in mind something more . . . imaginative. Let's have lunch.'

And so *Monsters and Marvels* had its genesis. Not a work his peers approved of particularly, but one that sold well and gained James a celebrity he at first found embarrassing and later useful. He had forgotten by then that its inspiration had been the desire to catch the interest of a pale-eyed girl in the front row of a stuffy lecture hall one summer evening long ago.

Chapter 14

'Oakley, a word . . .'

James fell into step with the housemaster and they walked in silence for a moment or two. He was used to this: masters needed time to construct their well-rounded phrases. He sometimes thought it must be all that Latin, with the verbs at that end of the sentence.

'Mmm . . . Half-term . . . coming up . . .'

Half-term was often a difficult time for boys like James. He would be spending it, as usual, at school.

'Yes, sir.'

'Mmm . . . If you have not already made – Mmm – plans – ' (tactful, James thought: a polite way of saying 'I know you have nothing to do ').

' – I'm thinking of going up to . . . Mmm . . . Town on Saturday . . . spend a little time at one of the museums, take in a theatre. Would you . . . Mmm . . . care to . . . ?' He added, casually, 'I have a spare ticket, you would be doing me a . . . Mmm . . . favour.'

James had grown rapidly in the last year or two: at fourteen he was already as tall as the housemaster and his awkward, slightly spastic gestures made him seem overgrown, gangling. He moved his arms about stiffly, making flapping movements in the air. He liked Mr Johnson, who seemed kind, and hoped, cautiously, that Mr Johnson liked him.

'Are you sure I shall not be in the way, sir?'

'On the contrary. I dislike attending the theatre alone.'

The day began well but at lunch James became increasingly agitated when the waiter offered a choice between roast beef and wild duck: obviously one would be better than the other, the problem being, how to know? How to choose wisely.

'What are you having, sir?'

'I'm in the – um – mood for wild duck.'

James, who had hoped to be encouraged in the direction of the beef, looked unhappy. He stared at the menu, then at the waiter, frowning accusingly. There was a pause.

'The roast beef is always good,' Mr Johnson said helpfully. James dashed at a decision.

'I shall have the beef!'

The waiter took the menus and began to move off. James suddenly had a picture of Mr Johnson's duck: glistening and plump on the plate, and of slices of beef, flat and greyish, being passed to *him*. He coughed nervously and caught the waiter's eye. 'May I change my order? I would like the wild duck.'

The duck arrived. Mr Johnson was served his plump and golden portion. The waiter turned to James. On to his plate slid a piece of an altogether different creature, a scrawnier, flabbier cut off a clearly undernourished barnyard quacker. James frowned, upset. It was not the first time such a thing had happened: at Aunt Laura's on his last birthday, a roast capon was placed on the table with a flourish.

'Your favourite, James!' his aunt prompted.

'Yes. Lovely.' His tone was muted: such a magnificent offering, everyone would want a lot; there would be less for him. Aunt Laura served the chicken – 'I know you prefer the white meat' – and delicate slices of breast were passed to James. His neighbour got a leg. James eyed it covetously: true, he preferred white meat, but there was more to a leg, of course. His own plate suddenly looked less appealing. The breast was consumed in moments and he felt cheated. He could see Aunt Laura was puzzled, upset: she had meant it to be a celebratory meal. He felt sorry for her, but not sorry enough to make up for his own disappointment. As with the duck, now.

The Natural History Museum was busy and Mr Johnson threaded purposefully through the more crowded rooms, avoiding the dinosaurs and the whales. James stayed close, his long legs easily keeping up with the pace Mr Johnson was setting. A loose shoe-lace caught under his foot, almost tripping him up and he paused, crouching, to retie it, and saw the housemaster disappearing through an arched entrance into the Insect Gallery. James hurried after him, then stopped, staring about him, appalled.

Butterflies were everywhere: in glass cases, in drawers, on walls. But here there was no shimmering, no faint disturbance of the air as a thousand silken fragments danced in the sunlight. Here the jewelled creatures lay quite still. Pinned down, skewered to their unnatural resting places, they flaunted their painted, useless wings.

James remembered his mother standing very still in the garden or on the hillside, leaning slightly forward, head bent, intently observing the butterflies, sketching, documenting, later attempting to capture something of their brilliance in watercolours – and failing. But she never tried to catch them. She refused to use the jar with arsenical soap. Now he saw why: tray after tray of poisoned corpses confronted him; objects of delight classified as specimens, examples of species. The room was full of death.

Quite near to James two boys about his own age stood by one of the mahogany display chests, opening and closing the shallow drawers of butterflies, slamming them shut with great force. He caught their eye and one of them grinned conspiratorially.

'If you bang the drawer really hard,' he said, 'sometimes the heads fall off.'

James hurried after Mr Johnson.

'Remarkable collection . . .' Mr Johnson said.

'Yes.'

James glanced from side to side without actually looking at any of the glass cases. He felt hot and anxious and shifted restlessly from one foot to the other, wriggling his shoulders. Mr Johnson noted the movements and the air of impatience. He made an attempt to compare one rare specimen with another, discuss migration patterns, draw the boy into conversation. It occurred to him that perhaps Oakley felt trapped, forced into the company of a master. He offered a temporary escape route:

'James, you might prefer to go round at your own pace . . . I shall . . . um . . . probably spend some time renewing acquaintance with the diatoms – not to everyone's . . . Mmm . . . taste. Shall we meet on the front steps in – say – an hour?'

'The front steps.' James nodded, and hurried away, head and shoulders moving nervously. Mr Johnson had obviously had enough of him, he was being shaken off. He moved through gallery after gallery, seeing nothing. At the theatre he was monosyllabic, blocking any attempts to discuss the play, the actors or the production. Mr Johnson grew irritated: he wondered what had gone wrong. The outing was not repeated.

*

It was hard for Daisy to find ways of giving James pleasure. This was, paradoxically, because everything about her delighted him. Thus, the sight of her approaching the restaurant table, the fragrance of her mouth, the touch of her thigh against his in the cinema, any of these and his face came alive, his pulse quickened. He met her friends and was pleasant to them, but the circle never expanded to include him, and in time re-formed without Daisy. He felt guilty about this, about separating her from her ex-colleagues and old friends, but as he pointed out disarmingly, she was all he needed. He loved to surprise her. Conversely, he hated being surprised: secret weekends, pleasur-

142

able shocks, small, thoughtful gifts, these were his offerings to her. It was unfair, she told him once, that just because he had lived longer he seemed to have so much more experience of giving. No experience, he could have answered, just a long-delayed opportunity. But it also had to be acknowledged that he had very particular tastes. She found his preferences unfathomable: a well-reviewed novel might remain unread; an unplanned visit to the theatre could misfire. An opera stood greater chances of success if he had chosen the evening. Cuff links and ties were not to be attempted.

They saw the writing desk in the window of a Chelsea antique shop late one night: a portable Victorian writing desk of mahogany, with green leather surface tooled in gold, its edges inlaid with brass. It had an inkwell with a domed lid, and a place for quill pens. Its tiny drawers (cunningly displayed half open) held pins and sticks of red sealing wax. It was just the right size to sit comfortably on a gentleman's knees in coach, railway carriage or ocean liner.

For James it was love at first sight: he pressed his nose to the window, noting the satiny patina of the wood, the tiny but solid brass hinges, the perfection of the object. It must, he said, be his.

Next day, at noon, he stepped out of a taxi and paused to admire the writing desk before claiming it: the mahogany glowed softly among the shadows, the brass caught the light, as did the square red sticker which now adorned it. Sold.

Telling Freddy about it later, Daisy described what followed as 'James doing his disappointment number': dismay, subdued anger, bitterness and a faint aura of satisfaction – life, of course, was like that. He should have known.

On his birthday, by special delivery, a parcel arrived at his flat: the writing desk. He was still staring at it in amazed delight when Daisy revealed herself as the engineer of the plot, explaining through the laughter and the kisses that followed, how she had telephoned the shop on the dot of opening time to reserve the prize, swearing them to secrecy, collecting it later. There had been so much laughter, so many kisses in those early days, 'but what an unselfish gift!' James declared, for she would never benefit from it. 'I shan't use it to write you long, Victorian letters because we shall never be separated, we'll be together, always.' And she laughed and kissed him again, as yet unaware that there are more ways than one of being separated.

Chapter 15

Henry was due Home again on leave. These meetings, separated by years, unnatural, were hollow affairs with neither father nor son capable of jumping the rails of circumscribed conversation. Last time they had barely recognised each other: James tended to think of his father as he had been when the photograph, the snapshot in the leather frame was taken: smooth haired, sunburnt, angular, a military-looking man. Henry, too, had snapshots and in them, as in his dreams, he saw his son as he had been when he went Home to school: not quite eight, small, serious and beautiful, pale skin flowing over bones with the unblemished smoothness of marble. Now, when they met under the clock at Victoria Station at the end of term there was a moment, a fraction of a second, when each refused to credit the other's identity: this grey man with loose wattles and an unhealthy, blotched skin, this was clearly not Henry. And this youth whose flannel trousers stopped well short of his ankles, whose sharp features were set in an enquiring frown and who was already nearly six feet tall, this could not possibly be little Jamie.

They hesitated, then laughed about their hesitation, Henry remarking on how James had grown, James insisting how well Henry looked. They found it hard to talk.

They never mentioned Elizabeth: it was almost as though she had never been. Her presence was of course always with them and created strange convolutions in their talks. They had to avoid bumping into her even in words, because as time passed she became more dangerous, like a submerged wreck, invisible, but capable of rending the flesh of an unwary swimmer.

When they took walks in the woods Henry found he could discern the angle of her cheek in his son's half-averted profile. When they dined with Laura, he saw that James had a way of leaning over the table, searching for salt cellar or pepper pot to hand to his aunt that recalled Elizabeth's habit of scanning the dinner table, hovering, head bent, like a guardian angel, making sure Henry had everything he needed, her gold-flecked brown eyes moving from plate to plate, then up to meet his gaze, softening into a smile. What sort of a smile? he asked himself sometimes. Was it a smile of tenderness, as he had believed? Was it a smile of reassurance, a smile to say 'Have no fear. I shall always be here'? Or was it a mask concealing her own feelings? Her secret thoughts? Plans?

Henry walled up his grief and anger behind a façade of everyday activity; of visits to the tailor, his solicitors, the bank, the club. And James no longer knew how to breach the barrier. He was too old now to make an unselfconscious leap from the ordinary to the agonising.

He contemplated ways and means: should he attempt to lead up to it gradually, talk of the past in general terms – 'I remember so little of my childhood, tell me . . .' What? How address the question?

Or should it be the approach direct: 'Tell me how my mother died. Tell me the truth.'

The word surprised him. The truth. There had always been unanswered questions, but now he saw that there was more to it. That he mistrusted the answers he had received. Where had she drowned? Not swimming off the cove.

At sea, his father had told him. On a boat, Aunt Laura said.

A boat? What boat? Going where? Why? But she knew no more.

Freddy had an explanation of course: 'It's my opinion she was doing a bunk. Bolting. Didn't you tell me about some chap

146

from London, a writer on some newspaper? It sounded a bit fishy, I thought. A lot of that sort of thing went on you know. He could have been poodle-faking and it got serious.'

James was startled. He recalled hearing the phrase, years before, when Bertie Raith was dominating the tennis court, gallantly sending the ball back to one of the ladies, deliberately within her reach. 'Poodle-faker', one of the husbands had commented, sotto voce, with a sour laugh.

Could it be that his mother, fragrant and smooth skinned, with her pale gold hair and eyes gleaming like sandstone, had kissed him goodbye forever that day on Hope Town jetty? That she had planned her own escape with the poodle-faker?

But he could say none of this to his father. They shared a sense of loss that could not unite them. Unspoken, the words each held in check corroded their peace of mind.

And when Henry next came Home on leave they met for lunch in town and spent the school holiday together. On Sunday morning, when Laura went to church, they went walking with the dogs, Henry becoming aware that there seemed to be more uphill than down these days. He said he was thinking of retiring. Taking up something – possibly tea-planting. Conversation lapsed.

'Turn back at the beech trees, shall we?'

'Yes, we don't want to be late for lunch.'

They walked on, chatting of this and that, and turned back at the beech trees, heading home, or rather, back to Aunt Laura's, Henry noting with a sideways glance the curve of his son's cheek, James taking care his hand did not brush against his father's as they walked.

Chapter 16

James was six feet two – slightly taller than Henry – by the time he was sixteen. He had a weakness for fine shoes, affected a walking stick and could summon up the necessary authority to order a meal in a restaurant and choose an acceptable wine if accompanying his aunt. His fingernails, bitten to the quick, and his occasional social gaucheries were put down to the normal problems of puberty. He talked more easily to strangers than to people he knew, and gazed with inarticulate longing at the few young women who crossed his path.

Earlier on, Aunt Laura sometimes suggested he might like to ask one of the boys to stay at the house and he would agree – 'Good idea'. But it always seemed difficult to settle on a convenient date, 'and anyway,' he said, 'they would be sure to get bored.'

At Oxford, arriving a virgin, James found the condition difficult to discard: the right circumstances were not often to be found; the girls either too shy or too aggressively New Woman, and after a couple of muffed and fumbling attempts at sexual adventure he decided to retreat to the safer plateau of social intercourse: a punt, a picnic, a walk. With the more serious-minded young women there might be the occasional analytical discussion over coffee after a lecture. He avoided balls, banquets and gaudy nights in general. Freddy had been painlessly ingested into Cambridge society. The Bergers were at Oxford but James avoided them: David had made the early mistake of trying to be friendly – 'Sarah is among us. She got her degree and has decided to pursue some frightfully complicated research at Somerville. She seems rather keen for you to have tea with her one day.' James made vague noises of agreement, quite sure that the invitation would not be followed up.

He turned, increasingly, to the safely distant past, to Homeric voyages and battles not with men but with the elements: he knew the purple-sailed Phoenicians who were the first to dare the open seas by night and out of sight of land. Vicariously, he charted the world, conquering not men but land and ocean. He won the Geography Prize for his essay on an old Christchurch man, Richard Hakluyt (1551 [or 2] – 1616), author of the crisply titled: 'The Principall Navigations, Voiages and Discoueries of the English Nation made by Sea or over Land in the most remote and farthest distant Quarters of the Earth at any time within the compasse of these 1500 years'. Between the pages of an atlas he felt at home.

He suffered physical frustration, even occasional torment. On an evening when the smell of honeysuckle drifted down the river and muted laughter came from open windows across the quad, he felt an ache, a stirring in his blood and longed to surrender recklessly to the beauty of the night with someone at least congenial. Reading Keats hardly assuaged the pain.

When it happened, his great initiation took him by surprise: Madge, a jolly girl – the sort who generally took her turn at punting – accepted an invitation to a picnic on the river.

James was a perfunctory navigator at best and, at his ease with Madge, he simply treated the boat as an extension of a debating forum.

'We have to ask: is a map a scientific instrument or a work of art?'

'Look where you're going,' Madge advised.

Pausing to manoeuvre a tricky curve of the river, he returned to his subject.

'Where does philosophy mesh with cartography?' he demanded, driving the punt forward violently.

'James,' Madge began, but failed to catch his attention. He

waved his arm at the sky: 'Kepler took his concept of a universe centred on the sun from the symbol of God in the Holy Trinity – '

'James!' Madge broke in.

'Pytheas the Greek – ' he was declaiming when an overhanging branch swept him off the punt and he disappeared in a thrashing of limbs, fortunately deprived of speech for a moment by the shock of the immersion, which prevented him from screaming for help. Fortunately, because he discovered as he struggled frenziedly to the surface that the river rose no higher than his knees. With Madge's help they tied up to the overhanging tree and she suggested he take his trousers off to help dry them out.

The last time James had exposed his limbs to a woman he was seven and the ayah had been busily scrubbing mud off his knees. He sat, draped in weeds, water streaming off him and collecting in the bottom of the punt, giving unhappy glances about him as though seeking outside help. Madge was amused.

'Jamie dear, I do not intend to launch an assault on your manly virtue,' she said reassuringly.

'Oh but I wish you would,' he said, the words out before he could stop them. She gave a shout of laughter and climbed over to his bit of the punt.

'Well the very least you can do then,' she suggested, 'is to get out of those wet things before we start.' In the deep shade of the willow tree she took charge of matters and James gasped and groaned and surrendered as he had longed to do. It was wonderful in its own way, and Madge was nice about it, but he could not help noticing that she glanced at her wrist-watch at one point and then suggested that as long as it had been all right for him she rather thought she would save her climax for another occasion: the punt was due back in half an hour. It was not at all the way it sounded from John Donne and he was left feeling somehow dissatisfied.

PART THREE

Chapter 17

There were to be many journeys: trips for research, lecture tours, stints at this or that university, but the first, and because it was like no other, the best journey, was the guest-lecture trip on the Bergers' Nile boat. It was the one Daisy remembered most vividly, to be summoned up on difficult days later, when she, like everyone else, had become the enemy, to be scored off, checked, mistrusted, weighed and so often found wanting. It was the journey when she and James were completely happy.

Honeymoon moments were snatched between tombs, temples, deckside lectures, camel rides, museum visits; the day's timetable starting with a pre-dawn alarm call so that the Bergers' discerning flock of graduates, teachers and academics could experience the sites in solitude, unspoiled by later-rising mere tourists.

They clustered about their satisfyingly well-informed lecturer, following him on the trail of the oldest surviving Egyptian map, a papyrus plan of the roads leading to the sea, 'past the mountains where the gold is washed', he declaimed, eyes gleaming as though gold itself lay at the end of the journey, not mere enlightenment. They peered closely to look at directions written in hieratic text as he explained them; compared old charts with new.

They trailed after him on the toughest routes, scrambling up the rubble in the Valley of the Kings to look at an ostracon scratched by a tomb-builder; he told them stories filled with blood and treachery that brought the wall carvings to life as they followed his guiding finger.

He was good at the little details: the revealing drapery on a robe, the gesture in stone that spoke of love. On an outer, sun-bleached wall in the temple of Karnak he showed them a bas-relief of a battle fought by Rameses II, a turbulent scene of infantry, slaughtered captives and chariots of war; of severed limbs and – detail again – a hillock of foreskins clipped from conquered enemies . . .

One day they took a felucca trip on the river and James explained embalming rituals while the sails flapped noisily in the wind and the Nubian boatman lolled at his ease, gripping the rope between his toes and singing quietly to himself.

At the back of the boat, Daisy did not listen to the lecture as closely as the others. Her eyes rested on James, his hair glittering in the sun, so tall, so imbued with authority that there seemed something godlike about him, and for a moment she felt dazzled, transported. Her heart swelled and she gasped, breathless, then laughed, aware of the embarrassing girlishness of her reaction. But when, over the heads of the others, he caught her eye with a glance full of intensity and desire, her body burned for him.

When she looked back at that first journey, she seemed always to see James in that setting, on the deck of the felucca, blazing with light; hair, eyes, his very skin burnished, like a figure on a golden shield.

Happily captive, the flock learned how geometry was used to re-establish boundaries after the Nile floods, and studied the plan of an Egyptian garden found at Thebes. Links and correspondences were established: 'The ancient Egyptians drew pictures as though they were making maps: they drew this garden accurately, looking down on it from above, laying out pool, trees, paths. But the birds and animals were seen as though from ground level – just as in Europe we later drew sailing ships naturalistically, floating in the oceans of our maps.'

Arriving on a proprietorial visit of inspection, David Berger was astonished by James's energy and his fiery style. He walked with Daisy on the deck one twilight and watched her vivid face as she talked, the bronze curls darkening in the gloom.

'You've worked a miracle. He's a changed man.'

She shrugged off the idea, having no experience of what David Berger called 'the old James'.

'But he was always lovely, to me!'

She wore a white kaftan of fluid silk, purchased in a dark little shop in Luxor, and David Berger suddenly felt impelled to ask her to dance, although dancing was not something he enjoyed. He led her round the dance floor, his thin, dark face puzzled. 'How did James manage it? How did he catch you?'

'By finally allowing me to catch him!' she laughed. 'It took so long.'

Day after day, dropping with fatigue, the lecturer and his bride would totter back to the boat, available for questions and conversation during and after dinner, and edge away to their cabin while the septuagenarians were still arguing the pros and cons of Hatshepsut's regency or the likelihood of a family connection between Akhnaten and Moses.

James was a conscientious lecturer, working on his notes, checking details in reference books. He sat in secluded corners scribbling on the portable Victorian writing desk that had been Daisy's present to him. Occasionally he broke off from work to write her one-line love letters.

The cabin was cramped; the bunks narrow, intimacy unavoidable. James, usually so meticulous, so private, found himself in frequent physical contact with his recently acquired wife, and discovered it was exciting to explore this new-found land, finding always something to delight him.

Freddy's speech at the wedding, affectionate, light-hearted, had touched on an aspect of 'the old James': 'We all realise what a momentous step this is for our Jamie. Kafka described the decision to live with his woman as "a reckless move which can only be compared to some great historical event, like Napoleon's Russian campaign." Well, unlike Napoleon, Jamie pursued *his* campaign to victory – and what a prize he has captured!'

Dancing with Daisy later, he said, 'You'll have to make some allowances: he's lived alone a long time.'

She was buoyed up with confidence and champagne. 'He'll have to make allowances too – I'm not perfect, you know!'

Freddy shook his head with mock dismay. 'I'm sorry to hear that. The received wisdom is that you *are* perfect, and Jamie isn't accustomed to compromise. You *are* aware of the problem?'

She laughed. 'Freddy, I've survived two mergers and a takeover bid, it was like the Ides of March on the executive floor last year: I'm a toughie. Surely I can cope with marriage to the man I've loved all my life? I mean: who could want anything more?'

'Well dear, you know what Shaw said: there are two tragedies in life. One is not to get your heart's desire. The other is to get it.'

He whirled her round so that her skirt ballooned out into a bell of ivory silk. 'I love your frock.'

'James wanted a white wedding but I felt off-white was as near as my conscience would allow.'

He hugged her affectionately. 'What luck that you're a girl so sex needn't come into it. We're going to be *such* good friends.'

But Freddy had drifted away, growing more impersonal as the years passed. They met at dinner parties, private views, little gatherings to celebrate the publication of one of his Greek translations. He was still warm and funny and they laughed a lot but it was surface stuff somehow. She asked him why, one day. He looked helpless, made a joke of it. Then he said, 'I think the bonds of friendship scare Jamie. He feels constricted. He's never had much practice in intimate exchanges – basically he's a hermit crab, but of course you know that, ma chère Desirée.'

James had learned Daisy's real name only on the eve of their marriage:

'Desirée! But then – why Daisy?'

It had begun at school: unable to take 'Desirée' seriously, they called her Daisy-Ray and it stuck. And besides, she had always hated her name, 'ghastly, typical of my mother – '

Under other circumstances, he might have agreed: it was not a name a sensible British parent would choose. But at that stage everything about Daisy delighted and astonished him. In their cabin nest, floating just above the water, with the banks of the Nile gliding silently past, he dwelt on the smooth angle of her elbow, the nape of her neck, the dark bronze wings of her eyebrows, her mouth . . . singling out portions of her anatomy for praise and celebration, as though they had an independent existence, he could rhapsodise on a detail, studying a curve, a declivity, with wonder. Her name said it all: she was desired, every inch of her.

'Have you met Desirée?'

'My wife, Desirée . . .'

'Desirée . . .'

He worshipped her, piecemeal and in her entirety. Sometimes she teasingly made light of his adoration. How, later, she was to regret that lost and loving time; yearn for a moment when even some small part of her might be found perfect.

Chapter 18

The first birth had been anticipated with apprehension: ignorant, frightened, frantically reading up on the pros and cons of natural childbirth and the need for paternal participation, Daisy had approached the event in a state of nerves. The birth was straightforward; someone handed her a small, messy bundle which she held awkwardly in her arms and regarded with some astonishment. 'Elizabeth,' she mumbled, 'hullo Elizabeth.' The literature had prepared her for struggle, for fortitude. This had been so easy.

The second confinement was slower, with attendant problems. The contractions were erratic, the dilation did not please the theatre sister. The whole affair was slow to proceed. Daisy, obedient, stoical, pushed and panted and controlled her breathing, to no avail. She was given what the young nurse called 'help' but found it less than helpful. She grew tired.

This birth, she decided, was proving an unpleasant and squalid affair and she was glad James was not present. He was, however, nearby, pacing the hospital corridor, asking questions, making himself – as is the way with expectant fathers – something of a nuisance. He had cancelled a lecture, and Lizzie was staying with Daisy's mother. He bought paper cups of coffee and left them untasted. He asked for progress reports when it was clear there was no progress to report.

Hours later the night staff took over and a whole new group of nurses were placed in a position to tell him nothing.

The young Indian doctor, hurrying from the labour ward,

was anxious, cloaking his anxiety with urbanity. 'We cannot tell you anything useful at the present time, Dr Oakley. Your wife is being very good – '

'Good?' James cut in, 'I'm sure she is. But why is it taking so long?'

'We have to arrive at the correct procedure. The birth is proving . . . a little complicated. We have to take every precaution, we don't want to endanger the child – '

And James fell apart, swept with the vertigo of one who stares down at the pit beneath his feet and sees that the being his life depends on may be about to disappear into it.

'Fuck the child!' he screamed at the astonished young intern. 'Don't worry about the *child* – ' He stopped, hearing the words inside his head. Fuck the child. The woman was all that counted. He had broken his own rule: never trust people who say they love you. People you depend on. They let you down. They go off, die, disappear. Abandon you. Flashes of darkness. Terror flickered at the edge of vision.

The doctor was accustomed to nervous fathers, to crises and the bitter imperatives of decision-making. People suffer. But James suddenly stopped behaving like an anxious father. He walked away. He turned to marble, unreachable; he waited silently to hear the expected worst.

But Daisy was strong. She and the baby formed a winning alliance against the various problems. Many needles, much pain and some humiliation later, there came the oblivion of a general anaesthetic. A birth took place. No terrible decision had to be made. The doctor brought the news to the father with justifiable self-satisfaction: 'Mother and son doing well!'

James seemed to hear the news from a long way off, as though his own exhaustion were the result of a momentous struggle. It was too late: the damage was done. Daisy too had let him down.

Chapter 19

The Third International Conference on the history of cartography was held in Brussels in 1969. James renewed acquaintance with some old enemies and made a few new ones. His latest book, *The Heirs of Marco Polo*, was actually available in a local bookshop and he was in demand for several impromptu round-table discussions.

Daisy spent the days in art galleries and the evenings sitting silently between James and his fellow delegates, her eyes going from left to right and back again, following the progress of the conversational ball as the men talked across her and around her. Once it had been established that she was there as a wife she ceased to exist as a person; this was the form at conferences. Usually, at a dead point while the plates were being removed by the waiters, someone would turn to her and ask if she had children and how was she enjoying her stay in the city? Sometimes they asked how old her children were and when she told them, they exclaimed that she did not look old enough to be the mother of a teenage boy and girl. She had learned to smile graciously at this and assure them she was indeed quite old enough. On this occasion one persistently attentive German delegate asked her, unexpectedly, how she and 'the esteemed Doktor Oakley' had first met. Had it been, perhaps, in some way connected with work?

As Daisy hesitated James cut in, leaning across her.

'Are you giving your paper tomorrow morning? I have some questions . . .'

'Yes,' the German said, 'tomorrow morning.' He leaned closer to Daisy, his shoulder touched hers. 'So, Frau Doktor Oakley: something tells me that you have a romantic story to recount.' He had, she suspected, drunk more during dinner than was wise.

She caught James's irritated narrowing of the eyes; the stiffening of the spine and restless shoulder movements. Her mouth went dry and she gulped at her wine.

'So I shall give you my guesses: you were perhaps his student – '

'We – '

'Mutual friends,' James said shortly. 'The usual English middle-class courtship. Quite banal.'

But it was not banal, she wanted to cry out; it was beautiful. It was –

'Actually it was a ship-board romance; we met on a boat,' she said abruptly. 'I took one look at him and it was *le coup de foudre*. And then he took off his jacket and wrapped it round me to protect me from the wind.'

'But how chivalrous!' exclaimed the German, delighted to have his hunch proved right.

'My wife is joking,' James said with a firmness that ended the discussion. He hissed furiously at Daisy, 'They'll think you're drunk. You know Continentals don't understand jokes.' There was an awkward pause. A kindly American across the table saw that a delegate wife was at a loss. 'If you can take the time, Mrs Oakley, you really should try and get to Bruges; take a look at the Archaeological Museum, there's a fine example of sixteenth-century work: a Pierre Pourbus map of the Franc de Bruges – enormous, nearly twenty feet long – painted on cloth, one of the best of the topographical items of the period – '

' – It's on canvas, in fact, not cloth,' James said curtly and turned away to answer a question from his neighbour.

Daisy offered her most ingratiating smile to the American: 'Thank you. It would have been nice. But I don't think there's time; we have to get back to London.'

She picked up her coffee cup and sipped the dark liquid. Then she replaced her cup very carefully on the saucer. She had to be careful because, just for a moment, she had been possessed of a powerful urge to tip the hot coffee over James's wiry hair, scatter him with the lump sugar and then sweep regally out of the room. After which she might possibly have hailed a horse-drawn carriage and driven off into the night. Hair flying in the wind, she might have raised her face to the moon and howled . . . But the moment passed and she took a second sip of coffee.

On the last morning, James announced over breakfast that in his view the conference was a success: his paper on 'Travellers' Routes and Coastal Charts of India 1752–1791' had been received particularly well. He decided that a detour to Bruges would be a pleasant way to round off the trip.

'I'm sure you'd like to see the Memlings and so forth,' he said generously.

Daisy, who had no fierce desire to see the Memlings, knew that this was not the moment to express reservations.

'Lovely,' she said. 'It'll be your birthday; we could celebrate with a special dinner.'

'You know I hate birthdays. The less said about that the better.'

They chose the hotel with care: quiet, slightly away from the centre of town, overlooking a canal. 'Friendly management', promised the guidebook. A footnote mentioned delightful personal touches – a bouquet of flowers or a bottle of wine if a guest had a birthday during the stay. Daisy rather hoped James had not read down to the bottom of the page: personal touches of that sort were usually discouraged. She looked up at him warily but he merely agreed that the place sounded agreeable.

Bright sun formed a pattern of little silver wings on the choppy waters of the canal, as though a flock of tiny birds hovered on the surface.

Daisy stood at the hotel bedroom window, so intent on the

glittering water that she did not hear the knock on the door. James had to let in the maid carrying the breakfast tray. She wished them good morning and closed the door behind her. James examined the tray, smiling fixedly.

'That looks nice,' Daisy said.

'No bottle of wine,' he noted with grim satisfaction. 'No flowers. I see the much vaunted birthday greeting is not in evidence.'

He had, after all, read to the bottom of the page in the guidebook.

'Oh. Perhaps they didn't realise – '

'They only have to look at the passport. I imagine that's the way it's usually done.' His shoulders were tense. 'I would be willing to bet that I am the only person in ten years whose birthday they haven't remembered!' he burst out bitterly. 'I should have known.' It was a bad start.

He announced that he would be in the Archaeological Museum for most of the day.

'I'll come too,' Daisy said. She was about to mention the American in Brussels who had told her it was not to be missed, but stopped herself in time: James disliked taking other people's advice, and a wrong word might cause him to avoid the museum altogether. So she simply said, 'I'll see the Van Eycks tomorrow.'

James shrugged but she had a feeling he was pleased. He helped her on with her coat and began to list the highlights of the museum.

The mood did not last long. He hated Bruges, a safe, cosy city with emblematic images of the faithful loving mother everywhere – the various Adoration of the Magi, the sycophantic groups ranged round Mother and Child in absurdly idealised stables; the Pietas in which the bereaved Mother drooped with such artful grace over her dead Son; the Flights into Egypt, babe wrapped warmly against the night, held close in maternal arms . . . on practically every street corner, above their heads, in little niches were tiny statuettes and carvings of the Madonna

163

and Child – 'the whole place is a ghastly, sentimentalised hymn to matriarchy, the dependable, loving mother always there, to the bitter end,' he said with distaste. He preferred not to have her pushed in his face at every turn.

*

James never carried snapshots of Daisy and the children around in his wallet, and there were no family portraits in silver frames or laughing groups spanning the years on piano top, or tucked into the dressing-table mirror. Having no tradition of photographic *aides-mémoire* in his life, he explained early on to Daisy, he found the idea of family pictures alien to him. After a while she put away her own collection: the parents, the brother who failed to return from Alamein, the married sister in Australia. The walls of their flat, later their house, were taken over by books and English watercolours.

Her father noticed, on one of the rare parental visits: 'Been banished, have we? Another of James's little diktats?'

'No, of course not, just some rearranging . . .

He did have photographs of course. They had arrived, decades ago, after Henry's death, neatly packed in cardboard boxes sent on to James with the rest of the 'effects of the deceased'. He had looked through them once: wedding pictures of Henry and Elizabeth taken outside a small country church . . . little sepia snapshots, corners slightly bent, of a child playing in a sandpit . . . smiling through the bars of a drop-side cot . . .

'Sweet dreams,' Elizabeth would say, leaning to kiss the child.

'What shall I bring you back from my dream?' he would ask.

'A peacock's feather,' she might suggest, or 'a fluffy white cloud'. One night she said. 'A snowflake'.

He had never seen snow, so she had to describe it for him. He must know what it looked like before he could dream it. Staring at the child in the picture, James saw that some things had not changed: he still liked to know where and what things were, know their shape, pin them down. This gave him a sense of reality, stopped him floating.

There were other pictures: military groups, and garden parties under trees, sunlight dappling the guests, bearers patiently standing to one side with trays of drinks. And there were two formal portraits, undated, in a double leather frame: Henry, tall, attenuated, elegant, a cane held lightly in one gloved hand, looked straight into the camera. The other, of Elizabeth, showed her half-turned away, looking back, glancing almost provocatively from beneath the brim of her hat, one hand poised to draw her long skirt aside. In both of them he detected a composure, a slight aloofness. They looked certain of themselves, their place, eyes veiled in ambiguity. Staring from one to the other James sensed a wordless communication taking place.

What message was it that passed between these two, so sure of themselves? What plans? Closeness or rupture? Had there been passion? he wondered. Or merely the politeness of conventional companionship? Frustrated, he longed to tear off the calm faces, flay them, find out their inner secrets. He felt again a sense of exclusion and loss and later, as he slept, was brushed by the wings of butterflies, perfume from a dress drifting out of reach above the trees, troubled by flashes of darkness heralding pain – and woke with a blinding migraine.

On their travels photographs were discouraged: there were no shots of Daisy against ancient monuments or James declaiming to his encircling Berger flock on some wild shore. Rebelling against this, the children learned to use a camera early and, to James's dismay, Lizzie acquired a second-hand 8mm cine-camera and captured family moments in the teeth of her father's opposition. He saw no need for this trapping of souls, to be conjured up later to go through their paces, re-creating long-forgotten incidents taking place in the forsaken foreign country of the past.

Once, at Christmas, when Lizzie was showing them videos of her work with what James called pop groups and she called innovative musicians, she ran some old home movies she had transferred to cassettes. There they were in some rural setting, James and Daisy setting out a picnic.

Daisy looked young, her face unlined, but when Lizzie's camera came in close on her kneeling by the hamper Bill remarked how red her eyes looked – 'Did you have hay fever or something, Ma? You look as if you've been crying.'

Packing the picnic basket Daisy had checked the contents with James as usual:

'Shall I put in lager or white wine, James?'

'Wholemeal or white for you, James?'

'Cheddar or Brie, James?'

She no longer felt confident about choosing their menu: doing so in the past had drawn down on her the slightly disappointed reaction from James that presaged failed outings.

Perhaps it would have been easier if she had not been regarded, in the beginning, as perfect.

She had hesitated, prompted by some superstitious fear, to let him know the depth of her feeling for him. In those early days, conscious that she might frighten him off, she had adopted a light-hearted, carefree tone, parried his declarations with gentle teasing. Later, when she recognised the importance of the pedestal she occupied, she grew frightened of toppling, and began to try always to do and say the right thing. The first falls from grace had not been dramatic, but she came to dread the perplexed, and then steely, look that James took on when she proved fallible. She grew determined that mistakes would not be made, that she would at all times ensure that things were as he desired. So she got into the way of checking things with him – what records to choose, what plays to see, what flowers to plant . . .

Around the same time she stopped shopping for clothes because she no longer knew what to buy. Does it suit me? she would wonder, jostled in the changing rooms by young women trying on skinny dresses and older women zipping themselves comfortably into tweed skirts. She no longer knew what she was – was she French Connection or Jean Muir? Laura Ashley or Jaeger? Once, in a small dark boutique she picked up a rough silk ethnic garment woven in gold and the colours of peacock feathers, with fringes at the hem. She held it against her longingly. But it cost a ransom and when would she wear it? And what would James think? Once, long ago, she might have appeared in their bedroom, wrapped in the golden fringes, and twirled confidently before him, but more than time had passed since those days, and such a move could only call forth James's surprise, that slightly pained lowering of the eyes that made her shrink and die a little.

That day of the picnic for example, when, smiling, he asked her for the Branston pickle:

'Branston pickle?' She repeated the words blankly, realising too late that –

'Yes.' Patiently: 'To go with the cheddar.'

And there she was, red-eyed on the video screen and it was taking place all over again.

'I had a cold,' she said, watching the woman on the screen painstakingly lay out the picnic. 'Can't you fast forward to something more interesting, Lizzie?' And remembered, on the instant, what had happened just afterwards: looking for a convenient, sheltering bush, she and Lizzie had come out on to a shoulder of the hillside, and Lizzie had lost her footing. Daisy, attempting to save her, had slipped too, and the two of them had gone rolling down the hill, over and over in the rough grass like two soft logs, calling out, shrieking, and finally, when they reached the bottom tangled up in a heap, laughing uncontrollably despite their grazes and scratches from thistles, nettles and turf.

Memory was worse than video: here they all were, those scenes good and bad, the ones she longed to erase, others she hardly believed now could have happened, but which once were taken for granted, treated so casually that she never thought to cry 'Stop! Stay a moment!' before the speeding instant had receded into the past.

Whoever it was, she thought, who said that those who do not remember the past are condemned to relive it, got it all wrong: it is those who remember the past, who cannot forget, who do the reliving. Over and over again. Rewind. Playback.

Chapter 20

The P & O liner seemed at first unchanged by time, yet not altogether as he remembered it: he recalled the smell of hot rolls and breakfast coffee in the panelled, windowless dining room which had so awed the seven-year-old, and which now offered merely a bland and unsurprising anonymity. He had been seated, then, by avuncular stewards who brought him lemonade and were understanding about spinach. He was lifted on to his chair, raised to the correct table level by a fat cushion, hearing without understanding the talk that eddied around him like waves.

Now, an eligible young man, he was led to his table with proper deferential style; invitations to cocktail parties found their way to his cabin.

The ship had been full of wonders, that first time: the ominous, echoing boom of the fog-horn when they moved through enveloping whiteness; the presence of an Indian prince, surrounded always by his retinue, loaded with jewels and suffused with the heady fragrance of sandalwood. The prince, it was rumoured, carried with him six solid silver vats as tall as a man, filled with Ganges water – enough to last him till he returned home – to avoid polluting himself with English water. The adults seemed unsurprised, but James was astounded: he had never seen this kind of Indian before: on the Andamans there were no maharajas, no palaces. Elephants cleared the jungle and carried timber, not silk-clad noblemen. So he hovered, staring, when the royal party appeared.

Fourteen years later there was no prince on board, but everything else seemed unchanged: the thrumming of the engines deep in the ship, the slow surge beneath his feet, a tilting pull that strengthened in bad weather so that he staggered as he set off on his early morning circuits of the deck.

Last time the deck had seemed huge, the task of circling the ship daunting. Adults had watched, amused, as the small boy with his serious expression marched past them. From time to time the child stopped and peered over the rail. Before he left home, his mother had described the magical green light which she had seen glowing on the water, the light she had tried to capture like a genie in a bottle. But for James on that first trip there seemed always to be some reason to be below after sunset: changing for dinner – even a child was expected to do that – eating, and then off to bed, so that he never saw the magic light. And when the voyage was over he forgot about it. Now he remembered and waited for the ship to enter warmer waters, to see the phosphoric light shimmering on the waves, remembering his mother's rueful advice: 'Do not attempt to imprison the light – you will only kill it.'

He found ship-board society difficult: others spontaneously formed groups, deckchairs pulled into intimate circles, drinks ordered by the trayful, jokes exchanged amid sudden bursts of laughter; complicity. There were tournaments, deck quoits and competitions. Dances, fancy-dress evenings. Young men played flirtatious games with slim, pale-skinned women in slithery frocks. People surrendered their privacy with alarming ease; he caught fragments of their lives as he strode past:

'My first husband lacked understanding.'

'– a trial separation – '

'Later, tonight, in your cabin?'

He felt, as always, excluded. Freddy, who was with him, was clearly amusing himself, though quite how, James was uncertain: Freddy was elsewhere much of the time, always last to show up at meal times, full of disarming but vague apologies to the table; then off again, returning to the cabin late, when

James was already asleep; his days seemed filled with critically timed appointments. From what hints he gleaned, James guessed that Freddy was juggling acquaintances who needed placating in turn – 'I adore ship-board life,' he said one morning when they managed to coincide over breakfast, 'but I don't think I could keep up the pace indefinitely.'

James was aware, and Freddy knew that he knew, that the women in snakelike frocks with lips dark red against smooth white skin, were not the partners that kept him so busy. But James was incapable of discussing the matter.

He spent a lot of time reading, and found himself talking to old people and children. The old people were usually going back to India for good, disappointed with an England they no longer recognised. 'Nobody has manners any more, prices have become a nonsense – and as for Income Tax! . . .' He listened politely.

Children were different: blithely breaching his defences, they stood by his deckchair, staring, until he took notice. Then they monopolised him, climbing on to his lap, tugging at his jacket, asking questions. Perhaps that was why he liked young children: they asked questions, and in turn answered them. Endless questions: why, how, when. Answers.

It was, of course, a matter of questions and answers that had brought him on to the ship, drawn him across oceans to the destination that was only days away now.

'My father wants to see me,' he told Freddy when the letter arrived. 'He's not well enough to travel and he wants to have some sort of ghastly twenty-first-birthday affair – '

'A party!' Freddy exclaimed. 'In India! I'll come too. Get some tropical gear from that place in Cambridge Circus. What a wheeze. Irresistible.'

'Not *at all* irresistible,' James contradicted. 'It will be awful. We shall have nothing to say to each other.'

And then Freddy, who never seemed to be listening, whose daily crises and 'amusing' disasters always appeared to occupy centre stage in his private theatre, added, 'You could ask him about your mother.'

'What?'

'About your mother. And the poodle-faker. What was really going on. You used to say you wanted to know the truth.'

The poodle-faker. Handsome Bertie Raith, who had taken the last photograph of Elizabeth, the one James used to keep in his bedside drawer at school, and later, in another drawer in his room at Oxford. Elizabeth, smiling at the camera – or at the person holding the camera. His father was in the photograph, and Bertie Raith was there that day, it was quite possible he had asked them to pose, keep very still, while he aimed the Box Brownie. Perhaps it was at him that Elizabeth was smiling, her eyes unreadable, black in the sunlight.

He used to tell himself he wanted to know what really happened. At school, opening and closing the drawer by his bed so that Elizabeth and Henry, bleached into sepia, appeared and disappeared like a magic-lantern show, he had longed bitterly to know more, to know 'the truth'. And now he had the opportunity. As Freddy said, it was irresistible.

Chapter 21

The Bergers had prospered: the little Nile boat had spawned the SS *Argo*, a liner with swimming pool that steamed round the Ionian, the Mediterranean, the Adriatic. The flock was larger too: the loyal teachers and academics, many of them retired now, still formed its core, but there was a wider cross-section, passengers who required a little time for shopping between antiquities; a sprinkling of younger ones who wanted more than a slide show and a hot drink to send them happy to bed. But some things did not change: David Berger still flew out, unannounced, to join each cruise for a few days. It kept the staff on their toes and the passengers reassured that the personal touch had not been lost. And every now and then, when his schedule permitted, James went along as guest lecturer, talking of ancient maritime empires or cartographical mysteries, giving the sun-bronzed passengers the comforting reassurance that this was no mere idling in warm climes, but an educational and ennobling experience:

'Men are we, and must grieve when even the shade
Of that which once was great is passed away . . .'

Suitably moved by the extinction of the Venetian republic they could move on to the consumption of fegato alla Veneziana at a local trattoria without undue guilt.

James was a lecturer they could respect: true he had been known to reduce the odd wife to tears if her classroom behaviour irritated him; true too that arguments or theories running counter to his own were not encouraged. But his passion for his subject was evident, and his enthusiasm seized his listeners' attention, even though some of them would have gone hungry rather than share his prickly presence at the dining table.

The cabins too were bigger, less cramped than the little Nile nest Daisy still recalled. She and James could unpack, move to wash-basin or wardrobe without that enforced intimacy, that contact of elbow or thigh that had seemed so delightful, then, when she had been newly Desirée. Now, when he introduced her – and he did not always do so – she was once more Daisy, more often, simply 'my wife'. At some stage, she was unsure quite when, James had decided that Desirée was, after all, rather a long and over-ornate name for everyday use.

Daisy was pitied by the women and patronised by the men, perceived as one of those doormats who clearly asks to be walked on; a tiresomely indecisive woman, too eager to please, a bore. There were the usual questions: children? Which university? Subject? They no longer asked if she had a job: clearly she was not professional material. Once, long ago, for a while, she had struggled, divided herself between two lives, exhausted herself serving two masters. Now she rested on the plateau of the unstressed housewife. Not good value in the conversation stakes. Mostly they ignored her and addressed themselves to James. He could be sarcastic, cutting on occasion, but an intelligent interest in his subject drew the best from him.

He showed them prints and facsimiles of rare and beautiful old maps – 'Visual aids, James!' David Berger said, with a mixture of approval and mockery, 'You're becoming a showman.' They learned some unfamiliar truths behind the public movements of fleets and armies: the *realpolitik* of historical trade and expansion, the cynical underpinning of great enterprises: 'In matters of foreign policy,' James said, 'then as now, self-interest guided morality. What greatness and glory there was lay with a few individual voyagers.' And, he conceded, the myths; though Ulysses and Jason were equivocal enough heroes, and the gods whose paths he also traced for his arm-chair-bound Argonauts frequently proved devious and insincere. The listeners got good value: James displayed a particular gusto in his descriptions of family treachery, betrayal and abandonment. Clytemnestra, faithless wife; Ariadne, deserted on Naxos, Medea . . .

Craggy, his sharp-boned face ruddy after a few days lecturing on deck, he led them through the centuries and across the continents (noting, for future settlement of accounts, who was paying attention and who snoozing in the sun).

'The men, most of them anonymous, who made the first voyages, made history. They opened up the world and took away men's fear. I dealt with some of this in my last book, *Portolans, Rutters and Perilous Seas* – our floating shop has a few copies, I believe.' ('Nice title, James,' David Berger commented with his brief, malicious grin. 'A touch of technical jargon, a little mystery and excitement – we'll make a feature of it in the brochure.')

So the new Argonauts did their homework, read up the subject by night, and by day assembled at the appointed hour for James's little talks. They followed him in the footsteps of the navigators, the men who made the first charts, the Greek *periplus* of the ancient classical world, the *isolario* – the island atlas; the early Italian portolans, the Portuguese manuscript rutters, these navigators were his true heroes, inching their way into the haven of a bay past dangerous reefs and rocks, round unknown coastlines, from island to island, down great rivers and finally, with the stars to guide them, on to an ocean which, for all they knew, might be endless –

' "O unprofitable man," the Genoese replied when Christopher Columbus asked for two ships to explore what we call the Atlantic, "can an end or limit be found to the Western Sea? Its vapour is full of darkness." Those men embarked, knowing the ocean could be endless. Or it could end all too suddenly, its cataract sending them hurtling from the rim of the earth's disc.'

How and where and why they journeyed, these men, and the records they made so that others might follow, this was the theme, the linking thread of his lectures.

Daisy wondered about the women, their lives uncharted in the ancient histories: had there been some wives who waved goodbye to their brave explorers and settled back with a sigh of relief to get on with the spinning and the weaving? (Penelope, as it were, waving goodbye to Ulysses and the boys, loosening her girdle and thinking to herself: now for a bit of peace? . . .) But there was no question of Daisy remaining at home: James required her presence. He never said he needed her, and showed no sign of doing so, but the first – and only – time she suggested he might go alone, a terrible silence had followed, and then an accurately gauged, wounding recital of her shortcomings, her inadequacies, her fear of burglars and intruders, her near-phobic reaction to rates demands and the sight of the bank paying-in book. In short, her clear need for someone to rely on, refer to, defer to. When they were younger, the children had come too, gobbling peanuts from the little dishes on the lounge tables, reluctantly attending their father's lectures, acquiring enviable tans. Now they went backpacking with friends or got themselves invited to villas in Spain.

Without help from James or the stars, the SS *Argo* cut its way in and out of bays, across dark-blue seas from island to island. The stops were brief: time to see the ruined temple, the amphitheatre, the monastery; buy some local honey and get in an on-site lecture. Then it was back to the ship for an air-conditioned lunch and a spot of sunbathing. Occasionally, they were granted a more modern note, the Dardanelles summoning up not only the Hellespont but also Gallipoli; a monastery in ruins not through the depredations of time but destroyed by World War II bombers, and high above the sea on Achilles' isle, rather than some corner of a foreign field, an English poet, a larger than life, kitsch nude with rolled-up manuscript: Rupert Brooke, in effigy.

But James never forgot what linked the more distant past with their living present: the clues men left to guide those who came after, finding their way across land and sea.

'Homer tells us that Calypso instructed Ulysses to keep the Great Bear or the Plough on his left hand as he made his way across the open sea. So long as he kept that constellation – "the only one that never bathes in ocean's stream" to port, he would reach home. If you and I set sail today without a compass, setting off from Malta to Greece, if we kept the Plough on our left as Homer tells us to, we too, like Ulysses, would be sailing East – to Ithaka!'

Chapter 22

He remembered it green but everywhere there was colour: trees lining the roadside from the jetty were covered in golden flowers, blazing like beacons. The gardens of the little houses dotted about on the low hills above the town were filled with blossom and flowering shrubs. Wild orchids drooped from the branches of looming rain trees.

As they drove into Port Blair – 'Horse-drawn carriage!' Freddy muttered into James's ear, 'Heaven!' – James noticed a Hindu temple set back from the road; the holy trees at the entrance were thick with yellow trumpets, and lotus blossoms floated on a stagnant pool.

Captain and Mrs Johnson were chatty without actually saying much: they talked in counterpoint, her gruff delivery mimicking his. The young men were bidden to dinner that night, and there was a dance at the Club. Did they play golf? A boating party was being organised . . . Had Mr Tremayne noted the presence of the aboriginals? Onges coming in to barter for sugar and cloth. Mrs Johnson discreetly indicated a group of small, very black natives moving unhurriedly up the road from the sea, carrying shells – mother of pearl and tortoise-shell. Virtually naked, faces and bodies painted with greyish-white patterns, they wore belts or aprons of string and bark and some of the men carried long bows and arrows. Freddy studied them narrowly.

'One assumes they're friendly?'

'Reasonably. But I would not care to be on any boat wrecked

on one of their islands.' Captain Johnson cut in, 'Even Onges are quite capable of murdering survivors so that they may be free to loot the wreck.'

The scene around them was busy: in the little bazaar people crowded round stalls heaped with fruit and vegetables, a few small, open-fronted shops sold saris, pots and pans, spices and household stores. There were wattle-walled village houses thatched with palm, and children played by the roadside.

James said, 'I think the bazaar is bigger than it was.'

'Oh yes. The place is flourishing. We've taught them a lot, you know.'

Freddy said, provocatively, 'I suppose the convicts are kept out of sight, away from the residential areas?'

Mrs Johnson raised her eyebrows. 'Hardly. Aboriginals apart, everyone you see is a convict, or convict's family.'

'Not quite the hell on earth you were led to expect by reports in the British newspapers?' Captain Johnson turned to James. 'We knew your aunt Laura. Sorry to hear about that . . .'

'How is my father?'

'Henry? Not too bad.'

'He's been a bit down, you know. Chesty.'

'Quite a few of the natives still remember Henry; they've got a lot of respect for the old hands . . .'

What would Henry look like? James wondered. Last time they met, his father had still acted the military man, as though retirement were simply a detail, not a metamorphosis that changed a whole life. What did a military man *do* when he ceased to be a military man? Henry had dabbled in tea, then business, but he had no gift for it.

'Is he staying with you?' James asked.

'No, no. He was over on Ross for a bit, but now – '

The carriage stopped outside a low, square building and Freddy jumped down to help Mrs Johnson out. James glanced at the white sign by the entrance.

'I didn't realise he was in hospital!' He felt stupid, ill-informed: a son should have known a thing like that.

'Oh. Didn't you?' Captain Johnson led the way. 'He'll be expecting us.'

They paused outside a door in a dim corridor. Freddy said, 'Look here, I'll wait outside, Jamie. There seems to be a garden at the back.'

And then the Johnsons were waving James into a shadowy room where a small, white-haired man with a congested blue face lay propped up on high pillows in a narrow iron bed.

James smiled politely, looking round, puzzled. The white-haired man was straining to speak: he wheezed and gasped, his face darkening, flecks of foam appearing at the corners of his mouth. Finally he spoke, in a reedy quaver that sounded theatrical: the last act of Lear.

'James?' he managed. 'Is that you, James?'

So it was his father who lay like a dummy, unmoving in the narrow bed. Henry who had been so upright, a tall man with a straight back, good on the polo field and the golf course. Who had to stoop, head bent, to catch his wife's murmured words. Henry had shrunk, lost his substance. He was a bundle of twiglike bones, a thing of parchment skin and faint blue veins, whose lungs had become enemies as he fought them for breath, shaking with the effort, exhausted by each phrase he wrenched out.

James felt let down, angry: he had not sought this reunion but, offered it, he had seen the possibility of questions and answers banishing some of the shadows that had lurked for so long; perhaps there could be some frank speaking, he and Henry could make peace instead of conversation. But it was not to be. He must make do with odd words, be understanding, act the affectionate son as Henry would act the good father, when in fact they had both forgotten what the other looked like. He had thought this trip might clear the air, he had come here full of hope. But he saw that Henry had come back to die.

The Johnsons, with a sort of gruff tact which James found

irritating, left them on their own, and James sat by the bed, wondering what to say.

'Is there anything you need? Can I . . . ?'

Henry shook his head, continuing to make the distressing whooping noises. His chest, James saw with a stab of revulsion, had become enlarged, barrel-shaped, sticking up misshapen from the bedclothes. Henry pushed the sheet away impatiently and made convulsive grabbing movements in the general area of his heart, as though trying to tear it free of his uncooperative body. As his fingers squeezed his chest it gave out a horrifying sound like the crackling of brittle paper.

James watched him coldly, wondering if they would sit here in silence till night fell. But, gasping and choking, Henry finally forced out some words; pausing between them, building up strength for the next battle, not always making it to the end.

'You look well . . . Are you . . . well?'

'Yes.'

'Good.' Pause. '. . . Glad you came.' Another pause. 'Any plans? Future . . .'

Had he hoped James would follow him into the army? It was too late to ask that, too late for so many questions.

'I plan to teach for a bit,' James said, leaning forward and articulating carefully, as though Henry's hearing too was impaired. His father nodded.

'Teach . . .'

'Just for a while you know. I may go back to Oxford, do some research. Geography . . .'

Henry crumpled into a fit of coughing, dragging breath up into his mouth noisily, his throat rasping.

'Damn . . . lungs.' A pause. 'You'll go across? House . . . still there.'

'Of course.' With sudden brutality, a surge of resentment that took him by surprise, James said loudly, 'I shall go to the cemetery. Visit my mother's grave.'

The old eyes bulged, grew watery. Henry's hand described a vague movement in the air. He seemed to shrink into the bed.

'She . . . it was at sea.' Frantic wheezing. 'We tried, we – '
Gasping breaths, unpleasant gulping sounds. 'Ah . . . but . . .
you know . . .'

No, James wanted to shout at him, I *don't* know. Why don't
you tell me? He had an almost overwhelming urge to grab the
old man by his bony shoulders and shake him till the tight,
blown-up chest burst like a paper bag full of air.

With a virtuous, holier-than-thou tone James said, 'It must
have been lonely for her here. Did you consider that?'

Henry gasped and choked, his watery eyes full of hurt and
distress. 'We . . . I – She was happy – '

'What happened, exactly?' James asked loudly.

'The . . . boat . . .'

'What boat?'

'Boat she was – on.'

Impossible to ask, was she leaving you? Was she simply
going on a trip, or was she going off with the poodle-faker?

'Hurricane . . .' More wheezing.

Behind James the door opened and a man in a white coat
stood watching them. He said crisply, 'No more talking,
Henry.' James got to his feet. 'You can see your visitor
tomorrow.'

He held out his hand. 'You must be James. I'm Dr Williams.'

Henry's eyes flicked from one to the other. Then his gaze
returned to his son. In an attempt at intimacy James reached
for Henry's hand but his father had clutched the sheet, twisting
it in his fingers, fighting for precious parting words. James
leaned closer: perhaps after all he was to learn something.

'Duck,' Henry whispered. He gulped for air. 'Dinner. Have
the duck.'

Have the duck? James began to grin, then forced his features
into seriousness. It was extraordinarily kind of his father to
worry about what he should eat for dinner.

'The duck,' he said. 'Right.'

He walked down the corridor with the doctor, heard how

much Henry had been looking forward to seeing him. He cut in.

'What is it that's wrong with him?'

'Emphysema. Air in the connective tissues of the body. Means less aerating surface of the lung, shortness of breath – heart has to work harder to drive the blood through the lung. In lay terms, he can't get enough air.'

'Can it be cured?'

They had reached a junction in the corridor. Williams said, 'I go this way. Tour of inspection. No, it cannot be "cured" as you put it. It can only be endured.'

On the veranda, amid hanging ferns and greenery, Freddy was chatting animatedly to two young men in dressing gowns. When he saw James he jumped up, nodded goodbye, and hurried over.

'Well? How is he?'

'Not too good. Pretty bad actually.'

'I'm sorry.'

They walked round the side of the building, under swags of crimson bougainvillaea and up the drive towards the gate.

'Did he manage to say anything?'

James nodded. 'He said I should be sure to – ' His voice began to wobble. 'Be sure to have the duck at dinner.'

Freddy stared at him. They began to laugh, uncontrollably. The laughter seized them and they reeled about helplessly, punching each other, trying to regain a proper gravity, laughing till it hurt, till tears came to their eyes and they leaned against the brick wall, out of breath, exhausted. James caught sight of a white coat at one of the windows. Dr Williams was staring at him, incredulous. Then he turned away.

The little ferry ploughed like a rocking-horse across the choppy waters of the bay. Looking back at Port Blair James saw a long stone building dominating the promontory high above the town, the sun gleaming on its crenellated walls.

'What is that place?' he asked a crew member at the rail.

'Sahib, that is Cellular Jail.'

James felt a fool: how could he not have realised it must be the Jail. But the jail had been only a dim memory; he had forgotten what it looked like, had imagined it taller, darker, grimmer. This looked like a stage set for an operatic prison.

The ferry tied up at the jetty and James stepped ashore reluctantly, looking around at the neat, almost smug little houses. Everything was immaculate. As though lined up for inspection. Could it possibly be so unchanged after fourteen years? It seemed unreal, like some model village spruced up for a royal visit. Why did he have a feeling of being deceived, of not being allowed to see the reality of things? But who could be guilty of deception in this genteel backwater? Once again he felt foolish. And self-dramatising: he was behaving like some Greek avenging figure. Whereas this was merely a chance to tidy up loose ends, no more.

The path ran through the trees and up the hill, just as he remembered. Everything was just as he remembered. He saw British soldiers from the barracks and native servants at work, and an occasional European woman crossing her garden in a straw hat or solar topi.

And then he was there, at the house. He stood by the gate staring at the red roof, the first-floor veranda. At the corner where long ago he used to lie prone, eavesdropping on the adults. One of the wooden railings was worn thin at the bottom, victim of his whittling knife. They must have repainted the building – probably several times, it looked immaculate – but they had not noticed the worn railing.

The garden was well tended, but not tumbling in drifts of colour and drenched in fragrance as it had been when Elizabeth was in charge. She had encouraged plumbago and jasmine – 'But Elizabeth! Such *Indian* plants! Don't you find them somewhat . . . vulgar?' 'No,' Elizabeth had replied to the dismayed mem, 'I like the smell.' She grew old roses sent from England, put in buddleia that smelled like honey to attract the butterflies – he looked around: there were no butterflies. But it was not, of course, the butterfly season.

A woman came out on to the veranda and stared down at him coldly. James hurried away, towards the church. The wind blew through the branches of the tall trees, a soothing 'Hush . . . hush' endlessly repeated among the leaves. He saw the church sitting on its plateau at the top of the flight of stone steps, and went on, past the vicarage, climbing steeply till he came to the cemetery wall and stopped, suddenly nervous.

The cemetery was shady and quiet and neatly tended, as he remembered it, but there seemed to be more graves now. Well, there would be. He picked his way among the marble plinths and crosses, and came to a familiar small grave.

'James, son of Elizabeth and Henry Oakley. Born April 1st Died October 29th 1902.' His name, his other self. James the first. The seven-month wonder.

What was it he died of, the first James, his brother? He had asked his mother once and she said pneumonia. She told him children and horses died of pneumonia, the climate was treacherous, but he was strong and healthy, she said, and soon he would be going Home, to bracing winds and a gentle northern sun, to strawberries in summer and snow in winter. To school.

Nearby there was another gravestone: that of Maria Henrietta Oakley, born June 1905, died the same day. He stayed, staring at the small grave, putting off a little longer the moment so long awaited.

A few feet away there was a larger grave with an ornate, carved headstone. He approached it hesitantly, wishing he had brought flowers, but then he saw that it belonged to an old soldier loaded with honours. James looked around, uneasy, peering at grave after grave, at the names, dates. Flashes of darkness. Dizziness. He felt the pain start up in his head as he went very carefully round the cemetery for a second time. He realised finally that Elizabeth was not there.

He had planned it for so long: the moment at the graveside when he would unburden himself of the sobs so long held in, perhaps find peace the way people were said to do. Grieving, he would be healed, watering her grave with his tears – wonderful, comforting emotional clichés which now had been suddenly snatched away. He felt cheated.

The cemetery, the neat rectangular dwellings of those who lay where they belonged, blurred. Hot, painful tears of rage filled his eyes. Tears that did not heal.

He stumbled away, towards the church. But inside he found only an elderly Indian caretaker who told him the vicar would be back next week.

'How long has he been here, on Ross?' James asked.

'The Reverend? He is arriving some two years ago, sahib.'

A newcomer. Useless.

'I was looking for the grave of Mrs Oakley. Mrs Elizabeth Oakley.'

The caretaker stared at him, the liquid brown eyes expressionless. James tried again.

'She lived here, on Ross.'

'Yes sahib, I know.'

'You knew her?'

'Yes, sahib.'

'Where is she buried?'

'Sahib must speak to Chief Commissioner – '

'I am a member of the family.' No reaction. He spoke more loudly. 'Mrs Oakley was my mother.'

The man looked astonished. 'You are Jamis sahib!'

It was a long time since he had heard the Indian variant of his name. He saw with embarrassment that the man's eyes had filled with tears.

'I'm sorry – '

'No, no! You will not recall me. I was cook's boy, mostly in kitchen.' An affectionate smile. 'You have become tall like your father. A very fine man, Oakley sahib.'

'Yes,' James said impatiently, not wanting to waste time on Henry. 'Please tell me about my mother.'

'Jamis sahib, it was hurricane, dangerous currents, rocks, many reefs. Many boats are lost.'

'But still . . . They must have found the wreckage . . . Bodies?'

'Sahib, they are not finding the body.'

In the background he heard the surf gently crashing and withdrawing, crunching on the shingle, lapping at the rocks, the rustling murmur that always accompanied memories of picnics, walks, butterfly-spotting trips with Elizabeth. 'Sahib, they are not finding the body.' He said goodbye and walked slowly towards the jetty. Where was the body then? Or had Elizabeth, as in his nightmares, flown away that day, to some other life, abandoning them?

He did not intend to stop when he reached the house, but he found the woman waiting for him in the shade of a peema tree.

'You must be James Oakley,' she called out in a high, clear voice. 'I'm sorry, I didn't realise just now. Do come in, would you care for some tea?'

About to refuse, he found his mouth was parched, lips cracking, and he followed her into the house. Dazed, he was incapable of conversation, but she did all the necessary talking. There were introductions, condolences and tea on the veranda. The clear voice, brittle as glass, rang in the air. Abruptly, brutally, James broke in:

'Did you ever hear any details – about my mother's death?'

She stopped in mid-sentence, staring at him, mouth open. He heard her say, 'Well only rumours – '

'What rumours?' he asked.

'Oh . . . nothing worth repeating. You know how it is with shipwrecks . . . things get muddled.' She stood up. 'If you've finished your tea . . . a walk round the garden? You'll find it has been well looked after.'

She led the way, at a brisk pace, keeping ahead of him. And suddenly, down at the far end where a small summerhouse stood, James stopped and exclaimed 'The duck house!'

He must have been about six when Henry announced one day that they were to have a duck house: the ducks would be enclosed in suitable quarters and given food and drink, encouraged to breed. The family would have a plentiful supply of delicious duck to add variety to a rather dull diet.

The duck house was built, an ambitious affair with an expanse of water for the birds, and shelter, the whole thing enclosed in strong netting. Elizabeth never liked the duck house; birds should not be captives, she said, but Henry said she was being illogical since she consented to eat them once caught.

The plan worked well, and the ducks flourished until one morning, early, James trotted down the path ahead of the ayah and found the ducks – or what was left of them – scattered about the duck run. Blood was everywhere, rusting the leaves, turning the mud a dark terracotta; feathers, bits of raw red flesh and a head or two, eyes staring blindly, were all that remained. Some predator had got into the enclosure and run wild, killing and gorging. The wind blew feathers on to James's lips and cheeks, sticky, smelling of blood. The ayah began to shriek with superstitious fear, brushing the feathers away. When his mother arrived she saw the blood on the child's mouth, his small teeth gleaming against the red smear.

She shouted for the mali, and when he came running she ordered him to clear up at once: 'Get rid of all this! At once!'

'Memsahib, I cannot.'

'At once!'

'Memsahib, not possible. Not my caste. Dead birds. I cannot touch.'

Her voice was shaking. 'I don't care who does it. *Get it done.*'

Elizabeth spoke quietly to Henry that night and the duck house was dismantled. But she never replanted the area where it had stood.

'You're admiring the summerhouse,' the woman said to James in her clear, penetrating voice.

'Yes.'

'This part of the garden was completely overgrown when we took it on. Like a little jungle. I don't suppose you would remember how it was.'

Chapter 23

The dinner was agreeable. Or so Freddy said. James, never at
ease with strangers, found to his horror that he was to be
introduced to everyone, trundled round from couple to couple:
'one of the Andaman babies, home on a visit'. Daughters of
marriageable age brightened at the sight of a new and eligible
young man. The older people informed him how things had
changed since 'his day'.

Some of the changes he could see for himself: electric light
bulbs shone coldly where he had known oil lamps and candles.
The combustion engine brought the noise of the factory
machine into the village roads where he remembered the clop
of horses' hooves and the creaking wheels of a Victoria. But
could there really have been, in the old days, as Freddy assured
him, a sign at the Club entrance reading 'No dogs or Indians
admitted'? Or was that just one of Freddy's bad jokes?

The dance was, as usual, in Government House on Ross, a
place grander than James had ever realised, with gardens worthy
of a minor palace. The wood carvings done by Burmese convict
servants writhed against the walls and on the staircase, and the
floor of the ballroom gleamed like silk.

'Of course, in your day, James,' a dark-eyed young woman
in a green silk frock said gaily, 'they polished the floor with
convicts.'

He smiled cautiously, waiting for some Raj-style witticism,
but it seemed she was serious. 'Truly. Two convicts held a third

man by his legs and pulled him up and down the floor for hours. It worked marvellously.'

'And how do they do it now?'

'I'm *told* they got in some wonderful new gadget from Whiteleys or the Army and Navy, but,' she leaned closer and he smelled her mango-scented breath, 'it's my belief they still do it the old way when no one's looking.' She giggled.

The caretaker at the church remembered his parents, had known him as a child; the ex-convicts were here for life, but the Europeans were all relative newcomers.

'Did you ever meet a newspaperman called Bertie Raith? He wrote an article about the Andamans – '

'Oh, the infamous newspaper article! I heard about it. Someone wrote a letter to the paper saying the man was no better than a Bolshevik troublemaker. But, of course, all that was before my time.'

None of them had known Elizabeth. And those who knew Henry now seemed incapable of setting him in the context of his marriage and its tragic end.

'Sad business,' one the men said tersely. 'Of course, the navigation channels round here are dangerous at the best of times. In the hurricane season . . .' He shrugged.

'I never had much in the way of details – ' James began.

'I only heard stories myself. It was before my time. And rumours tend to get things wrong, don't they? Sleeping dogs you know . . . Best to let the past lie.'

But did the past lie? That was what James wanted to know.

'Another whisky?'

He was tempted to rupture the social fabric, refuse to let the past be washed away like last season's leaves in the monsoon. To ask 'What rumours?'

But training proved too strong. 'Thank you. Just a small one.'

He got away early and went to the guest-room Henry had arranged for him.

Flashes of darkness. The stab of pain. Troubled and confused half wakefulness. Dreams invaded by the scent of violets. It was not a good night.

James was at the hospital early, crossing on the first ferry, determined to pin Henry down: shortness of breath could be circumvented. He could phrase his questions so that a nod or a shake of the head would provide an answer.

Last night he had begun to wonder, head spinning with the thought, whether there had even been a shipwreck: could his father have invented the story of the ship lost at sea to cover the shameful truth that his wife had run away with another man? To cut short the spreading of rumours? Rumours which had persisted nevertheless. He realised it might seem brutal to trouble a sick, frail man, but he intended to do so. He hoped Williams would not be around.

To his dismay, as he reached the entrance steps he found the doctor waiting for him. He looked stern, disapproving.

'I hope I'm not too early,' James said mechanically.

Unexpectedly, Dr Williams said, 'I'm sorry.' He paused. 'I'm very sorry.'

'What for?'

'There was nothing we could do.'

James stared at him in disbelief. 'Why wasn't I told? Why wasn't I sent for? I should have *been* here, that's what he wanted – '

Yesterday he had stood by the gate with Freddy, laughing at his father's parting words, not knowing they would also be his last. Today he was to have pinned Henry down, willing or not, but Henry too had escaped, like the butterflies over the treetops, and now James must do the right thing: mourn for a departed father. The problem was that he felt nothing.

He tried to visualise his father, propped up in bed, his chest crackling like five-pound notes as he squeezed at his heart, but instead he saw Henry as he had been one day on a school visit years before, on the day of a cricket match. Fathers v. boys. Henry had looked impressive when he arrived, tall and hand-some in his summer-weight suit and regimental tie, his bony face sunburnt, very much the soldier. James had been proud of him and led him the long way round to the playing fields so that the boys would see him. And then one of them asked about the war. Indian soldiers fought in France; at Ypres there had been some sort of pathetic cavalry charge, doomed bravery, a slaughter of turbanned innocents. Nobody said 'no dogs or Indians admitted' in the trenches. They assumed he too had been there, showing the flag, going over the top.

But – 'Somebody had to look after the Empire,' Henry said, smiling down sadly at the smooth young faces. 'Orders are orders so I had to stay put, I'm afraid.'

So no glory for Henry, no medals or wounds to be displayed. He had been guarding convicts on an island penal colony five thousand miles away from danger.

James had been ashamed, and hurried his unsatisfactory father away from further questions. He had wiped the scene from his memory, or so he thought, but now it rose up, vivid with the sunshine and green lawn of that summer day, and now he looked into Henry's face, really looked, not glancing quickly away as he had then, and saw how his father had felt, and now he found tears trickling down his face quite effortlessly. After all, he was behaving like a son.

Chapter 24

The wind blew hot and fierce all day, and at sunset they came into Tinos harbour, almost blown ashore, the frail Argonauts clutching the gangplank handrail as they ventured on to land, pushing their way through a shifting crowd that filled every street and café.

The sun had gone but a glowing afterlight of apricot and violet hung over the town. On any other day, Tinos would have been like any other Ionian island. But this was the Feast of the Assumption and thousands of pilgrims from all over Greece had come to give thanks, or in the hope of a miraculous cure. The church of Panaghia Evangelistria gleamed white at the top of a steep incline, and towards it, like a river of humanity running uphill, the crowd moved up the long, straight street, laughing, shouting, carrying James and Daisy with it. Children played in the gutter, young girls in flimsy dresses threaded with gold and silver, with flowers in their hair, tripped in their high heels up the cobbled street, and all the while there was the noise of the wind, the banging of shutters, the tinkle of plastic mobiles and shell decorations hanging outside souvenir shops, all mixed up with the voices in a wind-drunk euphoria.

Lingering by one of the stalls that lined the street, holding down her skirt, blinking away the dust whipped up by the dancing wind, Daisy was jostled by people buying religious souvenirs, candles as tall as themselves and votive offerings, cheap little rectangles of wafer-thin tin, embossed with an arm or a leg or an eye. First diagnose your ailment, then pick your tin wish. The man behind the stall ignored her. He was busy: this was not a night when British tourists were needed. She examined the flimsy metal wafers set out in neat stacks: would there be one she could use? Something for an unnamed, unspecific ache? For a sense of something mislaid? Missed? It seemed suddenly important that she should find her ailment pictured. She riffled through the tin discs, anxiously – ah! One of the wafers showed a heart: probably intended for a cardiovascular complaint, but it would serve. She held it out and the stallholder picked coins from her palm.

'Daisy!'

She spun round guiltily, pocketing her purchase. James was very cross: 'I nearly lost you; it's most unwise to wander off under these conditions – '

'I'm sorry; I didn't realise – '

'I thought you'd want to see inside the church before they close the doors.' He strode off, ahead of her.

Swimming with the crowd, James and Daisy surged up the wide steps and into the church, out of the windswept dusk and into the dark, stuffy interior, the only sound the shuffling of feet and the murmured incantations; the smell of hot candle wax competing with the emanations of tight-packed humanity. In the darkness the gold of the icons glowed dimly. Shielded by glass, loaded with jewels and silver, Mary and the Infant accepted the homage of the multitude who filed past, reverently kissing the glass cover, blithely disregarding the transmission of germs, and dropping their little discs into a container with a slot like a ballot-box.

'Shall we go?' James had had enough. 'Perhaps we can find a cup of coffee somewhere. Instant, no doubt.' She was about to follow without protest, give up her secret plan, but a curious yearning filled her, making her heavy so that her feet remained rooted to the ground. She stood, eyes brimming with tears of disappointment. James, pushing ahead, came back to find her.

'Is something wrong?'

'I – so wanted to join the line, see the icon . . .'

'What on earth for? It's just superstitious nonsense and it's the most appalling bit of kitsch – '

'I just wanted to.'

'Well in that case,' he said reasonably, 'you'd better get in there right away, hadn't you?'

She was amazed, staring at him. He shrugged: 'I didn't realise it was that important.'

Hastily she joined the queue, shuffling towards the Madonna. In the dimness she dropped her wafer heart into the box, barely glancing at the Mother and Child. She hurried back to James, smiling. He raised his eyebrows. 'Worth the body odour?'

'Yes, in a way.'

'Good. Now perhaps we can find some coffee.'

The vast, carved doors were closed. And locked. For a panic-stricken moment Daisy thought they were in for the night. They would be stranded, miss the boat. The possibilities for disaster multiplied in her mind, and it was all her fault – but, of course, James knew the way to a side entrance.

In the courtyards of the church, birds were busy settling down for the night in the cypress trees. Beneath them, people did the same, unrolling their sleeping bags on the stone paving, setting out supper, feeding babies.

At his lecture that morning James had set the scene for Tinos, whose fleet, as he showed in detail, ingeniously opposed the Persian invasion under Xerxes. In passing, he told them why the people crowded in, on this one night, to sleep huddled together in the church courtyard: 'Incubation was what the ancient Greeks called it: sleeping on holy ground in the hope that while they slept the god would come to them, cure them. They still do it. Different god. Same hope.'

In the street, the darkness dispelled by glaring electric lights strung between the stalls, people were still buying souvenirs, and still the wind blustered, blew skirts high, whipped hair free of pins or flower circlets, and still the shell necklaces and plastic mobiles tinkled, filling the air with their continuous, formless music.

When they weighed anchor, after midnight, the voices and the sounds of the town still came to them, carried on the wind. Daisy leaned against the rail and listened to the Argonauts comparing notes on their evening's adventures: one had tasted squid, grilled on charcoal by the roadside, another had joined in the dancing, someone had bought honey and walnut sweetmeats and a gypsy had read another's palm. 'A long life line, she said . . .'

Daisy looked back, up at the church. Offering accepted? she wondered.

On Delos, earlier that day, with the sunlight harsh on the white ruined columns, she had listened while James conjured up the island's heyday as a classical trading centre, its ships full of merchandise and slaves. Listening, she felt herself there, she too moving in the annual procession Homer spoke of, when the freemen and their ladies danced and gave thanks, her light robe moving in the breeze, girdled in soft leather, her hair caught up in a fillet of gold . . .

> A man who encountered the Ionians then,
> Might think them ageless, deathless,
> Such grace he would survey,
> Such joy would he feel . . .

Oh, to be ageless for a moment, to feel grace and joy and dance among the white columns carrying wreaths and fruit and sacrificial oil. To feel the rock under her bare feet and sip wine from a lover's cup. Once, her lover's hair was golden and took fire from the sun. It was silvery now, but in the bright light it still glittered.

'I'm going below,' James said. 'Try not to dawdle. Epidaurus tomorrow, early start. I'd like to get some sleep.'

Chapter 25

In the days following the funeral James was left to himself: it was clear to him that no one wanted a spectre at the feast, no one wanted to be lumbered with an orphan, not even an eligible orphan, so he was greeted sympathetically and smiled at but no invitations were issued to dine or lunch.

Freddy, on the other hand, had found someone who knew someone in Bloomsbury and was immediately part of a social set.

They moved into a guest-house on the hill above Port Blair and James sat on the veranda and stared at the sea. Behind him the low hills rose, covered with spindly coconut palms and rain trees. He felt empty, limbs drained of blood and energy, a straw man fit to stand in a field and scare the birds away, not capable of independent movement or decisions.

On the fourth day, Freddy was up for breakfast and sat, wrapped in a silk dressing gown, reading Cavafy's poems, nibbling at some pineapple. He laid down the book with a sigh.

'I must go to Alexandria one day. I suppose you wouldn't . . . ?' He watched James morosely chewing his leathery toast.

'Time you had a change of scene, Jamie,' he said firmly. 'There's to be a picnic on some island where the turtles lay their eggs: we are to go in a boat and you shall come too.'

James frowned. 'I'm not invited. I'll clearly be in the way.'

'Rubbish, Everyone is worried about you. They just didn't

want to intrude. I, as you know, am an insensitive swine and know better. You'll come to the picnic.'

The blue dome of the sky hung over the deeper blue of the sea, sealed by an unbroken horizon, trapping the heat. Even the breeze created by the movement of the little boat was warm.

Standing on deck next to the helmsman, James watched tiny patches of land come into sight and fall behind them: thickly forested, the tall trees packed close, looming like a palisade above the mangroves that reached their bony fingers into the water. The islands were undisturbed by any sign of human habitation; only the birds swooping in the high branches and an occasional fish leaping to catch an insect on the wing broke the stillness. In the glaring sunlight the islands had no depth: like carved jade screens they floated on the deep blue water.

The helmsman knew their names, identifying them as they came in view: 'Rutland . . . Boat . . . Snob, Grub, Redskin, Jolly Boy'. Others, he said, had no name, had not even been explored. He had Burmese features and spoke English with no more than a slight inflection. Small and sinewy, he had a sea-soned, weather-hardened look, skin scorched and pickled by sun and sea, hands scarred. Next to him James felt ineffectual, untried.

They crossed a stretch of open water. An island came into view, far off.

'North Sentinel. No landing. If you know what's good for you. The Jarawa are bad enough: the Sentinelese are worse. They'll see off their own kind if they get too close.'

As the perspective shifted, beyond North Sentinel, another island blurred the horizon: 'South Sentinel. Uninhabited.'

James stared at the nearest island, trying to see through the dense undergrowth, trying to visualise the life that went on, hidden from outside eyes, picturing the naked black bodies that moved surely, effortlessly through the rain forests which the white intruder stumbled and trekked through so clumsily, hacking a path only to see the forest implacably growing back, covering his traces.

Dimly he recalled figures from long ago, small dark shapes clustered round Henry and Elizabeth on the jetty, Onges holding out shells, live lobsters and baskets of prawns. A moment came suddenly into sharp focus: one of the British officers, knowing the aboriginal love of honey, had opened a tin of condensed milk for them to try. They tasted it in turn, licking their fingers and grinning appreciatively.

There had been something puzzling at the end: one of the women, young and laughing, wanted more. She tilted back her head and made signs to the officer. She was barely four feet tall and he stood over her, holding the upended tin and she slowly swallowed the last of the thick, creamy liquid as it trickled into her open mouth.

His hand must have shaken or moved slightly then because a few drops missed her mouth and fell on to her naked pointed breasts. One of the tribesmen, no taller than the woman, had stepped closer and begun to lick the yellowish droplets from her tight black breasts. The memory blanked out abruptly and James could recall only being hurried back up the little path and Elizabeth ordering the ayah to give him his bath.

James scanned the tiny islets. 'Is there a good coastal chart of this area?'

The helmsman shrugged. 'I'd be surprised. Lot of islands. Two hundred? Four hundred? Big job.'

'But a chart would tell us how many islands there are. Size and shape. Show the reefs and navigational channels.'

The helmsman shrugged again. 'You want a good chart, you better draw one.'

There was a wind-up gramophone on board which someone had found. Now, as the little steam launch chugged on, it left a trail of noise hanging in the air behind it above the wake. The song wavered and slowed, words slurring until someone quickly wound up the handle to set the singer and the song back at the correct pitch and tempo, the voices of the picnic party – cheerful, enthusiastic and frequently out of tune – joining in the chorus.

'If I wanted to charter a boat to have a good look, take a little time, not just cruise past like this – who should I speak to?'

'Try me.'

'You know your way round all the islands?'

'More than most.'

'I want to charter the boat. How do I find you?'

'There's some village houses over by Chatham Causeway. Ask for Andy at the boatyard.'

'Mr Oakley!' One of the young women waved insistently from the other end of the deck. 'Mr Oakley! We need you!'

The helmsman glanced at James questioningly. 'Oakley? Any relation to – '

'He was my father.'

There was a silence. Then, 'Good man.'

'Really?' James was surprised that the man should know Henry: he could see that, despite the wrinkled, wind-whipped skin, Andy was not much older than he was.

'You didn't think so?'

'What?'

'That he was a good man?'

'Oh! Of course.'

A pause.

'You knew him well?'

'He was kind to me.' The Burmese features were expressionless, the helmsman's eyes fixed on the water. James felt in some way at fault. He moved away, embarrassed.

They anchored off one of the islands. Servants rowed the picnic party ashore and transferred hampers and rugs, cushions and parasols. Then they waded into the sea and began to beat the surface frenziedly. 'It's to frighten off the sharks,' Freddy said knowledgeably.

'Yes Freddy,' James said. 'I know.'

Frightening the sharks. Picnics and teaparties at Corbyn's

Cove, and his parents swimming off Ross. The servants always went in first, beating the water. And suppose there *had* been a shark? And suppose one of the servants had been attacked? No one asked those questions in his memories.

Further along the shore people splashed about in the surf, shouting and laughing at nothing in particular in a way James found oddly irritating.

One of the girls left the others and came across to the shady clearing where the hampers were piled up.

'Aren't you coming in the sea, James?' It was the green frock, translated now to a boldly striped swimsuit. 'You must be so hot and uncomfortable.'

He looked down his nose and frowned. 'I hate water except hot in a tub or iced in a glass,' he said rebukingly. 'I'm perfectly all right here.' Pause. 'Thank you.' She retreated.

The helmsman had remained on board and James could see him sitting, chin resting on crossed arms, by the rail. Whether he was asleep or watching them it was impossible to tell.

The house was built on stilts with wattle walls and the usual banana-palm thatch. James climbed the steep ladder to the living quarters and paused in the low doorway. He attempted to find something to knock on, but the bamboo-and-cane door surround was unpromising. He called out instead.

'Good morning. May I come in?'

He felt ridiculous. By now Freddy in his place would have been on first-name terms with the helmsman. He, in contrast, was incapable of pronouncing Andy's name: they barely knew each other; it seemed presumptuous.

The floor was springy, made of tightly woven straw which bounced slightly as James walked across it to where Andy sat cross-legged on a mat, drinking whisky and studying a grubby sheet of paper in the dim light that came from the doorway.

For a moment James wavered between remaining on his feet and sitting down uninvited. Shifting uncertainly from one foot to another on the disconcertingly flexible flooring he almost lost his balance and collapsed abruptly on to the rush matting.

Andy glanced up from the sheet of paper and jerked his head towards the whisky bottle. 'Help yourself.'

'No thanks.' He suspected that the usual mode of business on the islands was serpentine in approach but he lacked the training. He said baldly, 'About chartering the launch . . .'

Andy seemed bored. 'I'm pretty booked up.'

'Oh. I got the impression the other day that you were available – '

'I didn't say I'm not available, I said I'm pretty booked up. Where exactly d'you want to go?'

James smiled stiffly. 'That's the problem: I'm not sure exactly where. But I could explain, and you could advise me. I want to have a look at the outlying islands. Spend a bit of time going in close, maybe even landing, if possible.'

'We're talking about a lot of islands. You got six months?'

James said, 'If there was a hurricane and a ship on its way to Madras from Port Blair got blown off course, lost . . . With your knowledge of how the wind and currents behave, would you know . . . well, where it might end up?'

The helmsman did not look up or alter his expression; he seemed hardly to have heard James's question. He continued to scrutinise the creased sheet of paper in his hand and took another slug of whisky.

'Is there something in particular you're looking for, or have you just got time to waste?'

James said hesitantly, 'Fourteen years ago a ship was lost during a hurricane. They never found the wreckage. I wondered whether it might have been thrown up on one of the distant islands? One of the islands that aren't visited.' He paused, but Andy remained silent. 'I wondered . . . If someone was clever enough to know where to look, could there be something . . . remains of a hull, cargo – '

'You're looking for the treasure ship.' He sounded disappointed. 'There never was a treasure ship. But once the rumours got started . . .'

'What rumours?'

The islands were full of rumours. They were the stuff of conversation, nourishing the small community who had long ago run out of anything new to say to one another. This one concerned a so-called treasure ship, a steamer laden with a maharajah's gems and gold, bound for some secret destination beyond the reach of the British inventory-makers and revenue collectors.

'But nobody with treasure on board would come this way. It doesn't make sense. It was just one of those stories that got started . . . There are always stories.'

And from time to time some outsider or other got wind of them, and then boats were chartered and expeditions organised and islands circled, all in the cause of finding the long lost steamship.

'There never was any treasure,' Andy repeated, 'but people don't want to be told that. They go snooping round the islands and sooner or later the tribals come rushing down to the shore – Sentinelese or Jarawa – and the strangers back off in a shower of arrows. But someone gets a look at one of the aborigines wearing a bit of gold round his neck, or in his hair, and before long it all starts up again.'

'But where does the gold come from then?' James asked.

'It isn't gold, it's brass. Brass buttons off uniforms. The tribals loot wrecks for two things: they want iron for their arrow-heads – that's something they've learned from us – and they love those brass buttons.'

'And what happens to the survivors, if there *are* any?'

'Well, they kill 'em, of course.'

Chapter 26

On the last night of the cruise there was a gala dinner with champagne and speeches, and the retired headmaster who had emerged as the natural leader of the Argonauts proposed a vote of thanks to 'our erudite and entertaining Mentor, who guided us through the ancient places and explained their secrets'.

Portolans, Rutters and Perilous Seas had sold out in the ship's bookshop, and the mood on board was expansive.

Daisy was subdued. Dressing for dinner, she had put on a white silk kaftan purchased long ago in Luxor. It still, she noted with satisfaction, fitted perfectly, and her tanned skin looked almost golden against the shimmering cloth. James came out of the shower as she was pinning up her hair with a diamanté clip. He stopped dead, staring at her. She tried, smiling nervously, to read his expression: not anger. Horror would be too strong. Dismay, that was it. He was looking at her with dismay.

'Is something wrong, James?'

'No, no.' A pause. 'Is that what you're wearing tonight?'

She was tempted for the most fleeting of moments to reply in level tones that since the garment was encasing her body and the dinner gong was about to go, he might hazard that guess, yes. But a flutter began in the pit of her stomach and she said, lightly, 'I just thought I'd see what it looked like . . .'

He was drying his face vigorously. 'Well . . . you'll certainly stand out in the crowd.'

Silently she unzipped the kaftan and dropped it on to the floor of the wardrobe. She put on a blouse and a beige skirt and brushed her hair out very hard so that it hung unbecomingly round her face. When they joined the throng in the lounge she saw that some women were wearing brightly coloured ethnic finery purchased on Santorini; others wore 'good' long frocks in taffeta or silk. Real jewels sparkled alongside market baubles. Daisy blended with the curtains and the upholstery and was virtually invisible, which presumably was what James desired.

In the bar, David Berger presented James with a bottle of champagne.

'No, no! Quite unnecessary!'

'Nonsense James, we're old friends – '

'We're not really old friends; we have simply known each other a long time.'

David asked, interestedly, 'Who *are* your old friends?'

'You wouldn't know them.'

'No. But you would. Name me ten old friends.'

James stared at him with hostility and remained silent.

'Five?' There was a pause. David shrugged. 'You see,' he said, 'I'm the best you can do.' He shook his head, the smile for once missing: 'What is it with you James? Why d'you always act like I'm about to pick your pocket?'

James chewed his lips nervously. He burst out angrily, 'I was outside the door that day, you know. At Oxford.'

'*What* day? For Christ's sake James, it was nearly forty years ago.'

'You were talking about me. "The possibility of wounds" – '

'What?' David looked bemused. 'Wounds? Sorry James, you've lost me.'

'It's really not important.'

Over dinner, reunions were planned and highlights of the holiday selected:

'Well, I thought Delos . . .'

'Oh, surely – the Palace of Nestor . . .'

'Dr Oakley?'

'Nauplion, probably. The bronze Mycenaean suit of armour, and that excellent fresco . . .'

They had anchored overnight in Nauplion, to visit Mycenae and Epidaurus, learning at the last minute that there was to be a performance of a play by Sophocles in the ancient, open-air theatre.

'Not one of the jollier items in the repertory, I'm afraid,' James said with relish. '*Philoctetes*. There are several copies of the translation in the ship's library. I suggest you do your homework.'

The more conscientious Argonauts immediately lined up to borrow a copy, and one or two old hands were to be seen ploughing through it in the original. 'Won't help you much,' James commented with a hint of sadism, 'it will be in *modern* Greek, of course.'

They drove out of town through the thickening dusk, across the plain of Argos, past the vast grim walls of Tyrrhens. Bumping through the darkness, Daisy lost any sense of place – it might have been a coach ride to Southampton – until they pulled up under some trees and joined the locals on a path through the pines. Then they came out of the trees and the vast bowl of the theatre rose above them, stone steps ringing the circle of the stage. People were scrambling in all directions, up towards the cheaper seats at the back where families with prams and pushchairs were gathered, chatting and smoking, down to the expensive seats near the stage, with cushions supplied.

When the lights went out the audience fell silent, the great bowl thrumming with anticipation, cicadas noisy in the trees all around. Then the floodlights came on, throwing the stage into glowing focus. A moth, caught in the beam, beat its way frantically towards the source of the light. Bats swooped low over the heads of the audience, squeaking, and Daisy flinched. She heard James murmur to the woman next to him, 'My wife is afraid of bats.' The woman gave a little laugh and Daisy flushed with shame, grateful for the darkness. Melting from the shadows, a group of black-clad men, white masked, padded silently towards the stage from beyond the trees: the chorus. The play had begun.

Trying to match what she saw against her quick read-through of the play, understanding not a word though every syllable rose sonorously from the stage, Daisy watched closely as Philoctetes emerged from his cave, white, horrific, a thing of rags, a Lazarus figure, his face, hair, clothes, all bleached, save for the splotch of crimson seeping through the white of his ragged leggings: his festering wound. A cool wind blew through the trees; the music wavered across the open spaces, the Greeks chanted melodiously, ethics were debated, a choice of truths offered, and a dubious solution, a cure of sorts.

And then it was over. The audience applauded and began to drift back towards the car parks.

'Poor man,' Daisy said, half to herself. 'So unfair.'

'What?'

'Well, of course he was tricked into going off to Troy to help them, wasn't he? He didn't know what to believe or who to trust. He was lied to. I think they treated him very badly.'

James said nothing for a moment or two. Then, to her surprise, he took her arm in a brisk way.

'The path's pretty rough here, you might trip . . .'

The touch of his hand on her arm, the light, firm grip guiding her, paradoxically made her feel shaky. Somewhere nearby, hidden in the darkness, was the temple of Asclepius, the sanctuary of healing. As they walked through the night, surrounded by the smell of pine and wild pepper trees, Daisy felt the healing powers of the Asclepeion flow into them both like balm. The uneven ground was smooth beneath her feet, and the warm, scented air felt like silk. She laughed, for no reason.

When they reached the coach James got into a discussion with David Berger about some arcane philosophical reference. He grew tense, his face stiff with anger and everything was as it always was, but still, for a few minutes, as James guided her, his hand on her arm, her heart had been eased. Perhaps after all her little tin disc had been an appropriate offering.

'Mrs Oakley: what did you enjoy most?'

Lost in her thoughts, Daisy did not at once reply. James prompted her with brittle jocularity.

'Wake up Daisy, you're being spoken to.'

'I heard the question. I was thinking,' she said. She took a sip of wine and then, to torment James, to irritate him as she knew it would, she said with a deprecating little smile, 'Oh, coming home is always what I like best.'

There was a tiny pause around the table: how typical, they must be thinking, the boring woman can't even pick out one highlight from the entire trip.

A last walk on deck. She saw David Berger standing alone, leaning on the rails, his head flung back as he stared fixedly up at the sky. Straightening up to flex his neck muscles for a moment, he saw her and gave his enigmatic smile.

'Falling stars, Daisy. I never get over the thrill of it, that moment, that brief, glittering drop through space, almost too quick for the eye. Makes me want to cry. Silly, isn't it?'

'Not at all. I want to cry all the time. Life's so full of unbearably moving things I wonder we manage to stay dry eyed at all.'

He looked at her curiously. 'You don't talk much as a rule.'

'I don't have much to say.'

'That doesn't stop most people.'

She laughed. 'Oh, David. I always enjoy seeing you.'

He said, his eyes on the stars again, 'You used to have a thing you wore, on the Nile. Long, white – '

'A kaftan.'

'That's the thing. You looked marvellous in it. One night everyone dressed up for the gala night, did themselves up in sheets and waste-paper baskets and God knows what as fancy dress. You made yourself a head-dress out of gold chains and some blue-and-purple-striped stuff – '

'It was a pair of designer Y-fronts I got James at Harrods, actually,' Daisy said. 'He refused to wear them.'

'You surprise me. Anyway, you looked marvellous. Like a Pharoah's queen. What became of the white thing?'

'Oh . . . I've still got it,' Daisy said, and clamped her lips shut, and blinked rapidly several times and turned slightly so that her face was shadowed.

'You should wear white, it suits you,' David Berger said, and was about to say more, but a star fell across the sky and he cried out in delight.

Chapter 27

'You want a chart, draw one,' Andy had suggested curtly when James first raised the subject. But James's was a very personal cartographic task: what he was creating on the cabin table of the little steam launch was a precise duplication of an imagined world, while the original lay before him in all its shifting, ambiguous reality.

Where to start? With the names and number of islands, surely – but it seemed no one knew exactly how many there were. Guesses varied between two hundred and seventy to over five hundred if the tiny outcroppings were included. Include them all? Make size a criterion? Population was hardly a significant factor: only twenty-six were inhabited. The helmsman was unhelpful, difficult to pin down.

Over a rare dinner together Freddy raised the subject of departure: the liner was due to sail from Madras in ten days. 'Which means we should really take the next boat to the mainland.' A pause. 'Unless you're staying longer, of course.'

James was busily helping himself to prawn curry and did not reply.

'Look here,' Freddy said cheerfully, 'I'm quite happy to hang on for a bit to keep you company. I don't have to rush back; the bank can wait, I rather think we own it anyway. Shall I see about changing our P & O reservations?'

James began to look unhappy. He studied his plate as though checking all prawns were present and correct, then glanced up at Freddy.

'Don't put yourself out, Freddy. I really am quite happy to be on my own. I'm not sure how long this is going to take.'

'You think you've embarked on your own little Odyssey, don't you, Jamie? Finding your way back to Ithaka?' Freddy's anger was born of anxiety: 'But what you really are is Peter Pan trying to get back to jolly old Never-Never Land.'

Two days later, as James was about to take a rickshaw to the harbour, Freddy came out to say goodbye. He gave James a brief, sad hug. 'Phone me when you get back to London.'

The islands lay scattered like a broken bracelet, seven hundred and fifty miles from the mouth of Calcutta's river Hooghly, seven hundred miles from Madras and less than a hundred miles from the Burma coast. The most northerly was Landfall Island, the southernmost point was on Little Andaman – the headland that jutted out below Hut Bay. Then came the Ten Degree Channel, ninety miles wide, and over seven hundred fathoms deep, tricky and dangerous navigational water that separated the Andamans from the Nicobars.

'You want a chart, you draw one.'

Staring at the islands rising out of a tranquil sea, James found it all too easy to see them for what they really were: the visible part of a submerged mountain chain running from Burma to Sumatra, only the highest points rising above the surface of the sea. The narrow strip of sand he sat on was no more than a footpath to one of the peaks of the great range that once towered free of the ocean, its slopes breathing air. Then came upheaval and inundation; the forests sank below the sea, the fringing coral reefs continued to grow and the looming, craggy landscape became an underwater world in which fish ate fish and dugong moved placidly across the shallow sea floor like sea-cows grazing in aquatic meadows. Who was it who told him that the tribes living on the islands collected and ate the dugong – trepang was the official name, but some people described them as sea-slugs. It must have been Elizabeth who had called them sea-cows, certainly he remembered hearing stories of dugong that could grow to eight feet long, and were probably the origin of the mermaid legend, because the female held its young to its mammary breasts by means of its flippers. James peered into the clear water trying to see them browsing in the swaying sea grasses but all he could make out were shoals of tiny fish above the brilliantly coloured coral, turning and darting in perfect unison like formation dancers.

Starting with his blank sheet, James began to assemble his statistics, facts, position and shape. The islands accumulated on paper as he encountered them: Interview Island off the west coast, Ritchie's archipelago on the east. Rutland in the extreme south, and outlying North Sentinel. Viewed from the sea they appeared as a series of small hills, nowhere of any great height, covered from skyline to high-water mark with dense and lofty forest. From Andy he learned there were no streams of any size: the water drained from the hills into tidal creeks running through miles of mangrove swamp. And always, it seemed, there was another island further off, tantalisingly out of reach. He nodded questioningly at a smudge, barely visible on the horizon: 'Andy?'

'North Sanctuary. Uninhabited. Beyond that, south Sanctuary. Uninhabited. But nobody lands there anyway. Bad reefs and currents. Rough water.' They chugged on, veering away from the choppy straits.

'You want a chart, draw one.'

James took him at his word: from books he found in the library on Ross he made notes; using an existing small-scale map of the area as his matrix he drew his own; enlarging, adding detail, checking reefs and rocks, submerged wrecks, measuring the curve of a half-hidden harbour, the effect of tidal pulls, all while Andy's little steam launch chugged from island to island through the narrow straits and navigational channels whose ways the helmsman had learned over the years.

At first he was amused, watching James crouched at the cabin table, checking, marking, calculating. Gradually, he was drawn in, offering comments and incidental information, adding a mark here or there, watching the chart take shape, leaving wet rings from his whisky glass on the edges of the paper.

As the little boat crisscrossed the blue waters, pausing occasionally to anchor, skirting the razor-sharp coral, he began to feed James's hunger for information, throwing him a bone of history, an anecdote, some geographical data, keeping the quest alive.

'He's just leading you up the garden path,' Freddy had said warningly, before he left. 'It's good business: you must be the best customer he's had for years. And how long is this going on? When are you planning to come home?'

As though he had not spoken, James said, 'We were down by one of the swamps yesterday . . . at low tide in the mangroves you can hear the popping of oyster shells. Everything around you is breathing, reaching up; sap in the plants, roots inching their way through the earth – I swear I could hear buds opening, a sort of creaking sound of leaves unfolding, everything growing so fast you can almost see it happening.'

'Which I find faintly disagreeable,' Freddy said. 'I get the feeling that if I were to stand too close to some of the more flamboyant plants I might be swallowed up, ingested into the jungle system and never seen again. And think what a loss *that* would be to the world.' He smiled, uneasy, and added, 'Don't get swallowed up, Jamie.'

But James was busy making yet another entry in one of his little lined notepads.

Strange things happened to wrecks and their contents beneath that endless surface. Washed by the salt water, dragged and rubbed against the coral, alterations took place, disintegration. Had Elizabeth, too, suffered a sea-change so that, diving for the wreck, might he find her become an underwater deity whose eyes were pearls, whose bones had grown a lacy coral gown?

Questions about long-ago shipwrecks were answered vaguely on the islands: there had been so many, over the years . . . was it one of the old shipwrecks he meant, the East Indiaman that went aground on – No? . . . Or the two sailing ships blown on to the same island one night in a great storm? . . . Or the coastal ferry smashed on the rocks below Aberdeen when the women convicts formed a human chain and pulled the sailors ashore . . . No? Ah, then . . . Sorry, can't help, old boy.

And he saw that he was becoming a nuisance: one of those people who are unable or unwilling to let well alone. Worse, one of those people who persist with something when it has lost its interest for others.

There had been so many wrecks, over the years: there were memorial plaques in the church on Ross; monuments commemorating tragic events, old stories told and retold. There was little of help to James.

'Before my time, I'm afraid . . .' Army personnel moved on, new people replaced them, links were broken.

He managed to locate an old plantation owner who remembered his parents but then he got things wrong, describing Henry as a 'remarkable man', talking of his wisdom and humour. He recalled James as a toddler being carried into the sea, sitting on his father's shoulders.

'He taught you to open your eyes under water – '

James recalled, fleetingly, a moment when he had opened his eyes on a magical world of fish striped like zebras, others with glowing eyes and manes like lions, but surely it had been Elizabeth?

'He was telling you a yarn about a kingdom under the sea, inventing some nonsense about underwater pirates who raided the oyster beds and stole the pearls, and sometimes carried off the trepang in their boats, bouncing on the ocean bed. You asked him what trepang was and he said if you were to find yourself in the right place at the right time you might see one or two grazing on the sea floor. He told you they were sea-cows, who lived in underwater meadows.'

'No,' James corrected him, 'that was my mother. It was my mother who called them sea-cows.'

'I don't know about that, she may have, later. But that day, when you asked about the dugong he said "sea-cows" and he taught you to keep a look-out for them. He told you sailors saw them holding their young with their flippers and that's how the legend of mermaids got started – ' He gave a snort of laughter. "Course he didn't mention they have dugs for suck-ling their young – might have given the sailors a few ideas . . .'

James was confused: so it was Henry who had told him about the dugong. But he had no memory of that. He hardly remembered talking to Henry at all. Certainly later, on those visits to England Henry had seemed distant, they had conversed awkwardly, with little to say to one another. Had it been different, once?

He should have gone home, but he hung on, sailing round the islands with Andy, building up his picture, gradually filling in more and more details on the chart: coves and creeks, shelv-ing coral and lagoons; currents and quirks of tidal waters. He put in diagrams, drew wind roses that showed the relative frequency and force of the winds, and badgered Andy for information on the effect of the two monsoons.

It was from Andy that he learned of the stick-charts used by islanders to steer on the open sea: the framework of coconut palm with cowrie shells lashed to the reeds to mark the islands and atolls; the ribs of the palm leaf curved to show the swells and currents and navigational channels, marking the deflections round islands following the paths of oceanic currents and deep-sea swells. They showed how the surface looked to a navigator of an outrigger sailing canoe, so that, memorising the chart, he could fix his direction or position by watching the wave pat-terns, reading them to locate islands, even those still invisible, below the line of the horizon. The Micronesians were known to have such stick-charts; according to Andy the local islanders used something similar – certainly the Jarawa on the outlying islands used the sun, the stars, the flying routes of certain birds, even the movements of shoals of fish, to steer by.

Listening to Andy's measured, flat-vowelled voice delivering a string of arcane facts, questioning him further and more deeply, there were times when James forgot for the moment why he was here, overspending on his allowance, shutting out the world. He would have been shocked had anyone suggested that Elizabeth had become, like Helen among the Greeks, an idea, an excuse to justify action. So he hired the boat for another week, another three days, another two, and asked Andy more questions.

And his chart grew. Not all the islands had names, but gradually they acquired shape and size and category.

When his money finally ran out he told Andy they were on their last trip.

'I'll be leaving soon.'

But there were islands still unseen, islands not even circum-navigated, their shape and size unrecorded.

'We'll go south today. I want to have a closer look at North and South Sanctuary, I'd like to establish their position.'

Andy studied the sky, checked the tops of the rain trees, the movements of the birds, his face, as always, impassive.

'I'm not happy with the weather.'

James looked at him incredulously. 'Clear sky, calm sea – '

'Watch the birds. They always know. Sky can change in an hour.' He paused. 'You'd do better to stay ashore.'

But James persisted, and they set off, chugging out of harbour towards the first of the misty grey-green shapes which had become so familiar, the originals of those which lay before him on his chart, shaped, measured, known. Some, at least. But he fretted: beyond the outlying islands there were others, always there were others still to be pinned down. Perhaps today he would add one more detail to his inevitably incomplete picture.

It was early afternoon when the sky began to turn yellow, then gunmetal, the sun blotted out by a thick, sullen haze. Andy pointed to the darkening horizon, dirty-looking clouds massing low.

'I'm turning back.'

James was childishly disappointed. His last journey cut short.

Surely the storm was far away? The sea was flat, the air still. He wanted to go round one more headland, see what lay beyond the farthest point they had so far explored, have a look at that southerly island. Get its measure, fasten it down on his chart, banish its mystery.

Andy, unexpectedly, lost his temper: 'There's always another island, another headland. This one's nothing special, see, I'll draw it for you now – '

He grabbed James's notebook, rapidly sketching an island that bulged on one side, deeply indented on the other, a deformed horseshore whose ends almost met. Oily fingers clenched on the stubby pencil, he added a creek, a central hill, a lagoon.

He threw down the pencil and swung the boat round, heading home. The noise of the engine drowned out James's protest, his attempt at authority. He seethed impotently as Andy drove the boat forward, ignoring him.

They slapped their way through the waves, and James watched the island receding behind them. He picked up the notebook and studied the confident sketch, puzzled.

'How is it you know the shape of the inner harbour? I thought you said . . .'

Andy had slackened off the throttle and James's voice, pitched loud, came as almost a shout, heard against a sudden absence of sound. He stopped, a knot of alarm tightening at the pit of his stomach, and looked up. From far across the water a long shadow was racing towards them like the wing of a vast black bird. There was a beat, a hush like an indrawn breath. Then the boat reared up beneath them; air and water merged into a churning, seething whiteness: blinding, choking, the wind lashing like whips as a howling, high pitched and shrill, came out of the sky.

A wall of boiling sea hit the boat, sending it spinning, knocking it deep into a dark hole in the green inferno. Andy yelled something at him but the words were torn away by the wind. He clutched at spars, hooks, rail. He wanted to sob out prayers, cry, scream. but he hung on grimly, fingers slipping, bleeding. Barely conscious, he was filled suddenly with a sense of closeness to Elizabeth. He thought dimly, was this how it was for her, that day? Was this how she spent her last moments, soaked, terrified, beaten almost senseless by the sea and wind and rain? In his head a voice repeated, almost listlessly, as if observing it all from afar, 'What a pity, what a pity, to end like this.'

There were no waves, no towering undulations, simply a wall of water that seemed to be everywhere, rising up beneath them to carry the little boat on its back racing through the churning atmosphere, throwing it this way and that, up, up, a great slope, and with shattering force flung it on to something that could be solid land, though the water still crashed over their heads and dragged them, flailing, as the wind howled, and lightning crackled through the black sky. Then, as suddenly as it had arrived, the storm was gone, sweeping on its way, leaving a sea heaving uneasily, a landscape of smashed trees, flattened undergrowth and the remains of a shattered boat strewn untidily across the knife-points of a coral reef that lay like a defensive boom across the entrance to a small, horseshoe-shaped island.

PART FOUR

Chapter 28

To be away from home was in itself a stressful condition; unexpected solitude compounded the anxiety. Daisy tidied the hotel room, brushed her hair, made some notes for her diary and still James had not reappeared. So unlike him, to leave her drifting, undirected.

She hovered in the lobby, watching the Russians stride off yet again for the beach, sunburn glowing lobster-red on their shoulders. The British were preparing to go scuba-diving, loading the taxis with oxygen cylinders, weights, underwater camera.

Where could he be? 'Looking for someone,' the receptionist had said blandly.

He had always been looking for someone or something, some piece missing from the jigsaw puzzle of the past, a key, an answer, she knew that. But answers had a way of playing tricks. Freddy had said as much, once, years ago when they were still in touch.

'We all know how Jamie gets upset by things, feels everyone's against him. Well of course Elizabeth's "betrayal" is the real cause, abandoning him. *Hinc illae lachrymae.* He's scratching away, eternally searching for justification for her disappearance. Fearing all the while that she ran off with the poodle-faker.'

'Do *you* think she did?'

'I don't even care, Daisy dear. For all I know she may have run off with one of the sailors – which has its appeal, of course . . .' He gave his radiant, rueful smile.

'I'll tell you a story,' Freddy said. 'Goya's model for the Naked Maja is supposed to have been the Duchess of Alba, although he painted a different face on the nude to protect her reputation. A hundred years later, as though World War II wasn't enough to occupy his mind, the then Duke of Alba was so upset by the old stories of his great-grandmother cavorting with a jobbing painter that he had her body dug up and got in medical experts to measure her skeleton – by then in none too good a state – to decide whether or not the body could possibly have matched the model for the Naked Maja.'

'And could it?'

'Opinion among the good doctors remained tactfully inconclusive.'

'The Duke must have been disappointed.'

Freddy shrugged. 'Perhaps that's what they really want, these pickers at ancient scabs: an indefinite postponement of a climax.' And maybe there was, too, an element of fear: 'Last time he nearly got himself killed; maybe he's superstitious, maybe he thinks he may have to barter something too precious in return. Ulysses was a wily old bird. In a funny way, Jamie's protected his own innocence.'

The hotel canned music blasted her ears and she decided – daringly – that she would go for a walk. She said as much to the friendly young New Zealand couple who had come over on the same plane and seemed already to have explored most of the island, striding around purposefully in huge walking boots and very short shorts. The girl waved towards the green hill that rose steeply behind the hotel. 'Try Mount Horton; it's an easy walk, isn't it, Kevin?'

Kevin pondered: 'Sure.' He squinted up at the sky. 'You don't want to be out at sunset though, it's pretty quick. Maybe you should try it tomorrow.'

She nodded gratefully, and with a perverse spurt of defiance immediately decided to ignore his advice: it was a modest enough hill, a friendly hill; sandals would do. She set off briskly, climbing a steep path cut like a tunnel through the undergrowth. The air was thick and hot, held in by the tight-packed bushes, and she began to sweat. Her feet, moist and slippery in the sandals, rubbed against the leather thongs. She should have worn walking shoes. Limping now, she reached a palm grove and came out on to velvety turf. A gentle breeze blew into her face; the air felt clean. As she climbed higher, she looked out over the island: hills, misty, fold upon fold, a soft green of many tones shaded into the horizon. Behind her the sea lay flat as a steel plate. With no James to twitch impatiently by her side she stood for a while, taking in the scene, enjoying it. Then she rested under a palm tree.

She left a marker at the edge of the palm grove – a handful of dried leaves and some bright fallen feathers – to guide her back to the path through the undergrowth, and continued to climb.

The sun had seemed high in the sky when she set out, but it was dropping more quickly than she had expected – good old Kevin: he would never have embarked on a walk to the top so late in the day. Of course, she should have taken his advice; she should have known what would happen, what always happened. The sun swung lower, dark gold and heavy. She paused for a moment, trying to gauge how long it would take to touch the horizon. She was three-quarters of the way to the top, it seemed a pity to turn back now.

Abruptly she began to retrace her steps and almost at once she was lost: no sign of her marker. The undergrowth seemed at first unbroken by any path, then offered several. Which to choose? She found herself sweating and breathless as she stumbled back and forth looking for a way down. The sun was very low now, and bigger, the sky colourless, darkening at the eastern rim.

She plunged into the bushes, choosing what looked like her path. After ten minutes the 'path' petered out and she found herself surrounded by thick greenery that seemed to press in, catching on her straw hat, dragging at her arms and legs. She turned this way and that, trying new paths, always coming to a dead end.

Even in the bright sunlight earlier she had felt uneasy. Now as the gold deepened to a plumlike purple she felt panic sweep over her, perspiration chilling on her skin, mouth dry, breathing at first difficult, then painful, her throat rasping as she gasped for air.

Earlier she had not noticed the thorns; now they scratched and tore at her, snatched her hat from her head. She should have worn jeans, not a stupid cotton dress! And the straw hat was a liability. Filled with self-pity and helplessness, she began to cry, moaning, whimpering. And then she saw him: an elderly Indian, thin, gnarled, immobile. He could have materialised out of the tree trunks. How long had he been there, so still, expressionless, watching her, waiting, as Indians always seemed to wait, with their maddening composure? Angrily she shrieked 'Hotel? Hotel!'

She thought for a moment that he had failed to understand her. He stood, unmoving; then, unhurriedly, he pointed at an opening in the undergrowth. She hurled herself down through the bushes, stumbling over roots, almost falling headlong into holes and ditches, and without warning came out on to the road that skirted the shore. As though dragged off course by a current, she found she was much further from the hotel, round the far end of the bay. The air had grown misty, palms were silhouetted against the sky. A stillness had fallen over the scene; no birds, no wind except for the light rattling of the palm leaves on the spindly coconut trees. No sound of surf. Drowning beneath the horizon, the sun had swallowed up colour and light. She walked through the dusk back towards the hotel, passing Indians, their cars parked by the shore, come to watch the sun set. Some ignored her. Most called hullo or good evening and she returned the greetings shakily, feet sore, eyes tight from the frightened hilltop tears. With a lifting of the heart she thought: he'll be back. I'll walk into the bedroom and just say I went for a walk. To watch the sun set. No harm done.

The hotel lights glimmered from the end of the drive; a faint sound of music drew her on and she was almost running by the time she reached the steps. She threw open the door of their room, smiling, determined not to question, not to reproach, simply to welcome James quite casually after a day spent apart, and certainly to make no mention of her own misadventure. But the room was empty.

She showered, dressed and he had still not reappeared. It was time for dinner and he remained absent. Daisy hovered, watching people take their places, uncertain what to do. After a while a waiter noticed her standing by the door and beckoned her towards the tables.

On the far side of the room, next to the kitchens, the Russians filled six tables. The Italians had commandeered two tables by the windows, pushed them together and formed themselves instantly into one of those intimate, noisy and utterly confident groups who always seem to occupy tables laden with desirable food under Mediterranean skies in restaurant gardens glimpsed from the passing cars of the less fortunate. They were not merely seated at their long, comfortable table: they *owned* it.

Daisy sat by herself at a table for four in the middle of the room. She glanced frequently towards the lobby, but James did not appear. She chewed her food carefully, but found it hard to swallow. She studied her knife and fork, admired the chromium-plated cruet on the table, checked that the flowers in the vase were real. She simply did not know where to look and felt her face stiffening with the effort to appear natural.

A burst of laughter from the Russian tables, and the sound of clapping allowed her to look across unselfconsciously: it was something of a party; Russian pink champagne was poured, toasts drunk. The Italians encouraged the celebration, raising their glasses of wine to the Russians, calling over greetings. And to her acute embarrassment, one of the big, crumpled men, the one with the luxuriant moustache, who had danced barefoot, ambled across the dining room, bottle in hand, and stopped at her table.

'Yuri,' he announced, introducing himself. 'From Caucasus. All.' He searched for words. 'Is our – um – Men's Day,' he explained, haltingly. 'In Soviet Union, celebration. We celebrate!' He poured some of the bright-pink champagne into her glass. 'Drink.'

'Yes of course!' Daisy smiled up at him brightly and took a large gulp. It was sweet and warm but she was grateful: it gave her something to do with her hands, and sipping, she could glance about, observe. At the next table the two honeymoon couples had joined up, the young men fashionably casual in Lacoste polo shirts and slacks cut sharp and tight; the brides in silk tunics and trousers, printed with subtle batik swirls of colour. Their hair shone in the lamplight, smooth, heavy, black, and their slender hands were painted from wrist to fingertip with elaborate and delicately executed patterns in a deep reddish brown, the colour of freckles. Daisy found herself staring at their hands, at the spirals and dots and wavy lines, intrigued, curious.

'Coffee in the lounge tonight, Mrs Oakley.' The manageress, elegant in a red-and-gold sari, murmured in Daisy's ear. 'The Russians will be getting a little noisy, I'm afraid.' She shrugged and sighed. 'These tourist packages are a little . . . unfortunate.'

The lamplight shone coldly on the drive, bleaching the dusty earth. Framed by the dark mass of oleander and hibiscus bushes, it looked like the empty stage set for an opera, awaiting the arrival of a leading character. In Handel or Cavalli he could descend seated on a cloud or a crescent moon; in Mozart he might step from a galleon gliding across a painted harbour. In real life he would emerge from a battered taxi clunking and grinding its way to the door. But no *deus ex machina* appeared, no James.

'Your coffee is growing cold.' One of the newlyweds stood at her shoulder, smiling encouragingly. Perfect teeth gleamed against her flawlessly scarlet lips (how could she look so untouched after a meal? Why had her lipstick not succumbed to soup or oily dressing? Daisy knew from experience that her own mouth would by now be patchy at best: a rim of red edging unbecomingly pallid lips).

'I was just looking to see – ' Daisy paused, uncertain how to go on: 'My husband should have been back by now . . . I . . .'

'You are worried. But no harm can come to him here.'

'Of course not,' Daisy agreed, and added impulsively, 'What beautiful patterns, on your hands.'

'Yes.' The bride glanced down at her hands: a detached, impersonal appraisal. 'It's traditional you know. For weddings. Frightful bore, it takes hours, but they expect it, the parents and so forth. It's done with *mindhi* – henna isn't it? – it lasts for weeks.'

'I thought you must be honeymoon couples,' Daisy said, 'you look so happy.'

'Well . . .' another perfect smile, snow-white, blood-red, 'this is a good place to get to know a person.'

'You haven't known each other long, then?'

'We met at the wedding.' Unsurprised by Daisy's startled reaction, she added helpfully, 'Arranged marriage. You know?'

'I didn't realise . . .' Daisy floundered, afraid of offending, wondering how to express her sympathy in tactful terms, admiring the girl for the brave face she was putting on the appalling situation.

'Did you not,' she said cautiously, 'find that . . . difficult?'

'Not at all. It is quite preferable. There are no divorces or separations in such marriages.'

'But – ' Daisy was at a loss.

'Ah, love, isn't it? Romance? No, that's the secret: we don't fall into the trap of romance. That variety of "love" is a delusion, a sort of dream. And when you wake up from the dream, you face disappointment with reality. People fall what they call in love with quite unsuitable partners, you know? Then they have to live with someone who is oh dear me, altogether incompatible. Unromantic marriage will be happier. No one disappointed, you see.'

Perhaps realising that her certainties might seem discourteous, she added graciously, 'Of course, there must always be exceptions. You married for love?'

'Oh yes!'

'Do you have children?'

'A boy and a girl – ' Daisy shrugged, embarrassed. 'Silly to call them that; they're older than you are!'

She strained her eyes out into the night, trying to see past the sharp light and shade of the drive, into the darkness beyond.

The slender, beautiful creature put her hand reassuringly on Daisy's shoulder. 'He will be home soon. And no harm can come to him: this isn't Bombay, you know!'

Chapter 29

He was looking for a man whose full name he had forgotten – had he ever known it? Andy . . . Andy something. An old man, perhaps a man long since dead.

The taxi bumped its way along the coast road, past empty beaches, palms, occasional fishing boats riding at anchor.

James bore the discomfort without complaint: the erratic steering, the non-existence of any suspension and the windows thick with dust – all this he could put up with. But when the driver swivelled in his seat to ask if he was familiar with the town, James rapped out a curt affirmative and advised the man to keep his eyes on the road.

Familiar with the town? Well of course . . . except that the little one-street bazaar now seemed to spread for miles, boasted a Fax 'Centre' and video shops. What would Chatham look like? Would there be a smart marina for tourists chartering fun-boats? Water-ski facilities? A floating disco? It was still early but he felt sweat trickling a zigzag path from armpits to groin.

Across the causeway to Chatham he could see elephants in the sawmill yard obediently lifting and stacking timber just as he remembered, and then the driver asked, 'Which house?'

James said brusquely, 'Just drop me here, I'll walk.'

Which house? He had not anticipated this indecision: in his thoughts he had found himself in the place without difficulty. In his dreams he simply knew the way. But everything looked different. Suburban villas where he remembered native huts on stilts; parked motor vehicles, dusty and dented, where brightly painted rickshaws used to wait. He stared about him, at a loss.

An immaculate, silk-suited Indian hurrying past, briefcase in hand, glanced at James, hesitated, then turned back: 'Are you in need of assistance perhaps?'

'I'm looking for . . .' James paused. 'It's a long time since I was here, things have changed – '

'Oh my word, yes. It's all riff-raff now. Jumped-up shop-keepers and wheeler-dealer wallahs from Madras. No class any more, I'm afraid.'

'There used to be someone called Andy, he had a boat – '

'Possibly you are wanting the Anderson boatyard, they are over Junglighat way now. Too far to walk. Taxi will be required.'

'Oh. Thank you – '

' – mind you are fixing the fare before you get in. Those devils will fleece you if you don't watch out.'

He hurried on, and disappeared into a scruffy-looking office block. James approached a car which might or might not be a taxi. The driver straightened up, looking keen.

'Taxi?'

'Junglighat,' James said, 'Anderson boatyard,' and got in. Prepared for the usual haggling, the driver wrenched at the gears, disappointed, and roared off in a cloud of exhaust fumes.

When Freddy first heard the story, when he and James were boys, he had been sympathetic, understanding: a mother vanished into thin air; a child abandoned, an island Eden no longer accessible. Later, worry crept in: 'Picking over the past doesn't really help, Jamie. Does it matter where she was going, or why? What happened, happened.' And later still, after Henry's death and the messy end to that botched reunion, when yet again James talked of 'going back, one day', he said, cautioning, 'Don't expect too much, Jamie. People change, places change, life moves on. Don't pin all your hopes on Ithaka.'

Aberdeen – 'just an ordinary bazaar', Daisy had called it dismissively, and looking at it now as the taxi drove through, swerving to avoid bullock-carts, braking at the last moment to avoid head-on collisions with rusty trucks, James had to admit she was right. And Junglighat, which had once been a convict settlement, was now a thriving commercial district. But the old Hindu temple, set back from the road, almost masked now by stained and cracking concrete buildings, was just as he remembered, with its tree of bright yellow trumpet-shaped flowers, and its sacred pool. That, at least, was still there.

The Anderson boatyard looked deserted; the building shabby with peeling paintwork and splintered wooden steps. There was no one in the office, and when he had called and banged on the counter a few times, James walked round to the back of the house and stood at the foot of the steps leading to a shaded veranda and he looked along the veranda to a big wicker arm-chair where a shrunken, yellow-skinned figure sat, eyes closed, clawlike hands betraying the tremor of a palsy that regularly set his head wobbling. James said,

'Andy?'

The old man's eyes flew open and he stared down at James, frowning, head poking forward like a turtle in search of food. His face was covered in fine lines like an old vase that has been shattered and its parts skilfully reassembled. The shaking of his head gave the impression he was denying the identity James suggested, but he said in a slurred, exhausted voice,

'If you want a boat, my grandson will be back soon.'

James said, 'I want to talk to you. I'm James Oakley.'

'Well, how are you? Good to see you.'

James felt a dizzying relief surge through him: after all, there would be no difficulty. Here was Andy, alive and mentally alert and now the questions could begin. He hesitated, flapping his arms awkwardly, turning his head from side to side as though to work it free.

'May I sit down?'

'Sure.'

'Last time I saw you, that day on the boat, you were telling me – '

'He doesn't know who you are, mister.'

James had not heard him approach, a scrawny boy in his twenties, clothes and hands blackened with engine oil, eyes suspicious.

'Oh, I think he does. He knew my name at once. I just wanted – '

'He won't remember.'

James said loudly, 'You remember me, don't you, Andy?'

The old man smiled. 'Sure. What did you say your name was? Weren't you one of the scuba-diving party last month? Camped out on Cinque Island?'

The disappointment was worse because his hopes had been raised. But people's memories could be jogged; if he worked at it, perhaps –

The young man was polite, but James felt hostility beneath the surface: unspoken, there was a suggestion that strangers had no business to come bothering the old man who now seemed to be asleep, eyes once more closed, head drooping.

'Look, there's no point – '

'I just wanted to talk to him, talk about a trip we made together, a long time ago – ' He raised his voice, 'Andy and I went round the islands together – '

The Buddha-like figure in the wicker armchair shifted, the eyes opened and he looked at James, puzzled.

'Who's that?'

'It's no one, Grandpa – '

James said loudly, 'Andy, it's James Oakley. Oakley. Do you remember we sailed round the islands? I was making a chart? And looking for a shipwreck – '

' – You and your bloody chart,' Andy said without heat. 'You damn near got us both killed.'

James leaned forward excitedly. 'Do you remember?'

'I knew the storm was heading our way. We should never have set off. The boat finished up . . .' He tailed off, his eyes glazing.

'Yes?' James prompted. The old man's head shook uncontrollably, the palsy taking over. James tried again.

'Andy. That day: we were a long way south, off an island. You were telling me about it. Then the storm hit us – '

'That bugger tore the boat apart, you know that? Lucky to get out alive. I wondered about you.'

James, clinging to a portion of the hull that kept him afloat, carried by the surging waves, half drowned, barely conscious, delirious. How long had he drifted, and how far, before he was picked up by a passing steamer, taken on to Madras?

Everything became confused: communication with the islands depended on the four-day ferries; fretting in hospital with a broken leg, dehydration, exposure, James found the British Consulate had organised him on to a P & O liner, arranged for his belongings to be forwarded.

'What about the man who owned the boat? Andy? Was he – '

'Got picked up. He'll be all right. Probably make a pretty penny out of the insurance.'

'But I was planning to go back, spend some more time on the islands – '

'I would advise you to get that leg home,' the young man from the Consulate said earnestly. 'Germs, Lord knows what. It really is the best thing.'

The old man had grown suddenly distressed, head shaking uncontrollably, feet shuffling about, cheeks wet – were those tears, James wondered, or was it simply that his eyes watered as part of the general degeneration of the system? The grandson, his cheerful face grim, gathered Andy up in his arms like a bundle of crumpled laundry. He headed for the door to the house.

'I'm putting him to bed.'

'Could I wait? See him a little later?'

'Another day. If it's that important. But he may not remember.'

Chapter 30

The Italians were having a party: the muffled thump-thump-thump of the music filled the hotel, coming up through the floor of the bedroom in a tormenting sub-sound. Daisy felt the bed reverberate, pulsating in time to the beat. She lay in the darkness trying to work out from the rhythm what the tune might be, but of course it would almost certainly be unknown to her. Instant recognition, she acknowledged, stopped with the Beatles.

The music was not, in any case, keeping her awake: anxiety was doing that. Worry about James. She could tell from his steady, even breathing, the way he lay unmoving in his bed, that he was awake: he always breathed with heavy regularity when he wanted to fool her, unaware that while really sleeping he threshed restlessly, twitched, talked aloud, sometimes moaned in distress – and on good nights, snored. But he, of course, knew nothing of all that. Daisy guessed that she was the one who breathed steadily when asleep, giving James his model. Over the years the pattern was set: he pretended to be asleep, she pretended to believe it.

Now she decided, on impulse, to break the rules, over-ride the programming. She said conversationally,

'Where were you today, James?'

'*What?*'

'Where – '

'Do you realise you woke me up? It's the middle of the – '

'Please don't go on with that pretence, it's too boring.'

Silence. She had disconcerted him and, as always, faced with the embarrassment of revelation or confessional demands, he withdrew. She heard him heaving about, turning his back, the springs squeaking. He said, indistinctly, 'Hotel beds . . . never make them long enough.'

Thinking aloud in the way she knew he found irritating, Daisy said, 'I wonder what Ross will be like? Will there still be people living there? Shall we see your house?'

The silence grew, crackling with tension and, as usual, she now wished she had not spoken. Her heart began to thump: she felt it throbbing in her fingertips, her head, her chest, its thudding so loud in her ears that it blocked out the Italians' music. Heat enveloped her, sweat prickling her scalp. She opened her mouth to gulp in air and heard herself say, voice pitched too high, 'James?'

'For God's *sake*! Give me some peace!'

Without putting on the light she reached for the sleeping pills, the tumbler of water, oblivion on demand.

James lay rigid, wide awake, afraid to sleep. He contemplated the day's ironies: he had found the man he came looking for, but to what purpose? Grown senile, his memory and strength gone, what could he reveal, now? James realised that in his fantasies he had always seen Andy as he had been on the boat that last day, ageless, tough arms fighting the little boat as they ran before the storm, eyes narrowed against the wind that came down on them, howling, that picked up the boat and smashed it against the razor edges of the coral reef as it passed.

Had he known more than he said? Why did James once again have the feeling, that day, of things being concealed? And now, so far from the event, when the old man might have talked, it seemed he no longer had anything to recount.

'Why did you wait so long to come back?' Daisy had asked when they landed. He had answered her impatiently, treating the question as irrelevant – he had a gift for that – but in truth he hardly knew himself. The years pass so fast. You tell yourself: one day I'll go back there, attend to unfinished business, clear things up. Instead you take on another lecture tour, another cruise, do another book, keep busy. Put it off again.

He had begun to drift off. At the edge of consciousness, not quite out of sight, there came a shimmering as of butterfly wings, a pale vision, the sound of a woman's laughter. He gave a cry, threshed violently for a moment and fell through the darkness into a troubled sleep.

The taxi was late and they only just made it to the ferry, Daisy flustered, frightened of tripping as they jumped on board; James furious: he hated being late for anything. He was always punctual, why could other people not be the same?

They were the only Europeans on the little ferry. Middle-class Indian families were seated buttock to buttock on the padded benches of the saloon, ladies in silk saris, men in well-cut Western suits, children in immaculate T-shirts, jeans and white trainers. Daisy thought of Lizzie and Bill, who used to rub their new jeans over the patio paving to break them in, and dip them in the algae-covered lily pond to give them a suitably aged, grimy look. The heavy boots they favoured had street credibility only when their original sheen was overlaid with a verdigris acquired through regular exposure to puddles, mud, and the vagaries of English weather.

What would an Indian mother have done? These parents seemed to have an altogether firmer hold on the behaviour of their young. She had accepted the ripped and filthy jeans, as she had accepted spiked hair, ear-rings, junk food, as part of childhood. As she later accepted the existence of marijuana, and live-in lovers as part of teenage mores. Perhaps she should have forbidden it all, but then she had always felt uncertain of her ground. In truth, she rather enjoyed their scene, vicariously. She had been a teenager just a little too early to make full use of the condition.

One of the children, an exquisitely well-groomed little girl, knelt on the padded bench, pointing through the window of the ferry as she called out to her parents. Even the soles of her fragile, dainty shoes looked clean. Daisy craned her neck to stare out of the window; the crossing took fifteen minutes: they must be approaching Ross.

The sea slapped the boat harder as the wind sprang up, sending the spray high, drenching the people leaning on the rail up at the front. James had refused to join Daisy in the covered saloon – 'Stuffy, and those children will be whining in two minutes flat.' She visualised him out on deck, rearing back in affronted disarray, hair plastered to his scalp, shirt soaked, blaming helmsman or skipper, outraged . . .

'Sir? You are becoming wet. You should – '

'It's just a bit of spray.' James sounded testy and the ferry attendant moved away. He glanced at James from across the deck: the British were always a little odd when they came back. If this one wanted to get soaked, that was his own affair entirely.

James stared ahead as the island approached. This was as he remembered: a frieze of trees, a fringe of coconut palms. Beyond . . . hard to see, from the boat, the salt spray stinging his eyes.

A surging of saris, a confusion of children, a crossfire of calls and domestic instructions, then the families were ashore, hurrying to their sight-seeing, voices growing fainter, and James and Daisy were left to themselves, with only the hushed growling of the surf to disturb the silence.

What had she expected? Nothing very dramatic, she supposed. It was not, after all, Pompeii or Akrotiri. The British had left, hurriedly, in 1941, abandoning the islands to the Japanese. She expected . . . dilapidation, the odd derelict structure, war damage perhaps, gaps in brickwork. What confronted her was a dreamscape, a surrealist view of a vanished civilisation.

Chapter 31

He looked first for the clubhouse on the shore, but where it had stood were only trees. The tennis courts were now a coconut grove lapped by the sea. And the little general store where Elizabeth sent the cook to buy small household items, where was the store? Surely it stood just here? A cluster of rain trees, growing out of the rubble, towered above him, sheets of rusted corrugated iron caught up in their topmost branches, dangling high overhead. A roofless wall of masonry buttressed by gigantic roots and lianas was all that remained of what had once been a four-square building. A small, rusty sign caught his eyes: The Farsandeli Store. He turned away quickly, and began to stride up the harsh white cement path that led into the trees. The path was new, laid down for visitors who came now to see what remained of Ross which had once been a little showplace of British India.

Almost at once he was lost: he looked fretfully about, trying to identify the sad ruins that confronted him, trying to place them where they belonged.

What place is this? he wanted to ask someone; this can't be Ross, they've set me down on the wrong island, this can't be that neat English suburb with its bungalows and churches, its library and tennis courts, its gardens full of hollyhocks, plumbago and roses. But it was: left unchecked, the forest had crept back and taken over again. Vast trees thrust through what were once solid floors, their surface roots showing strong as hawsers.

The ruins of the old settlement stood festooned with creeper; banyan trees and palms grew out of walls and broken floors.

And where was the house with the red roof and the veranda with the railing worn thin by a child's whittling knife? Surely it stood just here? In a reversal of process, its beams had grown into trees, the window panes crumbled to sand, the walls turned to dust –

'James,' Daisy began, but he was already hurrying ahead of her up the cement path.

'*James!*'

Reluctantly, he turned back. 'Why don't you just wander around? You won't want to look at everything, you'll be bored – '

'But I don't know where anything is! I'll get lost!'

Her voice trailed after him as he hurried on, leaving her to pick her way up the bleak white cement path through the trees.

From the scraps that remained he began to rebuild it: a flight of curving stone steps that led only to a circle of palm trees and a scrap of root-clad brick wall – this must be the house where the captain of the S S *Maharaja* lived in such style between trips . . . and that cloister of short, stumpy stone pillars . . . a small sign prompted his imagination: 'Subordinates' Club'. In front of the cloister a huge, exposed root looked dead, but branches growing out of it had turned into trees, towering high as a cathedral. He hurried on up the hill, out of breath, not looking where he trod, gazing about him, searching.

The church was still there, just about, its porch held up by a stout plank of wood. He picked his way inside the grey brick shell that remained, open to the sky, its cracked stucco walls bright with yellow lichen, its only roof a trellis of wild vines. The spire stood swathed in tightly clinging ivy, clasped by the engulfing greenery in an embrace that had first destroyed, but now supported the structure. From the top of the spire a slender tree grew, towering almost as high again. Sunlight came through the tall, narrow windows, throwing colours on to the earth floor from the tiny panes that remained intact.

Daisy had left the cement path, and was climbing up the hillside, sandals slipping on the dry, crumbling earth, coming upon half-buried walls leaning at crazy angles, gate-posts, broken columns, shafts of sunlight piercing the rain trees and gleaming on scraps of marble, a broken urn – they might almost have been ancient relics but they were just the remains of the English colony who had as always imported into an unwelcoming environment the surroundings they felt at ease in: cosy houses, neo-classical pediments and ornamentation, all set down in a green island where the tropical vegetation had – for a while – been banished. She found it extraordinarily romantic, operatic, mysterious. Wherever she walked she heard the sound of the surf, slapping, surging, whispering, withdrawing to surge again. A gusty breeze blew off her straw hat and sent it rolling down the hill, startling her. She scrambled after it, watching helplessly as it rolled further and further away, bouncing on the cement path, bouncing finally to the feet of a man coming up the hill, walking carefully in highly polished leather shoes, his Western suit uncreased. He stopped to retrieve it, glancing about for its owner. Daisy waved and called, 'Hullo! That's my hat.'

He waited while she slithered down to join him, brushing dried leaves and pine needles from the straw. As she reached him, breathless, he bowed and handed her the hat.

'Thank you.' She jammed it firmly back on her head. He was fastidiously brushing specks of earth from his fingers; Daisy felt rumpled and grubby in contrast. She glanced left and right indecisively: she had assumed that if she set off down the hill she would find herself back at the harbour, but she saw now that the path dropped away only to rise steeply again, heading towards a grove of tall palms. Nothing looked familiar and she was uncertain which way to go.

'I seem to have lost my way . . .'

James would have sighed patiently, lips thinning into one of his unamused smiles. Naturally. That is what Daisy had a tendency to do: lose her way. That was why she needed him to be there with her, to aid her faulty navigation, to correct her hazy sense of direction. To prevent her making a fool of herself. But the man who had saved her hat did not smile loftily. He merely nodded. 'Bit of a snakes-and-ladders affair, this path. You British – ' he said it kindly, 'You British never did like straight roads. Look at the way the Romans tried to help you. No use, of course. You continued to go your devious ways.' He added hastily, 'I use devious in the dictionary definition to mean winding and erratic.' He took a small plan of the island from his pocket and studied it for a moment.

'We should be approaching the house of the Assistant Commissioner, Major Bird.' Perched on the side of the hill, the Assistant Commissioner's house was now a nest of broken bricks from which a grove of slender trees reached up to the sky.

'Poor man,' her guide murmured, 'he stayed on, you know, when the rest of the administration left. The Japanese gave him a bad time: tortured him, deprived him of water and then executed him in a dramatic fashion – '

'How dreadful!'

'Oh yes. Very dreadful,' he said casually. 'Well. That one we cannot blame on the British.' He added politely, 'Have you seen the gaol?'

'Not yet.'

'Oh, it's not to be missed. Quite an irony: the British built it to lock up naughty fellows, keep things peaceful, you might say. And it has become a shrine to our freedom-fighters. Quite a tourist attraction.'

Daisy thought it was perhaps time to continue her exploration. 'If you could just tell me which way . . .'

'No, no. I shall accompany you. Sometimes young hooligans come over on the ferry. No real harm in the chaps, you know, but best for a lady to be accompanied.'

James stood by the pillars to the gates of Government House. The long flight of stone steps was still there, though cracked and sunken on one side, but they led nowhere, or rather, they led only to a bare plateau of broken floors divided rectangularly into the shapes of the rooms they had once supported. James stepped from one room to another, like a ghost passing through walls. What room had this been? The black-and-crimson marble floor was inlaid with intricate geometrical patterns, the colours showing through the sand and leaf-mould. Perhaps this had been the great hall, with the staircase whose newel-posts were carved by Burmese convicts, the staircase that led to the ball-room, its gleaming wooden floor long since consumed by fire or termites.

In the distance he heard the warning hooter of the ferry. He turned and went slowly down the long flight of stone steps. On the brow of the hill a deer was poised, watching him.

James avoided the cement path that cut so brutally through the trees, its white gash had nothing to do with the island. It was a walkway constructed for the comfort of tourists, turning a place of memories into a museum. Instead, he scrambled through the undergrowth, quickly finding himself out of breath, and worked his way back down to the harbour, past the shell of the parsonage, past the cemetery. Strangely, the wall remained largely intact, and much of the encroaching undergrowth had been cleared away. A huge banyan tree grew among the graves, surrounded by a grove of palms leaning at steep angles. He stood for a moment, regaining his breath, listening to the soft roar of the surf.

James Oakley's grave had vanished, buried in some upheaval, or overgrown by palms. The unknown brother, dust to dust, had left no trace. And this time there was no need to walk around, studying the cracked and broken headstones, searching for the grave that was not there.

He found Daisy sitting under a palm tree by the jetty, drink-ing coconut milk from the shell and chatting to a plump matron in a pink sari. She waved to him: 'James! Why don't you have some coconut milk, the man over there is selling it, it's quite safe, he hacks off the top of the coconut with his machete and hands it over, look, you drink from the hole, no dirty glasses, it's delicious – '

'I think we'd better get aboard: you'll find the ferry is about to leave.'

The pink sari waved a confident hand: 'Oh, plenty of time yet!'

James glanced at his watch: 'Not according to my calculations.'

But of course the pink sari was correct: after the warning hoots and much activity on deck, the ferry remained tied to the jetty until the last straggler had come on board. James strode up and down, radiating impatience, glancing pointedly at his watch; Daisy knew there was no point in attempting a conversation. His shoulders were stiff and high, eyes flicking cold blue flames. Why did we come here? she wondered. Why did we have to travel so far for him to be so very much the same as usual?

As the ferry drew away and headed back to Port Blair Daisy said, 'I thought you told me there were butterflies, didn't you say there were butterflies on Ross?' He moved away, further along the deck. Wrong time of year of course. When was it, the butterfly season, when every bush quivered with fugitive life, when on a certain day they rose up in a cloud that covered the sun and flew away?

Across the harbour the hillside was dotted with houses, their roofs and walls visible through the trees.

'Which is the jail?'

'What?'

'The Cellular Jail. Didn't you say you can see it from here?'

He pointed at the tip of the headland and she screwed up her eyes to examine the building that lay along the top of the hill, its crenellated walls pale pink in the sunlight, partially screened by tall palms.

'But it looks quite attractive!' she exclaimed, surprised. 'I thought it would be gloomier . . .'

It was grim enough in its day, he thought, though Henry

always said it was better than most of the jails on the mainland: airy, uncrowded. But today it seemed there was a quite different view of the place.

After leaving Andy's boatyard, depressed, at a loss, he had taken a taxi up to the jail, astounded to find it crowded with Indian visitors touring the premises in groups, guided by confident young men who ran through their patter in a mixture of Hindi and English.

The walls were covered with large photographs, portraits of men, and with lists of names, hundreds of names set out in columns.

James lurked at the back of a group, his gaunt pale face looking raw and unfinished, sticking up above the smooth, brown skins around him. These were the martyrs, the guide explained, waving at the photographs. Killed, he added, by the British. Martyrs who died trying to set their country free.

'This is a shrine to the freedom-fighters of our First War of Independence, and the later struggles.'

The First War of Independence, James realised, was what he had known as the Indian Mutiny.

Nobody stared at the Englishman, the interloper in the group: they were all far too polite, but James was aware of their awareness of his presence. He said, loudly and abruptly, 'What about the Japanese? The Japanese Occupation? Shouldn't you mention the atrocities?'

'They were our enemies. You don't expect kindness from your enemies. We thought you were our friends.'

'We *were* – are,' James protested.

'But you imprisoned those who wanted freedom for their country.'

'They weren't all freedom-fighters!' James was red in the face, his mouth dry, sweat running down his body. 'What about the murderers?'

'There will always be murderers. That is their role. Their karma. One way and another we must all die.'

There was something very important James had to say; he

had to remind the man about the difference between politics and crime, but there was a word he needed to do so, and the word refused to come to mind. He stood staring at the guide, at the portraits, his brain failing to respond. He kept feeding it the prompt, like a man trying to start a car, turning the ignition again and again when the engine fails to fire. Once again the mental filing system was failing to deliver. He faced a blank. He tried sifting words, rejecting, searching. Something told him the word he sought had an 'a' in the first syllable and a rat-tat-tat rhythm, like bannister, or acolyte, or radishes. He tried words at random, hoping they might lead him to the one he sought. Farandole, no. Parasol . . . The word lurked obstinately out of reach. His head throbbed.

As the group of tourists moved on, up the stairs to look at cells, the guide feeding them the approved historical myths, James felt frustration surging up: there could be no understanding. These people had not been there, how could they know? But then, a small voice added, he had not been there either.

Daisy was still gazing up at the jail from the deck. 'I can't wait for us to see it, see how it's changed.'

James said absently, 'I went yesterday.'

She looked at him, quite stunned for a moment. The enormity of it, shutting her out of an experience that he had so often discussed sharing with her. But really it was just another stage in everyday exclusion: even when she was by his side he was elsewhere. She turned and stepped down into the saloon. She sat on the padded bench, tears welling from her eyes, trickling, dripping off her chin. Children stared, nudging parents. A sari-clad granny, small, bony, leaned across and enquired with Indian lack of self-consciousness if she was grieving for a loved one?

Daisy stared at her, the tears welling, dripping. In a way she was doing just that. 'Yes.'

'It is a recent bereavement?'

Not really: I lost him long ago, Daisy wanted to reply. Instead she nodded, feeling a fraud as the woman patted her arm consolingly, because she was filled not with sadness but with rage, and a furious self-pity. The boat bumped against the landing stage and she clambered off without looking at James. She hurried to where the taxi waited and got in, keeping her head averted, gazing unfocused through the window, using her straw hat as a screen. In silence they drove back to the hotel. In silence crossed the lobby.

The manager was bustling about, organising the guests into groups for the following day. He intercepted James and Daisy: 'We have a party going to Jolly Buoy for snorkelling tormorrow morning – '

Curtly James vetoed the snorkelling.

Daisy said calmly, 'I shall go. Please put my name down.'

James swivelled an incredulous blue glance in her direction but she was already halfway up the stairs.

She changed into her swimsuit and picked up a towel.

'What are you doing?'

'I should have thought it was obvious. I'm going for a swim.'

'It's almost lunchtime.'

'Yes. Don't wait for me.' She strode briskly out of the room.

The sun was high overhead, a small silver disc hidden by a heat haze. The palms along the beach cast only the smallest of shadows, directly at their own base. Daisy threw her towel down, kicked off her sandals and went into the sea, swimming steadily, her rage giving her strength. After a while she turned on her back and floated, looking back towards the shore, rising and falling with the swell of the surf. A man was making his way into the sea, splashing water on to his face, his arms. The tide was on the turn and Daisy saw that he was being pulled by the deceptively gentle, inexorable current, into the rocky section of the bay, though the sharp rocks were still hidden by the high water. As he stood, irresolute, a wave nudged the back of his knees. Daisy called out a warning, but too late: it was the smallest of waves but taken unawares he lost his balance and fell over. He began to flail helplessly in the shallow water, his head vanishing beneath the surface.

She swam the few yards that separated them, stood over him, grasped his arms, and hauled him to his feet. 'You want to look out for the rocks, over there behind you.'

Coughing out sea water and choking, he looked up at Daisy and exclaimed, 'Ah! We meet again!'

She peered at him, myopic, uncertain. 'On Ross,' he said, 'we examined the ruins. You have undoubtedly saved my life.'

'Hardly. It's just that the rocks – '

'Rocks can on occasion prove fatal – ' he went into a small fit of coughing, then added, 'You saved me.'

He paused for a moment, gulping to get his breath, then said, with a formality Daisy found decidedly ludicrous under the circumstances, 'Allow me to introduce myself: T. A. Ramachander.'

'Oh!' she had a quick mental picture of James hustling her out of an antiquarian bookshop as the bookseller called after them –

She said diffidently, 'I believe I've met your brother . . . in Madras . . .'

The Ramachanders' father knew the inside of the Cellular Jail: 'He was one of the politicals, incarcerated in the Thirties, you know. You could say my brother and I imbibed Marx and Engels with our mother's milk. Matter of fact, *Das Kapital* was my first reading book, but I regret to say my brother preferred *Gulliver's Travels* and *Alice*. There were,' a pause, 'ructions at home.'

Guided by Daisy, Mr Ramachander staggered across the beach, still talking, and subsided in the minimal shade of a palm. 'I always felt . . . you might say an affinity with Engels: cotton was his family's business, like ours – ' a deprecating smile and wave of the arms, 'on a rather different level of course. But I always felt they understood our problems. You will recall what Marx wrote about the extinction of our hand-loom weavers in the last century:' He coughed delicately. ' "The misery hardly finds a parallel in the history of commerce.

The bones of the cotton-weavers are bleaching the plains of India." '

Chapter 32

James brushed his teeth, splashed his face and very deliberately switched off the light. Daisy would have to undress in the dark.

Once, he used to watch her undress, marvelling at the flow and harmony of flesh and hair, catching her at odd moments, as she paused to unfasten a hook or a zip, frozen in an attitude of grace like a figure on a Greek vase.

Things change. He remembered a story about Richard Strauss attending a recording of *Don Quixote* after the war: the venerable composer sat listening, eyes closed, nodding in approval, until a certain moment, when he stepped in with a word of advice: 'You are playing as if Don Quixote is still young. He is old, very old and very sick. And he remembers. Play it like a memory . . .'

With time things change. Cease to touch one. Lose their charm. The first snowfall, the smell of lavender after rain, the whistle of a distant train carried on the air at dusk . . . Once magical, now aspects of meteorology, olfactory and aural experience. When does it happen? All part of growing old. A certain Schubert phrase that brought him close to tears . . . the tremulous quality in Daisy that had touched his heart . . . What once seemed miraculous aroused no more than a mild interest. He acknowledged all this without being moved, involved. Feelings he had believed eternal proved to be mutable as shadows, shifting with time, melting away. Her arms, white and round, that had drawn exclamations of wonder from him, were now simply limbs that rubbed against his in planes and trains. A memory.

The Italians were dancing on the terrace, the girls in very short, skin-tight skirts, long legs flashing. The English party, enjoying an after-dinner brandy under the stars, stoically slapping away mosquitoes, found their quiet enclave overwhelmed with music and laughter. They exchanged glances, raised eyebrows in wordless communication and withdrew to bed. The Russians had danced earlier: 'folklorick', they announced, forming a circle, attuned as termites. Daisy, sipping an unfortunate choice of liqueur, watched the Italians dancing. She could get up and join them, she would not look ridiculous: her hips and waist remained much as they were thirty years before, and she still had good legs. 'But nobody notices!' To her embarrassment she found she had spoken aloud. But nobody noticed.

In her twenties she knew a lot of men: colleagues, friends of colleagues, friends of friends . . . they met casually, sometimes in the course of work, for drinks; flirted lightheartedly over lunch. Some were her age or a little more. And there were the – infinitely more interesting – Older Men, their faces pouchy, attractively lined. They looked rumpled, but full of vitality. Sometimes they were accompanied by wives, women with greying hair cut sensibly short, whose bodies tended to be dumpy, clothes discreet. She thought of them as the Salt and Pepper Women, creatures of faded, indeterminate colouring, their features blurred into middle-aged blobs. These women smiled at her when they met. They knew her name and asked interested questions but she had difficulty in recognising them. Often she failed to notice they were present. They were to all intents and purposes invisible.

Sometimes, of late, when Lizzie or Bill dropped in, en route to somewhere more interesting, they brought along friends, cool young people of immense poise and confidence and Daisy beamed bright, interested smiles at them, asked them bright, informed questions, genuinely seeking to know what they were thinking, listening while they talked. And talked.

Occasionally, a silent rebellion threatened: I could contribute to their discourse. My brain has not atrophied. But they don't see me. I have become invisible. Of no interest.

There was a song Buddy Holly used to sing when she was young and he was unaware how little time was left, a catchy, heart-achingly perky number with a refrain that went: 'I Guess It Doesn't Matter Any More'. It could serve as a title for the lament of a Salt and Pepper Woman. There was grey in her hair. Young men no longer suddenly caught their breath as she was passing. That was Yeats not Buddy Holly, but she guessed it didn't matter any more.

He could hear the music thumping through the floor. What on earth did Daisy think she was doing? She had been behaving oddly all day. Another time he would have dealt with the matter firmly, but his own agitation at the moment was too great. He tried to breathe evenly, to lie still, but panic filled his nostrils, clogged his throat, crawled over his skin like ants. His veins pulsed with blood, threatening to burst. Pins and needles in his fingers, his face stiff, muscles unresponsive. Could this be a stroke? Was his brain failing? Numbers, lines of poetry, geographical locations, could he still call them up? What was that word he had sought earlier? Was his memory permanently impaired? Like a spool of film spinning out of control, images engulfed him. He tried to get out of the bed but the weight of darkness pressed down on him.

Awake, asleep, between the two, he sidled into nightmare: the figure writhing on the pillows, the bed swathed in mosquito net, and looming above it, ghostly, not clearly seen, a thing of shimmering pallor –

The door rattled as Daisy came into the room.

'You woke me.' Accusingly.

She did not apologise.

Chapter 33

The whisky tumblers were encrusted with grease and dust, layer after layer, to the pearly thickness of alabaster. 'It's bad for you, that stuff,' the boy protested, worried and resentful, but Andy ignored him, upending the glass clumsily so that whisky ran down his chin. The room smelled of unaired linen and old flesh and the slow overhead fan merely moved the stale air around, neither cooling nor refreshing the atmosphere. James talked, doggedly, of their last encounter, undeterred by the lack of any reaction, trying to conjure up the past, the days spent charting the islands, the search for the wreckage that might have told him . . . what? That Elizabeth really had been shipwrecked? (But what did it matter in the end whether she drowned, choked by a watery shroud, or suffered a horrible death, butchered by savages?)

To encourage response James left questions hanging in the air, wondered aloud, paused encouragingly. The blades of the fan stirred the silence; the smeared windows diffused the harsh sunlight giving the room a cavelike dimness.

The old man sat huddled in his cane armchair, immobile except for the occasional movement of whisky glass to lips. Was he listening? His eyes were veiled, his face blank. Once, his expression brightened with interest and he leaned forward, smiling sweetly: 'How d'you like our islands? Been here before?' James faltered in mid-sentence and the boy shot him a triumphant glance. Senile. Lives in a dream. 'He doesn't even know who you are.'

James drained his tumbler, suddenly defeated. He got up, rubbing his hands briskly, slapping his pockets, making vague, distracted gestures to blur the awkwardness of departure. Andy waved the empty bottle at his grandson – 'Get's another, Joseph boy.' Was it the whisky or his physical decline that caused him to slur his words? The small, wrinkled face cracked into a malicious grin as he stared up at James: 'I thought you were done for, storm like that. Lost your precious chart, I bet.' He cackled.

One of the prompt-cards had worked. But how reliable was the response? James said, cautiously, 'Not that it mattered, did it? There were other charts. I found out, later.'

'Sure there were charts.'

'Why did you lie to me then? "You want a chart, draw one", that's what you said. Why?'

The old man rubbed at his face as though trying to locate an elusive itch.

'Well, first off, the charts didn't have it *all*. Lot of gaps. Better off doing it yourself. And then . . .' His voice trailed off.

'And then?'

'There were difficulties.'

More whisky. The boy yawned and watched them from across the room until his grandfather sent him away. The fan moved overhead. They sat in silence.

'You took your time, coming back.'

James looked surprised. 'It's just a couple of days, and you said – '

'To the islands. In a hurry, were you? What is it, fifty years?'

Fear had been part of the problem. Fear of what he might learn: just before that last trip with Andy, after Freddy had gone back, with an affectionate hug and a sad joke – 'You're not Ulysses, you're just Peter Pan trying to get back to Never Never Land, Jamie' – James had wandered round Aberdeen bazaar. The little stalls of his childhood were giving way already to shops; modest, hardly more than shacks, but one at least had a counter and a few shelves filled with household goods.

'Surely this used to be a little stall selling cloth by the yard?'

'Quite right, good sir.' The shopkeeper smiled, displaying several gold teeth. 'You are an old Andaman hand, I see.'

'My – ' James paused, 'my family was here for a while.'

They reminisced about the old days and then James said he must go, he was off on a boat trip round the outlying islands. The shopkeeper waved a finger in a jocular warning – 'Keep a weather-eye open, good sir, tricky waters round there.'

'Well I certainly don't want to become another of the mysterious Andaman shipwrecks.'

'Oh we have no mysteries. Shipwrecks, yes, my goodness, but no mysteries.'

'I heard of one where the wife of a British officer was lost at sea. They never found – '

'Oh, you are talking of Mrs Oakley. Well, some funny business there, I agree. There were stories, rumours at the time – '

'Rumours?'

'Well, some people were saying that maybe she did not drown at all you know, but was rescued, crazy nonsense. People are shipwrecked. They drown or they die of thirst and hunger. It is also possible to arrive at an inhabited island. Poor souls, they face a Jarawa reception party. Poisoned arrows and, forgive me for sounding somewhat ghoulish, my dear sir, the cooking pot.' He raised plump hands in humorous deprecation, 'In a manner of speaking. The aboriginals do not, I believe, bother too much with cooking utensils – '

Elizabeth, her white body in flames, puffing up, the skin flayed, exploding –

'You're saying they are cannibals? But I thought – '

A shrug. 'Maybe. Maybe not. There is only one way of testing for sure!' He roared with laughter. 'But in a place like this there is always gossip, rumours, people having nothing better to do, so rumours are persisting.'

The next day James took his last trip with Andy.

James accepted another shot of whisky. 'I didn't know you sailed as a cabin boy, that you did the Madras run.' The wrinkled yellow face smoothed out for a moment. 'How'd you hear about that?'

'The big boatyard down the road. I was looking for you and took a wrong turning. We got talking.'

Andy reached for the almost empty bottle. 'Those bastards. Other people's business . . .' He gargled another glassful. 'I meant to tell you. But like I said, there were difficulties. Your father – '

'What has he to do with it?'

'Good man, your father . . .'

It seemed Andy was changing the subject, rambling again: 'I was small for my age.'

'What – '

'Small for my age, just a tyke. She talked to me.'

Inside James's head a sudden turmoil, a roaring began, so loud that it blanked out Andy's voice.

'She?' The nightmare circled –

'You were on that ship? Her ship – '

'She said she had a boy smaller'n me she'd be seeing soon, when she got home . . .'

James asked, trying to sound casual, 'She was alone?'

The old man pondered. 'Alone?' He frowned. He had lost the thread again. A pause. 'I was small for my age, you see. Brought out the maternal feelings, I guess.' He fell silent; he seemed to have forgotten James again.

He was small for his age, but quick, and he had almost finished cleaning the cabin when the Englishwoman appeared, smiling, apologising for getting in his way. 'I forgot my diary.' She scooped up the leather-bound book and turned to leave. The child stood, a duster dangling from his hand. He said nothing, waiting for her to go, accustomed to passengers who treated him as a piece of furniture. She paused in the cabin doorway. He noticed that beneath her close-fitting hat her hair was pale yellow. 'What is your name?' she asked.

She asked his name, his age and told him she had a son a

little younger than he was – 'I shall see him, very soon, in England.'

She told him about England; about the winter with snow and ice – he had never seen snow, and knew ice only from the cold-boxes that kept food fresh and the lumps that clinked in the glasses of passengers. The idea that ice could grow on water like a skin astonished him. She told him how black fog filled the city streets in England the way smoke billowed from a damp fire. Perhaps he would become a sailor and one day see all this for himself.

That evening he carried fresh water to her cabin and neatened the bunk. And seeing the leather-bound book on the shelf, he opened it, curious to see what it contained.

The sky has turned dull, curdled looking. The cabin boy says we are in for bad weather. Andy is not much older than my little James, but he works like a full-grown man, without complaint, his small hands roughened from labouring. James will play cricket on smooth lawns and learn the dates and names of kings and battles – and then? Join the Army perhaps? The Civil Service? What will he have learned from his years of education? To be kind, I hope. And to be curious. And to be brave. A child is so vulnerable, and we send them away when we should be binding them to us; we distance ourselves when we should be close. We must, it seems. But is this what we want?

A dream of water-melons, they say, betokens a happy life. But I find myself reflecting once again on the Indian proverb: whether the knife falls on the melon or the melon on the knife, it is all the same. I wonder now, is it the woman or the child who meets the knife? And whose bitterness is the greater?

He glanced at the neatly filled pages without comprehension, replaced the book and left the cabin.

Elizabeth came out on to the deck, walking briskly to work up an appetite for dinner. At the far end of the deck some of the crew scurried about, securing hatches and ropes. As she rounded the ship to windward, Elizabeth saw what looked like a wall of darkness, a gathering together where the water joined the sky. She was watching it approach when one of the sailors screamed something at her. He grabbed her arm and pulled her through the companionway as darkness fell on them and the hurricane struck. The ship reeled, hurling Elizabeth against the wall. Shrieks and cries of alarm were drowned out by a roar like a wild beast breaking out of a cage. Then the wind came down on them, and all distinction between air and water was lost, everything boiling as if enveloped in steam. It hit the little ship with a spiteful, destructive force, battering from every direction at once. Lightning flashed blindingly through the portholes. The wind drove downwards, punching holes in the sea big enough to swallow a small boat. Those on board, like beans shaken in a box, were thrown violently from side to side as the vessel see-sawed on the mountainous waves. It seemed it could get no worse when the sea suddenly bunched itself together and rose in the air. The ship rose with it, poised on the crest, carried along at giddy speed, helpless, gripped in the wind's fist, whirling through the darkness, hurtling on and on until there came a terrible, juddering, splintering crash, and then the wind was gone and everything was silent and still.

Some knelt to pray, others wept with joy, a few were too dazed and battered to do more than stagger across the sharply tilting floor and stare out into the darkness. They were alive. And on dry land. They could hear the sound of the sea but they were stuck fast, unmoving.

Between the splintered shambles of the saloon and the cabins people crawled and clung, trying to find their way through the once-familiar surroundings. Without lights they moved like blind creatures, feeling surfaces, tapping, reaching before them with splayed fingers, calling out.

As the first light dawned they gathered, huddled together, crew and passengers no longer separated by social distinctions or the barriers of race, and wrenched open companionways to the deck. At first they saw nothing but the tops of trees black against the sky. The deck sloped upwards and they climbed its steep side, clinging to the rail. They were beached in a mangrove swamp, the prow sunk in the ground, the stern hanging high in the air. The force of the hurricane had lifted the vessel over the reef, across the beach and hurled it to the far side of the lagoon, to bury it among the mangroves and the creepers.

The cabin boy noticed the Englishwoman further along the deck. Unlike the others she looked neither happy nor fearful: pale hair hanging loose around her face, clothes oil-stained and torn, she stood examining what was visible of the island, her expression one of interest and expectation. She saw him and beckoned. Clinging to the rail, he inched his way along to her. She was a small woman, but she seemed formidable as she put an arm round his shoulders.

'It seems we are saved, Andy.'

A senior member of the crew beside her at the rail, overheard. 'Madam, we are perhaps not quite saved.' He was looking carefully at the shadowy trees beyond the mangroves. 'It will depend on what sort of island we find ourselves on.'

James tapped his empty glass to break the lengthy silence. 'Andy – ' The old man jerked upright, startled. His face took on the glow of interest that accompanied an amnesiac spell. He nodded wisely at James: 'You want to try scuba-diving, that's the thing these days. They take you down in a group, show you the coral reefs . . .' In mid-sentence he fell asleep.

James tried to shake him awake, reaching forward frantically, knocking over his glass, all as slowly as a man moving through water. He slumped back in his chair, and he too slept.

The English party went off in three taxis: Daisy watched them leave, supplied with beach umbrellas, cushions, packed lunches in hampers. Servants of various sorts were crammed into the front seats next to the taxi-drivers and the expedition had a touch of Raj-style shikaree about it, even though the aim was to sample the underwater life rather than shoot tigers or crocs. She had opted to join the Russian group. With them she need not make polite conversation, nor be identified as part of a social structure. With the Russians she would simply be a foreigner swimming alongside.

The dancing Russians had gone and another group had taken their place. They seemed at first to be identical, but their songs were not the same – from Georgia, they said – and Daisy rather missed Yuri with his luxuriant moustache and nimble footwork.

The air-conditioning in the coach had, inevitably, broken down. Daisy fanned herself with an old London Transport map lurking, forgotten, at the bottom of her handbag, and stared through the windows as the bus bumped its way along a cracked and pot-holed road.

The trees on either side rose dark and green, sun filtering through the topmost branches. Away from the rusting corrugated-iron and concrete industrial development of Port Blair, the true nature of the island began to reveal itself. Reluctantly, she conceded that James had not been wrong: there was beauty here, in the gloom of the rain forest, the wild hibiscus flowers gaping like scarlet mouths, the morning glory spinning its web over bushes and trees like delicate green and purple lacework. By the roadside, deep pink lotus flowers floated on pools as still as black glass.

As soon as they were afloat, the Russians began to sing the predictable 'folklorick songs'. The repertoire was extensive, and after a while Daisy lost the urge to hear more. She no longer smiled benevolently at the broad-cheeked women and the men in their ill-cut, open-necked shirts. She craved for silence, the opportunity to observe each new island, tiny, dense with rain forest, the mangrove branches inching into the water from beneath the tall trees. They glided past, lying in the sunlight as though enchanted, no sign of life disturbing their stillness. In an occasional Russian pause she heard the shriek of parrots, the cry of a bird, but saw no flash of colour in the branches. On the ground there was no movement. No life.

Along the Nile, she recalled, their boat had moved through a hive of activity without disturbing it, lent a sort of invisibility, insulated by the water. Women carried on washing clothes, men loaded enormous bales of hay or reeds on to the backs of tiny donkeys with delicate, twiglike legs. The harvesting and water-carrying went on as it always had. Only the children broke the rules, waving and calling out to the passing boats, grinning and capering with absurd grace in their cotton djellabas.

Here, the silent islands came in sight, hovered alongside and were left behind, unreal as illustrations in a children's story book with their white sand and bright green mangroves rising out of a dark turquoise sea.

On some islands landing was forbidden, for the protection of both the aboriginals and the visitors: if the natives were friendly, they risked further contamination, disease, erosion of their way of life. If they were not friendly, it was the visitors who faced a rather more immediate risk.

They anchored off Jolly Buoy and were rowed, six at a time, to the beach. Only when she was handed her flippers, mask and breathing tube did Daisy suddenly quiver into the realisation that this was what they were here for: not to admire the passing scenery but to strap on unwieldy plastic equipment and venture below the surface of the ocean. Perhaps she could explain that she felt unwell, that there had been some misunderstanding, she was on the wrong trip . . .

But, of course, she did none of those things. She slipped out of her sundress, sat down on the beach and began to struggle into her flippers and tight rubber mask, peering through the glass porthole uneasily. The mouthpiece of the breathing tube felt uncomfortably like a piece of dentist's equipment. The Russians were already dotted about in the sea, calling out, wallowing like walruses.

Ready to pull back, convinced she would drown, Daisy launched herself nervously into the sea, floated face down and opened her eyes.

Astonished by the clarity, the vividness of the colours, for a moment she had the weird sensation that there was no water beneath her – that she hung suspended in air. The merest wave of her flippers sent her gliding forward among tiny fish, some zebra-striped in black and white, others darting like splinters of bright blue glass, some colourless, transparent, revealing their spines and organs, or splodged with rainbow colours like an artist's palette. She floated on, further out, over fantastic growths of reef, drunk on the shapes and colours. Time did not exist, or effort, just this translucency, this cradle that held her, gently rocking. The surface hung above her like a canopy of pearly silk; below lay the clean sandy bed dotted with coral shapes: yellow mushrooms, purple cactus, skeletal pink bushes, bulbous fingers reaching upwards towards the light; fronds and tendrils and globes of a dozen different shapes and colours. She felt safe and calm, almost drugged, as she drifted further from the shore. Ahead she was dimly aware of a rim, like the edge of a plate, coming closer. And then a cliff opened beneath her on to dark blue emptiness. The reef had ended and the sea floor dropped away into what seemed a bottomless void. It was like stepping off the edge of a skyscraper. For a moment she hung there, gazing down into the darkness, frozen with terror. Then she recoiled, as though clawing back from the edge, and screamed, and all her safety, her drugged ease was lost in choking, churning clumsiness. Coughing, blinded, swallowing sea water, her body suddenly heavy and unwieldy, she threshed, shouting for help.

But she had drifted out of earshot, and neither the splashing Russians nor the crew could see that she was drowning. Salt water filled her throat, her nostrils, her ears. Painful, hateful, it slapped at her, stinging, tumbling her cruelly.

She was sinking. There was no strength in her limbs, no fight left. She felt herself spiralling downwards into the void. And there was something else: far beneath her, in the dimness, had there been a vague shape, a blurred movement? ('The servants beat the water to frighten away the sharks . . .') She knew with absolute certainty that there was a shark in the depths. Frenziedly she fought her way to the surface and began to tread water: she slowed her movements. Heart pounding, she forced herself to float. She knew how to float, for God's sake. She lay, gathering her strength, waiting for the teeth to snap, the sharp, wrenching agony, the sea reddening. She knew what she must do – if she could manage it. She rammed the flap of the mouthpiece against her teeth, slowed her breathing, and then, fearfully, she forced herself to look below the surface.

She had pulled back from the rim. There was, of course, no shark. She saw a few yards away a rounded rock like a huge mushroom cap sticking up from the sandy bottom. She hovered over it. How deep was the water here? She let her flippered feet sink and found her feet just touching the stone mushroom, and balanced upright until she was standing, head sticking out above the water, looking about her like some sea-bird. She stood, regaining her breath, swaying with the movement of the water, for a long time, until gradually the terror receded. She swam back, breathing steadily through the tube, watching the coral pass beneath her. When the water was too shallow to continue, she walked up the last few feet of shelving sand and collapsed on to the shore, shaking. Gradually calmness filtered into her.

The sea was clear as glass at the shoreline, shading into pale turquoise, then bright blue. Like a shadow beneath the surface lay the coral reef. The sun flooded the palm leaves and mangroves so that they seemed to glow with light from within. Tiny hermit crabs and huge ants scuttled about on the blinding white sand, searching for food. She lay with the sun on her back, a light breeze cooling her skin, her feet washed by the water. Everything – air, water, blood, lungs, thoughts – flowed together in harmony: no feeling of anxiety, no lurch in the pit of the stomach, no sudden tears, spasms of alarm, no sense of regret. No Daisy. Just a great, oceanic surge that lifted her with it. She felt herself melting into the elements.

Chapter 34

James jerked into wakefulness, stiff with cramp, head aching,
surroundings unfamiliar, aware that something was different.
He knew that dying had to be the most interesting thing that
lay ahead for someone of his age. This could be it: he could be
about to complete the process begun so long ago. Then he saw
Andy, slumped in the cane armchair, and remembered where
he was. The old man lay so still, with no sign of breathing,
that James knew he was dead. It was Henry all over again; he
had left his visit too late. As he lumbered stiffly to his feet the
old man's eyes flipped open, like a doll with movable lids.

The boy had never faced danger – not on land anyway. He
knew about wind and high waves, storms and unsteady decks,
but when the Jarawa appeared – dancing black silhouettes
against the blinding sand – he hung, powerless to move, as
though lashed to the rail.

From a distance they looked like insects: sticklike arms and
legs, long bows and arrows waving in the air. They streamed
across the beach towards the stranded ship with the concentration of ants advancing on a source of nourishment. On the
ship, people blundered about, panic-stricken, tripping, falling,
struggling to escape. One of them knocked him aside and he
lost his balance, rolled down the deck and lay, dazed, where
the tilting deck met the superstructure. The Jarawa were closer
now, he could hear them howling like wild animals. He lay,
unable to move. And why bother? He knew that when they

boarded the ship they would finish him off. Someone grabbed his arm and began to drag him along the deck towards the prow: it was the Englishwoman. She had lost her shoes, her toes stuck through her ripped white stockings and her hands were raw, almost bleeding.

Some of the others were jumping off the ship, leaping from high above the ground, running into the sea or heading further along the shore – those who could – or lying injured, calling out piteously. Others had run back into the saloon, to try and barricade themselves in. She pushed him ahead of her, forcing him on.

The boy and the Englishwoman crawled off the sunken prow and slid into the mangrove swamp. He was terrified: beneath him lay a yielding sludge that pulled him down, sucking at his feet. She whispered that he must grip the mangrove branches, use them like horizontal ladders. Clumsily they hauled and clambered their way across the swamp towards the beach. To his bewilderment they were heading not away from the savages but towards them. She flattened him as he jerked upright in panic, held him down, and they both fell together into the thick pool of mud, the syrupy liquid coating them with an evil-smelling sheen.

The islanders had passed them now, one carrying a flaming torch, and in the distance he heard the sounds, the screams and cries. They lay very still, breathing in the swamp air, foul from rotting fish and dead sea creatures washed in and trapped by the intricate web of roots. Then she beckoned him to follow. On the beach the Jarawa had started a fire. The flames licked round the first bodies. From the ship came crashes, more screams. The sickly smell of burning flesh drifted across to the swamp. The boy began to whimper. Sternly she shook him, drew him on.

They had rounded the headland, still under cover of the mangrove, and he realised that they were now hidden from the capering, victorious aboriginals. Then she pulled him from the swamp and on to the firm, powdery sand. As they prepared to run, he glanced for a moment behind him, to where he could see smoke and flames rising in the air. He felt her fingers tighten on his wrist and when he turned he saw the figure: a warrior holding a two-yard-long bow stood a few feet away, directly in their path, watching them.

'He didn't move, he just stood there, that great bow taller'n he was, held in his hand, watching us. We must've looked like swamp creatures, both of us covered in mud to the eyeballs: faces, arms, everything coated with the stuff; her dress stuck to her body like a soaked bandage.'

Only her hair had escaped the mud, hanging in a wild yellow bush. They stood, the three of them, unmoving: the two muddy fugitives and the Jarawa, watching each other. He was small, hardly taller than the Englishwoman, with no fat or excess flesh on his body. His skin was smooth and hairless and so intensely black that it had an almost blue gleam in the sunlight. His frizzy hair was shorn close to his scalp, in a pattern, as though his head was studded with peppercorns. Apart from a belt of woven vines he was naked. His face was expressionless. He fitted an arrow into the long bow, raised it and stood, waiting –

'Waiting for us to run, I guess.'

The Englishwoman, quite slowly, making no sudden movements, snapped a twig from a mangrove and began to draw a pattern in the sand. She worked without haste, frequently glancing up at the warrior, meeting his gaze, holding his attention. Then she stepped back, drawing the child close to her. The Jarawa moved closer, but not too close, suspiciously, craning his neck to look at the pattern she had created in the sand. He stared down at it, puzzled, surprised.

Andy, his face grey with exhaustion, was dribbling, one side of his mouth pulled down like a grimace; he shook slightly with a palsy. His eyes drooped. His mind was pulling away from the past, the pain, the questions, the sense of helplessness. It was all bad for him. He longed to stop. If Joseph was here he would say Andy must rest, send the man away. But James loomed over him with questions, his gaunt figure twitching, tense, demanding more, more.

'How about some food?' Andy muttered, his voice slurred. 'Could do with some food.'

James went into the kitchen. It smelt sour, a combination of rancid fat, over-ripe fruit and stale curry. He looked around helplessly. Andy called out to him feebly, 'There's some rice . . . you'll find rice and peas in the fridge . . .'

James fed him spoonfuls of cold rice and peas, and whisky from the dirty tumbler. Andy laughed: 'Joseph'll be mad. Not allowed whisky in daytime. Not – '

James broke in: 'What happened? What happened after that?'

It was hard to remember. 'It was so long ago, I was just a tyke . . .'

Then, as he tried to recall it, the scene swam back into his head. No words, there could be no words, there had been no words at first, just patterns, the shapes of people, their bodies, faces, eyes. The others came running from the fire, whooping, angry. They circled the two, flourishing bows, the iron-tipped arrows ready. There were women too, carrying sharply pointed sticks, their heads shorn like the men. He stared at the small conical breasts, the mysterious smooth place with a dark fold like a gash, where their legs joined their body. Standing very straight, the Englishwoman held him close against her. One of the Jarawa moved towards them, reaching out angrily, but the first, with a sweep of the bow, pointed to the pattern in the sand. They all stared, held back from action. Then the warrior stepped forward, putting the woman and the child behind him, and turned to face the rest: it was a statement of ownership, in its own way, of protection.

The shipwreck, and what followed, had left them dazed, numb. They were prodded from place to place with pointed sticks, like cattle being moved; they knew nothing, understood nothing. The women plucked at them curiously, pinching their arms and legs, feeling their hair. The Englishwoman's shaggy yellow mane intrigued them all. The boy, with his sallow skin and Asiatic features, was less interesting.

The expectation persisted that at any moment they might be killed. They were, after all, the only survivors, the rest burning to ash on the shore. One protector in an entire community surely would prove a fragile shield? Each day they waited for the moment to arrive.

Much later he asked her about the pattern in the sand, and she replied only that it was a pattern she had seen drawn by an aboriginal child once, when he was lost and in need of protection. To draw a pattern in the sand, she said, had seemed important at the time, a way of staving off something.

The women, in the beginning, were against her; they dragged her with them to search for edible roots and grubs in the forest – she was given a sharp stick like the others – and she spent hour after hour digging in the sandy soil, digging deeper and longer to fill her basket from which the others, spitefully, stole. They made her climb tall trees for fruit and berries growing beyond reach of the long, hooked poles they carried. They pushed her into streams to find freshwater crayfish and into stagnant pools to fetch lotus roots. Sometimes she crawled back to the bank, leeches fastened to her arms and legs, stuck fast to her flesh or dangling and nesting in her pale pubic hair. She beat the women at their own game, once, when they sent her up a tree to bring down a honeycomb. She had seen how the men chewed the leaves of a particular plant – a species of Alpinia that smelt pungently of ginger – before approaching the hives: spreading the chewed pulp over themselves. Unnoticed, she gathered the Alpinia leaves and climbed slowly, chewing, spitting the pulp into her palms, anointing face, hands and hair, blowing at the bees the way the men did, as though extinguishing candles. Buzzing in alarm they retreated, and she took the comb – and threw it to the women below. At once the bees followed, zooming down on the women who scattered, shrieking. They did not repeat the game.

The Englishwoman – Andy knew now that her name was Elizabeth – never complained. She puzzled them by wading into the stream each day to wash: something they never thought of doing. But mostly she did as they did, eating fruits and berries, and honey from the comb, fish, turtles, sea creatures. They could make fire but preferred to borrow it from a tree struck by lightning, and the boy learned quickly to play his part in keeping the fire burning day and night in the encampment. When the men caught a wild pig in the forest they roasted it at once, and gorged on the whole animal until only the largest bones were left.

They slept in family groups, in huts, each with its own small fire that burned through the night, their sleeping platforms raised off the ground. On nights when the men went out in their canoes to hunt turtles, she went with the women at ebb tide to gather fish and sea creatures in nets that she held in one hand while she poked in the shallow water, searching out fish with her pointed stick. Sometimes the boy went too, and he saw how, now and then, she stopped to stare out at the sea, where the phosphorescence lay like a green fire on the surface. When the turtle swam away in fright, its movement caused a fiery wake to spread behind it, a glittering arrow guiding the hunters to their prey.

They both suffered from vicious insect bites, and their flesh was torn and scratched by thorns and sharp vines in the forest. The islanders had extraordinarily elastic, smooth skin; thorns slid over them without piercing their bodies. Their skin was unwrinkled, and even the oldest among them had the same gleaming ebony skin and unlined faces as the young.

She worked hard: the constant search for food, the laborious tasks – gathering firewood, fetching water, stripping leaves, weaving baskets, the rebuilding of huts damaged by termites, the days lost when storms lashed the island, sending seas high over the land – left little time for leisure, but there were seasonal feasts, celebrations, and ceremonial dances, driven on by the beat of the sounding board and the chanting of voices, which lasted through the day and far into the night.

At first sight the islanders had appeared ferocious, their eyes glittering wildly, sharp teeth menacing, but gradually this impression changed: it was the contrast between the whites of their eyes and their pointed teeth with the blue-black skin that gave them their apparent fierceness. Their smiles and sudden laughter – which overcame them sometimes without visible cause – altered their aspect completely: they became childish, radiant.

They took the boy for her son, which permitted closeness, and because he was small for his age, at first he stayed with the women when the men went hunting, and was allowed to help her. But now and then they drew him forward and examined him: at a certain stage, boys underwent a ritual, a rite to mark their step into manhood and he knew the time would come for him before long.

One day they ventured back to the ship. It had settled in the swamp, and already plant life had encroached, and the deck had grown a lush green carpet. Lianas clasped the hull and wound their way up the mast like rigging. A mangrove grew out of a porthole like a plant in a windowbox. The ship seemed to be floating on a sea of leaves.

They climbed on board and cautiously made their way below. The seas, the salt wind, the tenacious plants, gave it the smell and look of a wreck rescued from the deep. Lying on the floor unbroken was a screwtop jar that had once contained food of some sort. The white ants had found their way to it, crawling through the thread of the lid, and invaded the jar. Now it seethed, packed tight with insect life. She stared at the ants pulsing within the glass jar, then with a movement of revulsion, hurled it through the broken porthole.

Termites and ants had been busy elsewhere: any fabric that had survived the elements was now reduced to a grubby, greyish dust. In what had been her cabin, the leather-bound diary still, astonishingly, lay on its narrow shelf, but when she reached for it, it crumbled in her hands. It was the only time he saw her weep.

Knowing no words to help her, he patted her arm helplessly, nuzzling her with his shorn head like a puppy.

'There is nothing for us here,' she said. But they found a metal water container, undamaged, and she hung it round his neck. Later, before reaching the settlement, she paused and took it from him, concealing it under an hibiscus bush.

The islanders grew no crops, so there was no sowing or harvesting, but the year had its shape: at one time they all searched for a soft, red, cherrylike fruit that hung in bunches from tall trees, carrying them to the village to eat and string into garlands. Later came a fruit with a hard, leathery skin that they cracked open with their teeth. There were blackish-red globes and wild jackfruit, and big, bulbous growths that smelled of pineapple when the women slit them open with the edge of a sharp shell. And on one particular day, when the pilchard shoals drifted close to the island, the men raced out in their canoes and scooped the fish from the sea, loading the boats till they could hold no more, pulling them ashore brimming, heavy with their living silver cargo.

The women grew accustomed to her presence. She learned to read the signs they left to mark their paths through the interior and became at home in the dense undergrowth, wandering through the moist dimness of the rain forest, slipping past thorns and spikes with a new-learned agility. The tall trees shut out the sun so that the whole forest, the ferns and palms and padauks, lay in a dreaming, dripping green glow as though under water and even the silence seemed liquid.

The islanders had canoes; light, fast outriggers made from hollow tree trunks. They used them for fishing, and sometimes, further afield, going from island to island, carrying fire with them, knowing on which islands water and food were to be found, navigating by means of wave swells, prevailing winds, the paths of birds, mysterious guidelines but dependable. Elizabeth watched the warriors in their frail, buoyant craft leaping the waves and told the boy he must memorise their secret sea-charts, he too must learn the wave patterns and the language of the wind. This was when they talked of escape.

Chapter 35

After they had watched the sunset, the snorkelling party climbed back into the coach and drove home. For a while the Russians continued to sing, the melancholy side of 'folklorick' brought out by the lavender-grey sky that rapidly darkened to indigo and then a velvety near-black. The voices blended: the women's true and clear, the men's deeper, growling. The singing grew softer, became sporadic as they fell asleep, mouths open, heads drooping. They slept on as the coach bounced over rocks and fallen branches, and into pot-holes and back through the forest, past little villages lit by flaring oil lamps that wavered in the roadside breeze and glowed through the walls of the thatched huts, while goats and chickens and stray dogs leapt out of the path of the roaring intruder.

From the veranda James watched the coach drive up to the entrance, the Russians with their burnt red shoulders emerging, then Daisy. From this distance her face looked unlined, and against her pale dress her skin was dark brown. For a moment, stepping down from the bus, she seemed to have stepped through a doorway to the past: years before, on a boat in the Mediterranean, he had come into their cabin, drying his face, and looked up to see Daisy – safe, middle-aged Daisy, clad in white silk that lay close to her body. Her hair was piled up, caught with some jewel, her skin glowed. He had stared at her in dismay – in terror – sensing an old pull; demands, desires, arousal, all part of a terrain he had withdrawn from. Too dangerous. He had steeled himself, stopped up his ears to the siren call of the senses. It was so easy to be cruel, and see her face sag, go blank. Now, stepping from the bus, she was as she had been then and, like someone flinching from a blow, James hurriedly glanced away.

When the receptionist told Daisy, as though to reassure her, that her husband was back, guilt of an unfamiliar kind assailed her: she realised that for the last few hours he had not entered her mind.

She saw him sitting out on the veranda when she came in. She turned on the light, then turned it off again and joined him, breathing in the dark air. From the garden came the intermittent sound of the cicadas and frogs. He stirred.

'How was the snorkelling?'

'Fine. They drove us back a long way round so that we could see the sunset at Chiriyatapu. You probably know it.'

He thought for a moment. 'Bare, swampy beaches, huge bits of driftwood littering the shoreline like something out of Dali.'

'That's the place. It was rather weird, completely deserted. I walked into the forest for a bit. Hot as a Turkish bath.'

'And how was the sunset?'

'Rather a washout I'm afraid. Quite grey and hazy.'

They were like strangers talking politely at a bus-stop or a railway station, she thought: none of the usual irritability and impatience on his part or fluttery hysteria on hers; instead a calm, an exhaustion that was new. What is happening? she wondered.

'I'll have a shower.' She paused. 'Your day: was it . . . ?'

'It was . . .' She waited. She knew he sometimes sought in vain for the right word these days, frustrated, upset, so after a moment she nodded at the back of his head and said, 'Good,' saving him the necessity of finishing the sentence.

She took a long time showering and when she came out of the bathroom he was asleep on top of the bedcover in his clothes and shoes, lying like a felled log. She dressed in the dark and went down to dinner. He was still asleep when she came back, but next morning when she stirred and glanced

275

across, he was already up, on the veranda, the old mahogany portable writing desk on his knees. She wandered out, pulling on her dressing gown, squinting at the sun as it floated on the silver horizon.

He had been writing; several sheets of paper were covered with his minute, crabbed hand, and she saw that he was still wearing the same clothes, rumpled and sweat stained. Should she refer to the fact? Question him?

'James?'

He carried on writing. 'I just want to finish this.'

'In that case I'll have a swim before breakfast.'

'Yes, why don't you.'

He spoke mechanically, and went on scribbling. He must try and remember everything, get everything down.

All day they had gorged on honey brought down from the highest treetop hives in hollow logs, the combs oozing dark, rich syrup. There had been dancing.

The moon was almost full, painting the tops of the rain trees bright silver. She said this was to be the night. He was nervous; he knew it would be dangerous, but she had prepared them well for it. They had watched from the hilltop the distant smoke from ships that passed on certain days, never changing course or coming closer: amid so many hundred islands, hostile or uninhabited, this was just another that went unexplored. But one of the ships would be bound to spot a canoe, bobbing on the waves.

The village slept as they crept down through the forest to the beached canoes. When they dragged the outrigger down to the surf-line the tide was on the turn: the canoe would be tugged out, needing no more than a guiding hand. A night of bright moon, and fireflies thick among the blackness of the trees, glimmering points of light like splintered stars brightening the darkness with their green glow.

Ankle-deep in the water, they held the boat as it rose and fell. The sea, so often rough here, had gentled its waves tonight.

She handed him the water container salvaged from the wreck and urged him on as he hesitated, his eyes drawn towards the black immensity of the sea: before its vastness, its power, for a moment he wavered. It was only a moment, then he turned back to help her in, turned back as he had done that first day on the island, and saw – as he had then – the warrior, the long bow held in one hand, standing where the trees met the beach, watching them.

Andy whispered urgently for her to jump in, hurry, he could push the canoe out, the tide would carry them away, arrows would miss a moving target and quickly they would be out of range.

She said, without haste, 'You will not be harmed. Get in.' And he understood then that she had been readying him for a solitary journey. Confused, angry, frightened, he looked from one to the other, the small black figure merging with the trees, the whites of his eyes glittering, his bow held loosely in one hand, carrying no arrows, and Elizabeth, her head stark as an exposed skull, the yellow hair shorn to a cap of pale fur, her body gleaming like marble in the moonlight –

'Gleaming?' James broke in. 'Her body was gleaming?'

It was only then, visualising the scene, that James realised Elizabeth had been naked all along.

Beyond the reef the waves grew rougher; the wind filled its lungs and blew the canoe far off the trade routes. Nothing came about as they had planned. A boy in a hollowed-out tree trunk challenged a great ocean and the sea played with him, a cruel game.

It was so long ago, but he still recalled the feeling, the way he knew he could fight the sea and win, the certainty that neither hurricane nor waves nor jagged reef, nor the shattered bones of the outrigger, could stop him. He would surge through the water and survive, he would live forever . . . He did not know then, the way the soaring spirit, the fire in the heart, dims, cools, shrinks with the passing of the years. Yes, he had survived, but the spirit had been extinguished, its immortality had proved illusory.

Andy made no mention of Elizabeth when he was picked up, half dead, clinging to what remained of the canoe. He was feverish, delirious for a while, and escaped close questioning.

When he got back to Port Blair he waited a few weeks, and then he tried to sell her ring. Later that day he was arrested and accused of theft: how would a Burmese cabin boy acquire a diamond-and-emerald ring but by theft? In desperation, the boy asked to see Major Oakley. Only to him would he explain how the ring came into his possession.

Henry saw him alone.

'I recognise the ring, of course.'

'Yes, sir.'

'It is my wife's.'

'Yes, sir.'

The boy was filled with fear in case his story was disbelieved, but he was also uncertain and confused about his story. The last two years – they had been prisoners, of course, but there was indecision too: how much to tell?

'The ring – '

The ring had been woven into a belt of vines and placed round the waist of the boy holding an outrigger that rose and fell in the surf. A present of a new life.

'She did not attempt to escape?'

'No, sir.'

He felt regret, sorrow that a man must grieve twice over, learn after so long that his wife was lost in a way worse than death, that she had been tainted, ruined. It had not seemed like that at the time, but as he talked, and watched Henry's face, he saw that shame entered into all this, and a revulsion, a horror. And now he saw why Elizabeth had made her final decision.

'We must send an armed force, to rescue her,' Henry said. And then added, with a sort of awkwardness, 'Must we not?'

The child, coming to certain conclusions, became older than the adult in the answering of the question.

There was a long silence, the boy staring at his feet and then up into the tall man's eyes. He shook his head.

'You could never get to her. They'd kill her first.' Did Henry believe him? Or did he take refuge in the statement, a solution that saved Elizabeth from public shame?

Nothing more was said. The ring was handed over to Henry, who paid Andy its true worth, rather more than the price the merchant from Madras had offered. He bought his first boat.

James, distraught, baffled, demanded, 'But why did you say that? Why did you say no to the idea of rescuing her?'

The beach, the moonlight gleaming on the woman's white body, the warrior standing at the edge of the trees, unarmed, his bow held loosely, no arrows. The woman's body as she half turned, glancing back at the man before she spoke, white skin gleaming, her belly firm and round as a turtle's back, big, heavy with the child she carried.

The boy had said nothing about that to Henry. The old man told James the truth now because he had forgotten the reasons for discretion.

He had kept silent, told no one. The matter might have ended there. But in his delirium, when he was rescued, Mrs Oakley's name had escaped him, a few words, jumbled, vague. Conclusions were drawn, and the rumours began. There were even people who claimed the impossible: to have glimpsed a white woman living among the savages.

*

He walked down the hotel drive to the beach and met Daisy as she came back, shaking sea water from her hair. She looked surprised, but said nothing and they walked in silence, in this new, exhausted calm that lay between them.

The portable writing desk was on his bed, pages scattered

around it. James picked up a grey, much-folded sheet of paper, brittle with age. He waved it at Daisy.

'I found this.'

She glanced at the sheet of paper. 'What is it? No glasses; I can't see.'

'It's what you wrote when you gave me the writing desk.'

'You kept it? All this time?' She sounded surprised.

'It was stuck at the back, inside one of the little drawers. I just found it.'

Daisy, her glasses now in position, saw him studying the letter with close attention, as if for the first time.

'Do you want a drink?' she asked. 'Fresh lime or anything?'

He looked up at her as though puzzled to find her there. As though wondering who she was. He looked back at the faded writing on the brittle paper, a letter written a lifetime ago. For a moment he saw the bright girl, shaking her bronze curls: the laughter he had helped put out lived again in the scrawled page.

He said, wonderingly, 'How you loved me, then.'

'Then?' she echoed. 'What d'you mean, "then"? I've loved you for fifty years.'

'Don't be absurd.' There was no force in his voice. 'You *are* only fifty-four.'

'We met when I was four,' she reminded him, as though explaining to a stranger, 'I thought you were the most important person in my life and I never changed my mind. When I was eleven I dragged my mother to a lecture you gave and I sat and loved you from the front row, and when I was sixteen and boys kissed me I still loved you and when I was nineteen and allowed myself to be deflowered one Saturday night by a selected youth, I wished it had been you.

'And when I was twenty-two you sat next to me at dinner and the roaring in my head was so loud that I could hardly hear a word you said and I thought: if he goes away now I shall die. And you said, "How do I find you?" How do I *find* you?'

'One.'

'What?'

'I asked, "How does *one* find you?" And you said, "One could look me up in the book." ' He added, as though thinking aloud, 'It's nonsense, you know. No one loves anyone at four. Except their mother.'

'I didn't care much for mine,' Daisy said. 'She didn't leave much of an impression – I hardly noticed whether she was there or not. But I thought about you . . . every day – no, there were whole days sometimes when I didn't. But never a whole week.'

'When you still loved me,' he said, prompting her.

'Yes,' she said. Because that was what he wanted her to say.

He needed a shower, a change of clothes, he told her. But when she had finished breakfast, he was gone again.

The morning was fine and clear. Around lunchtime the sky took on an ominous tinge and the sun disappeared behind a yellow haze. There was no sunset. On other evenings the sky had been briefly flamboyant, vulgar even, with a display of blazing orange, the palm trees silhouetted black against it as on cheap postcards. That night he did not return. She wondered whether to report him missing, and had a mental glimpse of James, face contorted in irritation and dismay, being picked up by the local police as he went about some perfectly reasonable activity he had not thought to tell her about. She decided to give it another day.

Walking on the beach next morning, searching with small success for shells, Daisy found Mr Ramachander sitting on a large, flat rock, contemplating the sea. This morning he had exchanged his Western suit for baggy cotton trousers and a Nehru jacket. He saw her and called out at once.

'Mrs Oakley! Good day to you. Enjoy the sunshine while you may, we will be having unsettled weather, I fear.'

'Surely not. It looks – '

'Deceptive.' He looked up towards the hotel. 'And how is your husband? How is Doctor Oakley? Back yet?'

She was surprised: certainly she had not mentioned James's absence to anyone.

'Er – no. Not yet.'

'Possibly he has business to take care of.'

'My husband is not engaged in business, Mr Ramachander.'

'Ah, but there is business and business. Possibly loose ends of some description.'

Again she was surprised: James, on the way to India, had used the expression, 'Tie up some loose ends.' She remained silent.

'So you are getting to know our mysterious Andamans?'

'Not really. There's something I find rather disturbing: everyone talks about the aboriginals, everyone knows they're here – but they're invisible. These are their islands, but they are the only people you cannot see. We have effectively pushed them out of sight.'

'Ah! I see you have been thinking! A dangerous exercise for a holidaymaker.'

Sitting cross-legged on his rock, smooth hands resting on his knees, Mr Ramachander reminded Daisy of the caterpillar in *Alice*: he had the same unsettling omniscience and sudden mood-switches.

He shrugged. 'The usual colonisation agenda has been followed: the imperialists moved in, took over the islands, imported convicts and disease from the mainland and killed off any aboriginals who objected. Thus they have become somewhat scarce.'

'Can't we make amends?'

'Best not to try. Just leave them alone. The Indian government is doing quite enough harm without outside help. "Benevolent non-intervention" they call it. But they still keep trying with the old ploys: beware of officials bearing gifts! Gradually the wretched tribals will succumb, become exhibits in a sort of rain-forest zoo, I daresay.'

He looked quite ill tempered, and Daisy shed her plastic

sandals and waded into the sea. 'Well, goodbye!' she called as she struck out.

When she emerged about twenty minutes later she found not one but two Ramachanders on the rock.

'My brother has arrived. You have encountered one another already, of course.'

The bookseller beamed at her.

'How pleasant to renew our acquaintance under these circumstances! I understand your husband is elsewhere.'

From T.A. a swift sentence in Hindi, and then, to Daisy, 'Dr Oakley was born on the Andamans. Perhaps he is in search of the past. Marx once said, you know, that the consciousness of the past weighs like a nightmare on the brain of the living.'

Too personal, Daisy decided. I think I should be offended. But the bookseller was ahead of her.

'Don't talk rubbish, my dear. Marx got everything wrong! St Augustine said past and future do not exist except in the present. There is only a present of past things, a present of present things and a present of future things. The present of past things is the memory, the present of present things is what we are perceiving as present, and the present of future things is expectation. I myself incline towards Whitehead who said that what we perceive as present is in fact the vivid fringe of memory tinged with anticipation.'

Daisy began to feel dizzy: already T.A. was ready to leap in with a counter-argument. She must cut off the flow of words.

'If you will excuse me . . .'

They both rose gracefully to their feet, shook her hand and subsided.

'À bientôt,' said the bookseller.

Daisy paused. 'I wouldn't settle down for too long just there: the tide will cover that rock completely quite soon.'

They leaped up in consternation. 'The bloody rocks again!' T.A. exclaimed. 'No peace for the wicked, eh?'

By afternoon a gunmetal haze had blanked out the sun and black clouds were spreading across the sky. The air was still and humid and even the sound of the surf had died away: the sea heaved, moving with an oily swell. A flurry of wind set the leaves rustling, and then the rain began, pattering steadily on the roof, on palm leaves, on steps and terraces. There was a smell of wetness. Saturation. The foliage glowed with an intense green. Without the bleaching effect of sunlight the flowers stood out, brilliant against the glittering leaves. The rain grew heavier, drumming on the roof; it fell like a curtain beyond the veranda, cutting Daisy off from the world outside.

Chapter 36

The day passed in waiting. James was patient: he brought offerings – whisky, freshly grilled fish wrapped in palm leaves, tins of fruit salad, which Andy preferred to the fresh variety available on the island. He handed them in at the door and the grandson took them without comment, hostile, convinced that this stranger threatened them in some obscure way.

James circled the house, walking carefully among the litter – tin cans, dog turds, plastic cartons, discarded coconut shells . . . When it began to rain he stood for a while under a jacaranda tree, then ducked into a little general store down the street and looked around for something to buy. He picked up a pen-knife and hurried back to the house. When the rain grew heavier he moved under the shelter of the overhanging eaves, and edged on to the veranda. He stood whittling a stick, something he had not done or thought of doing for sixty years. The rain battered the hibiscus bushes, crushing the scarlet blooms, pulping them into splotches that looked like clotted blood; forming treacherous puddles in the pot-holed street. Beyond the rain a hidden sun was spinning westward, dragging inky clouds in its wake. Joseph came out of the house and stared up at James angrily.

'I can't stop you seeing him. But if you cause him harm I'll have to throw you out – you'll be on the next plane back to Madras. We don't want you here.'

'Why do you imagine I want to harm him?' James was puzzled. 'I just want to talk to him.'

'He's frightened. I never saw him like this. But he won't listen to me. Do what you want.' He walked away down the steps into the rain.

The house was dark, the light from the windows barely penetrating the gloom, the rain hitting the roof with a sound like distant drums. James waited, his eyes gradually adjusting to the dimness.

'Andy?'

Daisy slept little that night. From time to time she thought she heard a taxi pull up, a door slam, footsteps. But James did not return. At dawn she dressed and waited. From below came breakfast sounds. No James. On the table by his bed he had placed the portable writing desk. She noticed the corner of an envelope sticking out from one side. They did not read each other's letters; normally Daisy would not even have lifted the lid, but today was not normal and today she not only lifted the lid, she picked up the envelope. It was not, she discovered, addressed to anyone, nor was it sealed. With a twinge of shame she drew out several pages covered in James's handwriting. It was not really a letter, more an account, part nightmare, part history, dwelling obsessively on details, posing rhetorical questions, supplying hypothetical answers, acknowledging that there could be no definitive solution, yet craving one. The last page was different. The last page followed the finding of Daisy's letter, written to James so long ago and forgotten, wedged at the back of the tiny drawer. It was addressed to her. She read it slowly, and when she had finished she wept, not shaken with bitter sobs or wrenched with regret, as had been the way so often in the past, but quietly, filled with an understanding she had supposed dead.

She must let someone know he was missing: embarrassment, his possible fury must be risked. First she burned the letter in an ashtray, page by page, as he requested. Then she walked down the stairs to the deserted lobby and waited for someone to appear. Today's snorkelling parties and excursions had already left, and there was a sense of activity from kitchens and corridors: sounds of chopping, scrubbing and sweeping. A blocked drain was noisily cleared, breakfast trays removed. This was the underside of hotel life, which took place while the guests enjoyed their pleasure elsewhere.

A small truck came fast up the drive and squealed to a halt. A young man in oil-stained jeans banged open the glass doors of the lobby. He stared at Daisy. 'I'm looking for Mrs Oakley.'

She was astonished, then filled with dread. 'I am Mrs Oakley.'

'They've gone. My grandfather – your husband has abducted my grandfather.'

'Don't be absurd,' Daisy said. 'My husband is English. He would not know how to abduct someone.' She realised the words sounded foolish. 'I mean my husband would never *abduct* anyone.'

'Is that so? Well they've taken a boat and they've gone. My grandfather can't walk, he can barely speak some days, so you tell me how he went of his own free will. I should never have left him. I knew no good would come of that man.'

The rain had stopped during the night and a fresh wind was blowing the sky clear.

There had been interviews and interrogations, disapproving officials and puzzled locals gathering to share the rumours – and to add to them. The known facts were sparse: it seemed that James and Andy had taken a boat and left the harbour.

Consternation was expressed: 'A *sailing* boat!'

Daisy said reassuringly, 'My husband is a skilled sailor – '

'– But unfamiliar with these waters!'

And, she reminded herself, he is an old man: shaky on bad days, over-ambitious on good ones. Neither condition augured well for this escapade.

A huge sheet of plastic, blown off some building site, had been caught up on the branches of a tall tree and hung there like the damaged sails of a ship, billowing out and sagging in the erratic wind, fluttering with a noise like wet sheets on a laundry line. The plastic sail gave the curving quay the look of a deck and Daisy stood, braced against the wind, feeling the spray in her face, sensing the surge of a sea beneath her feet stronger than the solid rock.

A small crowd gathered. For a while the mood was jolly, the scene took on something of a party atmosphere. Everyone knew the British were eccentric, doubtless Dr Oakley would reappear shortly, like some naughty boy who had played truant. It was just a matter of time, the boat was probably on its way back already.

She felt a gentle touch, a hand on her arm, and turned: N. K. and T. A. Ramachander, and a third, unmistakably a relative: 'My cousin Gopal, he lives on Andaman, he works as a soil analyst on the spice farm.'

G. Ramachander bowed briefly over joined fingertips. The bookseller said diffidently, 'Mrs Oakley, we have brought you a seat, you cannot remain standing all day.' The cousin placed a small, folding stool before her and waved towards it gracefully. 'I am utilising it for bird-watching. Please to be seated.'

Suddenly weary, Daisy lowered herself on to the seat. The three Ramachanders stood protectively round her forming a human screen from inquisitive eyes.

Gopal said warmly, 'Mrs Oakley, perhaps I could recite to you some verses from the *Bhagavad Gita* – '

'No thank you.' But he had begun.

> 'End and beginning are dreams
> Birthless and deathless and changeless
> Remaineth the spirit for ever
> Death hath not touched it at all
> Dead though the house of it seems.'

'Eliot said something of the sort –' N. K. broke in, ' – and in fewer words: "to make an end is to make a beginning . . .

The end is where we start from." Gopal's reading is very narrow I'm afraid.'

As the hours passed the crowd grew quieter. Patrol boats had returned without news. The locals began to cast glances of sympathy towards Daisy. Someone offered her a cup of hot, sweet tea. She took it and gulped it absently, wondering if James had taken food or water with him. She felt no uncertainty about his destination though she had said nothing to the official questions. What should she say? My husband has gone in search of . . . what? A ghost? The source of a rumour? A wrecked ship in a mangrove swamp? His peace of mind? She would in any case have been unable to help them: among three hundred or more islands, with bays, lagoons, inlets, creeks, dangerous straits and unpredictable currents, her information would have been useless: James had given the island no name.

'Would you care to rest in a convenient nearby house?' The soil analyst squatted beside her. 'We can arrange – '

'I shall remain here, thank you.'

'Of course.'

He continued to talk in his mellifluous, singsong voice, caressing the words, soothing, smiling, radiating goodwill. He talked of the cycle of life, of dream and reality. It was impossible to be rude to the round-eyed, cherubic man. Nor could she bat him away or flatten him with sarcasm. Like one of those weighted, round-based dolls he would simply bob upright again, still smiling.

'May I enquire your husband's age?'

'Seventy-six.'

'Nearing the end of his appointed span,' he said gently, 'a man feels the need to go in search of God – '

'– a Hindu feels the need,' R. K. said impatiently. 'I don't suppose – '

'– A need to leave wife and business and home. To prepare,' said G. Ramachander. 'A man can be called by God.'

'Well, I'll go on waiting just the same,' Daisy said.

'You do not know how long this waiting may continue.'

'Nevertheless.'

The old man was slumped in a corner of the deck where James had set him down. Wrapped in a blanket against the dawn chill, he stared up at the sky while James steered. He had been so firm, so definite as they drank their whisky together: he could navigate, tell James which route to take. He gave orders. For a while the shrunken frame had regained strength, the voice was clear. He gave more instructions. But there were things he kept to himself: he had always meant to go back one day, keep faith with her, make his way stealthily through the gloom of the tall trees, find her, rescue her perhaps. At least try or die in the attempt. But such heroics faded with sunlight and the journey was never made. Until now.

They counted off the hours by the passing islands. They left the sheltered waters and headed out into an open strait that set the little boat bucking, keeling over, the sail almost horizontal to the water. The sun's heat was fierce now. They were getting nearer. Even on a fine day the sea was always squally here. The island was protected by rough water. Andy knew the ways of the tides and currents: he had seen the outriggers dancing their way across the waves with a skill he had thought magical until he studied the charts, the palm leaves and cowrie shells lashed into patterns that marked the safe channels. Memory came and went. Moments stood out sharply against a tantalising blur. Honey – dark, almost bitter, oozing from the comb, and the way they never got stung, funny that . . . the turtle thrown live on to the fire and eaten, torn piecemeal from the shell . . . a day when he had cried out, frightened, thinking her wounded, at the sight of blood staining her legs, trickling from her body, something which he grew accustomed to . . . the fishing trips, the plaiting of vine sinews, and one particular belt that held a ring. Fireflies hovering like a net of emeralds over the black vegetation that came down to the shore . . . He must have slept at one point for he became aware of James shouting at him, 'Which way, for Christ's sake! Which way?'

James followed the mumbled directions, watching anxiously as the waves lifted the boat, slid away and gathered again to slap viciously at the hull. He felt the sun on his head and back, tempered by the breeze. He should be wearing a hat. He must keep the boat on course. And he must keep awake. He felt the roughness of the line between his fingers, the tilt of the deck beneath his feet – (there was a felucca trip once, the wind blowing steady up the Nile. A white silk kaftan that slipped over nakedness in a small dark cabin. The sweet softness of her flesh, her welcoming hands, mouth, thighs . . .) His eyes were sore, the lids heavy. Between waking and sleeping he hung, pinioned. The flashes of darkness came at him, presaging pain.

His mind churned, circling, covering the same ground over and over, the pattern shifting, now playing the scene one way, now another. The dream hovered just beyond reach, solving no problems. Dreams could solve problems, he knew. But James's dreamscape was enigmatic, amorphous, the inhabitants unreliable.

When had he first begun to hate Elizabeth? Not at the beginning, then it had been all grief, despair, loss. Anger, yes, but it had been the pain of love deprived.

When had he started to hate her? When had the original nightmare – the dress like butterfly wings, the scent of violets, the woman with pale hair who turned away and floated out of reach above the treetops, when had that changed? Darkness blinded him like a fierce light. Then, swimming out of the darkness came the other, the woman flung back on the bed, body arched in sensuous abandonment, something evil lurking, a succubus, the pale horse watching sightlessly.

He must have seen it before he dreamed it, in a book or at some art show. This nightmare was Fuseli's before it was his, an artist's vision that dealt with a quite different story, but he had claimed it, the woman was now his troubled dreamer, he merely a part of her dream, another insubstantial figure lurking in the shadows, crying silently to be made real.

As a small child he had tried to pronounce his mother's name

– Elizabeth had become a lisped Lilith amid indulgent adult laughter. But Lilith went away one day, abandoned him, betrayed them all. Another Lilith, he learned later, abandoned those who loved her. Had she been unhappy in Eden? Why did she go, leaving Adam unprotected? If she had stayed, paradise might never have been lost: Lilith would not have listened to the serpent, she was strong. But the screech-owl, the night-fiend she became, brought fear in the night, danger to children, terror of darkness. She was not to be trusted. Elizabeth turned Lilith was not to be trusted either. No one was to be trusted. Certainly no one who said they loved you. Sooner or later they left you crying alone.

Across the deck Andy breathed noisily, eyes bleared and rheumy. He was gripped by a sudden attack of palsy that shook him free of the blanket. He clawed at the rail, fighting his own uncontrollable limbs, the wizened face twisted with the effort.

The island lay blurred in the mist that always surrounded it, hiding it from passing ships. It was ringed by an atoll, a circle of coral that rose up from beneath the ocean, a wall with a surface like twisted razors and broken glass that kept the ships away, and the surf pounded ceaselessly on the reef, mist rising in a white pall. He whispered instructions, hanging over the side, staring down at the shadow that lay beneath the surface. A little to starboard . . . then port . . . straight on . . . until with the sigh of a lifting wave they lay rocking gently in the lagoon.

That night as the outrigger had slipped out through the reef and away to sea, Andy had looked back before the beach and trees vanished into the darkness. He could see nothing – except the moonlight on the tight-packed tops of the towering rain trees.

But the last image of Elizabeth would haunt him forever, the ragged skullcap of pale hair, the face, so different from the powdered mask that had smiled at him that first day on the ship. This was a face with skin toughened by rain and sun, whose muscles had learned new tasks – the chewing of bark and rending of meat; the features, the very aspect, changed by the habits of survival, eyes red rimmed, white teeth more prominent, lips drawn back in a smile like the snarl of a dog as she let go of the canoe.

The trees grew almost to the water's edge, rising up like a shield. There was a stillness to the place that seemed baleful. A watcher would get no clue to the life, if life there were, that went on in the interior. Long ago, men armed with bows taller than themselves had come streaming out of those trees with warlike cries, to greet the shipwrecked strangers with arrows tipped with iron and poisonous juices . . . there had been screams, a fire on the beach . . .

This was the place. James brought her about and they lay quiet, the sail hanging slack. He strained his eyes, seeking for some sign, a fragment of hull looming from the mud, a rusted sheet of metal.

A dead tree, skinny, attenuated, rose from the centre of the swamp, forming a mast. Creepers trailed from the bare branches like rigging. On the treetop, a bright-feathered bird fluttered in the wind, a living pennant. Were he to dig down into the ooze there might be an anchor, corroded and lumpy; the petrified remains of ships' instruments, fossils from the past.

A pattern drawn in the sand. Survival. Bondage, or a release from bondage of another sort, perhaps. What had the island been? A penitentiary, or a place of freedom? And it was all so long ago, it was, after all, an island like any other. Elizabeth's island. Her decision, and her right to make it. How devious his search had been. And the mourning, endlessly prolonged, had been less, perhaps, for her than for himself. He saw that now, and with a curious lightening of the heart, he let her go.

They had drifted closer to the shore. Among the trees there was a movement, a figure slowly emerged. Small, very black against the sand he raised his long bow and stood, arrow aimed at the boat, waiting. At first sight he seemed young, a warrior, the body lean, flesh unwrinkled. But James saw that his shorn head was silver. He heard Andy wheeze from behind him.

'Never saw a Jarawa with grey hair.'

This was an old warrior, tired and part of a dying island race.

It was perhaps – fanciful thought – his brother. A last link with Elizabeth. The Jarawa waited, bow drawn, composed. It was a statement of territory, not a challenge. They stared at one another across the water. Then James drew in the rope, turned into the wind and they headed out.

People had lost interest after a while, and even the Ramachanders, who brought Daisy coconut milk in the shell and a ripe mango; who offered, beseechingly, a 'nice clean bed' in a nearby guest-house, even they had things that had to be attended to, so she was alone, sitting on the folding stool, when she saw a speck on the horizon, a speck that grew into a sail, then a small boat. It was heading for the jetty with two figures visible, one small and hunched, curled up like a sleeping dog, and James, steering the boat. As they came nearer, Daisy saw with a stab of fear how changed he was: how had she failed to see that he had grown so thin, the limbs wasted, the face so gaunt. The late sun caught the silver hair, the metallic stubble on his cheeks. The boat skimmed the waves, following the path of the sun, borne on a river of gold that flowed through the dark sea. The sun blinded her and for a moment she saw him as he had been that day on the Nile, blazing with light, glittering, a god from another age. The little boat came alongside the jetty where she waited and she saw him smile at her in recognition of a moment that had come full circle; the two of them, a small boat at the end of a day. She was four and her head came to his knees. I shall write you letters, she said, when I have learned to write, and when I grow up we shall be married. When you are grown up, he said, I shall be an old man. I shan't mind, she said, I shall marry you and look after you.

Now others were running, calling, the boat had been seen. The grandson had leaped on board, kneeling to cradle Andy, but James with his air of authority looked so strong, eyes flashing blue, hair bright in the sun, that they held back, hesitating. But Daisy saw the colour ebb from his face, the light leave his eyes and reached him first, and it was Daisy who caught him as he fell.

About the author . . .

Lee Langley was born in Calcutta of Scottish parents. She travelled widely in India during her childhood, until her family returned to Britain. She is married to a writer, has three grown-up children, and lives in Richmond-upon-Thames near London.

Her first novel, *The Only Person*, was published in 1973, followed by *Sunday Girl, From the Broken Tree* (Book of the Month Club Alternate Choice in the US), and *The Dying Art*. Her fifth novel, the highly autobiographical *Changes of Address*, was set in India—a portrait of a mother and child that received critical acclaim and was shortlisted for the Hawthornden Prize. Her sixth novel, *Persistent Rumours,* won the Writers' Guild of Great Britain Best Fiction Award and the 1993 Commonwealth Writers' Prize for Best Novel in the Eurasia Region.

As well as novels, she has written poetry and a stage play, produced in London's West End and several other countries. Her scriptwriting has included a feature movie and work for British and American television, including a highly praised dramatisation of Graham Greene's *The Tenth Man*, shown as a Hallmark Movie of the Week on CBS. She has written arts and travel journalism, which has taken her to many parts of the world including Japan, Peru, Egypt, and the United States.

Before writing *Persistent Rumours,* Lee Langley went to the Andaman Islands 700 miles out in the Indian Ocean, to the old British penal colony, now in ruins, which forms the setting of her book both in the past and the present day, where dangerous aboriginal tribes still survive on the outlying islands.

More fiction from Milkweed Editions:

Larabi's Ox
Tony Ardizzone

Circe's Mountain
Marie Luise Kaschnitz

Agassiz
Sandra Birdsell

Ganado Red
Susan Lowell

What We Save for Last
Corinne Demas Bliss

Tokens of Grace
Sheila O'Connor

Backbone
Carol Bly

The Boy Without a Flag
Abraham Rodriguez, Jr.

The Clay That Breathes
Catherine Browder

An American Brat
Bapsi Sidhwa

Street Games
Rosellen Brown

Cracking India
Bapsi Sidhwa

A Keeper of Sheep
William Carpenter

The Crow Eaters
Bapsi Sidhwa

Winter Roads, Summer Fields
Marjorie Dorner

The Country I Come From
Maura Stanton

Blue Taxis
Eileen Drew

Traveling Light
Jim Stowell

The Historian
Eugene Garber

Aquaboogie
Susan Straight

Kingfishers Catch Fire
Rumer Godden

Montana 1948
Larry Watson

The Importance of High Places
Joanna Higgins